A Twirl in Time
Upon A Time
Book Four
By
Stella May

A TWIRL IN TIME

First edition. May 31, 2023.

ISBN: 978-1737647478

Written by Stella May.

Table of Contents

To my grandmother Vera, my beautiful guardian angel.

CHAPTER ONE

V*erochka* leaned against the wing backed chair, gazing out the oversized bay window. A relieved smile tugged at her lips as gentle, diamond studded blue waves washed onto the sand beach. She turned at the sound of shoes shuffling along the hardwood floor.

Abby, *Verochka's* granddaughter by marriage, waddled into the great room, rubbing her enormous belly with both hands. Carefully, but ungracefully, she plopped her pregnant body onto the sofa with a contended sigh. Experience proved Abby sat for just a few moments, before struggling to her feet, and started pacing again. The poor thing was definitely unsettled and uncomfortable. First pregnancies can be quite difficult for young women.

A little chitchat was in order. Just to take Abby's mind off her condition for a few moments.

"It's hard to believe that only two days ago the Atlantic Ocean churned as if possessed by demons from hell and spewed its mighty wrath onto our tiny Amelia Island." *Verochka* glanced at Abby who seemed lost in her own thoughts and still rubbing her belly.

Okay, strike one.

"They named that hurricane Ian, can you believe it?" *Verochka* forced a laugh, "isn't that a ridiculously lovely name for such a monster?"

No comment, not even a nod.

Strike two.

Undeterred, *Verochka* plowed ahead. "They said it was the deadliest hurricane to pound Florida in almost a century."

Abby finally nodded and continued to massage her belly.

"The reporter said it left a path of demolished homes and businesses." *Verochka* shivered, grateful their house escaped serious damage. Not a shingle was torn off its roof. Not a single board ripped from the wraparound wooden deck. Its concrete pillars withstood the storm just as the architect promised. A couple of broken windows were minor compared to the chaos their little town was plunged into. A jewel by the sea, Fernandina Beach was forever encapsulated in an Edwardian era, and proud of it. Its historic downtown once again weathered the storm, but bore the visible scars.

Abby looked up. A mix of pride and stubbornness lit her face. "The residents of the Amelia Island are used to the hurricanes. We are, after all, the descendants of the pirates and fishermen and always faced the whims of nature straight on, never bending under." Haughty, her voice reminded *Verochka* of an old Abby, the Coleman heiress, born and bred on Amelia Island.

Finally!

Relief washed over *Verochka* now that the girl was talking. "You are so right, Sweetie. It's a hardy community and will endure, shaking off the disaster, then move on to clear out the debris and rebuild this beautiful little town back to its former glory. They always have and always will."

Even after the deadliest storm of the century, life marched on.

"I'm glad we stayed here in the house and not raced for the mainland." Abby wrestled herself off the chair. "Worrywart Alex wanted to evacuate but I knew it was because of the baby and me. I'm happy he listened to me. I would never have felt safe anywhere but here. Our home."

Verochka nodded in agreement. Due any day now, her granddaughter was antsy and prowled the house like a ghost. No chance of her being comfortable anywhere, not even in *Verochka's* luxurious hotel suite. Home was not just a structure, but a sanctuary. She truly believed in its healing power and protection. So, all three of them stayed put, and rode out the storm together.

Although relieved when calm finally returned, *Verochka* continued to worry about Abby. Every day the girl grew increasingly restless.

"Are you okay with Alex in Jacksonville for that two-day realtors' orientation class?" What new could a seasoned real estate broker and owner of a successful business learn from that, was a mystery to *Verochka*. As an eleven-year-old veteran of the industry, her grandson Alex could give his own orientation classes.

Merde. Verochka let loose a gentle breath. No point to dwell on it now.

Hoping to keep the girl distracted, *Verochka* chimed in, "Abs? Do you need anything?"

"Like what?" A petulant expression on Abby's face didn't promise any easy way out of her current funk. Always the optimist, *Verochka* ignored the snappish reply, and fluffed her hair cut in a short sassy bob. Briefly wondering if she was as peevish in her last days of pregnancy as Abby, she bore down on her irritation.

"Like drink, or food." *Or good spanking.* "Are you hungry?"

"I'm always hungry nowadays, Grandmother." A loud sniff accompanied her answer. "How much food does that baby need, anyway? I've gotten so fat, I swear that soon I won't be able to squeeze through the doorway."

Verochka sat on the corner of the sofa, and patted Abby's hand. "Hang on, Sweetie. Only another few days."

"It's just so unbearable!" Almost wailing, Abby grabbed a throw pillow, and hugged it against her breasts. "I'm peeing every five minutes, my ankles are swollen, and my face got round like a full moon!" Closing her face with her hands, the girl burst into tears, something she did a lot lately. "I feel so ugly!"

Verochka placed a box of tissues onto Abby's lap. She took one, covered her face with it, and sobbed her little heart out.

Merde.

Enough was enough.

"Stop it. Just stop. What are you, a weakling?"

Abby blinked, then hiccupped. She stared at *Verochka,* as if undecided to be offended or ashamed of herself. But her tears began to slow.

In a gentler voice, *Verochka* continued, "You are as beautiful as ever. Even more so. As to your body, it gets to its normal size as soon as she or he will make an appearance."

Verochka was dying to know the gender of the baby, and impatient to start buying some adorable tiny clothing. Designers, of course, as only the best of the best was appropriate for her great-grandbaby. But to her utter dismay, both Alex and Abby stubbornly refused to learn the sex of their first offspring, claiming that they wanted to be surprised.

Kids! Oh, well.

As soon as the baby was born, *Verochka* promised herself a huge shopping spree. She planned to fly to Milan for a day. Or Paris. Or maybe London. She'd decide later.

But for now, she must curb her impatience, and wait. A couple of days. Three at the most.

Merde.

Abby's wistful voice interrupted her inner debate. "You really think so, *Verochka*? Honestly?"

"I really know so, Sweet Pea. Been there, done that, got a t-shirt."

Abby gave her a wobbly grin. "I bet your 't-shirt' was a satin Hermes *peignoir.*"

At least, she managed to distract the girl enough to make a joke. Good.

Deadpan, *Verochka* pursed her lips. "Actually, it was a Chanel, a mulberry silk that cost an arm and leg, but," she shrugged negligently, "I so deserved it after giving birth to twins."

"Ugh." A delicate shudder later, Abby shook her head. "I really don't know if I could have managed. Twins! That boggles the mind."

"Yes, well, I'm sure you'll do it brilliantly, Sweetie, but for your sake, I'm really happy that your child is a solo number."

"Oh, Lord, me too." After a long pause, Abby's eyes lit up with curiosity. "Grandmother?"

"Hmm?"

"I meant to ask you, how did you meet Grandfather?"

A tug at *Verochka's* heart was tender and soft.

Oh, JJ would have loved to be called grandfather.

Ten years after his passing, and she still wasn't used to the separation. To her, JJ was alive and well, but somewhere in a better place. He was always with her.

In her thoughts, in her heart, in her soul.

Verochka smiled through the sheen of mist that clouded her eyes. "I met him quite by accident, really. From that moment on, my life spun off its axis, and has never been the same."

"Aww…" Abby's voice became dreamy. She scooted closer. "Was it love at first sight?"

Verochka chuckled. "Well, first I fell in love with his music, and only later I lost my heart to the man."

"Music?" Abby puckered her brows. "I thought he was a businessman. Or was it a banker?"

"JJ was the CEO of the Morris' family holding. In the sixties, he was called a magnate, a mogul, a tycoon. But in his heart, he was a musician, first and foremost."

"Tell me, Grandmother. Please. Tell me everything."

"It's a long story, Sweetie. Are you sure you're up to it?"

"Of course, I am! I'm dying of curiosity here."

"Well, then." And turning back to the window, *Verochka* opened the floodgates to the memories...

CHAPTER TWO

The sound of a saxophone halted her steps. That deep, velvety voice grabbed her by her throat, and refused to let go. Holding her breath, mesmerized, *Verochka* stopped, then pivoted. Where did it come from? Straining her ears, she looked around, searching the almost empty street. Guided by her hearing, she glanced at the closed doors on her right. The Broome Street Bar. Inside, the sax murmured its enchanting tale, sad, and touching, and heartbreaking.

Mon Dieu! *What must one feel to play like that?*

Verochka closed her eyes and swayed to the music. Her arms by their own volition lifted and moved in a lazy, unhurried wave. She visualized the dance in her mind, something slow and sensual. Strange, but she never paid attention to jazz before. Then again, she was never partial to any music except classical.

To *Verochka*, there was nothing and no one compared to Tchaikovsky. But the soulful notes of that sax fascinated her as much as the famous opening theme from Swan Lake. When the sound trailed off, she felt almost bereft. She craved to hear more. Will the musician play again? Oh, she hopped so. She'd wait for it.

Outside? On the sidewalk at almost ten at night?

Unwise, not to mention quite dangerous. Granted, this spot in SoHo was not prone to crime. But still. A young woman alone was bound to attract some attention. *Verochka* looked at the closed door of the bar, biting her lip.

To go inside, or continue on her way? The wisest thing to do, of course, was to turn around, and go home, to her tiny apartment. It was late. She must rest before her wake-up call at 5:30 AM. All morning classes of Madame Valeska started at precisely 6 AM, and God forbid if any of the dancers was late even by a minute. The wrath of her teacher definitely equaled to her worldwide fame as a former principal dancer of The Royal Ballet.

Tired after the long day of classes and rehearsals, then cleaning the premises, *Verochka* barely kept upright. She hated her after-hours janitorial obligations, but promise was a promise. And *Verochka Osipoff* never broke her word.

No matter how spent she was, each and every evening, after all the dancers went home, and the school was closed, she headed to the closet for a broom and a bucket. At first, she didn't mind it at all. It was an arrangement made in heaven. An eighteen-year-old orphan from France, determined to reach her dream, *Verochka* arrived at the doors of the famous New York ballet school with nothing but fifty dollars to her name and a small satchel that belonged to her father.

After her initial shock faded, the formidable Madame Valeska, the owner of the school, ordered *Verochka* to change into her leotards, and dance.

Her final verdict delivered in a grumbling voice was like a heavenly music to *Verochka's* ears.

"You have a potential, Miss Osipoff. I'll take a chance on you, and let you stay for a probationary period of three months. After that, we'll see."

Verochka's elation was huge, but temporary. The school was obscenely expensive. No way she was able to afford the tuition. There was a stipend, but applying for it took only God knew how long, with no guarantee that it will be granted in the end.

On top of it, she was a foreigner, all alone in the strange country, and barely able to speak English.

Madame Valeska, quickly assessing the situation— more accurately, feeling sorry for her— offered *Verochka* a deal: the education in exchange for cleaning services. A tiny room in the attic as a temporary place to live was added to that offer. To *Verochka*, it was like a Christmas gift she could never have dreamt about.

Overwhelmed, moved to tears, *Verochka* grabbed the opportunity with both hands. After a while, she got her stipend for the gifted and unprivileged students, thanks to Madame Valeska's help, and was able to cover most of her tuition.

The convenience of living on the premises saved her the expense of a rent, and occasional participation in corps de ballet's performances made everything else manageable. She didn't need a lot of food, as her extremely strict diet fell mostly into yogurt and fruit category. As to clothes— she learned at her dancing parents knee the skill to mend tears and repair pointe shoes.

Two years later, *Verochka* was still living in the attic, and still mopped the floors, and cleaned the premises. But it didn't matter. Her main goal to become a prima ballerina of The Royal Ballet took the precedence over everything else.

Ambitious? Maybe. But, as her father always said, you must dream big. Otherwise, what was the point? So, she dreamed big, and worked like a woman possessed in order to reach that dream. She was content, and happy, and along the way, fell in love with New York, her new home. Her only home. She learned English, and became quite fluent in it, even though her accent stubbornly refused to be erased.

Of course, she missed France, and Paris, and small street cafes, and long strolls along the Seine. Oh, the aroma of freshly brewed coffee and sprinkled with powdered sugar beignets! Sometimes, she could smell them in her dreams.

But most of all, she missed her parents. She was sure they were looking at her from heaven, smiling, proud of her accomplishments.

Her occasional nostalgia was usually sweet, and short, like a children's lullaby.

But not tonight.

After finishing her duties, *Verochka* was ambushed by a sadness so huge, she almost doubled down with it. Suffocated in the large empty building that housed the ballet school, she was lonely, isolated, until she couldn't bear another minute longer locked inside. Hence, her impromptu evening walk that brought her in the middle of SoHo, to the Broome Street Bar.

The plaintive sounds of sax reached her ears again.

Oh, yeas, please.

Listening to those seductive low rumbles, she wondered about the player.

Who was he? Or was it a she? Why was that melody so sad, so sorrowful?

The pull of it was irresistible. Like drown by a magnet, *Verochka* took a couple of steps toward the bar, then stopped. Did she dare go inside? She'd never been to such an establishment before. She bit her lip and considered as her common sense battled with longing. At the end, the pull of that melody and her innate curiosity won. Squaring her shoulders, *Verochka* marched forward, then opened the door.

CHAPTER THREE

Inside, the bar was larger than she expected. The tantalizing aroma of food ambushed her. Despite the dim light, and the snaking trails of the patron's cigarettes, the atmosphere was cozy, homey, and welcoming. The long wooden bar on her right gleamed like a mirror. The walls were peppered with photographs and sketches of musical instruments, with the saxophone reining supreme. The combination of it all, and the nice mellow ambiance of the place quieted her nerves. After her eyes adjusted to the muted light, *Verochka* scanned the room, searching for the sax player. Almost immediately her gaze arrowed onto the lone figure at the far corner. Tall and dark, cradling his sax in both hands, the musician was totally lost in the music, oblivious to his surroundings. Deep rumbling throb of the sax brought a sheen of tears to her eyes. Her heart squeezed, then trembled. The beauty of that melody, full of sadness and secrets, tugged at her soul. For the life of her, *Verochka* couldn't tear her gaze from the player.

Eyes closed, shoulders hunched, he seemed to be detached from everything and everybody. The musician and his instrument were like a single entity, like a natural and integral continuation of each other. And that melody...*Magnific!*

Only God knew how long she might stay enthralled, glued to the spot, if the bartender hadn't noticed her.

"Miss? May I help you?"

She glanced at the bald like an egg enormous bear of a man, squinting at her out of shrewd piercing eyes. In the dim light, their color seemed almost black.

"Ah...yes, I suppose so."

Pulling her bravado around her like a cloak, *Verochka* moved to the bar then, perched on a high stool. She aimed her gaze at the burly man.

No, not black.

The bartender's eyes turned out to be the darkest blue she'd ever seen. Indigo.

"What can I do for you, Little Sparrow?"

"Sparrow?" Amused more than insulted, she lifted her brows. "Why is that?"

"You seemed kind of lost, and shivering, just like a little birdy."

"I guess I was. Shivering that is. The music..." she shook her head, "it's something... magical."

"It is at that. JJ here is a pure magician with the sax."

"JJ? Is that his name?"

"Yep." The bartender turned away to take care of a patron, then switched his attention back to her. "Can I offer you anything, miss?"

"What?" Totally absorbed in the music, *Verochka* dragged her eyes from the player, and blinked at the bartender. "Sorry, I missed your question."

One corner of his mouth lifted in a warm smile. "That's okay. JJ has that effect on all the ladies."

"Oh, but I was listening to the melody, not looking at your JJ."

"No? Well, then, you're made of a stronger staff, Little Sparrow."

He laughed, all the while wiping the glass in his hands with a clean towel. He raised the glass high and nodded when it gleamed in the hanging light fixture.

"So, what's your pleasure? And please don't say whiskey or wine. Even without carding you, I could easy guess your age, and it ain't an inch closer to a legal one."

"I'm twenty." Maybe her declaration came out in a haughty manner, but she was sick and tired to be taken for a teenager.

"Sure you are." Laced with a mild sarcasm, his deep baritone tickled her ears.

"No, honestly. I'd show you my ID, but I currently don't have it on me."

"Huh," he squinted at her and shook his bald head. "Looks more like sixteen to me."

"It's my genes. I look deceptively young for my age."

The weathered face a breath short of being ugly, creased with a rueful smile.

"You can say that again. Anyway, what would you like, little one? Juice? Water?"

She'd love to have a glass of water, but *Verochka* realized that along with her ID, she left all her money at home. In a hurry to get out of the building, she forgot her purse. And what did she need it for? After all, she didn't plan on stopping anywhere, especially in a neighborhood bar.

Uncomfortable, *Verochka* flashed a fake smile. "Oh, nothing, *merci*. I'm totally fine."

With a loud harrumph, the bartender produced a tall glass, filled it to the brim with orange juice, and placed it front of her.

"On the house." After a brief pause, a basket full of chips joined the drink.

"Oh, but I couldn't..."

"My treat, Little Sparrow. Consider yourself Winston's guest tonight."

"*Merci*, Mr. Winston, you are very kind."

"Just Winston, like Churchill. Or cigarettes."

"Okay, Winston. I'm pleased to meet you."

"Pleasure's all mine, little one. And what's your name?"

"Not a Sparrow, for sure." She chucked, and offered her hand. "It's Vera Osipoff, but everybody calls me *Verochka*."

"Nice to meet you, *Verochka* Osipoff, and nice nickname." Her hand was swallowed by the huge rough palm, but the shake was surprisingly gentle. "Mind if I ask what's that accent?"

"Not at all. I was born in Paris."

"That's what I thought. All those soft nasal sounds."

"I've been trying very hard to eliminate my accent, but..." She shrugged.

"Don't. It's sexy as hell."

The wink that followed his shocking statement was positively mischievous.

A wide smile spread over his homely face, producing two little dimples on his cheeks. As unexpected as it was endearing, the sight of those dimples went straight to her heart. Suddenly, he no longer seemed so scary.

Appearances were deceiving for sure. And who should know that better than her?

Delighted, *Verochka* smiled. "If you say so."

"Don't mind if I do." Another wink made her laugh. " So, what do you do in New York, *Verochka* Osipoff with a sexy French accent?"

"Study. I am a ballerina."

"You don't say?" He gave her a curious glance, then nodded. "You got the body for it, too. Fluid, graceful, elegant. Not a Little Sparrow, then, but a Beautiful Swan, huh?"

"Why, *merci*, Mr., ah...I mean, Winston. And you? Is this your bar?"

"I'm a manager. The bar belongs to someone else."

"Oh, is he a good owner? Is he kind to you?"

"He is. JJ is a fair one, and a good friend to boot."

"I'm very glad to hear it. It is very important to be appreciated, *non*?" Then it struck her. Eyes wide she asked, "JJ? The sax player? He owns the bar?"

"Among other things."

She turned and studied the imposing figure of the musician. Presently, he was engaged in a conversation with a woman at a nearby booth. The smoldering glances that gorgeous brunette was sending in his direction were hot enough to ignite a fire.

As *Verochka* watched, the woman leaned forward, touched his hand, and sent a peal of laughed, low and sensual and intimate. The answering masculine laugh raised all fine hairs on *Verochka's* nape. Somehow, she knew his voice was deep and throaty, just like his sax. A helpless shiver ran along her spine.

Were they lovers? Possibly. Probably.

Merde.

And what if they were? Aucun de tes soucis. None of your concern.

Her jealousy was ridiculous. Deliberately tearing her eyes from the pair, she turned to Winston. The little smirk accompanied by the raised bushy brows were eloquent and damning. She winced. Was she so transparent? Apparently.

Merde.

Winston gently patted her hand. In reassurance? In pity?

Verochka would have bristled, if she weren't so ashamed.

Nodding at the basket of chips, Winston prompted, "Eat, little one. You're skinny enough to be blown away by a breeze."

"I'm not skinny, just slender." With a soft moan, she eyed the offerings, almost salivating at the sight of the forbidden golden treats. "And I am not allowed to eat at this time."

"Says who?"

"My teacher, Madame Valeska. She'd kill me for even looking at the food, much less eating."

"She's not here, is she? And a couple of chips won't hurt you. Eat, and drink that juice."

Her inner tug of war was brutal, but short. The hunger won.

"Well, maybe a little, then. *Merci*, Winston."

She nibbled on a single chip, and almost groaned with pleasure. When was the last time she ate anything so delicious? And the answer was never. Highly regimented even as a child, *Verochka* was not allowed to eat anything sweet, greasy, or fried. Never mind processed food. And carbs? It was a sacrilegious word, close to 'evil.' She tried not to think of how many cardinal rules of her formidable teacher she broke today. A late-night walk, a trip to a bar, a conversation with a complete stranger. Granted, Winston was not a stranger anymore, but still.

So, what's one little indulgence thrown in? Capitulating, Verochka reached for another chip. She raised the cold glass and inhaled, then sipped the orange juice. Positively sinful.

Magnific!

Bolstered, seduced by the banquet of tastes in her mouth, *Verochka* finished another chip, and drained her glass. God, she was full, and warm, and happy.

Her previous disquiet became a distant memory, silly and embarrassing.

Verochka smiled while gazing up at the face of the stranger that in a short period of time became familiar.

"*Merci*, Winston. It was quite delicious."

"You are very welcome, little one. I hope to see you more often."

"Oh, you will. After hearing that sax, you couldn't stop me from coming by."

"I'm glad. Want me to introduce you to JJ?"

"Oh," she bit her lip, considering. Tempting, so tempting, but... She firmly shook her head. "No, not today."

"Next time, then. Where is your jacket?"

"My what?"

"A jacket, or a coat."

"Oh." Verochka looked down, scrutinized her attire. *Merde.* In her haste to get out of that stifling empty building, she ran out in her regular clothes without anything warmer than a thin sweater over a pair of tights. "I'm afraid I forgot it at home."

"Girl, it's October. You could catch pneumonia as easy as that." He snapped his thick fingers. "No way I'm letting you out like this." Furrowing his brows, Winston disappeared through the swinging doors behind him. A moment later, he returned with a heavy knitted sweater. Considering its enormous size, it was his own. Without a word, he came forward, tugged her from the stool then pulled the garment over her head. Swallowed in it, *Verochka* blinked back tears. Moved, humbled, enormously grateful, she threw her arms around Winston. "*Merci.* Thank you so much."

Burrowing her nose in his chest, she closed her eyes, and just breathed him in.

For just a moment, he froze, then patted her on the back awkwardly.

"You are welcome, little girl."

"I'll return it to you tomorrow."

"No rush, but I'll sure be glad to see you again."

"Oh, you will." She stepped back, fingered away the unwanted moisture from her eyes. "You sure will."

He nodded, then called one of the young men bustling about. "Adam will walk you home."

"Oh, but there is no need. I live just around the corner."

"That's one corner too many. And it's after one in the morning, so—"

Alarmed, *Verochka* squinted at the wall clock, and almost wailed. "*Mon Dieu*, Madame would kill me now for sure!"

A husky rumble of Winston's chuckle accompanied her hasty retreat.

CHAPTER FOUR

JJ rubbed his bleary eyes then kneaded his aching shoulders. Dammit, he was exhausted. To quote Winston, "totally pooped.". He was embarrassed to be wiped out at barely three in the morning. He glanced into the cloudy mirror, plucked at a gray hair, and grimaced. Now there's proof he certainly wasn't getting any younger. Even a couple of years ago, he played his sax until the wee hours, then drink a half bottle of whiskey, and still be energized and revved enough for an amorous interlude.

Not anymore, laddie.

Even though thirty-two wasn't considered old by any stretch of the imagination, the added weight of ruling the Morris empire was bound to take its toll. Sometimes JJ felt ancient. Like today. Earlier, when he saw that tiny blonde girl perched atop of a bar stool, he cringed. She all but vibrated from the inside, watching him with open fascination. Oh, to be so young and vibrant. So energetic! He'd give his right arm to feel that again.

Right arm, huh? Then how will you play sax without it?

JJ tugged at his earlobe. The sad truth was, he became disillusioned and jaded during his two years at the helm of the family business.

Correction - businesses as in plural.

One bank, six hotels, two wineries, and too much real estate for any one company. The vast tentacles of the Morris Holding spread all over the country and overseas. If he knew the enormity of it all,

21

he'd probably have refused to step into the organization's CEO shoes after his father's death.

And who are you kidding, laddie?

JJ was too much of his father's son. To shun the responsibilities toward the business that his grandfather built on sheer determination and stubborn will to succeed was simply impossible.

Unfeasible.

Out of the question.

Even though at the time his mother had offered him two options — step up to the helm, and take over the reins, or turn them over to the board of directors. For JJ there was no choice. Morris through and through, he couldn't do anything differently.

And Madeline knew it, damn her cunning shrewd soul.

JJ heaved a sigh and rubbed his tired eyes. Their relationship was always strained, to put it mildly. Madeline's cold apathy, brusque indifference, blunt disdain— it hurt and confused him as a child. To earn his mother's approval, JJ tried hard to be the best at everything: school, sports, languages. But all for naught. Madeline totally ignored her only son, like he was invisible. If not for his father's unconditional love, JJ would have withered.

Charles Morris was a single stalwart in his life, his true champion. His anchor.

Despite being a busy man, he was always there for JJ, banishing monsters from under the bed, tending to the little boy's hurts, wiping his tears. And constantly reminding JJ of his own self-worth. But even all his father's love was unable to fill in the void. With a stubborn determination of a child, JJ craved his mother's attention, if not her love. But Madeline was incapable of love.

On some primordial level, he realized it even as a little boy.

Beautiful as she was cold, his mother lacked something vital, something essential he later identified as empathy.

JJ laughed, remembering his short but spectacular rebellious period, when he tried to gain his mother's attention with elaborate pranks such as dying his black hair electric blue or stealing his father's Bentley for a memorable night trip around Manhattan. How old was he? Sixteen, seventeen? Damn. Was he ever that young, that stupid? His desperate childish efforts went unnoticed or ignored by Madeline.

All he managed to achieve with his stupid infantile rebellion was humiliation of the only person who loved him unconditionally: his dad. That painful realization put an abrupt stop to JJ's folly. Shedding the obnoxious persona he had cultivated for quite some time, he manned up in a matter of hours. The revelation that his mother's callousness was not his fault crashed like a train at full speed.

He'd been such an idiot!

That simple truth brought an acceptance, then freedom, then pity toward the woman he started to perceive as Madeline.

Calm and contend, JJ finally learned to ignore her blatant indifference and disapproval. It didn't matter anymore. Shutting all the painful memories deep inside, he stopped calling her mother. Even in his mind, she was Madeline.

His father's death ripped JJ apart. But even in his grief he knew better than to turn to his mother. Incapable of compassion, totally unperturbed, Madeline didn't even pretend to mourn her husband. Instead, she firmly stepped forward, and took the reins of the family business into her elegant hands. More out of pure selfishness than anything else, she embarked on a quest to prove that a strong, independent woman had the talent to rule the Morris empire as well as any man.

However, she failed to take into consideration the long hours, the vast responsibilities, and the sheer enormity of the task. She soon realized her mistake.

In typical Madeline manner, instead of acknowledging her defeat, she decided to step back under a pretense of being too busy with her social obligations.

Turning the reigns of Morris Holdings to her only son, she blithely left the office, and never looked back. That was three years ago when JJ was barely twenty-nine.

The board of directors, even though apprehensive, grudgingly accepted the young CEO. Working like a man possessed, JJ quickly earned their approval and respect.

During the years of his leadership, the business expanded threefold, earning more money than all of them were able to spend in several lifetimes.

Was he proud of himself? Absolutely. Obscenely wealthy and independent at the age of thirty-two, JJ had the world at his feet. His every whim was attainable by a flick of his hand. As the most eligible bachelor, he could have any woman in the whole country, and beyond.

But was he happy?

Sex, even without deep emotional attachment, was quite pleasant and satisfying, indeed. But to a point. And how many Rolexes, exotic cars, yachts and airplanes did one need? JJ shook his head.

Getting cynical, laddie.

Maybe. Probably. Oh, hell. He raked all ten fingers through his hair.

More than tired, he was plagued by frustration. Deep, dark, and frightening.

Seemingly out of nowhere, a sudden discontent sprung forward, eating a hole in his gut. His life lacked something vital, something crucial and essential.

JJ was unhappy, and irritated, and dissatisfied. A sceptic with superficial values, an empty soul. In short, he was the male version of Madeline.

Dammit all to hell and back.

Out of habit, he poured himself a whiskey, then stared into the glass. He didn't want a drink.

"Sonovabitch," JJ cursed under his breath. Scanning his living room, his eyes landed on the black box with his cherished saxophone. His real joy. His only salvation. That, and his little bar on the quiet street in SoHo, where he escaped the hustle and bustle of the outside world, and become himself, even for a few hours. Only there was he able to relax and play his music to his heart content.

Lifting the sax gently, JJ cradled the familiar weight and shape of it against his chest, then brought the mouthpiece to his lips. The melody flew up, sad and soft, like his mood. Closing his eyes, JJ let out all his troubling thoughts, and dissolved into the music. The sudden image of the blonde girl from the bar drifted behind his closed eyelids. So out of place, awkwardly perched on the tall bar stool, she seemed like a tiny alien dropped there by accident. Who was she? A little rich girl defying her parents by visiting a grown-up bar in the middle of the night? Or a poor soul seeking refuge? Will he see her again? Doubtful. Did he want to? Maybe. She was so enraptured by the music, with a naked delight on her face, it was refreshing. And yes, invigorating.

So much so, JJ forced himself to concentrate on anyone else but her.

The little girl was gone by the time he finished playing. Ridiculously disappointed, JJ squelched his annoyance. That was for the best. She didn't belong in his bar. By now, she probably forgot all about him, and his sax, safe and sound in her own little world, wherever that might be.

JJ put down his instrument and ordered himself to forget that tiny blonde girl.

He'll never see her again. Or will he?

Winston might know who she was. Chuckling, JJ shook his head. Winston was one of a kind, indeed. Imposing, scary-looking, with a heart the size of Texas, and curiosity to match. No surprise if his bartender knew not only her name, but her entire damned life story.

Should he ask him? Better not. Some secrets were best left uncovered.

Let that brief encounter be a pleasant memory. Distant and sweet and unspoiled.

CHAPTER FIVE

Despite Madame's loud commanding voice, *Verochka* lost all ability to concentrate. Grabbing the barre with her left hand, she tried her damnedest to execute the perfect plie, but her leaden legs disobeyed. *Merde*, why were her knees so shaky and weak? And why, instead of the ballet music, the rumble of a sax teased her ears?

Snap out of it. Pay attention.

"And one, and two, and three. Brush your leg, rotate in, then out. Right arm up, legs straight, knees together. *Tendu point.* And one, and two..."

Why hadn't she noticed before how irritatingly high-pitched Madame Valeska's voice was? It droned on, and on, until *Verochka* was ready to scream.

"Miss Osipoff! Where is your arm? And why are you squatting like that? You are supposed to be a ballerina, for crying out loud, not a fricking baboon!"

Wincing, *Verochka* managed to murmur an apology.

Pay attention, you fool.

"Legs in first position, brush in, and out. *Tendu,* chin up. And one..."

Dieu merci, Madame Valeska switched her attention back to the class.

Letting out her breath, *Verochka* listened to the tongue-lashing aimed at another girl. Her legs were still disobeying, heavy and shaky and unresponsive.

27

Worse, her attention kept wandering. In her head, she was once again in the middle of a dimly lit bar, perched on the bar stool, listening to the soulful crying of a sax. She shivered as the image of the sexy musician swam before her eyes.

Mon Dieu, he was big. Not as big as Winston the bartender, but still. Tall, broad shouldered, with gorgeous black hair. Was it silky to the touch? Or coarse?

Merde, *and why are you even thinking about his hair? Think about your next step.*

Tendu point. Brush, in, and out. Chin up, back straight.

But the image of the handsome stranger refused to leave her alone.

What color were his eyes? Dark, or light?

She missed Madam Valeska's command to turn, which earned her another sharp reprimand. Ashamed of herself, mad at her body's stubborn refusal to listen to her brain's command, *Verochka* scowled.

Stop this foolishness. Listen to the music.

As if on cue, a rumble of a lone sax flew up, then scaled down to the lowest murmur. *Magnific!*

"Miss Osipoff! Where in the blue blazes are you? Pay attention!"

Darn. Missed another *plie.*

Calling herself a thousand bad names, *Verochka* strained her ears for the sounds of the piano.

"And one, and two, and three..."

She managed to follow the rhythm for the next sequence of steps. Barely.

Heureusement, the flow of morning exercises was as familiar as her own face. She could do them in her sleep. Usually. But not today. With an effort, she moved her leg behind, stretching, straining her toes. Her pointe shoes, that were like extensions of her feet, felt uncomfortable, painful. On top of it, in her haste to be on time for class, she forgot to bind her toes with tape. As a result, they pulsed like a rotten tooth. *Verochka* didn't need to look to know they were scraped raw and bleeding. *Merde.* How will she manage what comes next?

After one hour of barre, Madame will put each of them through a vigorous solo test. *Arabesque*, she'd carry it out. Probably. Maybe. But *jete*, or *sissonne?* That was a big challenge. Or, God forbid, a *fouette.* Praying silently to all the ballet gods, *Verochka* continued to struggle with her wooden legs and injured toes, waiting with trepidation to the final cords of the piano. Finally, the music stopped.

The room plunged into silence.

Please, God, please, please, please...

But her prayers were all for naught.

"Miss Osipoff, you are first, *s'il vous plait.*"

Verochka moved into the center of the room, wondering if that's how it felt when facing execution. She held her breath, lifted her face, and looked at Madame Valeska for instructions.

"And now, Miss Osipoff will demonstrate to us a *fouette.* Class! Your attention, please."

And with that, she aimed her hard stare at *Verochka*, and nodded for her to begin.

Here goes.

A fake smile on her face hurt as much as her feet, but the painful impact of landing onto her butt on the hard floor simply took her breath away. She managed just two twirls. Tears of humiliation sprung to *Verochka's* eyes, as the burning sensation in her rear end flared up.

"*Merde!*"

"You can say that again." Brutally hard, Madame Valeska's voice held not an ounce of compassion. "On your feet. Repeat."

Wincing, *Verochka* stood, wiped her tears, and assumed the starting position.

This time, she managed four revolutions, before her right leg gave out on her. She fell down as hard and ungraceful as an elephant in tutu. Her tailbone screamed in protest. As if that wasn't enough, a muscle cramp seized her right leg in brutal talons. Cursing under her breath, biting her lip, *Verochka* desperately massaged her calve with both hands. Damn, it was as hard as a stone. Oh, how she hated those debilitating cramps, the curse of all dancers!

Madame walked closer surveying *Verochka* in silence. Then she knelt. Surprisingly strong, Madame's hands kneaded for a long time, until the cramp dissolved. In a single fluid motion of a former prima-ballerina, Madame Valeska came to her feet. A deep disapproving scowl marred her face.

Uh-oh. Verochka knew that expression.

"You are dismissed, Miss Osipoff."

"Oh, but Madame, I—"

"Am in no position to resume dancing." A viciously cold voice bore no argument. "Go, soak your feet in ice, and put some salve on your toes. I'll see you in my office, later."

There was no reasoning with her formidable teacher. And the trip to her office? Talk about facing the firing squad. *Verochka* experienced that excursion only twice during her years in the school, and those were two times too many.

She shuddered in recollection.

Resigned, *Verochka* scrambled to her feet, grimacing in pain. Her imploring gaze did nothing to pacify the older woman. She drew in a deep breath and limped out of the room.

She'll soak her abused feet, baby her toes, and then go to the office to face well deserved scolding. After, she'll clean the floors as best as she can, hurt legs or not.

But nothing— not even Madam Valeska's wrath— could stop *Verochka* from going to the bar later. She shrugged away the wayward thought of a danger walking alone at night in SoHo. For crying out loud, it was 1962, not the dark ages, and her neighborhood was almost crime free. And there was the sweater to return to that wonderful kind bartender, Winston. Of course, she could easily send it to him by a courier. But he fed her, tended to her, then offered his own *un gilet* to ward off the cold. How could she not deliver it back personally?

And if by pure coincidence the tall, dark owner of that bar was there, playing his sax, it wouldn't matter to her. Not one damn bit.

CHAPTER SIX

That tiny blonde girl was here again. Seated at the bar, on the same stool as yesterday, she kept her eyes glued to JJ. He almost missed a note. Damn, he was losing his concentration. And it was all her fault. At the moment, she froze, closed her eyes. Her skinny arms lifted, one higher than other, as she swayed to music. Totally lost in the melody, oblivious to everything, the girl reminded him of a swan. Graceful, long-necked, heart-breaking elegant.

Geez, and where did that come from?

Irritated, JJ tore his eyes from the little intruder. Why had she come again? Who was she? Yesterday she might've wandered in by accident, tonight was different. She came here on purpose. But why? To see Winston, or to listen to his sax?

Look at them, heads bent together, chatting like two reunited relatives.

Winston hovered over her almost protectively, basking in a glow of her smile that was visible even from a distance. He never saw his bartender act so silly. It was embarrassing, really. On their own, JJ's eyes turned once again to that smiling creature. Tiny she might be, but her legs were sky-scraper long, shapely, and strong. The elegant column of her neck seemed almost translucent in the dim bar light. And why the hell was he paying attention to her legs or her neck?

Blonde and scrawny, she was nothing to look at compared to his usual female companions. JJ preferred his women tall, built, and beautiful. And brunettes.

And definitely old enough to know the stakes of the game.

In short, this girl was as far from his usual type as the minor scale from major. And still.

Dammit, he was aware of her. Annoyed with himself, JJ tried to rationalize his strange response. Just curious, that's all.

And who are you kidding, laddie?

As a result of his inner disquiet, he managed to execute a wrong note. The sax almost whined in protest.

Oh, hell no.

Now he was hopping mad. Who the hell was she, to come to *his* bar, his personal sanctuary, and spoil the perfect mood of the evening?

Disgusted, JJ put the sax into its protective box. He intended to find out who the hell she was, and where she came from. And shoo her away as fast as possible, dammit. A bar was no place for children.

He was about to take a step forward, when his longtime waitress Mimi stopped him. "Look at that blonde at three o'clock, Boss. She's been staring at you all evening."

Because Mimi was not only his employee, she was also one of the few he called friend, JJ didn't snap her head off. Instead, he grumbled under his breath, "Shit."

"Know her?"

"No."

Mimi nodded, swiveled her eyes in the direction of the girl, then back at him. "Want me to shake her off?"

And she'd do that, too. In a New York minute. Then he'd be free of the dubious honor to show her the door, earning Winston's wrath, and could resume his play. Oh, he was tempted. For a split second that is. But JJ was always honest with himself.

"That's the problem. I don't."

Mimi eyed him with open curiosity, then shrugged. "Oh, well. Good luck."

"Yeah, I sure need it."

Without another glance, JJ strolled toward the bar. He stopped a couple of feet from the girl. She leaned closer to Winston and let out a peal of laughter.

His insides clenched. His bartender was the first to notice him.

"Hey, there, Boss."

"Hey yourself."

The little blonde girl lifted her eyes, and looked straight at him. The impact was staggering. He'd tell himself later that it was her unusual eyes that prompted his heart to skip a few beats. Too large for her narrow face, those eerie colored eyes simply stopped his breath.

Violet.

Her eyes were violet without a hint of blue or grey. Like lavender or amethysts.

God have mercy.

He never saw anything more beautiful in his life. And that face! Not pretty in a classic sense, but...JJ fumbled for the word. Arresting. Striking. Heartbreaking.

She held his gaze, unwavering, eyeing him with an open admiration. His unruly heart lurched to his throat, then plunged all the way to his gut, and lower still. Shocked, JJ realized that he was becoming increasingly aroused. And all from a single glance.

Dammit. No way in hell.

Close up, she seemed even younger than he thought. Barely a teenager, with her hair in a ponytail. Talk about robbing the proverbial cradle. Feeling like a pervert, tense and uncomfortable, JJ frowned. And if he clamped his jaw any tighter, he'd reduce his teeth into a powder.

Moron.

JJ turned to Winston and glared. "She's not old enough to be a patron."

"*She* is sitting right here! In case you didn't notice." Light censure in that surprisingly rich haughty voice with a whisper of an accent was unmistakable. A shimmer of something exotic in it, and forbidden— and erotic as hell— made up a lethal combination.

Oh, he noticed, alright. So much that he was ready to implode.

The knot in his gut squeezed tighter. Still frowning, JJ turned his stare at her.

And lost his tongue.

Say something, you idiot.

For the life of him, JJ couldn't utter a single word. In the hushed, charged silence his heart was the only sound reverberating in his ears. He briefly wondered if she heard it.

After a moment, she obviously decided to take the initiative in her elegant hands.

"I'm Vera, *Verochka* Osipoff. And you are the owner of this wonderful place."

This time, her brilliant smile was aimed at him. The impact almost brought him to his knees.

"I love your music." She finished with a little catch in her voice.

"You love jazz?" Finally, his vocal cords unclenched enough to produce that gem of a question.

No nice to meet you, no how do you do, my name is JJ.

You love jazz? Really? She must think you're demented. Or rude. Or both.

"It seems that I do, although I never paid attention to it before."

Unperturbed, she kept those eerie mesmerizing eyes on his face.

"And what kind of music did you pay attention to before?" Almost angry, his question sounded more like an accusation than an inquiry.

Why was he acting so hostile? It wasn't her fault he was grabbed by the throat with lust. Sudden, brutal, hot as hell. It burned a hole in his gut.

Her reply came a second later. "Classical mostly."

Yeah, and why am I not surprised?

She had that look about her, elegant and ethereal, like a Debussy prelude.

"Miss *Verochka* here is a ballerina." Winston piped in with obvious pride.

That explained her mile long legs, and those fluid arms.

JJ cast a quick glance at Winston. The former patrol officer who stopped JJ that memorable night, cruising in his father's stolen Bentley, Winston looked ridiculous. A wide smile that split his craggy weathered face from ear to ear made him look even scarier, if that was possible. Bald, stocky, with bulging muscles and don't-fuck-with-me attitude, he was the image of a burly bouncer.

When Winston retired from the police force, JJ hired him on the spot. Based primarily on the gratitude for not arresting his stupid ass all those years ago, his decision paid off in spades. And Winston's imposing statue didn't hurt either. Currently, his tough as nails bartender was eyeing the pint of a girl in front of him with something close to a tenderness. Annoyed, JJ shook his head. If he didn't know better, he'd think that Winston was smitten. Well, maybe he was. Clearly, this girl managed to wrap him around her tiny pinky.

"She's all the way from Paris," Winston added this tidbit in a husky voice, all the while smiling like a besotted fool.

Paris, of course. That's why that sexy accent.

"And what are doing in New York, Miss *Verochka*?"

CHAPTER SEVEN

JJ's question was posed for her, but his bartender was on a roll. "She's studying in that famous dance school across the corner." Winston beamed another smile at his newly adopted protégé.

JJ narrowed his eyes and looked from Winston to the hot blonde perched on the bar stool then back to Winston.

And just what in hell do you intend to teach her, you old geezer?

Surprised and disgusted at the nasty thought, JJ gave himself a mental slap for acting like a jealous fool. What did he care. He didn't know the girl. Held no interest for her.

Yeah? Then why are your jeans feeling snug?

Sometimes he hated that damned inner voice.

Despite his current mood, JJ was impressed enough to give a soft whistle.

"The New York Ballet School?" That school and its owner, Madame Valeska, had a worldwide reputation. And who should know better than JJ, since he owned the building in which that famous school was located, and was well acquainted with its imposing leader.

"The one and the same." *Verochka* eyed him with a renewed interest. "Are you familiar with it?"

"Familiar? He is—"

JJ shot a quick glare at Winston, silently ordering him to shut up. Obviously, his message came through. The older man coughed, then nodded. For some unknown reason, JJ decided to conceal his true identity.

Turning back to the blonde girl, he nodded. "Yes, I am." Noncommittal. Short.

Momentarily confused, she frowned. As her mouth opened for another question, JJ forestalled it. "You are a long way from home, little *Verochka*."

"This is my home now." A typical Gaelic shrug of her shoulders was as exquisite as her face. "And I'm not little. I just look much younger than my years."

"And how old are you?"

"Twenty."

Dear God, practically a child. Never before had JJ felt the weight of his thirty-two years so acutely. Compared to that slip of a girl, he was ancient. The thought depressed him. He curved his lips into a fake smile.

Just look at her, so eager, so honest, so open.

It was a wonder a big bad city like New York hadn't wiped all that naiveté out of her. Given a few years, she'd probably learn to hide her feelings, guard her emotions under a cold indifferent mask. He sincerely hoped not.

And why do you care?

Opting for a safer subject, JJ asked a question that was burning his tongue. "Is this your real name?"

"My real name is Vera, but since my childhood, everybody calls me *Verochka*."

"Oh? And why is that?"

"That's how my parents called me. An endearing version of the very old name. Vera means 'faith' in Russian."

"Russian? I thought you were from France."

"Born and bred there, but my parents were immigrants from Russia."

He assimilated that information, tucking it inside to check out later.

"Where are they now, your parents?"

A hint of a shadow darkened her eyes before she replied, "They both perished two years ago. I came here on my own."

JJ did the math in his head then nodded at her with wonder and admiration. Two years ago she was eighteen. To embark on such a drastic move, at such a tender age? Too gutsy. This little girl seemed to have a courage that bellied her age.

"Why ballet?"

"My parents were ballet dancers, and I practically grew up in a variety of theaters. I loved everything about it. The smell. The feel. The atmosphere. I had potential since my early years, so, the decision was quite natural."

Her dazzling smile lit up her whole face.

"My father always said to me be fearless in what sets your soul on fire. Ballet sets my soul on fire." Another little shrug, before she finished, "Like your sax sets yours."

He must admit, she surprised him with that one. Was he so transparent, or was she so perceptive? In any event, the situation spelled trouble. With a capital T.

"Well, you know a lot about me," she quipped in that accented English that did nothing to pacify his discomfort, "but I still don't know anything about you, except that you play jazz, and own this bar. Oh, and that your name is JJ."

"That's about it, in a nutshell." That's all she needed to know. All he'd permit her to know. No need to reveal his true identity. Or his real name.

She cocked her head, eyeing him like a curious kitten. "Somehow, I doubt it"

Perceptive little thing, aren't you?

Okay, he'd humor her. "What do you want to know?"

"Oh, many things. Where did you learn to play sax? Is this your profession, or a vocation? And what does JJ stands for?"

Safe grounds. To a point. Despite himself, he grinned. "That's all?"

"For now."

"Well. I learned to play in my teens. It's my joy. It stands for Jacob Joseph."

"Such a grand biblical name. And how old are you, Jacob Joseph?"

"Too old."

"Too old for what?"

For you. He swallowed his answer before it sprang to his lips. Damn. *What the hell do you think you're doing?*

She's practically a baby, and he was all but salivating after her. Pervert.

Curter than he intended, JJ replied, "For a silly conversation."

Her eyes widened in surprise, as confusion bloomed on her expressive face. Winston frowned. An imperceptive shake of his head spoke volumes. Disapproval. Disappointment. Frankly, JJ was disappointed in himself.

You are an asshole, pal.

Cursing inwardly, he stepped back. "I kept patrons waiting long enough. Now I must play."

Without a wave goodbye, he turned away. A burning sensation in his back followed him all the way to his corner. Even without checking, JJ knew that two pair of eyes watched him in silent disbelief. Regret warred with his common sense.

Yes, his hasty retreat was abrupt, even rude, and definitely uncalled for. He swore under his breath.

A retreat? Who are you kidding, laddie?

He was running away, pure and simple. So what? Let her think whatever she wanted. And if she was insulted enough to never step a foot in his bar again, that's all the better. For her. And for him. Because JJ never wanted anything in his life like he wanted her. *Verochka,* with her violet eyes and tender, expressive face.

If he had an ounce of decency, he must protect this naive slip of a girl from himself. Gutsy she may be, but she has no defenses whatsoever where men like him—powerful, wordily, experienced—were concerned.

Let her dance, and enjoy her life, and forget all about him.

Swim away, Beautiful Swan. Swim as far and fast as you can.

CHAPTER EIGHT

"**I** will never go to that bar again. Ever! I'd rather break my leg. I'd rather break both legs!"

Fuming, *Verochka* drew in a deep breath, let it out with a loud whoosh. But her anger refused to evaporate. Instead, it flew hotter and stronger, increasing in force and intensity. She all but shook with it.

Merde.

But no matter what, she vowed to never step a foot inside of that bar. So what if she missed the company of Winston, and the sound of that heavenly sax? *Verochka* cursed out loud. Russian swearing words shot from her tongue like sharp bullets, followed by the more mellow but equally potent French profanity. Incensed, she ignored the prickly nick of embarrassment. *Verochka* rarely— if ever— used such unladylike language. But the moment clearly called for it, so she allowed herself the indulgence. As if on cue, her mother's voice laced with disapproval echoed in her mind,

You should be ashamed of yourself, mademoiselle. Cursing like a sailor? La honte!

With a careless shrug, *Verochka* disregarded that chiding. No one was around to hear her explosive tirade. She was free to express her disgust in any way she chose. Wasn't she? And she was entitled. Fuming and cursing, she stabbed her mop into the bucket with a vengeance.

The gall of that impossibly rude and overbearing man!

So, what if he played like a god? So, what if his hair was as black and gorgeous as starless night sky in Provence? So, what if his eyes were as dark and spectacular as Belgian chocolate? *Verochka* didn't care. Not one damn bit.

From now on, his image was forbidden to her like that sinful dark chocolate.

Forbidden but not forgotten.

She sampled that Belgian delight just once, long ago in Paris, but the taste of it was still fresh in her mouth. Would an experience be similar with that man? Afraid of the obvious answer, she shook her head. No way, no how.

Cheri, *who are you kidding?*

His dark velvet eyes framed by the impossibly long thick lashes were etched into her memory forever. And his chiseled unsmiling mouth.

And that stubborn strong chin. And...

Merde, *what are you doing,* Verochka?

Rhapsodizing about his looks was stupid, and foolish, and absolutely pointless.

He was rude, and insolent, and plain nasty. A shame, considering his talent with the sax. On top of it, he was a total stranger. Tall, dark, and hostile.

Silly to be disappointed in someone she barely knew. Even sillier to be hurt.

Hurt? Huh.

Straightening her shoulders, *Verochka* drew to her full height, and set her jaw. She was made of a tougher stuff. *Verochka* Osipoff was a fighter. Fearless, determined, and stubborn. She'd make herself forget him, and that foolish conversation, and his bar, and his music. So there!

Unexpectedly, the sound of a husky sax tickled her ears. It was so real, for a moment she forgot where she was. *Verochka* whirled around. But instead of a dim smoky bar, all she saw were rows of barre, and mirrored walls of the dance room. A phantom born out of memory, that melody flew up, then gradually dipped to a low murmur. A riot of goosebumps sprung along her arms. *Verochka* shook her head in a meager attempt to clear her mind of that seducing sound.

To no avail.

She tossed the mop to the floor and covered her ears with both hands. It continued to play. Then she squeezed her temples until her head ached. But that music, sad and soft and soul-searing, never let go. Giving in to the seductive sound, *Verochka* closed her eyes, swaying to the rhythm. Her arms lifted, her body moved, as if slowly pulled by invisible strings. But when her legs curved, assuming the dancing stance, she forcibly wrenched herself free of the illusion.

Merde! *What the hell are you doing? Stop this foolishness at once!*

Fuming, she turned away. She has duties to perform. The floor won't clean itself. She gripped the mop handle as if she were choking it to death then returned to scrubbing the scuffed hardwood floor. The old parquet was a poor substitute for the man she wished to punish, but at that moment *Verochka* didn't care. She attacked it like it was a living breathing thing. Like it was JJ, damn him.

Three days passed since that memorable evening. Three days, and she still was mad, and confused, and disheartened. And spellbound. By the music. And, yes, dammit, by the musician.

JJ. Jacob Joseph. She still didn't know his last name.

Like that made any difference.

Verochka snorted. Whatever his name was, he was still harsh and ill-mannered. But, *Dieu*, so handsome. Why did he treat her like a little girl? Didn't he see she was a woman grown? Instinctively, *Verochka* straitened her spine to her full height of five-four. Yes, she was slender, and small, just as a ballerina was supposed to be. But she was twenty, for goodness' sake, not twelve!

Even Winston didn't treat her like a child after their initial conversation. Instead of a Little Sparrow, he called her a Beautiful Swan, which pleased her enormously. So, why did his employer perceive her differently? And why did he cut their pleasant chatting in such an abrupt matter? Too old for a silly conversation?

Absurde!

Infuriated anew, *Verochka* plunged the mop into the bucked with an unnecessary force. As a result, a fountain of dirty water flew up, splashing all over the clean parquet.

"*Merde!* And look what you've done now, you silly cow!"

Resigned, she dropped the mop, and sank onto the middle of the wet floor. Her own reflection, multiplied by mirrored walls, added to the confusion.

She squirmed as water seeped into her leotard and berated herself for her childish behavior. Why was she so sad? Worse, she felt lost, like Alice from her favorite childhood book. The feeling of hurtling down a dark hole was disconcerting but exhilarating. Will she dare to travel all the way forward to discover the secrets and new paths? Or should she turn around, and climb back to safety and everything familiar? A tug of war between her mind and heart lasted a long time. Common sense finally won the battle.

Verochka rose to her feet. As great as the temptation was, she was better off to step back from it. There was no place in her life for anything besides ballet. Dancing was her mission, her vocation, her main goal.

You are a ballerina, first and foremost. Never forget it. Never question it.

Her soul belonged to dancing. It was her destiny.

And the dark stranger with his beautiful music? Just a distraction she couldn't afford. Her path to the ultimate dancing Olympus was clear, straightforward, and didn't allow any detours. She sacrificed so much, her childhood included, to finally get there. And when the victory was so close, she could all but taste it, *Verochka* had no right to stumble. No possible reason for doubts, or regrets, or second guessing. Why then did it depress her?

The life she led for the past two years suddenly lost all excitement. Normal, ordinary, ruthlessly organized, it now seemed boring and suffocating.

Her main goal to become a prima ballerina for The Royal Ballet appeared as an ephemeral, almost unattainable dream.

Stop it! What nonsense is that? If you won't believe in yourself, who will?

Dancing was in her blood, her one and only passion. Her salvation.

The beautiful stranger with chocolate eyes and magical sax was just a short and unexpected episode in her life, like a wonderful dream.

Enchanted.

Delightful.

Impossible.

Time to tuck those thoughts close to her heart, and hide them deep. And when loneliness swept over her, she'd allow herself to remember. And to wonder. And yearn.

Verochka swiped at that moisture trickling down her cheeks then stood and gathered her cleaning supplies, before leaving the room.

A soft and quiet murmur of a sax followed her all the way to her tiny apartment in the attic.

CHAPTER NINE

JJ called himself a thousand names, none of them complimentary. Through the windshield, he eyed the four-story grey building with something close to trepidation. Stately and dignified, with its row of tall Palladian windows on the third floor, it was one of the most prized pieces of real estate he owned in New York. This part of SoHo belonged to the historic district with its typical cast-iron architecture, trendy bars, and the former industrial buildings that were converted to pricy apartments sought after by the young artistic crowd. He loved this picturesque part of New York. He felt right at home here, especially in his little bar on Broome Street just around the corner. His gaze swept along 434th Avenue, then returned to the familiar grey structure towering ahead.

Why on earth did he come here? And why was he sitting in his car, in front of his own property, debating the wisdom of his impromptu visit? Maybe, because on the third floor of that building was the famous ballet school, he had no business to be interested in. That school should concern him, the landlord, only as a tenant.

No more. And it was, until now. Until he met the tiny blonde girl who was a student here. He missed her, dammit. Three nights in row he eyed the doors of the bar, waiting for her. He was so obvious, that Winston, and even Mimi, made a few joking comments. JJ ignored their good-natured needling. Instead, he became worried. What happened? Why did she fail to return for three nights? Maybe, she was sick?

Or maybe she was insulted by your asinine behavior?

Wasn't that what he wanted? For her to get angry enough to stay away? Dammit, wasn't it? JJ swore, plowing his fingers through his hair.

That one brief encounter affected him more than he was willing to admit. More than he was comfortable with. Her mesmerizing eyes haunted him so that JJ became distracted. Impatient and irritated, he found himself pacing his Midtown office, unable to concentrate on business matters. Even the smallest decision took a double effort to make. Only this morning, he read the financial report for the last quarter twice before he realized he didn't give a damn about a single effing thing.

JJ stopped caring about his duties and responsibilities, daydreaming instead of a pair of unusual violet eyes. That made him mad. Mostly at himself but also at her.

How dare she disrupt his well-structured life?

How dare she upend his world, and then disappear like damned smoke?

What right did she have? Showing up in *his* bar, befriending *his* bartender, listening to *his* sax, and then just poof, evaporate into thin air?

That little sprite went too far!

So what if those accusations sounded absurd even to him? JJ didn't care. His rational mind can go to hell, and take its logic along for the ride.

If she won't come to his place, he'll come to hers, and give her a piece of his mind. But first, he needs to come up with a plausible explanation for his impromptu visit for Madame Valeska. Would the pretense of an inspection fly? Maybe. Possibly. Hell, who was he kidding? A shrewd and astute woman, the owner of that renowned ballet school, will realize in no time that even the urgent inspection didn't warrant the visit from the Morris Holding CEO in the middle of a week. And, according to the lease, she must've been provided with a twenty-four-hour notification.

Damn, what was he thinking? He wasn't, that's the problem. He just reacted. Like a damned schoolboy.

And when did he start to ignore his brain, and listen to his heart? Three days ago, that's when. Dammit all to hell and back.

Everything changed three days ago. Suddenly, irrevocably. And there was nothing to be done about it. The real question was, did he *want* to do something?

Did he want to erase the memory of that evening from his mind? The answer was a firm and definite no.

It scared him. It excited him. It made his blood churn, and his gut burn. It made him alive for the first time in ages.

JJ frowned. He was turning into a teenager ruled by his glands. Pathetic.

Never before in his thirty-two years had he felt so uneasy, so anxious. Or so tempted.

Face it pal, you're losing it, and fast.

No way in hell. He was still in control. No problem forgetting about that little blonde urchin if he chose so. And he intended to. Soon. He had to satisfy his curiosity first. Who knew, maybe he imagined the whole damned thing, and blew it out of proportion.

Hope springs eternal, laddie.

JJ cursed out loud, something he was never in the habit of before. *Shit. What now?*

The smart thing to do was to turn around, and then head back to his office. There were enough pressing matters on hand to keep him busy. The bank in Manhattan, the hotel in Lisbon, the vinery in Tuscany, to name a few. And that cursed financial report.

And don't forget the upcoming annual ball.

To his utter annoyance, an extravagant gala at the Paradise Hotel The Morris Holding threw each year before Thanksgiving loomed on the horizon.

Attending that glitzy event went along with his duties as the head of the company. JJ hated every moment of it. Strolling along the ballroom with a flute of champagne, and making small talk with the patrons was not his cup of tea.

But he's gotta do what he's gotta do. Just one night a year, and then he'll forget all about it. Thankfully, that ball was his mother's domain. JJ was not required to participate in preparations, except to approve the budget, and disburse the funds. Thank God for small favors.

Briefly, he wondered what kind of monstrosity his mother created this time. Last year, it was themed as a Egyptian event, with all the guests dressed accordingly to that era. To JJ, it was pretentious, if not outright crazy. But hey, since the rich and famous patrons were only happy to fork out the exorbitant fee, what did he care whether they were in stupid costumes, or not? JJ shrugged it off. There was still time until November. Madeline will call him soon enough with the required budget. No reason to dwell on it now, when there was a more pressing matter at hand. Such as his on spur-of-the moment trip to the ballet school, and his upcoming visit with the little enchantress who turned his world upside down, and tighten his guts in knots. And maybe—please, God—it will be enough to exorcise her ghost out of his system, and leave him in peace.

But before that, JJ must come up with a spin for the formidable Madam Valeska.

But no pressure, laddie.

Despite everything, he laughed. Yeah, he's got his job cut out for him. Well, he'd treat it like any other challenge thrown at him. Visor off, head on, full speed ahead. And just in case, this time he'd add a prayer to the mix. Somehow he was sure he needed it.

So, what are you waiting for?

JJ sucked in a deep breath and flung the car door open, then stepped out.

CHAPTER TEN

"Leg up, chin up, hands up. Miss Osipoff! Stretch. More!"
Verochka winced. *Mon Dieu,* if she stretched any more, she was going to pull a muscle. Stifling her groan, she obeyed Madame Valeska's command. Thankfully, today her limbs were warm and supple, and didn't give her any trouble.

Unlike her wayward thoughts. Or her strange dreams.

More like a vision, those vivid dreams featuring the tall, dark, and handsome sax player, refused to dissipate with sunlight, and kept her in a constant state of breathless expectation. But expectation of what?

Her decision to avoid that rude man was firm and unquestionable. And easy to implement. All she had to do was stop her nocturnal trips to his bar. And she accomplished that, for three straight days. Three impossibly long, miserable days.

No, *Verochka* was not depressed. Just out of sorts. Temporarily. She was too busy to even think about him. But her unruly imagination disagreed. Slithering through *Verochka's* resolve, it managed to ambush her more often that she cared for.

Like right now.

"Miss Osipoff! Where have you gone?"

Merde.

Like a bucket of icy water, Madame Valeska's voice brought her crushing back. Calling herself a few unpleasant names, *Verochka* grabbed the barre with a white knuckled grip.

Pay attention, you fool.

To make up for her faux pow, she exercised a perfect plie, then lifted her leg as high as humanly possible. That warranted a murmur of approval from her mentor. Bolstered by that rare show of praise, *Verochka* doubled her efforts.

The creak of the opening doors interrupted her concentration.

Since *Verochka* was poised with her back to it, she disregarded the intrusion, and continued with her routine. Whoever broke Madame Valeska's cardinal rule, and barged in during class, was none of her business. Poor misguided soul was in for a very nasty tongue lashing. But at the very least, it will draw Madame's attention long enough for all of them to take a free breath.

But instead of the rude tirade she anticipated, Madame's exclamation was almost friendly.

"Oh, Mr. Morris! What a pleasant surprise!"

"I hope I'm not interrupting?"

The male voice sounded familiar. Deep, well-modulated, cultured.

Where had she heard that voice? Curious, *Verochka* strained her ears, all the while concentrating on her exercises. Distracted or not, Madame had no trouble keeping her attention on the class. Sometimes it seemed she wore an additional pair of eyes on her nape.

"Of course not. You are welcome here any time."

A moment later, Madame Valeska clapped her hands, and called out, "Class, your attention, *s'il vous plaît.*"

On cue, all the dancers stopped, and turned around to face their teacher and her guest. *Verochka* followed suit. As soon as her eyes landed on the newcomer, all the breath whooshed from her lungs. JJ! *Mon Dieu,* what was he doing here?

Her silly heart gave one heavy thump, then trembled painfully against her left breastbone. Had he come looking for her? Why? He all but bit her head off the other night, and sent her packing. And what if he tells Madame about her visits to the bar? She'd be in such trouble!

Then it hit her. A bubble of relief rose up. He must be here for an interview. He was a musician, *non*?

Just recently, their longtime pianist decided to retire, and Madame was searching for a replacement. But of course! That must be it. *Verochka* let out a calming breath.

And how would she cope with seeing him day after day in the class?

Merde.

Her decision to avoid him at all costs just got smashed to smithereens.

She'd think of something.

Like what?

Trying to look anywhere but the place where JJ was standing, *Verochka* cast her eyes downward. The prickling sensation of being watched was unmistakable. She felt it all the way from her burning ears to her hurting toes. Even without looking, she knew that he was staring right at her.

Verochka bit her lip. Keeping still took an enormous effort on her part, considering that her knees—and her whole body— began to tremble. The proverbial butterfly in the pit of her stomach flapped like crazy. Uncomfortably hot, with sweat rolling in rivulets down her back, *Verochka* didn't need a mirror to know that she was blushing. She shifted her shaky legs and grabbed the barre like an anchor.

Mon Dieu, *let him switch his attention to any other dancer. I beg you!*

Her desperate prayer was interrupted by Madame Valeska's stern voice.

"Class, let me introduce you to our esteemed landlord, Mister Reginald Morris."

At first, *Verochka* thought her ears were playing a trick on her. Startled, she whipped her gaze to her mentor. What? A landlord? But no, Madame must be mistaken. He was the bar owner and sax player. No way could a musician from the neighboring bar, however successful, own this building.

And what did Madame Valeska call him? *Reginald?*

Yes, a mistake for sure. His name was JJ. Wasn't it?

Slowly, *Verochka* dragged her eyes toward the man who disturbed her dreams.

Impossibly tall, incredibly handsome, dressed in a classically cut business suit, he exuded the wealth and power like an expensive perfume.

Mon Dieu, did he lie to her?

His sure stance, the expression on his face, the way he held his head— everything screamed rich and famous.

Mon Dieu, *I'm such a fool!*

Was it silly to feel so disillusioned, so betrayed?

Even sillier to hurt all over, like someone bashed her over the head.

Not someone. Mister Reginal Morris. *The bastard!*

Her anger surged up, hot and ferocious, obliterating all other emotions.

Shaking from the force of it, *Verochka* balled her fists until her nails dug into her palms. She welcomed the pain. It centered her as nothing else.

Enraged, *Verochka* glared at the impeccably dressed liar.

Sax player my butt.

Made a fool of her, didn't he? And she believed every bloody thing he said. Worse, she lapped up his fake story like a brainless, gullible idiot.

Seduced by the music and a pair of chocolate eyes. Shame on you, Verochka.

Mad at herself, at him, at the world in general, she fought to keep the treacherous tears at bay. She'd be damned if she cried in front of him!

Who did he think he was? The ruler of the Universe? The jerk. With a capital J.

Verochka Osipoff was no one's dummy. Maybe naïve, certainly young, but she was one strong woman. Proud, and self-reliant, and free willed.

She might be poor, and not of his elevated social strata, but she never belittled or hurt any living soul. She had more decency in her little pinky than this rich and conceited man. *Esteemed* landlord, was he? Well, landlord he might be, but esteemed was not a word she'd apply to JJ. He was a fraud, and a liar to boot. Nothing worse than that combination.

Fuming, shaking, *Verochka* narrowed her eyes and glued them to his face. A deep frown darkened his features, but his gaze never wavered.

That's right, frown away, you bastard. You are in for a big, unpleasant surprise, because this little Parisian is about to give you a piece of her mind.

But later. Without an audience of her classmates or her teacher.

Fortified by her decision, *Verochka* tore her eyes away from JJ—correction, *Reginald*—and contemplated her next step. If she didn't have a chance to corner him in the school, she intended to go to his bar. Tonight.

And may God have a mercy on his pitiful soul.

CHAPTER ELEVEN

U h-oh. He was in trouble, if *Verochka's* smoldering glare was any indication. Sizzling, molten, darkened to the deep amethyst, her eyes managed to convey her emotions as if she spoke them out loud. The Little Swan was mad. Magnificently so. All but vibrating from it, she stared at him with such fire, it was a miracle she didn't singe a layer of his skin.

The little hell-cat.

JJ had enough sense to smother his laugh. He'd give everything to channel all that heat into a more pleasurable venue! A treacherous thought, it knifed his gut, as his imagination flared with the pictures of *Verochka,* naked.

Panting.

Writhing.

Instantly, he became hard as rock. Damn. Mortified by his body's reaction, JJ shifted his stance, grateful for his fashionable wide trousers. But he was unable to tear his gaze off of her. That form hugging ballet attire left nothing hidden from his hungry eyes. He almost swallowed his tongue when his gaze dropped to her unencumbered by a bra breasts. They were small but firm, with nipples pocking at the tight lycra of her bodice. Her slender torso narrowed to an impossibly tiny waist that could be effortlessly encircled by two hands.

His hands.

Like two elegant wings, her fluid arms lay along her body. Fascinating.

And her legs! Milelong, shapely, beautifully proportioned, they seemed to go forever. JJ shook his head. How had he ever thought of her as a little girl? Moron. She was all woman, with a capital W. And she'll be his. Soon. As soon as he was able to break that fiery barrier of mistrust and anger she erected between them.

This woman is mine.

In the span of his lifetime, he was never more sure of anything than he was now.

Never wanted anything like he wanted her. Never needed anything more than her.

Damn, he was in trouble. Deep trouble.

JJ frowned. Wanting, even craving, was one thing, but *needing* another person? That was first. He should be shocked, or scared, or both. He was none of that.

Instead, he became elated.

Revved.

Determined.

The prospect of a long battle to win that little spitfire delighted him. JJ didn't have a single doubt that he will came out a victor. He always did.

A satisfied smile tipped JJ's mouth. That little blonde enchantress had no prayer. In no time at all, she'd share his bed.

And then what? Another one of your conquests?

No way in hell. *Verochka* was nothing like the other women he dated. She was unique. She was tender. She was impossibly young. Practically a girl, not even of the legal age. JJ shrugged it away. His mind was set. His heart thundered.

Anticipation burned in his gut, hungry and hot and impatient. Nothing can stop him now. As soon as possible, he promised to go to Cartier, and buy an engagement ring. He'll let her to become accustomed to his company, before he popped the question. Dead sure of her answer, JJ disregarded the nagging feeling that he was rushing into something unfamiliar, something huge and important. So not like him.

So what? There was the first time for everything, his spontaneous decision included.

Watching her blazing glare, JJ bit his cheek to prevent his smile from spreading wider.

If only she knew! She'd probably scratched his eyes out, before kicking his balls all the way to his throat with those magnificent and long legs.

Better bide your time, laddie.

Yes, he'd give her time, but not too long. Lengthy engagements were a nuisance. Thank God, they lived in 1962, not in the last century when it was customary to wait until the nuptials for a year or two.

He shuddered. A year? He'd be lucky if he lasted a week. By Christmas— New Year the latest—he planned to introduce the new Mrs. Morris to society, and his status as New York's most eligible bachelor will cease to exist. Best news ever.

But what of the ballet?

She was hellbent on making her mark, becoming a prima ballerina. What was it again, The Royal Ballet troupe in London?

Over my dead body.

One way or another, JJ intended to make sure she stayed in New York, with him.

Because whether she realized it or not, they belonged together. And if he has to interfere in her dancing carrier one way or another, so be it. Without a lick of guilt, he'd do it, and the consequences be damned. If she couldn't live without ballet, he'll indulge her, and buy her the finest troupe in the country. Her own ballet company. Let her dance to her heart content until she's ready to settle down.

Until she's pregnant with my child.

Yes, that was exactly what he planned to do. But *Verochka* Osipoff—soon to be Morris—was destined to live right here, in New York, happily ever after.

Enormously pleased with his decision, JJ turned his attention to Madame Valeska.

"I would greatly appreciate a private word with one of your pupils."

"Oh?" She creased her forehead and eyed JJ with suspicion. "And who might you like to speak with?"

"Miss Osipoff."

"*Verochka?* But...why?"

"With all due respect, Madame, this is between me and her."

Deep disapproval shone from her eyes. Guarding her little swans like a dragon, wasn't she? Well, there were two options disarm that dragon, or conquer it. Whichever worked best.

Frowning, Madame Valeska pursed her lips, clearly torn between her duties to her students and her obligations to her landlord.

Undeterred, JJ gave her his most engaging smile. Infusing the equal parts of authority and conviction into his voice, he addressed the formidable woman. "We both know I do not need your permission, and could easily approach Miss Osipoff on my own. But out of respect for you as her teacher and mentor, I'm asking you first."

"Well, since whatever I say will be irrelevant, you can talk to *Verochka*. But only after the class."

"But of course." Taking one of her small hands, JJ brushed a light kiss over her knuckles. "I truly appreciate it, Madame Valeska."

"Don't make me regret it, Mr. Morris."

"Whatever do you mean, Madame?"

Still frowning, she lowered her voice. "That girl had it rough. When she first arrived here, she was so thin, I could easily see through her. Malnourished, almost pitiful, with no family, and no money, and God, so young! Barely a child. How she managed to reach New York, guided by nothing else but sheer guts and stubbornness, is a pure miracle. Oh, but her talent! A true gift from above. Despite the lack of formal schooling, even then she could dance better than many prima ballerinas, and believe me, I've seen a lot of them. I took her in, let her stay in the storage place in the attic converted to an apartment. And never regretted it ever since. She became more than a pupil to me, Mr. Morris." Lifting her eyes, she squinted at JJ. "I have no right, but I'll ask you all the same: please, be careful with that girl." A deep sigh later, she snapped her back ramrod straight, and managed to look at him down her pert nose. "And if you hurt her, young man, you'll answer to me, landlord or not."

As warnings went, this one was truly ridiculous, even laughable, all things considering. Should he be amused, irritated, or insulted? Surprisingly, he was none of that. Instead, a surge of admiration for this tiny dragon of a woman flooded his heart. A caring nature, even deliberately camouflaged under a thick layer of sternness and indifference, was impossible to hide. And not many a man was brave enough to threaten JJ to his face, let alone a female, and live to tell about it.

Deeply touched, he cradled her hands in his.

"I promise I will never hurt *Verochka*."

I will marry her.

But he chose to keep that little detail secret for now. It was too new, and yes, a bit shocking, even to him.

"See that you don't, Mr. Morris." The gaze she aimed at him was a hair short from being hostile. But she no longer fooled him. JJ smiled.

"But you are mistaken, Madame."

Two raised brows almost disappeared under the ruler-strait bangs, as she stared at him quizzically. "You said Verochka didn't have any family. You were wrong. You are her family."

A genuine smile accompanied by a suspicious mist in Madame's eyes transformed her face. It looked almost gentle, and somehow vulnerable.

Surprised, JJ blinked. For as long as he knew this woman, she had never smiled. Ever. Always cool and composed, with a perpetual deep scowl on her smooth face, his famous tenant seemed intimidating, even frightening. As to her age? It was everybody's guess. Now, with her shining eyes and tender smile, she looked softer, and younger, and almost... fragile.

What do you know, the formidable tyrant is a softie.

In the next moment, as if coming to her senses, Madame Valeska pulled back her stern familiar mask. The dragon was back.

"If you want to wait for Miss Osipoff, you may certainly do that." Once again, her voice became curt, clipped, and cold. "But I must ask you to step out. The class is not yet finished."

"Of course." And pulling his own impersonal mask back to his face, JJ nodded. With the last brief glance at *Verochka,* he turned around and left the room.

The prickling sensation of being watched followed his every step. By the time JJ closed the door behind him, his backside almost smarted from the sharp little daggers thrown at it by a pair of sizzling violet eyes.

CHAPTER TWELVE

V*erochka* wasn't sure how she managed to finish her class. Sheer stubbornness kept her upright and moving, while her blazing anger fueled her resolve.

The gall of the man! The infuriating bastard! The pompous jerk! Just wait until she gets into his face.

Oh, you are in for a such big surprise, Mr. Reginald Morris.

Almost on autopilot, she stretched, pivoted, and twirled. Her legs hurt, her toes screamed bloody murder, but she ignored the familiar discomfort.

Pain was good. Pain was her friend. It centered her, and obliterated her mind, and reminded *Verochka* of who she was: a ballerina. First and foremost. A darn good one, if she dared to say so herself. Everything else was irrelevant.

Even her heart, or her disillusionment, or the overwhelming sense of betrayal.

Merde.

As soon as Madame Valeska announced the end of the class, *Verochka* bolted from the room. Her pointe shoes she forgot to remove clicked loudly against the parquet floor. Unmindful of the danger it presented for her legs, she bounded the staircase toward the attic, skipping two steps at the time. She slipped just once, but managed to catch herself in time. A fall was the last thing she needed. In six weeks, she was scheduled to dance before the panel of The Royal Ballet. *Verochka* refused to blow her chance. Oh, to be selected for that world renowned troupe! A dream come true. The imminent goal she sacrificed so much to reach. Jeopardizing her body before that monumental event was irresponsible and plain stupid.

Verochka stopped, removed her pointes, and barefooted continued up the stairs. Slow, and easy. For a couple of heartbeats. Oh, the hell with slow and easy! Holding her ballet shoes against her chest, she rounded the landing on the run. By the time she reached the door to her apartment, *Verochka* was out of breath.

So what? She was not on a dancing floor anymore.

Might as well breathe any way she wanted. Madame was not here to scold her. Nevertheless, she drew a couple of calming breaths. A fatigue she stubbornly ignored before, refused to stay offstage any longer. Weary, *Verochka* slumped her shoulders. There was one hour before her private lesson with Madame Valeska that was even more grueling than a group class. Her mentor relentlessly put her through every step of her solo from Swan Lake.

The Tchaikovsky masterpiece was one of the most demanding to perform in the entire history of ballet. The part of Odette was coveted by all ballerinas, but not everyone, even the most talented of them, were able to rise to the challenge. *Verochka* was determined to succeed. There was no choice if she wanted to join The Royal Ballet as their next prima.

Wanted? She desired it with every fiber of her being! She lived for it. She breathed for it. She sacrificed for it. She vowed to do anything—absolutely anything—to grab the opportunity with both hands, and make her teacher proud. And if she had to rehearse until she dropped, so be it.

She didn't want to think about her janitorial duties after class. No matter how exhausted she was, she never reneged on her chores. She owed Madame Valeska too much.

Lost in thoughts, she stood by her door for a long time. *Verochka* jolted. What time was it? There was no clock on the wall in this section of the building, but even without it, she was sure she had dawdled for quite some time.

Merde.

The rest she needed so badly must wait until later. There was just enough time to jump in the shower, gulp down some yogurt, before dawning a fresh leotard, and heading to the third floor for her class.

As soon as she finished, she promised herself to grab her cleaning supplies then scrub the floors. And then march straight to the Broome Street Bar for one last time. Oh, she'd let him have it, alright. And if there was an audience, all the better.

Let all the patrons of that miserable establishment know what a lying pig its owner was! Fortified by that decision, she grabbed the doorknob, and twisted it. She never locked her door. What was the point? She didn't have any valuables except her pointe shoes, and no one ever wandered up to the attic but her.

With a deep weary sigh, *Verochka* stepped inside. Damn, she was tired more than she realized. Wiping her sweaty forehead with one hand, she shut the door, slumped against it, and...froze.

Her mind went totally blank as the pair of familiar dark eyes met her gaze.

Here, in the middle of her tiny room, stood none other than JJ Morris.

No, Reginald Morris, remember, you silly goose?

But her brain's correction went unheeded. Mesmerized, she blinked a couple of times, but the picture stayed the same. A figment of her unruly imagination? An apparition? She'd pinch herself if her hands hadn't gone numb.

By their own volition, her fingers unclenched.

Bang!

Verochka's shoes clattered to the floor. In the hushed silence of the room that sound seemed deafening. A deep laugh confirmed her worst fear. The man who invaded her dreams was really here. Not a vision, but a living breathing entity.

He dwarfed her tiny space to the size of a postage stamp.

His rich and exotic fragrance permeated the room. Like an intoxicating mist, it enveloped her in its seductive fold. In close proximity, he seemed even more gorgeous than ever, if that was possible. Thick and wavy, ink black hair framed the face of a warrior. Or a fallen angel. Dark chocolate eyes gleamed with secrets and promises of something forbidden.

She shivered, hugged herself, but that mesmerizing gaze kept her riveted to the spot. Unwillingly, her eyes journeyed across his features.

Mon Dieu, it should be criminal for a man to have such long lashes. As if drawn by a magnet, her eyes dropped to his mouth. Such a beautifully carved mouth. Well defined upper lip, with a strong groove, a full lower one, almost puffy.

Her heart melted. All the air abandoned her lungs with a helpless *whoosh.* A hot tidal wave flooded her stomach. Her small breasts became heavy, pocking through the flimsy material of her leotard. She was inexperienced, but not a dummy not to recognize what was happening.

Awakened.

Aware.

Aroused.

Cheeks flaming, *Verochka* couldn't tear her gaze away.

The air became thicker, darker, as if charged by an electric current.

She swore a burst of sparks and a hiss of sizzling echoed in the small room.

Danger.

A satisfied smile curved those beautiful lips, and then a deep chuckle rumbled free. The sound broke the enchantment.

Verochka jerked back, shook her head. What just happened?

You know what, you fool. Snap out of it!

Burning from shame, she deliberately balled her fists. Mad at herself, *Verochka* glared at the man who reduced her to the pitiful state of jelly.

"What do you think you're doing?" *Dieu merci*, her voice betrayed her turmoil.

An indolent smile flashed across his face, setting her teeth on edge.

"Why, inspecting my property, and making sure my tenants are okay."

"I am not one of your tenants!"

Maybe stomping her feet for emphasis was childish, and definitely unwise, since she was still barefooted. As a result, she managed to abuse her heel. Wincing, *Verochka* ignored the pain, and concentrated on anger.

That was all his fault! In a matter of minutes, he managed to disturb, excite, and humiliate her, damn his gorgeous chocolate eyes.

"But you are."

Tilting his head in the manner that struck her as extremely arrogant, JJ gazed at her with something close to a smirk on his face.

"As a pupil of the ballet school that *is* my tenant, you fall under *that* category. And your door was unlocked."

And that tone of voice, like he was addressing a foolish child!

"*Merde!*"

His burst of laughter filled the room, sending a wave of goosebumps along her arms. Her body reaction insulted her, and ignited her anger all anew. "No matter what, you have no right to invade my privacy."

Congratulating herself on acting as a mature and sensible woman, *Verochka* schooled her face into what she hoped was an impersonal mask.

"You are correct, and I apologize for it. My only excuse is that I wanted to talk to you face to face, without an audience."

Despite her anger, her curiosity poked through. "Talk to me?"

"Yes, talk, and explain..." He hesitated, ran his hand through his hair.

"Explain what?"

"Well, everything. I didn't want you to think that I—"

"Deliberately made a fool out of me? That you lied to me?" Her loud snort was rude, and unladylike, but she didn't give a damn. "Don't bother. It really doesn't matter to me."

You are lying to yourself. Don't bother? Doesn't matter? *Really?*

Wasn't she going to confront him later? To demand an explanation?

Not anymore, she wasn't. Verochka shrugged her treacherous thoughts off.

I changed my mind. So what?

"I never lied to you." Serious and sincere, the tone of his voice did nothing to extinguished her anger. If anything, it added the proverbial water to oil.

The nerve of the wretched man!

Infuriated, she rounded on him, coming so close she noticed the golden specks in his irises.

"*Mon Dieu!* How can you say that? You told me that saxophone was your joy, that your name was JJ, and that you are the owner of the bar!"

"And all of that is true. I own the Broome Bar, among other things. My name is JJ, and the sax is my one and only joy. Or it was, until..."

"Until?"

"You won't believe me anyway, so let's skip it."

"By all means." She windmilled her arms for emphasis. "Skip whatever you wish. As a matter of fact, you can skip all the way back from where you came." She marched to the door then flung it open. "Leave this room at once!"

He didn't move. Shaking his head, he gave out one of his infuriating deep laughs.

"I won't, so you may as well save your breath, little—"

"If you call me 'little girl' just once, I swear, I won't answer for my actions!"

A loud hand clapping was mocking, almost insulting.

"Bravo. I always admired fiery spirited women. It's quite...invigorating."

Verochka saw red. "*I-invigorating*? Why you conceited, arrogant—"

But he rolled over her spattering with an ease and experience of a seasoned bouncer.

"I was about to say little hellcat. You, *Verochka* Osipoff, are many things, but 'little girl' is not one of them."

His gaze darkened, his face grew intense, almost frighteningly so.

Staring at her, he lifted a hand, reached over. Afraid that he was going to touch her, *Verochka* held her breath. Fear and anticipation waged war in her heart.

Oh, yes, please.

His hand dropped without making contact.

Merde.

As if shaking off a spell, JJ shuddered, then took a step back.

She'd scold herself later for feeling so ridiculously bereft.

You are a fool, Verochka. *Did you forget what a despicable liar this man is?*

She too took a step back. Bare, her feet made no noise on the carpeted floor. But her thundering heart pulsed in her ears. Briefly, she wondered if he heard it.

"Where was I before being so rudely interrupted?" Scrounging his forehead in concentration, he tapped a finger against his lips.

Look at him! Unruffled, cool and controlled, like nothing out of ordinary just happened. Probably nothing had. For him. But for her...

"Oh, yes. My alleged lying."

What! Did she hear him correctly?

Mon Dieu, the man was impossible! Infuriating, exasperating. Maddening.

"Alleged?" Her disbelief was short-lived, sliding comfortably into irritation. "Why, you have a nerve, Mr. Morris. Mr. *Reginald* Morris."

Her rebuke brought a slight nod of his head. "I believe I do have nerve, but that's irrelevant at the moment. I told you my name was JJ, which is the truth. My full legal name is Reginald Jacob Joseph, but since my childhood, I answer only to JJ."

"Why?"

"Why what?"

"Why three names?" *And that's all you're wondering about? Really!*

"Oh, that." After a negligent shrug JJ resumed his explanation. "My mother named me Reginald after some ancestor of hers, but my dad always wanted to name me after his father and grandfather—Jacob and Joseph, respectively. So, there you have it."

Another shrug, this one more self-conscious than careless. Sticking both hands in his pockets, JJ slowly scanned the room with his eyes. She bet he didn't see his surroundings. What did he see?

For some incomprehensive reason she felt sorry for him.

Have you lost your mind?

The man has everything, looks, money, position in society. His bar and saxophone, too. She had no doubt he had many friends. Many *girlfriends.*

When her mind veered into that direction, *Verochka* gave herself a hard mental shake.

I'm so not going to think about it!

Before her brain has a chance to process, she blurted out: "What kind of a name is Reginald?"

His short bark of a laughter lacked merriment. "A stupid and pompous one for sure. That's why I refuse to answer to it. My mother is the only one who calls me that."

"*Non*, not the only one. You forgot about Madame Valeska."

"Oh, yes, the formidable Madame Valeska, God bless her quick tongue and meddling heart."

Verochka bristled, as her anger flared. No one belittled her favorite mentor in her presence! Marching forward, she stabbed his chest with her index finger.

"Never say anything derogatory about that woman." She punctuated each word with a sharp poke to drive the meaning through. "Or else!"

"Or else what?"

"Oh, believe me, you don't want to find out."

"But what if I do?"

JJ covered her stabbing finger with his hand, then pressed her hand firmly against his heart. It vibrated under her open palm like a drum, strong and heavy. Her own heart skipped a beat, then trembled like a frightened bird desperate for escape. Lost, mesmerized, shocked, *Verochka* stopped dead. Dark as midnight, his eyes kept her immobilized.

She should be scared. She was elated.

Circling her waist with his other hand, he drew her closer. Their bodies bumped.

Her mind clouded.

Her gut clenched.

"What if I want to find out everything about you, Miss *Verochka* Osipoff?"

Deep like his eyes, the timbre of his voice was like a forbidden caress.

Spellbound, she lifted her free arm, placed it on his chest.

To push him away? Surely. Probably. Oh, who was she kidding?

The material of his suit felt like soft velvet under her fingertips. The skin of his hand still covering hers was softer, warmer. She shuddered, as a thousand butterflies flapped their tiny wings in the pit of her stomach.

Lightheaded.

Floating.

Doomed.

Her consciousness snapped into preservation mode.

Snap out of it. Step away. Now!

She deliberately ignored the warning. Instead, she moved even closer. Her bare feet made a connection with his shoes. Her aching breasts touched his torso. A hot hard ridge pressed into her soft belly.

"W-why?" She licked her dry lips, and repeated the question: "Why do you want to find out everything about me?"

"I'll tell you when I have an answer."

CHAPTER
THIRTEEN

Oh, he had the answer. And if he told her, she'd run screaming. Or think he was a lunatic on top of a liar. No way he was jeopardizing the tentative truce they established.

Truce? Is that what you call it?

Holding her in his embrace, trembling from anticipation, hard as a rock, JJ didn't give a damn about semantics. She felt right in his arms. Every square inch of her felt right, and familiar. His heart recognized her before his brain had a chance to catch up. She was the one. She was his woman. His destiny.

She made him alive.

Vibrant.

Whole.

The world be damned if he let her slip out of his fingers.

Gazing into her startled eyes, drowning in those enchanting violet pools, JJ emptied his rational mind, and let his emotions loose.

With both hands he framed her tiny waist, drew her so close he felt her beating heart against his chest, and kissed her.

Lightly.

Slowly.

Tenderly.

It cost him dearly, but he reigned in his impatience, keeping the kiss as gentle as possible. Their lips touched, one, twice. Their breathing meshed. The burning in his gut intensified, but he was still able to control himself. Barely.

Coaxing her lips apart, he dipped his tongue inside. The flavor of her, something sweet and exotic and exquisite, burst into his mouth. Shaking, delighted, he tilted his head, deepened the kiss. A soft moan. A heartbeat of hesitation. Then she looped her arms around his neck, and all but flown into him. And JJ was lost.

With a sharp little ping, his famous control snapped like a fragile bone.

He changed the angle, ground his lips against hers until he almost felt pain. She whimpered into his mouth. Damn, he was probably scaring her. With the last drop of a common sense left, JJ stopped the assault, and dragged his lips from hers.

God help him, he couldn't let go of her, not completely. Like a powerful poison, she tainted his blood, clouded his senses. Played havoc with his mind.

Just from a single kiss. He should be concerned. Hell, he should be scared.

It was too strong, too soon. Too bloody everything.

Instead, JJ was thrilled. Excited. Delirious.

Her closed eyelids fluttered open. Like in a mirror, he saw his own face reflected in those violet eyes. Wide and unblinking, they shone with wonder and awe.

His breath stuck in his throat. He was not alone. She was as lost as he.

Throwing all caution away, JJ lowered his head and took her mouth again. Hard.

Not enough. Not nearly enough.

He craved her flesh like a thirsty man for a gulp of water. When he dragged two thin straps of her leotard down, bearing her shoulders, JJ was a goner. In his mind the chant 'take, take, take' became as incessant litany. All but deaf from it, he fought his basic instinct to possess with an inhuman effort.

Too soon. Too much. Not enough!

He didn't know why he stopped. How he managed to stop.

If he stripped her of that pitiful excuse for clothing, and dragged her to the floor, he knew she'd never utter a single protest. She'd be willing, and eager, and happily satisfied at the end. But what might happen next, after the haze of madness passed?

Would she be ashamed? Feel guilty? Remorseful? Probably, all of the above.

No way in hell could JJ allow her to be ashamed of herself, or him.

And he'd die first rather than become a reason for her regret.

Accustomed to have his every wish satisfied, JJ nevertheless was always careful and conscious about the cost of his indulgence. He never took advantage of anyone, never hurt a single soul. Cruelty was as abhorrent to him as an abuse of his own power.

Looking at her now, all mussed, confused, with her swollen from kisses mouth and naked shoulders, he was swamped with a tenderness so huge, it grabbed him by the throat. Although still painfully aroused and hurting, JJ was enormously glad he managed to put on the brakes, and chain in his desire. After all, they have their whole life ahead of them to indulge in every blessed erotic fantasy he could think of. And, God knew, he was ready to think of many!

To spoil that bliss with a quick tumble on the floor, however satisfying it might be, was an inexcusable exercise in greed and stupidity.

Stepping back, JJ gazed at her in silence broken by their uneven breathing. Barefooted, almost naked to the waist, with her formfitting tights, she was exquisite like a Japanese ivory netsuke he was so partial to. But unlike those miniature figurines, she was flesh and blood, and all woman.

She simply took his breath away.

With the unsteady hands, he tugged her straps back into place, and almost wept with the regret.

Later, buddy.

She watched him in silence, confusion slowly clearing from her face. He expected anything from bewilderment to indignation to anger, prepared for it. But the first thing that jumped out of her mouth was, "What time is it?"

Taken aback, he blinked a couple of times before he found his voice.

"Pardon me?"

"Time! What is it?"

Without waiting for his reply, she grabbed his left hand, turned it, and looked at his wristwatch.

"*Merde!* I'm going to be late!"

"Late... for what?"

God help him, the woman managed to baffle him enough to lose his bearings.

She glanced up. "For my class. My private class with Madame Valeska!"

His little swan became a whirlpool of activity. Running to the wooden box that sat on the floor, she started to pull clothes out, all the while muttering under her breath in French. More amused than insulted for being so easily dismissed, JJ crossed his arms over his chest, and leaned against the wall. The space was miniscule, tidy and ruthlessly organized. Her meager belongings consisted of a single child-size cot, a crude box that doubled for her dresser and closet, and a tiny fridge jammed in the corner. His earlier inspection of her impeccably clean and uncluttered bathroom uncovered a bottle of shampoo, conditioner, and a humongous box of oversized Band-Aids. The puzzle of that item was solved when he glanced at her heavily bounded toes. No cosmetics, or medicine, safe for Epsom salt and a tube of antibiotic ointment.

"Oh, *Dieu,* I'm in a such trouble!" Her muttering gained volume and desperation.

Chuckling, JJ shook his head. Poor little swan. She was so terrified of her formidable teacher, she clearly forgot about their earlier encounter. Well, then, he must remind her about it. Soon. For now, he watched her in silence, amused and oddly delighted. But his amusement quickly faded as she plopped onto the floor, and began to peel away her tights from those skyscraper legs of her.

As entertainment went, this little striptease was extremely enjoyable. If it were deliberate instead of being accidental, that is. Still, it struck him as provocative as hell. The lady clearly forgot about her audience, acting on autopilot. But when she started to remove her leotard, JJ drew the line. Being entertained was one thing, but being tortured—quite another. He was many things, but masochist wasn't one of them. Deliberately, he cleared his throat. "Want me to turn around?"

"What?" She jerked her head up, looked at him as if she just realized that he was still here. "Oh, yes please."

A cold shower loomed in his near future. A helluva lot of cold showers. But no matter how many times he abused his body with icy water, the sight of that innocent striptease was impossible to erase from his subconsciousness. After a moment, the rustling behind him stopped. Testing the waters, he looked over his shoulder. Once again, she was fully dressed, more the pity.

Frustrated, JJ turned all the way around. "What's the hurry?"

"I'm late, and Madame will go ballistic."

"I'm sure she won't be mad at you."

"A lot you know. She hates tardiness."

"Want me to talk to her?"

"Absolutely not! I can take care of myself."

"Why am I not surprised." At least he was smart enough not to laugh.

When she was about to streak pass him, JJ grabbed her forearm. Soft as silk, her skin under his fingers felt incredibly delicate, almost fragile, but the muscles it covered were strong and unyielding as steel.

He loosened his grasp, afraid of marring that perfect skin, but still kept his hand in place. "Have dinner with me tonight."

"A what?" Slowly, she pivoted. Clouded with surprise and confusion her eyes locked onto his. "Dinner?"

"That's right, dinner. In a restaurant."

"But...but why?"

"Because we both need to eat. Why not do it together? And besides, your refrigerator is almost empty." He regretted that statement immediately.

Indignant, *Verochka* lifted her pointy little chin, and rounded on him. "Did you check my food, too?"

"If you call a pint of yogurt and two celery sticks food, then yes."

"You had no right to do so! And in any event, I can't eat anything rich on calories."

"How about rich on actual nutrition?"

"How about you mind your own business?"

"Oh, but you are my business, *Little Swan*."

"Since when?"

"Since the first time I set my eyes on you."

That shut her up. But just for a moment.

She narrowed her eyes. "If it is a joke, it is not funny."

"No joke, *ma petite*. A simple truth." Tucking a stray curl behind her ear was a mistake. As soon as his fingers brushed that delicate tiny shell, a zing of electricity shot up his arm. Did she feel it too? A helpless shudder ran through her body.

Oh, yeah, she definitely was not immune. Even as his joy soared, JJ opted to proceed with caution.

Easy, laddie, the girl is as skittish as a newborn filly.

Removing his fingers from her ear, he smiled down at her. "If you refuse to go to a restaurant, then come to the bar after your class."

She shuddered again, lowered her eyes.

"Oh, but I...I can't. After the class, I have my cleaning duties, so I—"

"Your what?" Harsher than he intended, his voice bounced around the tiny room like an echo. Dammit, did he hear her correctly? His hands landed on her shoulders. More softly, he repeated, "Your what?"

Unperturbed, she gazed at him straight on. "My cleaning duties. I scrub the floors every night. That was my agreement with Madame Valeska."

Damn that woman. Scrubbing floors? After all her exhausting classes? Really?

A mental check to himself to hire a professional janitorial service immediately.

Drawing a calming breath, JJ dropped his hands, took a deliberate step back.

The temptation to grab her, and finish what they have started a while ago was too strong. "You're free of your cleaning duties."

"What do you mean?"

"I mean, as of today, Madame will have a professional service for that. You are free of your janitorial obligation, *Verochka*."

Pleased with himself, he decided to apply a little shock therapy to erase the frown from that beautiful face. "Besides, the future wife of JJ Morris doesn't scrub anyone's floors. It's unseemly, and highly inappropriate."

CHAPTER FOURTEEN

*V*erochka froze. For a several heartbeats, she tried to decide whether he was joking or simply lost his mind. Unseemly? Inappropriate?

A wife!

That insufferable man went too far! Who the hell did he think he was?

Did he think she should be grateful for his attention, or his decision to relieve her of her cleaning duties? That a single kiss was enough for her to...to marry him?

Imbecile!

Outraged, she stepped closer, and glared at him with every ounce of resentment that churned inside of her. "If you think that I'm flattered, think again, Mr. *Reginald* Morris. I'm not going to marry you even if you were the greatest dancer on earth. And to scrub floors or not, is my decision. Mine! I don't need your imperial permission for that."

"I beg to differ. The decision to hire the professional cleaning services for my property is solely mine. As to marrying me..." A smile he aimed at her was self-indulgent, and arrogant, accompanied by a regal curve of one dark brow. "You will be my wife, you little spitfire. And soon. I bet by Thanksgiving we'll be engaged, and say our I dos by Christmas."

Torn between indignation and befuddlement, she gaped at JJ. *Mon Dieu*, has he lost his mind? Was he kidding?

"Are you... serious?"

"Like the IRS."

"Have you gone mad? Christmas?"

"Too soon? Well, how about New Year's then?"

"How about never?"

"Not an option."

He moved lightning fast. So fast, she didn't have a chance to foresee his next action, much less to avoid it. Sure and hard, his embrace enveloped her like a heavy blanket, immobilizing her body. Once again, she found herself pressed against his chest. But now her hands pushed firmly against it in an attempt to free herself.

A feeble and quite pitiful attempt, but still. She was not a match for his strength. Thrashing her limbs was impossible, stomping her bare feet useless. The only weapon left to her was her eyes and her mouth. She aimed what she hoped was a murderous glare at him as a string of foul curses in two languages flew free.

When her vast repertoire of swearing words was finally exhausted, she kept her eyes on his face. Out of breath, but still quivering from anger, *Verochka* hissed, "Let me go, you miserable brute!" She managed to infuse all her bubbling outrage in her demand. Or so she hoped. For a moment nothing happened.

He dropped his hands, as a deep rumbling laugh shook his body. "My God, I simply adore you, *Verochka*."

"And I simply hate you!"

He raised his brows and burst into laughter. *Verochka* saw red.

"I'll hate you 'till my last breath, Mr. Morris."

Gradually, his merriment subsided, but an indolent smile still curved those chiseled lips.

"A challenge, for sure. Well, I'll do my best to change your disposition toward me."

Mon Dieu! What was wrong with him?

Nothing. Absolutely nothing.

She shoved her treacherous thoughts from her mind. Afraid that her resolve was not a match for his persistence, she drew to her full unimpressive height of five-four. With the huge differences in their sizes, he still towered over her. *Merde.* But Mr. Arrogant now met his equal in stubbornness. He just wasn't aware of that yet. Well, then, *Verochka* will be more than happy to demonstrate. Baring her teeth, she rounded on him.

"You can take your challenge, and shove it!"

That earned her another chuckle. "Lord, what a temper, what a passion!"

"Temper? *Passion?* I'll show you passion, you arrogant prick!"

Never before in her life was *Verochka* so mad at another human being. But this man seemed to draw the worst out of her. Not a violent person, she shook from the impulse to break or destroy something.

Or hit someone!

Without a second thought, she picked up her pointe shoe from the floor. The pink satin slipper was not much of a weapon, but connected with bare flesh, its reinforced cardboard toe box was hard enough to cause some damage. Her own feet were testament to that. As an impromptu missile, it was guaranteed to be quite painful indeed. Aiming for the face, *Verochka* sent the pointe flying. God knew what may have happened if he hadn't caught it first. Effortlessly. One handed.

Merde!

She should be grateful for his fast reaction. Probably. But not for that little smirk on his lips. Laughing at her, was he? Enraged, she grabbed the second shoe. But before she was able to lift her arm, a firm grip on her wrist stopped her. Somehow, he managed to move and stand in front of her. Without hurting her, he held her right hand immobilize. The firm grasp of his fingers around her wrist was warm but unyielding, like a manacle. All her struggles to tug her hand free were futile. Humiliation added fuel to her resentment. Spiked to a boiling point, her anger bubbled up like fiery lava.

The horde of foul curses burst from her mouth like startled bats out of cave. She was almost breathless from the effort to extricate her hand from his, while the damn man didn't even break a sweat. She could have killed him for that alone.

A loud *tsk-tsk*ing of his tongue set *Verochka's* teeth on edge.

"Language, Little Swan, language. I ought to wash out your delectable mouth with soap."

"Just try it!"

Mindless, sizzling, she lifted her left arm. Unerringly, it was subjected to the same treatment as her other one. Now both her hands were imprisoned in his.

"Careful, *ma petite*. You might hurt yourself."

Just as suddenly as he grabbed her, his fingers loosened their grasps. Still smiling, he took a step back. "And now you are definitely late for your class."

"*Merde!*"

The insufferable jerk was right. She was late. Very late. Damn his chocolate eyes. And his mouth. And the rest of him. Their confrontation must wait.

With a silent promise to finish their fight later, *Verochka* bent to gather up her pointes. One was laying under her feet, but its twin landed in the middle of the room, where he dropped it after catching it on the fly.

Pressing her ballet shoes like a shield against her chest, she faced JJ straight on.

She'd be damned if she let him have the last word. Or the last laugh.

"For your information, Mr. Morris, I'm not going to marry. Ever. My life is dedicated to ballet. There is no place in it for anything—or anyone—else."

Holding her head high, she pivoted and flung the door open. A second later, his soft reply reached her ears, "We'll see about that."

A promise? A threat?

A ripple of goosebumps covered her skin, and set the all fine hairs on her body to standing alert. Shivering all over, *Verochka* hurried ahead.

We'll see about that, you jerk.

CHAPTER FIFTEEN

J J knew she'd come tonight. She couldn't resist to show up, and rub his nose in their morning match.

Oh, he knew her number, alright. Enormously pleased, he smiled around the mouthpiece of his sax as he eyed *Verochka*. Sitting across from him at the bar, she did her best to ignore him.

We'll see how long that lasts, Little Swan.

The obstinate little thing, she was too stubborn to let him win the first round. No doubt, she was here to finish their earlier argument.

Argument? Are you kidding?

It was a fight, a full-blown battle of wills. If not for her class, God knows what might have happened in that tiny attic room. Probably for the best he didn't have a chance to find out. But dear Lord, who'd have thought that under all that classy and elegant façade was hidden an explosive temper! Blonde she might be, but her spirit was that of a true redhead. And that passion! He couldn't wait to channel it into a more pleasurable venue. The images of *Verochka*, naked, panting, sweaty, swam in his mind. In an instant he became hard as a rock. The enormous erection was almost painful, pulsing and straining against the barrier of his pants.

Hell.

JJ shifted, adjusting his stance, praying that no one paid close attention.

As was his habit, he exchanged his business suite for jeans and a polo shirt before coming to the bar. Now he wished he wore something less formfitting than a pair of blue Levi's. Even though old, soft, and comfortable, they were still too revealing.

JJ's hands flexed on the fluid body of the sax. The melody soared, trembled, as his breath caught in his throat. Gently, gradually he relaxed his throat muscles.

The instrument in his hands obeyed, albeit grudgingly. As his breathing returned to normal, his thoughts jumped back to the earlier encounter with *Verochka*.

That kiss left him breathless, and greedy, and unsatisfied. He wanted more, much more. And he intended to have it. Soon. There was no way he'd let her out of his life now.

Touching her, kissing her blew his famous control to smithereens.

It was a pure miracle he managed to put on the brakes. As a businessman, and a darn good one, JJ always evaluated the risks, calculating ten steps ahead of the opponent. Like in his favorite game of chess. He always kept a cool head. Always.

For the first time in his life, *Verochka* made that impossible.

A cool head? What a joke. The only 'cool' he managed to maintain was his resolve to win that woman over. He wanted her too much for any calculations or evaluations, or anything rational.

Admit it, laddie, you have it bad.

Bad didn't even begin to describe it. The situation was explosive, he barely kept himself in check. Yes, it was for the best that he stopped. And only because JJ was determined to win the war, not just the first battle. And win he will. He always did.

He cast a quick glance at her, smiled when those enchanting violet eyes briefly met his. She spun away, but not before a delicate shudder passed through her body. Oh, she was aware, alright. Well, so was he. The anticipation churned in his gut, bubbling, burning.

Not now, not yet.

Let her stew for a while. Just a bit longer.

Finishing his current piece, JJ took a deep calming breath, and started to play Gershwin's "Summer Time."

As a reflection of his current mood, that famous lullaby turned into a sultry, seductive ballad. Unable to tear his eyes from her, JJ watched her body jolt. Then she froze. With her eyes closed, she began to sway to the rhythm of the melody, as if she was dancing in her mind. Fluid, eloquent, her arms lifted, then slowly flew down. Like two wings.

The Beautiful Swan.

And that swan was his. Forever. Didn't he read that those birds mated for life?

Amused, JJ chuckled. A swan he might not be, but he was determined to marry just once. Marry *Verochka*. She was his mate, his one and only. He wasn't sure how he knew that. Did it really matter? JJ gave a mental shrug. Nothing mattered except that deep seated feeling of recognition.

Here you are. I've been looking for you all my life.

It grabbed him by the throat from the first time he saw her.

God knew, he tried to fight it, to rationalize why he must forget all about her.

He was too old for her. They were from two different worlds.

She didn't belong in his society, didn't fit into his life.

All true. All valid reasons to stay away. And he had. For three days. Three unbearably long days, before he capitulated.

Looking at her now, JJ wondered how he managed to last those three days.

The few feet separating them became a chasm. He fought the urge to close that distance, to get physically closer to her.

Patience, JJ. Patience.

Perched onto the tall barstool, she was smiling at Winston who looked like a proud papa bear. Relaxed, she listened intently to whatever his bartender was saying. Probably a joke, since they both ended up laughing. Damn.

A stab of jealousy was as strong as it was silly. Jealous of Winston? Ridiculous.

He was old enough to be her grandfather. Calling himself an idiot, JJ tore his gaze from the laughing pair.

You are more upset at not being included on that joke, laddie.

And wasn't that pathetic? Wincing, JJ silently cursed. Dammit, he was behaving like an idiot, or a jealous fool.

Snap out of it.

Shaking his head vigorously, JJ blew into the mouthpiece with enough force to put Jericho's trumpet to shame. His lungs almost exploded. As a result, he executed the wrong note, sending a grumbling cacophony into the air.

Disgusted with himself, he cursed again and put the sax down.

He was in no mood to play.

Stepping down from a small elevated platform, he aimed his gaze at *Verochka*. As if sensing his eyes, she turned, met his stare. Held it. His breath stuck in his throat. His heart lurched. His blood churned.

Glaring at him, she cocked her head to the side. Defiance. Challenge.

Well, he was more than ready and able to accept her silent dare.

Patience be damned. Now or never.

Now.

Slowly, he started toward the bar. Something in his expression must have alerted her. Unblinking, she watched his progress, as her small hands grabbed the edge of the bar counter. Her whole posture was that of a startled little animal, poised to flee from an impending danger.

Not laughing anymore, are you, Little Swan?

Resolutely, he continued forward, closing the distance between them with the single goal in mind to drag her away from the audience of patrons—and Winston—and finish what they started that morning.

What you *have started.*

Impatiently, JJ shrugged it away. The hell with semantics. One way or another, they will have their face-to-face in private. There was just one place where they won't be disturbed: his office.

"Hiya, Boss."

Winston's cheerful greeting cut into his thoughts like a serrated knife. Frowning, JJ barely managed a single nod. For a long moment, the older man peered at him with a cocked eyebrow, before his mouth assumed a disapproving grimace. As a former cop and now bartender, Winston read people better than any lie detector. One glance at JJ was probably enough for him to come to an obvious conclusion that something was brewing. Something that concerned his favorite little protégé.

A loud harrumph rambled in Winston's throat, accompanied by an almost vicious stare. His displeasure was as clear as a crystal tumbler he was polishing.

JJ ignored him. Without a word, he took *Verochka's* hand and tugged her from the barstool. She stumbled, but managed to find her footing.

"Hey! What do you think you're doing?"

Her loud outcry of indignation failed to put a hitch in his step. Holding her small hand in a firm grasp, he continued to pull her after him. Maneuvering between the tables, he held his course aimed at the closed doors of his corner office.

An obstacle of a single chair on his way was dealt with quickly via a swift kick of his foot. It slid sideways, before upturning with a loud *clunk.*

"Hey! Stop this instant! Let go of my hand, you imbecile!"

Verochka's shouts started to draw attention. All conversations subsided to a half murmur as more people were catching on.

You are making a scene, buddy.

The hell with it.

Mimi, who was taking the orders nearby turned around. "Ah, Boss? Is everything okay?"

"No, it is not okay!" *Verochka* yelped before JJ had a chance to open his mouth. "Please help! I don't want to go wherever he's taking me!"

Mimi switched her gaze from JJ to *Verochka*, then back to him again. Whatever she read in his expression gave her pause. Mimi frowned, chewed her lip. After a heartbeat of hesitation, she gave an imperceptive nod, and turned back to her patrons.

"Is she deaf?" Enraged, *Verochka* scanned the place. Every single person in the room was watching them with curiosity mixed with a heavy dose of amusement. "*Mon Dieu*, this bar is full of lunatics! Just like its owner."

Unmindful of her struggles and vocal clamor, JJ walked to the door to his office, opened it one-handed, and propelled her inside. He locked the door, pocketed the key, and only then let go of her hand. Spitting mad, she marched forward, grabbed the doorknob. A twist and the few futile tugs later, *Verochka* turned her blazing eyes on him.

"You are a brute, a tyrant, and an obnoxious pig! Open that door at once!"

For emphasis, she tapped her foot, crossed her arms, and glared at him.

JJ cocked his head. As ridiculous as this situation was, he found himself enjoying it. Enjoying *her.*

Was it wrong of him? Possibly. Probably. But she was irresistible. Magnificent in her outrage, vibrating from within, *Verochka* balled her little fists, all but shooting daggers at him with her eyes. If eyes could kill, JJ was sure he'd have been long dead by now. Absently, he rubbed his chest just under his left breastbone, like some of those invisible daggers had indeed reached their target.

The little hellion was primed for the fight. Well, then, why not add a little sizzle to the flames? He came closer, and brushed a single fingertip along her jaw. As he predicted, she swatted his hand away, spitting out a string of cuss words.

"Connard! Tas de merde! Filse de pute!"

Since JJ knew the language well, there was no trouble understanding all the vile and inventive expletives thrown at him. Finally, she ran out of breath. As *Verochka* drew some air into her lungs, and opened her mouth again for the second act, JJ forestalled her. In perfect French, he addressed the little spitfire. "You may as well stop your childish behavior, because I'm not opening that door before we have a chance to talk."

That gave her pause. Looking at him with something close to shocking surprise, *Verochka* fell silent.

JJ silently congratulated himself for throwing her off. His accent might not be as naturally elegant like hers, but he prided himself on being fluent in French, among other foreign languages. It always came in handy while dealing with the international partners. Or one little feisty Parisian.

But his victory was short lived. Squaring her shoulders, she managed to glare at him down her perky little nose. With her eyes only, she communicated her emotions as eloquently as if she said them aloud.

God, what a woman! No wonder he was crazy about her.

You are *crazy, period.*

Finally, switching back to English, she replied in a clip and curt queen to a peasant manner, "I don't want to talk to you."

Somehow it came out more insulting than all her previous cursing combined.

"Tough. Because I do."

For the life of him, he couldn't remember what he was going to say. Not as tiny as her attic apartment, his office space suddenly seemed to shrink in size. They were standing too close to each other, the air thick with churning undercurrents, JJ was unable to draw a breath. Space. He needed some space between them.

Taking a step back, he shoved his hands into the pockets of his jeans.

Seemingly composed, she issued a direct order, "Okay, I'm listening. Talk."

Right. Talk. He must say something. But what, dammit?

"Fast, *sil vous plait*. I'm quite busy."

That irritated the hell out of him. "Yeah? Doing what? Laughing with Winston?"

"So, what? He's such a pleasant and kind man, unlike someone I have the *misfortune* to know."

Irked, JJ tried to ignore that little barb. He failed.

"A misfortune, is it? You didn't feel that misfortunate when I kissed you earlier."

He sounded like a petulant child which spiked his annoyance.

"An unforgivable mishap on my part." *Verochka* moved her shoulders in a typical Gaelic gesture only a true Parisian pulled off. This one was the Mercedes of all shrugs, negligent and dismissive and snobbish as all get out. JJ almost smiled. "I admit, I was curious. That's all."

And just like that, his merriment evaporated like morning fog.

"Curious, were you?"

Unable to stop himself, he closed the distance between them in two slow strides.

The hell with the space. "And did I manage to satisfy your curiosity?"

Deliberately mild, his tone of voice didn't betray his brewing anger. With a promise to congratulate himself later, JJ squinted at her.

"You did... okay." Another shrug, this one as insulting as slap in a face. "Not great, but not half bad either."

That does it. Fisting his hands, JJ took a couple of deep breath, and counted to ten.

With an effort, he schooled his face into a fake bland mask.

"I apologize. Usually I do better. Must've been all that negative energy coming from you at the time."

"Can you blame me? You invaded my space, pawed through my things—"

"I didn't paw, I checked." It cost him to keep his voice even, and his expression cool. That Little Swan tested his control as no one else.

"Whatever." Carelessly, she swiped his correction aside with a single word. "I was upset."

"Upset?" Despite everything, JJ let out a short bark of laughter. "*Ma petite*, you were mad as a wet hen. Pardon me, wet *cygnet*."

"I'm not your *petite* anything! I'm my own woman. And don't try to sidetrack me."

"God forbid. Let's stay on track, then, shall we?"

He lunged forward, and pulling her hard against his chest, covered her mouth.

CHAPTER SIXTEEN

There was no time to react. No time to think. Pressed hard against his body, she could only feel. And feel, and feel...

Her lips parted. Voluntarily. Eagerly. Impatiently.

She might lie to herself later that it was due to pure shock.

Taking advantage, JJ slanted his mouth to hers then swiped his tongue along her lower lip. Sure, and bold, he plunged inside, invading her mouth. A little whimper stuck in her throat. Helpless under the onslaught, she clung to his forearms like an anchor. Her head was spinning, and spinning like she was twirling in a *fouette*. But unlike that whipping pirouette, the sensation failed to stop on the magic number of thirty-two revolutions.

She was afraid of her own feelings.

Afraid of losing herself.

Afraid of spinning out of control.

Too much, too soon. Too... everything.

But still, she found herself unwilling to let go, to step away. To break the connection.

The kiss exploded. The flames between them flew hotter, higher, darker.

Wherever they touched, her skin got scorched. In the back of her mind the word 'danger' pulsed like a bright neon sign. Unmindful, *Verochka* parted her lips wider, giving him better access.

More. Mon Dieu, *more!*

Almost wild with desire, she tried to press closer. Her breasts were wedged against his chest. Her middle burned from the steel ridge pressed to her abdomen. Guided by pure instinct, she rubbed against it, drawing a low rumble deep from his throat. That tortured sound shot through her like an arrow, piercing her heart. Triumphant, bolstered by her own power, *Verochka* lifted her arms, grabbed two fistfuls of his hair, and dipped her tongue into his mouth. Rich and dark, his flavor burst like a tidal wave. His unique smell of something musky and citrusy overpowered her senses.

The contours of his body, large and strong, the silky softness of his hair, the texture of his warm taut skin— so familiar, and still shockingly new.

Lightheaded, elated, she continued her explorations, straining her body against him. His hands cupped her behind, drew her forward and up, all but grinding their pelvises together, until she wasn't sure where hers ended and his began. Lifting his mouth a fraction away, JJ looked into her eyes. Whatever he saw, made him suck in a sharp breath. Like a heavy cloud pregnant with a thunderstorm, silence clung in the air. The only sound in the room was their breathing, labored and fast and desperate. She returned his gaze and failed to prevent a shiver from racing along her spine. The pulling sensation was overwhelming, like she was slowly being sucked into quicksand. Another moment, and she was sure to be swallowed whole. Poised on the last tiny ledge of sanity, *Verochka* quivered. Fear? Anticipation? Excitement?

Get away! You won't survive the plunge.

Too late.

Recklessly, she let go, falling, falling...

Without warning, a shrilling noise cut through the haze of her euphoria.

What on earth ...?

Coming from somewhere inside the room, that annoying sound kept its high-pitched, intrusive clatter, until the mood was broken.

Verochka blinked in confusion. After a moment, JJ cursed under his breath. His arms slowly slid from her body, leaving her cold and oddly bereft.

The regret written on JJ's face was hard to misinterpret. He backed away, then raked both hands through his hair. He turned toward that persistent noise. In a second he glanced back at her.

"Sorry, I have to take this."

Take what?

Still shaken, *Verochka* tried to make sense of his words.

Only when JJ reached over his desk and picked up a phone receiver, the mystery of those sharp shrills was finally solved. The telephone. *Merde.*

She should be glad for the interruption. She should thank all the saints for interfering, and preventing her from making a colossal mistake. She has no time for romance. Not now, not ever. Especially, for romance with this man.

He overwhelmed her. Confused her. Disturbed her on the most basic level. It would be too easy to lose her head, and fall in love with him. She was lucky she managed to keep her common sense, and her heart intact.

And who are you kidding, you silly goose? You heart already belongs to him.

No way. She shook her head, then pressed both hands against her ears in a futile attempt to shut her inner voice. Her heart, along with every other part of her belonged to ballet. Period. She was born to dance. She will never marry. Ever.

You can lie to yourself for as long as you want, Verochka, *but you know the truth.*

Helplessly, she let her hands drop, and looked at the man who turned her world upside down.

Oh, Mon Dieu, *what have I done?*

Her poor heart squeezed. Like a little bird with broken wings, it trembled, forlorn and defeated. Yes, she could tell herself all the pretty lies, but she knew the truth. She was head over heels in love with JJ.

What now?

Before JJ brought the telephone to his ear, a soft oath broke from his lips. His following 'hello' was sharp enough to cut diamonds.

Despite *Verochka's* bewilderment, she wondered about the caller. Who was on the line to warrant such an icy greeting?

JJ froze for a moment before all the shutters came down his face. She almost heard a heavy *clang.* Utterly and frightenedly emotionless, he listened intently to the caller.

Unblinking, his eyes were focused on some spot on the opposite wall. She'd bet her best pointe shoes he was not seeing anything. All his responses were clipped, short, and terrifyingly calm.

"Yes, Madeline. I remember."

Madeline.

A woman.

A friend?

A *lover?*

Merde.

Jealousy was not something *Verochka* tolerated. It was a silly and pointless emotion, and quite demeaning. But now it grabbed her by the throat.

Who the hell was Madeline, and why was she calling JJ so late?

"Of course. No problem. A date?" A quick glance over his shoulder at her. Dark and cold, his eyes pinned her to the spot. Chilled to her bones, *Verochka* shivered. Whoever that woman was, she was definitely not a friend. Who then?

And what was that all about a date?

JJ turned away, listened for a moment, before replying, "No, you don't have to. I will bring my own date. Yes. Okay. Goodbye."

His own date? Really? After he kissed her brains off, and all but turned her into shaking jelly, he's bringing his own date? This man has a nerve!

Crossing her arms over her chest, *Verochka* tapped her right foot. The incorrigible rascal was about to receive a piece of her mind.

CHAPTER SEVENTEEN

Quivering from righteous indignation, *Verochka* continued to follow JJ's every move with her eyes. Finally, he put the receiver back, his gestures controlled, and measured. Then he drew a deep breath.

"That was my mother."

His mother? The one he called Madeline? In that brutally cold voice?

"Your...m-mother?"

"Yes."

When he turned around, *Verochka's* heart squeezed painfully. Bleak, shattered, his eyes seemed ageless. And somehow, he looked...vulnerable.

"You probably wonder why I called her by name."

She did, but at the moment she was more concerned with his sadness hidden under a layer of cool detachment. Something was off with their relationship. Something *Verochka* failed to grasp.

"It's really simple. She never loved me. No matter what I did, or how I tried, she never warmed up to me. I guess some women don't have a maternal instinct." A negligent shrug. "For as long as I remember, she treated me like a guest. An unwelcomed one at that."

Verochka went with her heart. "I doubt that was the case. She must love you, just deep down."

His humorless laughter didn't reach his eyes. "So deep that you couldn't unearth it with a bulldozer."

A gamut of emotions— from compassion to sadness to anger for the little boy—filled *Verochka*. Her face must've betrayed her turmoil.

JJ scrutinized her, long and hard, before his mouth curved into a sad smile. Lifting her chin with one finger, he murmured, "Feeling sorry for me, Little Swan?"

She supposed it was a testament of her current state that she let that moniker slide.

"What if I am?"

"Don't. It doesn't matter anymore. And besides, my dad overcompensated for Madeline's lack of feelings. He loved me unconditionally. I was lucky. I survived."

But at was cost?

Now she understood his aloofness, recognized it for what it was: a defense mechanism. Pure and simple. That little unloved boy was still lurking inside, still craving his mother's attention. Still hoping.

Oh, what she'd give at the moment to offer him a simple kindness, to erase those shadows of the past from his mind. But something in those dark assessing eyes stopped her. She instinctively knew he'd refuse her kindness. He'd refuse it, or worse, laugh at her. Their relationship was too fragile, too tentative. Too new.

Who were they? Not exactly friends, not strangers. Adversaries?

They sure circled around each other like two boxers in the ring.

Or two soloists before a *pa de deux*.

Teetering on murky ground, *Verochka* mentally shook herself. If he refused to accept her kindness, her only choice was the truth.

"I'm not feeling sorry for Reginald Morris, but for the little boy JJ."

He seemed to digest that for a moment, then nodded.

"Well, then, are you feeling sorry enough to go to the ball with the grown version of that boy?"

"A what? Ball?"

"Yes, a winter ball. An extravaganza my mother insists on holding every year before Thanksgiving."

"But...but..."

"But what?"

"I don't belong at that event."

"Neither do I. So what?"

"But you are a Morris."

"So will be you. Soon."

Instantly, her irritation took over. "*Merde,* how can you say it so flippantly?"

"I'm not being flippant, *Verochka*. I'm dead serious."

"You're impossible! I told you before I'm not going to marry anyone!"

"Not anyone—me. Make no mistake, Little Swan, you are going to be my wife. Before the end of the year, you'll promise to have and to hold, for richer or poorer—"

"Over my dead body!"

The gall of the man! Marry him? Before the end of the year? As if ever!

JJ's booming laughter grated on her nerves. *Verochka* gritted her teeth until her jaw hurt.

"You are so adorable when you're angry."

"And you are so obnoxious at any time!"

Merde. Feeling sorry for him? Really?

You ought to get your head examined, you idiot.

Instead of annoyed, JJ beamed, obviously pleased with her parrying response.

The cad! Amused, was he? How she wished to wipe that self-indulgent smirk from his face! *Verochka* curled her fingers until her nails bit into her palms. No one—absolutely no one—got on her nerves like JJ Morris.

No one ever befuddled and enraged her at the same time. And certainly, no one before threatened to upend her equilibrium so irrevocably. The man was lethal.

For her peace of mind, for her well-regulated normal life. For her heart.

She must stay away from him. She must get out of here. As soon as possible, or she might do or say something outrageous.

With an effort, *Verochka* drew her head high, and glared at him. "Please unlock the door. It's quite late. I must go back."

She'd congratulate herself later at how cool and dispassionate her voice sounded.

"I'll walk you home." He took a step forward. Sidestepping him, she moved back.

"I'll walk by myself, but thank you."

Keeping her gaze on him, *Verochka* inched closer to the threshold. After a long moment, JJ took a key from his pocket, and unlocked the door. The latch gave way with a tiny metallic click. Finally, she was free to go. Why then instead of relieved, did she feel so disappointed? Hesitant, she hovered at the door, calling herself a thousand names for a fool.

What is wrong with you? Go already! Just open the damned door and go!

After a moment of inner struggle, *Verochka* grabbed the doorknob, and tugged at it with an unnecessary force. The door flung open. Before she changed her mind, she hurried ahead.

"Oh, and *Verochka*?"

Poised to run, she cast a brief glance over her shoulder. A picture of negligence, JJ was leaning against his desk, a small smile playing on his lips.

"Don't worry about the gown for the ball. I'll buy you one."

The nerve of him! Did he really think she intended to go to that event with him?

With something close to a growl, she hissed through her clenched teeth, "I'll get my own *zut* gown!"

And kicking the door closed, she sprinted away.

CHAPTER EIGHTEEN

Did she realize she just committed to attend the ball with him? JJ grinned. Probably not. She was too aggravated to pay any attention to her last remark. But he did, and he'd be damned if he let her renege on her promise. This time, her sheer stubbornness played to his advantage. He needed to remind her of her parting words. And he will get her a gown, the most exquisite one money can buy. Guilt may well eat at him forever if she spent a penny for a dress. JJ wasn't privy to her financial situation, but from what he deduced, it was quite pitiful.

Dear God, she lived on yogurt alone! Was she starving? Two celery sticks in her fridge were a bad substitute for a meal, even for a ballerina. How could she endure her rigorous dancing classes without proper nutrition? Dammit. JJ cursed under his breath. Instead of dragging her to his office for an argument, he should've fed her to make sure she didn't go to bed hungry.

You are such a selfish bastard.

But it was too late for berating himself. He will order Winston to feed her every time she visited the bar. But what about other times? JJ frowned. It was impossible for him to be with *Verochka* twenty-four hours a day, no matter how much he wanted it. She had her own life, as did he. He'd gladly pay all her expenses, but knew without a doubt that accepting money was not a possibility. Not from him, or anybody else.

Verochka was too proud, too independent, too stubborn. Too self-reliant.

For goodness' sake, she scrubbed the floors for two years in order to pay for her education! JJ admired her for that, for her character, her strength, her spunk.

If left all alone and penniless, was he able to survive? Questionable.

Verochka not only survived, she flourished. With a single-minded determination, she moved toward her dream, refusing to accept anything but victory. She was the strongest person he had ever known.

Her independent streak was as spectacular as her unique violet eyes.

Never before JJ met a woman like *Verochka*. She humbled him. She enchanted him. She stirred something deep inside, something huge and unfamiliar he still had no name for. For the first time JJ not only wanted a woman on the most basic level, but needed to cherish and protect her, to shelter from all life's hardships.

The feeling was overwhelming. All consuming. And frustrating.

He desperately wanted to do something to help her. But what? If she won't accept money from him, then he must take a roundabout route. Buying decent food and have it delivered to the school incognito was a smart start. JJ nodded, pleased with his decision. Yes, that's exactly what he planned to do.

Then, a call Madame Valeska to learn what else *Verochka* needed. The woman might be a formidable dragon, but she cared about her students. And if he wasn't mistaken, his Little Swan was among Madame's most favorites. He'd play on her tender feelings.

From his brief inspection of *Verochka's* tiny room, he surmised that she didn't have many wordily possessions. Neat as a pin, that room reminded him of a military barrack. A child-size coat, a miniscule fridge, and a wooden chest that probably held all her wardrobe. She didn't have a desk, or a lamp, or a darn clock. A further search of the premises failed to produce any coat. Damn, how she managed to survive without warm winter clothes for two years in the New York climate? It was beyond him. Mindboggling.

How could she live in there, in that sterile barren space, with a tiny round window that barely let sunlight through? Pinned to the wall, a single unframed photograph caught his attention. A man and a woman with their arms around each other, smiling to the camera. The resemblance between the man in that picture and *Verochka* was almost uncanny. She had his eyes, and his coloring, but her smile was a mirror image of the woman's.

Her parents.

JJ wondered why that old photograph made him so sad. Or so forlorn.

Remembering it now, he let out a frustrated oath. *Verochka* was all alone in the world, save for her ballet teacher. And now him, whether she wanted it or not. Probably not, but JJ refused to let that deter him. Until they were married, he planned to improvise. Taking care of her from a distance made good sense. And for that he needed Madame Valeska's help. *Verochka* wouldn't accept anything from him, but from her teacher? Probably. He needed to swear Madame to secrecy as to the identity of *Verochka's* benefactor. Will the woman cooperate? Sure she will.

After she learned his intention to marry her star pupil.

As the future wife of JJ Morris, *Verochka* was entitled to all the comforts his wealth provided, but mentioning it to her was fraught with some serious consequences. Bodily harm to his person was less disconcerting than the barriers she might erect between them. That was simply unacceptable.

JJ was happy to rent a decent apartment for her, but knew she'd balk at the very idea. Pacifying himself that *Verochka* wouldn't be living in the attic longer than the next couple of months, JJ grudgingly capitulated.

By November, he was sure to wear her down enough to talk her into moving in with him.

By Christmas, or New Year at the latest, they'd be married. He was firm on the date. He smiled. A winter wedding in St. Patrick's Cathedral. Yes, that was perfect. Note to himself: call the church and book a date in advance. And put his personal assistant to the task of ordering a wedding gown. He was sure the House of Chanel was only too happy to accommodate his request, and send the most gorgeous wedding dress suited for royalty. White, with a lot of lace, and a long train. The reception will be held at his family hotel in Midtown. The very name of it—The Paradise— was a perfect reflection of their future together. He could hardly wait for it to begin.

Patience, laddie. Patience.

JJ swore under his breath. Until he put his ring onto her finger, he'd be a mess.

Damn, a ring! He had yet to buy her an engagement ring. No problem. Plenty of time for that. Definitely do it tomorrow. And JJ knew exactly the one that suited *Verochka*. Not a diamond, but a pearl. Ethereal, delicate and exquisite, like his Little Swan.

Smiling, pleased with his decision, JJ nodded. Yes, she was born for pearls.

As if on cue, his mind conjured a picture of *Verochka* wearing nothing but a long string of natural pearls draped around her swan-like neck.

Oh, hell yeah.

Instantly aroused, JJ lingered on that image for a few seconds, before deliberately shutting it away. No point in torturing himself with a fantasy.

The real deal is yours, laddie. Or will be. Soon.

Impatient, he looked at his wristwatch. Damn, was it two AM already? Time to close the bar, and head home. Alone. His quiet oath held no heat, but a great deal of frustration. Couldn't been helped for now. He just had to wait a few more weeks.

A few more weeks? How the hell will he survive?

Because you must, if you want to win the little spitfire over.

JJ never wanted anything more in his life. A groan of resignation wrenched another helpless curse. Raking fingers through his hair, JJ lectured himself on the virtue of patience. As much as he wanted to see her again, he must wait for a couple of days. Three were ideal. Let her simmer down. A short separation might do them both a world of good. Especially him. Until he got himself under control, and recaptured his equilibrium.

And who are you kidding, laddie?

No matter how long he managed to stay away from her, he'd never recapture his famous control, not to mention his equilibrium. And besides, to win *Verochka* over, he must get her accustomed to his presence, to get used to him. To feel comfortable around him. And how can he ensure that if he stayed away from her? No, patience be damned. He'd see her tomorrow. Already today. On the spur of the moment JJ decided to bring her flowers. Will she be surprised, or embarrassed? Probably both. He chuckled. Whatever the end result, it will keep his Little Swan a bit off a balance. And wasn't it justified? She managed to unbalance him enough to dream of a white wedding and happy ever after. As a payback goes, that one was just what the doctor ordered.

Did she have a preference? Lilies? Carnations? JJ shrugged. Start with the most classic approach— the long-stemmed roses. No woman he knew ever resisted red roses. Then again, all the women he was acquainted with were so different from *Verochka*. She was one of a kind, truly unique. Inside and out, from her bewitching violet eyes to her exotic accent to her steel backbone. She was *Verochka*.

And she was his.

JJ wondered briefly what may have happened if she hadn't stumbled into his bar a few nights ago. Will they meet eventually, or live their separate lives, totally unaware of each other? Somehow, he doubted it. Sooner or later, the Universe would have brought them together. Because they were meant. Destined. Fated.

Call him a fanciful fool, but JJ always believed that every person on earth had his or her other half. But the privilege of meeting, or even recognizing your mate was granted to a few exceptionally lucky ones. He was one of them. Thank God.

JJ hummed happy tune as he headed for the door. Although still frustrated, he found himself in a much better mood. The major plan was clear in his head. Every next step brought him closer to his goal. Not soon enough, but still.

He picked up his sax, carefully strapped it into its case. Despite the hour, a few patrons still lingered over their drinks. Tipsy, but not drunk, they were obviously having a good time, not ready to call it a night. JJ decided to overlook the loud laughter, and a few harmless insults. Winston will start hustling them out soon. Speaking of the devil. JJ cast a brief glance at the bar, and laughed. Clearly, his bartender was still mad at him, if the single glare he spared JJ was any indication. Let him stew. Of course, JJ must explain everything to Winston. Tomorrow. And ask him to be his best man at the wedding. That will surely blow the old man's socks off. JJ let out a bark of laughter. He laughed picturing Winston's face.

After crossing the almost deserted parking lot, he unlocked his car, carefully deposited his sax onto the back seat, and slid into the driver's seat.

As he imagined his Hulk of a bartender clad in a tux, with a cummerbund and a little bow, JJ burst into another bout of laughter. Winston was sure to leave a memorable impression on all the guests, especially Madeline. She'd be mortified, no doubt. What did he care? It was his wedding, after all. His decision, his choice.

Unorthodox? Hell yeah, but so what? Who knew JJ better than the old ex-policeman who almost arrested him once upon a time? And who was the best friend any man ever wanted?

Enormously pleased, JJ started the engine, and slowly pulled out of the parking space.

CHAPTER NINETEEN

Even at this late—or early—hour, a few cars still cruised along Broome Street. SoHo might not be as densely populated as Manhattan, but this neighborhood of artists and poets never slept. Streetlights cast a cheerful illumination, creating the carefree atmosphere of a perpetual Christmas. Boisterous and exuberant, this little piece of heaven pulsed with life and excitement even at almost three in the morning. JJ loved it with every fiber of his being. He felt more at home here than in his luxurious Midtown penthouse.

The on-again-off-again impulse of moving to SoHo permanently now held a special appeal. *Verochka* was accustomed to this neighborhood. His condo in a high-rise building may seemed cold and alien to her. Would she feel at home there? He tried to imagine *Verochka* in his penthouse, amongst the modern sleek furniture and abstract paintings. Questionable. Doubtful. Highly unlikely.

Well, then. He must choose something different, a place when she'd feel comfortable. Mentally, JJ scrolled through the list of properties he owned in SoHo. A few held some possibilities, but the old historic building in the cast-iron district was the most promising. It was close to her school, and just a short drive to his Manhattan office. Yes, it might work. For both of them. He needed to check it out personally, and take *Verochka* to see it later.

What were his chances to talk her into moving in with him? Even as impatient as JJ was, he was realist enough to understand that it might not happen soon. Probably not before the ball. He pacified himself with the fact that November was just around the corner. Just four short weeks until the ball. Four impossibly long weeks.

Dammit.

Impatient, JJ curled his hands around the steering wheel. Should he try to expedite the issue?

Rushing it, pal.

Verochka was still fidgety and hesitant around him. She still didn't trust him. And who could blame her? He was a stranger that barged in into her life just a few days ago. Well, *she* barged in into his bar first, but that was irrelevant. It was not her fault that his reaction to her was so strong or so powerful.

So overwhelming. He wasn't sure who was more shocked by it—him or her.

But initial shock aside, JJ was determined to win her over, no matter how long it took. And for that, he must earn her trust. Because without it, everything else—passion, need, even love—was pointless.

JJ drew in a deep breath. If he wanted a future with *Verochka*, he must be patient. He must court her relentlessly, properly, and wait for as long as was needed.

How long? A week? A month?

He swore out loud. That abstract period of 'long' went against his nature. As a businessman, he always operated and relied upon concrete numbers and firm boundaries. He must have a deadline in his head, even if a tentative one.

After a brief consideration, he decided to count the date of the winter ball, November fifteenth, as his time limit. He hoped he wouldn't need an extension, but if he did, he'd adjust his expectations accordingly. Even if it killed him.

JJ smiled thinking of that ball. Unlike before, this year he was only too happy to participate in Madeline's outlandish event. Hell, he could hardly wait for it. This ball was special, because *Verochka* was attending it with him. He sincerely hoped by that time, she'd be wearing his ring. And that was sure to raise some brows. His choice of bride may undoubtedly cause an uproar and a whirlpool of speculations. JJ tried to imagine *Verochka's* reaction on being the center of attention. Then again, as a performer, she was not a stranger to a spotlight. She was used to people staring at her on stage. Hell, she lived for it.

Professionally, yes. But in real life?

He was sure she'd take it in stride, with her head high, and her little nose upturned. No surprised if she exercised a perfect bow.

JJ smiled, then laughed out loud, envisioning that picture in his mind. Madeline will be mortified. Insulted to the tips of her pedicured toes.

A ballerina, a foreigner, without a cent to her name? Scandalous.

So what? Madeline might come around. And even if she didn't, who cares? Not him. Not one bit. JJ stopped caring, or seeking his mother's approval a long time ago. She never approved of any of his decisions, business or personal. He was used to it. Come to think of it, the only woman she ever warmed up to was Celeste. His ex-girlfriend was presently in town, of which Madeline happily informed him over the phone. She even offered to ask Celeste to accompany JJ to the ball, but he snipped that idea in the bud. Madeline was clearly disappointed. Was she hoping for a reconciliation between Celeste and him?

Wouldn't surprise JJ. Even the fact that his then steady girlfriend cheated on him, and married—and divorced—twice since then, hadn't deterred his mother. Nothing would. Celeste was from a wealthy family with an old pedigree, and even held a noble title to her name. To Madeline, that was an ultimate adulation, a pardon from all sins. Not to him. Even though JJ long ago forgave his old flame, he never forgot. Her betrayal was an ultimate deal breaker.

True, he didn't love Celeste. But he trusted her enough to live with her for almost a year. And she destroyed that trust in such a blasé offhanded manner, he was more stunned than angry at the time. Madeline refused to get it through her snobbish head that once the trust was broken, there was no repairing it. At least, not to JJ. Doesn't matter. Water under the bridge. And if Celeste hoped to rekindle their relationship, he'd disabuse her of that notion. Fast.

A ping of nostalgia was like prickling the skin with a tiny needle. Not enough to bring pain, but impossible to ignore. Like a papercut, irritating, mildly annoying.

Bold, brazen, self-centered, Celeste was exciting, and invigorating, like her favorite champagne. JJ never acquired a taste. Give him a single malt scotch every day, hot and honest and gut-churning. Like *Verochka*.

Comparing the two of them was probably not fair. Striking in their own way, they were as different as the sun and moon. *Or as a swan and a peacock.*

Celeste's features seemed shallow and artificial. As to her character?

It didn't come close to the strength and depths of the little cygnet who took his breath away. And her loyalty. JJ was sure than a subject of betrayal was as alien to Verochka as it was abhorrent. She vowed to never break her word, never renege on her promise. Once she made up her mind, nothing short of Armageddon could stop her. Was it any wonder he was crazy about her?

Slowly, the image of his old girlfriend faded away, as *Verochka's* expressive face swam in front of his eyes. Momentarily, his breath hitched, his heart lurched, then started to beat a mad staccato inside of his chest. She might act skittish, even weary, but there was nothing fidgety or hesitant in her response to him. Instantaneous, uninhibited, explosive, she was like a human inferno in his arms.

If kissing *Verochka* was so earth-shattering, what will happen when he takes her to bed? Shivers of anticipation shot through JJ's body.

A mind-boggling experience for sure. He could hardly wait.

Sooner or later, that Little Swan will be his, body, mind, and soul.

Sooner preferably, because JJ was all but exploding. Fried around the edges, his infamous control barely survived the evening. As to his patience? It was shredded into a gazillion tiny pieces. God knows what might have happened if Madeline's call hadn't interrupted that kiss.

Lost in thought, JJ almost didn't notice when he arrived at his destination. He shut the engine, and sat in the car, looking at the high-rise building he called home.

Why was he reluctant to exit the car? The prospect of spending another night at his penthouse alone suddenly seemed daunting. He always preferred his solitude, guarded it almost religiously. Surrounded by people during the day, JJ craved his privacy at night. His sax and his music were all the company he needed.

Being alone to him never meant being lonely. Until *Verochka*.

The impulse to turn around and drive aimlessly around the city was irresistible. He was about to start the car, but stopped his hand in mid-motion. Damn. Tomorrow was Tuesday, and there were several important conference calls scheduled in the morning, not to mention the bank board meeting in the afternoon.

And in between them, he must squeeze in a trip to Cartier, to buy an engagement ring. And order a food delivery to the school. And stop by the florist.

But the first thing in the morning, he'd put his assistant to search for the perfect wedding dress. The idea pleased him enormously, and bolstered him enough to shake off his reluctance to drag his lonely self upstairs. To be clear-headed tomorrow, he must get some rest. After a long cold shower, that is.

With an exhale of resignation, JJ turn to pick up his sax from the backseat, then stepped out of the car.

CHAPTER TWENTY

*V*erochka exercised a triple twirl listening with a half an ear to the music and Madame Valeska's occasional stern remarks. Hands above her head in imitation of swan wings, one leg bent at the knee, she held a pose created by Marius Petipa in 1895, the first choreographer of Swan Lake. A forward dip of the body, then sharp uplift, all the while standing on one *en pointe,* and keeping her back ramrod straight. Two male hands around her waist anchored her body, and kept her from losing balance. Aaron Swift, a fellow student from her class, was appointed by Madame to be Siegfried to her Odette. He was a dream partner any ballerina could ask for. Tall and athletic, he was built like a long-distance runner, with miles of beautifully sculptured muscular legs. His deceptively slender arms were strong enough to lift her effortlessly and hold her for long periods of time. With Aaron, *Verochka* wasn't afraid of being accidentally dropped, an ultimate nightmare of any ballerina. They trusted each other on stage, so attuned together, their movements, and breathings, were perfectly synchronized.

Why then had she managed to step on his toes several times during today's rehearsal?

Because she was not paying one hundred percent attention, that's why. Because she was still baffled and confused by the delivery that came early this morning for her.

The quantity of food was enough to feed the entire school, and then have leftovers for a week. Like that wasn't enough, a huge bouquet of three dozen red roses that was delivered shortly after, adding to her shock. Even without a small note attached, she knew who was it from.

Only one person was capable of such an extravagant gesture, JJ Morris.

Instead of being pleased, *Verochka* saw red. The nerve of the man!

Who did he think he was? Her benefactor? Is that his idea of softening her up for accepting his marriage proposal?

What proposal, for goodness' sake?

He didn't propose. He informed her of his intention to marry her. By Christmas, of all things! Like it was a given. Like she had nothing to say about it.

Merde!

Fuming, *Verochka* leaped, landed, and lifted her right arm high above her head. Behind her, Aaron put both hands on her shoulders, turned her around. By the libretto, they looked at each other, his gaze smoldering, hers imploring, then took a few steps together, before separating for her short solo. *Verochka* drew a deep breath, poised and alert, waiting for the musical cue.

An abrupt silence accompanied by loud clapping broke her concentration.

"Miss Osipoff, Mr. Swift, take a short break."

Saved by the clap. Rendre grace a Dieu!

Immensely grateful for the interruption, *Verochka* grabbed a towel hanging from a barre, then wiped her sweaty face. She plopped onto the floor feeling like she was granted a pardon from an execution, then stretched her achy legs.

Even though the Swan Lake second act *pa de deux* didn't have any *jete* or *fouette,* it was strenuous enough to make her muscles sing in protest. Every pose demanded a precise execution in excruciating slow motion. It was the first 'conversation' between the heroes, a tender and tentative duo when the bewitched princess in the guise of a swan meets her prince. Tchaikovsky's genius reflected it in music with a heartbreaking poignancy, intertwining cello and violin in an almost a human voice cadence. It always brought tears to *Verochka's* eyes. But even her favorite melody failed to captivate her today.

Soon, her breathing returned to normal, unlike the turmoil of her emotions. Inside, she was a bundle of confused thoughts and jumping nerves.

Damn the man for intruding on the most sacred part of her life—her ballet rehearsals. Wasn't it enough that he invaded her dreams?

Or trespass on her every waking hour.

He was a major thorn in her behind, infuriating, annoying, maddening.

Gorgeous.

Merde, his looks were not relevant! Under all that male glory, he was the most obnoxious human being she ever met. Controlling, stubborn, determined.

And so sure of himself, it was simply outrageous. Delivering her food, of all things. Why did he think she was starving? And even if she was, it was not up to him to take charge of her diet. Or any other aspect of her life!

She was a responsible mature woman, able to take care of herself. She didn't need a keeper. Two years she managed to live on her own. She might not have a lot of possessions, like beautiful clothes, or jewelry, or comfortable furniture, but she had everything she needed. She was content. Until this incorrigible man forced himself into her life, and made her yearn for something elusive *Verochka* had no name for.

She shook the unwanted thoughts off. If she cannot name that *something*, then she was better off without it. She was better off without JJ Morris, period.

Light as a shadow, a sadness crept over her, murmuring of regrets and unfulfilled wishes. Impossible. What regrets? *Verochka* didn't have a single regret. As to her wishes—all she ever wanted was to dance, to become a prima ballerina for The Royal Ballet. In three weeks, she will perform before the panel of that distinguished company, and hope to be chosen for the part of Odette in their upcoming production of Swan Lake. Her biggest dream was about to become a reality. But that dream may become a reality *only* if she fully concentrates on her rehearsals, and forgot about everything else. She must breathe and live for that event with no exceptions. Every minute of her life must be dedicated to ballet.

No more interruptions of any kind. No more late-night trips to the Broome Street bar, or silly daydreaming about its owner.

Stay focused, Verochka. *And get your head out of a cloud.*

Her pep talk was cut abruptly by none other than Madame Valeska. She walked closer then sat down on the floor beside *Verochka*. Her exceptional legs that once upon a time captivated ballet lovers around the world still managed to make all the female students green with envy. Crossing those outrageously long legs, Madame Valeska aimed her piercing eyes on *Verochka*.

"How are you, my dear?"

"Ah...very well, thank you."

"That's wonderful."

Why Madame was looking at her like that? If she wasn't pleased with *Verochka's* dancing, she'd say it without mincing words. A long pause made her uncomfortable, even twitchy. Wincing inwardly, *Verochka* waited for a reprimand. Madame's voice finally broke the silence.

"Now, as much as it is not my business, I still feel responsible for you. So I will ask anyway." She gazed at *Verochka*, frowning. Is she didn't know better, she'd swear Madame was uncomfortable. "Are you in love with Mr. Morris?"

Verochka blinked a couple of times at the unexpected question. If her teacher clubbed her over the head, she would be less shocked.

With an effort, *Verochka* swallowed, and at last found her voice. "What! Oh, *non*, Madame. *Absolument pas!*"

Madame Valeska kept her eyes on *Verochka's* face a bit longer than was comfortable. Finally, her mentor curved her lips in a half-smile. A light pat on *Verochka's* forearm was unexpected and highly unusual. Madame was not a toucher.

"Oh, child, don't fight it so hard. Love is a precious thing, a gift from above. Like your talent. And just like any gift, it is up to a person to accept it, nourish it, or to reject it. The choice is yours."

"I am not in love with Mr. Morris." She heard the desperation in her own voice, cringed, and rushed ahead, "And even if I was silly enough to fall for the man, I'd never act on it. I won't allow myself to get sidetracked from my main goal." Balling her fists to keep her hands from shaking, *Verochka* looked straight at her teacher. "Ballet is my life, Madame. Just like it is yours. You are my inspiration. Your example is my guiding star."

"Dear God, girl! Heavens forbid you follow my example."

Madame Valeska lowered her eyes. A deep sigh later, she turned to *Verochka*. Her next reply came out in a faraway manner, like every word was causing her pain. *Verochka* barely recognized Madame's voice.

"There was a man in my life once, when I was a bit older than you. He loved me. But I was young and ambitious. My single goal in life was to dance. To be better than any other ballerina. To become a principal dancer." Her gaze turned inward. A profound sadness settled like a heavy blanket around Madame's body, bowing her shoulders. "When he proposed, I rejected him. And regretted it ever since."

"But, Madame, you career...it was brilliant! Simply outstanding."

"Yes, it was. I was prima for fifteen years, longer than any ballerina ever dreamt of. I have danced many parts on the most famous stages around the world. But..." Madame Valeska drew her knees up, encircled them with her hands, "...after you take your final bow, what's next? The empty bed in an unfamiliar hotel room, the painful memories, and... regrets. There is nothing worst in this world than loneliness, child."

Uncomfortable and embarrassed, like she unwillingly witnessed something intimate, *Verochka* lowered her eyes. Madame words echoed in her head: *an empty bed, painful memories, regrets. Loneliness.*

Is that what awaited her in her own future? Disturbed more than she was willing to admit, *Verochka* swallowed around the lump in her throat. Before her brain registered her intention, she heard herself ask, "If you could go back, would you?"

"Would I decide differently? In a heartbeat. No ballet part, not even the most rewording one, can compare with the warmth of human companionship. With love. Remember that."

With a heavy sigh, Madame Valeska raised from the floor in a single fluid motion.

She snapped her back straight, tilted her head, and address the room in her regular no-nonsense voice, "Okay, the break is over. Everybody, on your positions, *sil vouis plait.*"

And just like that, her formidable teacher was back.

CHAPTER TWENTY-ONE

E xhausted after five hours of relentless rehearsals, *Verochka* dragged herself up to her tiny apartment. She was sweaty, and filthy, and aching all over. Standing under the weak spray of her miniscule shower, she quickly lathered shampoo onto her hair, hurrying with the overall process. From the experience, she knew there was only about two more minutes before a lukewarm water will cool off completely. If there was something *Verochka* truly hated, it was cold. In any form or way.

If she was able, she'd live in the place where there was perpetual summer, somewhere small and picturesque, with the gingerbread trimmed houses near the white sand beach. And a lot of sunshine. *Verochka* sighed. It was silly to dream of something she might never have. But indulging in her occasional fantasy was harmless. She closed her eyes and allowed herself to drift to that wonderful place in her mind. In her imaginary world, there was a house, a peculiar octagonal building overlooking the great ocean. She loved the wraparound deck on its second story, especially the large stripped umbrella. She'd sit on that deck every morning, drinking a cup of rich black coffee, and welcome the new day. Those visions were so vivid, so disturbingly real, *Verochka* almost believed she has really been there.

But when? And where was that place? Not in France, for sure, because there was no ocean in her native country. In America? But since her arrival here two years ago, she lived only in New York, and only in SoHo. So, why did she feel like she was familiar with that little slice of paradise? Deeply, intimately.

Shaking herself off, *Verochka* turned her face up toward a spray of water.

She was being silly. That place was in her imagination only. Oh, but what a wonderful spot it was. Joyful, cheery, peaceful. Maybe she'd find it, and make it her home. Someday. In the future. Someday, she'd travel all over the globe, see wonderful countries, eat delicious cuisine.

But she'd always return home, to that little sunny paradise near the ocean.

A trickle of cold water brought her back to reality in a flash. Damn, she stayed in the shower too long, daydreaming. As a result, she was cold, and shivering. She shut off the icy water then stepped onto a tiny bathmat, grabbed a towel, and wrapped it around herself. Almost threadbare, it was not large enough to cover her body past midthigh, leaving her legs exposed. Someday, she'd be able to afford thick, large towels, and a fluffy bathrobe. With a little sigh, she tucked her old towel more security around herself, and left the bathroom. The enormous bouquet or scarlet roses greeted her. There was so many of them, *Verochka* was forced to borrow a bucket from the custodian, and deposit the flowers into it. A pure shame to keep all that beauty in an ugly steel pail, but since she didn't own a vase, it must suffice.

The sweet fragrance of those roses permitted the air of her tiny room. She never received such a gorgeous bouquet. Enchanted, *Verochka* trailed a tip of her finger over one bud. Soft velvety petals caressed her skin, making it tingle. A delicate shudder rippled through. She smiled. Then she frowned. As much as she hated to do so, she must thank the man for his gifts. *Merde.* Turning away from the flowers, *Verochka* huffed in an exasperated breath. She must be grateful, and appreciative, even if she was irritated with him to no end. Her parents believed in good manners. Their frowns sprang into *Verochka's* mind if she didn't properly acknowledge the generosity bestowed upon her. If only it were any other person, but JJ Morris. On the spur of the moment, she decided to send him a thank you note.

Polite, cordial, impersonal.

It was a coward's way out, Verochka.

Cursing under her breath, she shook her head. No, it was simply unacceptable. Whatever flaws she had, cowardice was not one of them.

Well then. She must go to the bar, and thank him in person. Tomorrow. Today, she was beat. And too confused and unbalanced. By everything.

JJ's extravagant gifts, Madame's shocking confession, and her own turbulent emotions where that man was concerned. For the first time today, she lied to Madame. Not in love with him? And who was she trying to fool?

She was so hopelessly head over heels, it was outrageous. Even if she denied it until the doomsday, she was unable to hide from the truth. Or lie to herself.

Love, unexpected, unwelcomed, burst into her life with the speed of a tornado, and like that violent storm, obliterated every obstacle from its path. Her own willpower included. Was she brave enough, strong enough, to withstand this brutal attack?

The real question was, will she be able to come out unscathed?

Did she want to be in love with JJ? Absolutely not. But did she have a choice?

Of course, she did. She might be hopelessly in love with the man, but *Verochka* was far from helpless. She simply must avoid him, and concentrate on her career. Ballet was her destiny, her vocation. Her love of dancing was stronger than her feelings for JJ, wasn't it? Maybe she was not really in love, but simply infatuated? After all, she never met anyone such as him: gorgeous, bold, talented.

And rich like a proverbial Croesus.

They were on the opposite sides of the spectrum. So, what did a man like him possibly see in her? Was his interest spiked out of sheer curiosity? Or worst, out of boredom? *Mon Dieu*, she was so out of her depth!

She wished she had someone to talk to. But who? *Verochka* was not accustomed to sharing her troubles with anyone except her parents.

Her gaze traveled to the single photograph on her wall, the only precious memento from her childhood. Smiling, with their arms around each other, her parents were frozen in that happy moment, forever young and beautiful. Filled with sorrow, *Verochka's* heart stumbled in her chest. The grief has never gone away.

She learned to live with it by hiding it deep inside. But somedays, the pain grabbed her by the throat, huge and throbbing and merciless, and bring the flood of memories back...

"Don't fret, ma petite. I see a long life ahead of you, filled with love and joy and happiness. One day, you will marry a prince. He'll be dark and tall and so incredibly handsome."

"But how can you see that, Papa? Are you a magician?"

She heard her own voice as a child, high-pitched, excited.

Her father chuckled. "Almost. You see, ma petite, I have special eyes, just like you do. They are violet, and they are extraordinary. I can see what many people cannot. And sometimes, I can see far, far ahead, into the future. When you are older, you'll be able to see it, too."

"What about Maman? Can she see into the future too?"

"No, Ma Petite Belle. Only the people with the violet eyes can..."

Startled, *Verochka* looked around the room. She heard her father's voice so clearly, like he was standing next to her. But of course, he wasn't.

Both her parents died on that gloomy winter day in Paris, when they were returning home from a rehearsal. A drunk driver mowed them down just two short blocks from their flat. That was four years ago. It felt like yesterday.

Whoever said that time healed everything was a stinking liar. Her pain never faded. It crawled deeper inside. But her memories became more bittersweet, more poignant. She cherished every single one of them.

Strange, but she didn't remember that conversation with her father until now.

How old was she at the time? Five? Six? Had her *Papa* really believed their violet eyes were special, and saw what other people didn't?

Probably one of his fanciful stories. Her *Papa* loved to spin a tale for little *Verochka*, full of magic and enchantment, and happy-ever-after endings.

The memories of her childhood were precious to her, and every moment with her parents were etched into her heart forever.

One day, you will marry a prince. He'll be dark and tall and so incredibly handsome...

JJ's image swam in front of her eyes. Tall, dark, magnificent.

She shook her head so fast and hard she thought it might spring from her shoulders. He might be a prince, but not from her fairy tale. The end.

Feeling more miserable than she was willing to admit, *Verochka* donned her sleeping shirt from under the pillow, then tugged it on. The single renegade tear irritated her to no end. *Verochka* never cried, even when she buried her parents. She absolutely refused to shed tears now. Wiping the treacherous moisture from her face, she plopped onto the narrow cold bed.

Chilly drafts of air from a single tiny window covered her skin in goosebumps. Shivering, *Verochka* jerked the chenille cover from under her body, and covered herself to the chin. Her room, located just under the roof, was usually hot in summer, and cold in winter. Even though November this year was relatively mild for New York, yet it still made her living space nippier than she liked. She ought to invest in a portable heater, but those things were too pricy, and she was too forgetful to remember to turn it off every time she went out. God forbid, she burned the school down. Her only defense against cold was warm clothes and a hot shower. A very short one, that is, thanks to her finicky water system.

What a luxury it must be to enjoy a really long shower every day, and not hurry in fear the hot water will run out.

Someday, she will have a house, with lots of hot water.

The house by the ocean, with grey stilts, and blue trim, and a beautiful view...

CHAPTER TWENTY-TWO

Despite her unsettling emotions, *Verochka* started to drift as soon as her head hit the pillow. Almost floating, she smiled, as her mind conjured the image of a man, dark, tall, impossibly handsome, standing by her side. Two strong arms embracing her made her giddy with delight. She felt secure, protected, and wonderfully safe. Lifting her face up with two fingers under her chin, he smiled down at her, then lowered his head for a kiss. In her dream, *Verochka* felt his breath on her cheek, minty and warm and familiar. Rich and citrusy, his masculine aroma tickled her nose.

Anticipating that kiss, she lifted herself on her tiptoes, opened her mouth...

And jerked wide awake.

Merde.

Dragging both hands through her still wet hair, *Verochka* muttered a helpless oath. The face of that fantasy man in her dream was unmistakable. JJ Morris.

Appalled and embarrassed, she swore, using her entire repertoire of French curses. She didn't need or want any man sharing her dream, especially *him.* How on earth will she be able to avoid JJ if the rascal managed to invade her dreams? It was as if her subconsciousness sided with the almighty Reginald JJ Morris.

And you agreed to go to the ball with him.

Aggravated, *Verochka* jumped from the bed, then started to pace. Since her space was unbelievably tiny, it took her three steps in any direction before she hit the wall. Fuming, she fisted both hands. What on earth prompted her to agree to his crazy proposition? Because she was mad at him at the time, that's what.

Determined to have the last word, she blurted out about getting her own dress without a second though. By the time she realized what she roped herself into, it was already late.

Idiot.

Unwillingly, unmindfully, she gave her word to the rascal.

Merde!

But a deal was a deal.

She'd be damned if she broke her promise because she gave it in the heat of the moment. She'll go to that stupid ball with him, and then put a stop to their acquaintance, once and for all. So what if she was in love with the man? *Verochka* had no time or inclination to continue this folly, or to give him any hint of encouragement to his astounding notion of marriage.

Marry him? When the pigs fly!

She didn't need him. She was perfectly happy and content on her own. Or was she?

Madame Valeska's words cut into her memory.

"No ballet part, not even the most rewording one, can compare with the warmth of human companionship. With love. Remember that."

Was it true? And what if it was?

Restless, *Verochka* continued her pacing until she was ready to scream. The need to talk to someone was overwhelming. She looked at the small wristwatch on top of her wooden chest. Her mother's watch. The golden bracelet was too fragile for everyday wear, and too precious. In fear of damaging it, *Verochka* never put it on. Now, the tiny round face gleamed back at her with both hands poised at eleven.

She bit her lip, contemplating. It was too late. She needed her rest. Tomorrow she was scheduled for costume fittings, not to mention a morning class, and her afternoon rehearsals. Sleep was out of the question. How could she possibly sleep if she was all but bursting at the seams? A tug-of war between frustration and common sense ended in a spectacular defeat of logic. Emotions won.

Verochka grabbed her jeans and shirt hanging on the door, donned the only warm sweated she owned. Impatiently, she shoved her bare feet into a pair of sneakers. The hell with the socks. Her hair was still wet, but there was nothing to be done about it now. Securing it into a lose ponytail, *Verochka* tucked the ends underneath her sweater. On an impulse, she palmed an orange and apple from the basket of goodies delivered that morning, and stormed out of the door.

There was only one person she knew, older and wiser, who'd listen. And maybe, help her make sense out of all this confusion.

CHAPTER TWENTY-THREE

Winston greeted her with a warm smile and a tall glass of orange juice. He placed it in front of *Verochka* on the bar counter, then pointed at it.

"Drink, Little Swan. That'll hold you until I warm up a bowl of stew for you."

"Oh, but I can't eat. It's too late, and I'm not hungry."

"Sorry, boss's order." Winston turned around, fished under the counter, and came up with a huge ceramic bowl. "My stew is famous around here. You'll eat, and love every drop of it."

"But...I don't... I can't—"

"What are those?" He interrupted her, eyeing the two pieces of fruit she held in her hands.

"Oh, sorry. These are for you." Stretching her arms over the counter, she handed the fruit to Winston.

"For me? You brought me a gift? Aww, shucks, little one. You shouldn't."

"Of course, I should. You've done so much for me. It's just a thank you token."

Winston accepted the fruit, eyeing *Verochka* with suspiciously misty eyes.

A gamut of emotions—pleasure, bafflement, embarrassment—swam over his face, as he held an orange and apple in one humongous palm. It was so endearing, she leaned over the counter, then planted a smacking kiss onto his cheek, surprising them both.

Two crimson patches bloomed on Winston's ragged face. After a moment, he cleared his throat. "Ah...thank you for your gift, *Verochka*."

"You are very welcome. Technically, it's a gift from your boss. This fruit, along with other goodies, were delivered to the school this morning."

"You don't say?" He squinted at her, rubbing his chin with thick sausage-like fingers.

"And if that wasn't enough, he sent me a bunch of roses. Can you imagine?"

"You don't say!" A huge smile spread across Winston's face making the crow's-feet around his eyes more prominent.

"I do say! The man is incorrigible."

"The boy is smitten." Chuckling, Winston nodded his bald head.

"*Smitten?*" Momentarily speechless, *Verochka* gaped at him. It took her awhile to find her voice. "How can you say that? He is just being stubborn, and controlling, and...and..." Gaining in volume and outrage, her voice jumped up an octave, then broke on an exasperated huff.

"Caring. That's called caring, little girl. The boy is a goner, alright, and I for one, is very happy for him. And for you."

"For...me? Oh, you are impossible, Winston. Almost as much as your boss. And here I came to talk to you, and you—"

"Talk to me? What did you want to talk to me about, Little Swan? I'm all ears."

"You sidetracked me, and made me forget what I wanted to tell you."

"Take a deep breath, drink your juice, and calm down."

On autopilot, *Verochka* grabbed the tall glass, then upended it in a few angry gulps. Obviously pleased, Winston grunted, then placed a steaming bowl in front of her.

"Now, eat your stew, little one. Hot food will do you a world of good."

Food? How can she eat when he aggravated her? Still seething, *Verochka* snatched a spoon from his hand, dipped it into the bowl. She raked her scattered brain for an answer, but it refused to cooperate. What did she want to talk to Winston about before he blindsided her?

After a couple of spoonfuls, she had her eureka moment.

"I remembered!"

"Good. Now tell me everything."

Bracing both elbows onto the bar counter, he leaned closer. "And don't forget the stew. Eat and talk, Little Swan."

"This is really good," licking her lips, *Verochka* placed the spoon beside the bowl, "but I can't eat anymore."

"Okay, take a break. Now, to your question?"

She searched carefully for the next words. "You see, I'm...confused. And I have no one to talk to. Everything is happening so fast, so...unexpected."

"The best things usually come to us like that, fast and unexpected."

"I wouldn't know. I always preferred my life well-paced, and predetermined. I know what I want, I know my goal, and I'm doing my best to reach it." After a couple of calming breath, she continued, "Ballet is my whole life, my only passion. My salvation. If not for ballet, I don't know how I would have survived after the death of my parents. So, I came to America to study in the most prestigious school, to hone my skills. To become a prima ballerina. I want to dance more than I want to breathe. And...and I was happy and content, until..."

"Until?" He prodded gently after her voice trailed off.

"Until JJ. He burst into my life, and upturned everything normal and familiar, until I don't know right from left." Exasperated, *Verochka* drew both hands through her hair, dislodging her rubber band. With a little oath, she yanked it off, then wound it around her wrist. "He said he wanted to marry me."

Now, what on earth prompted her to blurt that out?

Idiot! Imbecile! Little fool!

Silently berating herself, *Verochka* held her breath.

"Hmm."

That's his reaction? Really? My earthshattering revelation earned a monosyllabic reply? Astonishing!

"What is that supposed to mean? I'm telling you that he *informed* me of his intention to be married by Christmas, and all you have to say is 'hmm'?"

Winston mulled that for a moment.

"By Christmas, is it? Well, I always knew when that boy makes up his mind, there is no stopping him."

"I don't care! I must stop him, one way or the other!"

"Why?"

"Why? Isn't that obvious?"

"Not from where I'm standing, it isn't."

"Winston, just think about it." Desperation crept into her voice, turning it to beseeching. "We are complete opposites of each other! He is...and I am..." she wind-milled her arms, then let them drop to her lap. "I don't belong in his circle."

"And what circle is that?"

"Rich and noble."

Frowning, Winston took his sweet time to reply. When he broke the silence, his usually gruff voice was soft and tender. "Nobility, Little Swan, is not something to be inherited. It's in your blood, in your soul. To me, you are more noble than many an aristocrat I've met during my lifetime."

Rendered speechless, *Verochka* blinked a couple of times. Did she hear him correctly? Her, noble? He must be kidding! She squinted at Winston, searching his expression. His gaze was unwavering and totally serious.

"As to being rich," he continued after a pause, "Money isn't everything, Little Swan. It doesn't determine who we are. Some people are wealthy, but they can never be happy. Some have not a penny to their names, but have a rich and fulfilling life. Like you, or me." Winston leaned forward and awkwardly patted her shoulder. "Now, JJ? He was born with a silver spoon in his mouth, but it didn't spoil him, or make him into a cold bastard. Unlike his mother, he managed to stay decent and kind and loyal. And that is what most counts, isn't it?" After a heartbeat of silence, he smiled. "What I'm trying to say, *Verochka*, money is not evil, nor is it an obstacle. Especially when two people are falling in love."

"But I'm not falling in love with JJ!"

Liar. Your nose should be sprouting branches.

"No, you are not." Calm and composed, Winston voice held a hint of pity. "You have already hit the bottom, little one. You just afraid to accept the truth."

And just like that, the proverbial nail was hammered all the way in.

"Mon Dieu!" She closed her eyes, pressed both palms into her sockets until she saw stars. "What have I done?"

"The most wonderful thing you could've done, girl. Love is a true gift. Not many fortunate enough to receive it."

"I already heard it today."

"From someone very smart, I wager."

"From my teacher, Madame Valeska."

"The same one who forbids you to eat at night?"

"Yes."

"Hmm."

She jumped to her mentor's defense with a renewed fervor.

"No 'hmm'! She is wise, and talented, and yes, very smart."

"Well, you should listen to your Madame, then. Not about your eating habits, mind you, but everything else."

Despite her mood, *Verochka* chuckled. Oh, the man has one-track mind, indeed. It was really endearing, even if a bit irritating. But her merriment was short lived. The situation was serious, almost grave, and she desperately needed advice.

"Winston, what should I do?"

He shrugged. "Why should you do anything? Just take it one day at the time, and see where it brings you. And listen to your heart, little one. My granddaddy always said, your heart might be on your left, but it's always right."

"Thank you for your sage advice, Winston. I'll be sure to follow it." A hint of good-natured censure was lost on the man. Pleased as he can be, he returned to his bartender's duties of polishing the tumbler in his hands.

"Feeling any better?"

Strange, but she was. No less confused, but marginally better.

"I think I am."

"Good. It's a pity JJ's not here. He'd hate to miss seeing you."

"Oh."

Verochka noticed the unusual quietness of the bar. Some conversations, an occasional burst of laughter, the waiters' efficient bustling. But the familiar husky voice of the saxophone was absent. How on earth did she miss that?

Was it her imagination, or the atmosphere tonight really seemed darker and emptier? Her eyes traveled to the little platform in the corner where JJ usually played. Vacant, it seemed almost forlorn like an abandoned child.

Her pang of disappointment was brief but sharp, like a prickle of a needle.

He is not here.

She should be glad and relieved by the reprieve. Now she didn't have to thank him in person. And wasn't it what she wanted? *Verochka* pushed her dismay away. Of course it was!

Why are you so upset? Do you miss him?

She bristled, more unsettled than she was willing to admit. Miss him? Nonsense! She just regretted that she failed to fulfill her obligation sooner rather than later. That's all. As much as she disliked it, she must make another trip to the bar some other day. And she was insanely busy with the upcoming tryout, and had no desire to continue these silly visits. It was aggravating how the man managed to disrupt all her careful plans. Why didn't he cooperate just this once?

Merde.

Irritated at herself, at him, at life in general, she turned to Winston.

"Where is he?"

"No idea. He called earlier to say that he won't be in tonight."

"Is this usual for him?"

"Nope. Highly unusual. JJ is here every night, first to come, last to leave."

The unwelcomed layer of concern coated her gut. She chewed on her top lip, frowning. Opting for nonchalance, *Verochka* schooled her face into a mask of polite indifference. "I hope everything is okay."

Her only hope was that Winston, currently busy with an order, missed the note of worry in her voice.

"Oh, I'm sure it is." Finishing with the customer, he turned back to *Verochka*. "Must be something business related. Morris is a vast international enterprise, and JJ's at the helm of that behemoth. Too young for that responsibility, if you ask me."

Letting go of the breath she was holding, *Verochka* silently chided herself.

So what if he missed one night at the bar? Like Winston said, it was probably business related, that's all. Nothing to worry about. He was fine, just busy.

Doing what?

The image of JJ in a company of some beautiful woman swam in her mind. *Merde.* She fisted her hands, cursing her unruly imagination. He was an unattached adult, free to court anyone he wanted.

The hell he was!

The clock above Winston's head caught her attention. One AM? Oh, Lord! How can it be so late? Startled, she shook her head. Time to go.

"I must be going, Winston." Reluctantly, she swung her legs sideways. The stool was so tall, her toes dangled without touching the floor. She extended her legs in an effort to find firm purchase. "Tomorrow is a very busy day. Ah, actually, already today. In a few hours, I must be in a class." With her butt halfway off the seat, and both legs still suspended in the air, *Verochka* hung in a precarious position.

"I'll ask Adam to walk you home." Winston signaled to the younger bartender.

"Oh, no. There is no need. The street is well lit, and you all are busy, so..."

"Adam will walk you home, little one." The younger man caught Winston's gesture and nodded. After a moment, he materialized beside *Verochka*. It was pointless to argue. She accepted the inevitable.

"Okay then. Thank you again for listening, and for the stew. It was truly delicious."

"You are very welcome."

"And Winston?" She lowered her eyes. "Please tell JJ I said thank you for the roses and the goodies, although it was absolutely unnecessary."

"You can tell him herself."

"Tell me what?" A familiar baritone inquired from somewhere behind her.

Verochka gasped, swiveled, and would have fallen off the stool if not for the two hands that caught her around the middle. Slowly she lifted her gaze. Dark as Belgian chocolate, the familiar eyes stopped her breath, and sent her heart skipping.

CHAPTER TWENTY-FOUR

As soon as JJ recognized the slender figure seated at the bar, all his exhaustion evaporated in a flash. *Verochka* was here. He didn't expect to see her tonight.

As a matter of fact, he was dead sure she'd avoid him like a plague. Not that he would allow her to do so, but still. She surprised him. Again.

Why was she here? Read him the riot act, no doubt. Well, then. Time to indulge her. After the day he had, JJ should be beat, but instead he found himself energized, and more than ready for the next argument with *Verochka*.

"Tell me what?" He repeated, keeping his eyes on her face.

"I...um, I wanted..."

Her breathing became fast and erratic, which pleased him enormously. She was nervous, fidgety, and if he wasn't mistaken, embarrassed. The combination worked in his favor.

"Yes?" He prodded. Try as he might, he held his lips from twitching.

"I wanted to thank you for your lavish gesture of sending me gifts. It was completely unnecessary, and highly embarrassing. I must ask you to never do that again."

Sweet Lord, only *Verochka* managed to thank and condemn him in the same sentence. And her tone of voice! Clipped, curt, with that lick of accent, she delivered her verdict in a single breath. Was she opting for a stern reprimand?

She'd be disappointed. If she only knew that to his ears it came as an alluring invitation. Or a challenge. Irresistible, erotic, seductive as any come-hither.

JJ never resisted a challenge.

"You are very welcome. I'm sorry if I embarrassed you."

"You did more than that. I might be a pauper by your standards, but I am not a beggar. Nor am I a charity case."

JJ frowned, cursed inwardly. Coming from his heart, his intention was pure, but he failed to take into consideration her pride. Unwittingly, he managed to wound her, scraping at her self-esteem.

Damn it.

"Let me assure you, that was not a charity. The last think I intended was to demonstrate my wealth, or damage your dignity. Please, believe me."

"I believe you. If I had the slightest doubt, all those boxes of goodies would have been returned to you untouched."

"I'm glad you didn't return them."

"But I shared the bounty with everybody, and gave the rest to our custodian. He has four little children."

JJ winced, then grinned. "Did you leave anything for yourself?"

"A basket of fruit."

Well, at least her intake of vitamins for the next few days should be satisfactory.

"If you didn't want to demonstrate your wealth, or damage my dignity, as you put it, what was your intention, then?"

"To please you."

"Huh? And why would you want to do that?"

"Why, because you are my future wife, and it is only natural that my most cherished wish is to please you." He deliberately lowered his voice to husky whisper, and added, "In any way I can."

If she caught his double entendre, she didn't let it show. *Verochka* drew a loud breath as she stepped back from him.

"Mr. Morris, listen to me, and listen good." With both fists propped on hips and her eyes spewing fire, *Verochka* leaned forward, "I will never marry you. Period."

She was so adorable. JJ barely suppressed the urge to hug her. "Never say never, *ma petite.*"

Verochka opened her mouth to reply, but he interrupted, hoping to throw her off, "By the way, did you like the roses?"

He succeeded, if her fast blinking and befuddled expression were any indication.

"What's not to like? They are spectacular." A reluctant grumble.

JJ smiled quite pleased with himself.

Stubborn little thing.

"Good. You'll have them every day for the rest of your life."

"*Mon Dieu!*" Her arms flew up like a pair of spooked butterflies. "Haven't you've been listening to me? Read my lips: I will not marry you!" She enunciated every word separately, sharply, as she glared at him out of molten eyes.

He shrugged. "What's that got to do with flowers? And I respectfully disagree. You *will* marry me. So, you'd better get used to the idea."

She gaped at him, clearly stunned. After a heartbeat of silence, *Verochka* blinked. Stuttering, she repeated, "B-better g-get used to? Who the hell do you think you are?" Heavy on disbelieve, her voice literally rose a full octave. He couldn't have been more pleased.

"The man who's crazy in love with you."

He didn't mean to say that. Not so soon. But the words flew out of his mouth, and it was too late to do anything about it. Shocked, Verochka gaped at him, with her mouth frozen on a perfect 'O.' Out of the corner of his eye JJ caught a movement. A deep chuckle disguised for a cough tickled his ears. Winston. Damn, he totally forgot about him. With his face arranged into something resembling a grin, Winston wasn't even trying not to eavesdrop. The younger bartender, Adam, was glued to his spot nearby, openly hanging on every word. Silently, JJ raised a brow in his direction. That was all it took for the younger man to jolt and scram.

JJ turned to face his other bartender. "Don't pretend that you didn't hear it, old man."

"Wouldn't dream of it, Boss."

"Since it's all in the open by now, I'd like to ask you to do me an honor, and be my best man at our wedding."

Two yelps rang simultaneously, one outraged, the second dumbfounded.

"Are you serious?"

"Sweet baby Jesus, Boss!"

"Do I look like I'm kidding?" He addressed his question to Winston, but he trained his eyes on *Verochka's* face. Pale, with two crimson patches high on her cheekbones, she was more astonished than angry.

"No, you're as serious as a heart attack." Winston's gruff voice fell onto its usual cadence. "It's me who's honored by your request, JJ. Say, are you sure? Your mother will have a hissy fit."

"My mother is not prone to fits, hissy or otherwise. More than likely, she'll refuse to attend, but who cares?"

"Well, not me. If you sure that what you want..."

"Dead sure. There is no one I'd rather have by my side on the most important day of my life than you."

"Then I accept. Thank you, boy."

"You are welcome, my friend."

"Have you both lost your marbles?" Quickly dispersing with her astonishment, his future wife balled her shaking hands, "In case it slipped your befuddled minds, I'm standing right here!"

Uh-oh. *Verochka* was about to fly off the handle. Despite everything, JJ grinned.

A huge mistake.

His mind flashed the warning, but it was already too late. With something close to a growl, *Verochka* charged forward, then hit his chest with both hands. It held enough punch to make him stumble a step backward.

"Whoa, Little Swan." Deceptively fragile, her slender arms were surprisingly strong. "Not that I'm a prude, but I am not into rough foreplay."

"I'll show you a rough foreplay, you bastard!"

With that, she bent her leg, most likely intended to knee him in the groin. If JJ's instincts weren't faster, his chance to have children someday may well dwindle to zero.

He sidestepped, then swept her tight to his chest.

"You little hellcat." Chuckling, he tightened his arms around her warm body. "I simply adore you."

She wiggled in his arms, agile like an eel. Spewing, her anger was almost palpable. "And I simply hate you!"

Unbounded, her silky blonde hair gleamed like polished gold. A single strand fell in her eyes. She blew at it, all the while glaring at him.

"No you don't. You are crazy about me."

"Why, you conceited, egotistical jerk! You pig! You..." The long and colorful string of curses erupted like a fiery volcano. Even though he didn't understand the unfamiliar language, it still sounded like the best music to his ears.

"Is it Russian?"

Instead of answering, she added more guttural sounding words. No doubt they were as foul as their French counterparts.

"Yep, definitely crazy about me. Admit it, *ma petite*."

"I will do no such thing! And stop manhandling me this instant!"

"If I let you go, will you aim for my family jewels again?"

"No."

"Are you sure?"

"*Absolument.*"

"Okay."

But as soon as he dropped his hands, she charged forward, as he predicted. He'd have been disappointed if she didn't. So, what if it was perverse of him? It gave him an excuse to haul her all the way against him, and plant a hard kiss onto her quivering mouth. She fought him. For about a heartbeat. Then her arms slid around his neck, and pressing fully against him, she returned the kiss.

Heat, instantaneous, scorching.

Lust, brutal, formidable.

Need to take, to plunder, overwhelmed him.

Scared him.

Shocked him.

Too soon, too much. Too everything.

He forcibly tore his lips away. His lungs struggled for air. His heart slammed against his ribs like a fist, repeatedly, mercilessly.

He felt like he had dragged himself off the edge of an abyss. It cost him enormously.

JJ lifted his head and looked at *Verochka*. Wide and unblinking, her violet eyes stared at him in helpless bewilderment.

"Tell me what you feel." It was imperative for him to hear it. "Tell me the truth."

"Poleaxed. Scared. Horrified."

"Why?"

"Because I have lost my mind. *Mon Dieu...*" Light as a sigh, soft as baby breath, her fingers trailed over his face, like she was trying to commit his features to memory. Curving one palm around his cheek, she returned his gaze. The intensity of her unblinking stare was eerie, almost uncanny. Hypnotic.

Uneasy but afraid to move, JJ held his breath. For a long moment he gazed at her, mesmerized. Her tiny hand on his face was like an anchor, a safe net that kept him firmly in place. He wanted to stay like that for eternity, lost in her eyes. Lost in her.

As if from a great distance, the sounds of whistling and clapping reached his ears. *Verochka* blinked, removed her hand. And the enchantment was broken.

CHAPTER TWENTY-FIVE

The mix of relief and disappointment left JJ shaky. Still bewildered, he turned, and gasped. Facing in their direction, all the patrons and the wait staff cheered and clapped loudly. Good-natured jokes and bold encouragements flew in the air, turning the ambience of the classy jazz bar into that of a boisterous carnival.

Sweet Lord, he totally forgot where they were! *Hell.*

JJ winced. It was one thing for him to become a subject of rowdy banter, but for her? *Verochka* must be mortified.

With a sincere apology at the ready, he switched his attention to her, and froze.

She extended her left hand upward, tilted her head, bent her knees, and executed a perfect curtsy. Then she repeated the process with her right arm, all the while smiling serenely at the audience. The entire bar erupted in thunderous applause.

She surprised him again. Damn, what a woman! Classy, chic, spunky. Add to that her ethereal beauty, her tough inner core, and that faint exotic accent that drove him crazy, and the package was irresistible. Was it any wonder he was nuts about her?

Delighted, JJ let out a bark of laughter, then took her offered hand, and mimicked her bow. Clumsy and humorous, that attempt earned another round of whistles and energetic claps. She took it like the seasoned performer she was—with grace and a grain of humor.

Still holding hands, they stood in the limelight, like two stars after a successful performance. They brought the house down. But like every event, this one was about to end. Uncomfortable being front and center of the attention, JJ sent an imperceptible nod toward Winston. If someone was able to quiet this overextended hilarity, it was his trusty old bartender.

"Okay, ladies and gentlemen, the show is over."

Like a Jericho trumpet, Winston's voice boomed around. All the noise halted immediately, turning to an occasional murmur.

To JJ, he whispered, "I suggest you take your Little Swan home now. Everybody has been entertained enough."

In contrast to his gruff stern voice, Winston's eyes sparkled with sly mischief. Then he winked at JJ, and addressed the bar in general, "As a consolation prize, the next round is on the house."

That prompted another wave of a boisterous cheer. Without further ado, JJ tugged *Verochka* by hand, and propelled her toward the exit.

"Wait, I didn't say goodbye to Winston!"

"He'll understand."

"*Mon Dieu*, where are you taking me?"

"Home."

"But...but..."

Resolutely, JJ approached his car with sputtering *Verochka* in tow. Quickly disengaging the locks, he literally poured her into the passenger seat. As soon as he was behind the wheel, *Verochka* rounded on him.

"What do you think you're doing?"

"I thought I made myself clear: I'm driving you back to school. Unless, you want to go to my place instead?"

She sent him a *get-real* glare, then settled deeper into the seat.

"I didn't think so." JJ turned the ignition. His 62 Bentley Continental came to life with an almost soundless hum. The memory of his father's car that he stole once upon a time, flashed in his mind. It was a Bentley too, an older model convertible in deep maroon. His father loved that car. And he stole it one memorable night, to embark on his foolish and irresponsible quest to drive around town. What an idiot.

A sadden pang of nostalgia was like an echo, hollow and dull. JJ shook it off.

He couldn't—wouldn't—regret that stupid act. If anything, it was a blessing in disguise. A major wake-up call. The consequences of that event forced him to recognize his own behavior as silly childish rebellion, totally pointless, and destructive. He wanted to get attention. Instead, he hurt his father, the only person who loved him. Dad didn't deserve that. That night, the dismay in his father's eyes made him ashamed of himself for the first time. And, JJ sincerely hoped, for the last. But most important, that night he met the Officer Winston Sullivan. And his life was never the same ever since.

Verochka's voice halted his bittersweet trip down memory lane.

"You didn't have to drive. It's just two short blocks from the school."

"We'll take a walk some other day. I'm not sure about you, but I am tired, and not in a mood for a leisurely stroll."

She sighed and leaned her head onto the leather headrest. If JJ needed further proof of her exhaustion, that was it. Poor Little Swan. She was barely holding herself upright. He pressed on the accelerator, and maneuver the car to the street. She needed rest, badly. He cast a quick glance at the indash clock. Almost two in the morning. She barely had four hours left before her morning class. Dammit, how will she function?

By sheer guts and determination, that's how.

Admiration and respect for her flooded JJ, even as a faint irritation flared up. Why was she torturing herself? Her everyday classes demanded a mindboggling quantity of strength. It was simply unbelievable what her tiny, slender body was capable of in terms of physical endurance. Was ballet worth it? Sacrifices, pain, endless rehearsals. And grueling training since early childhood. And all of this for the sake of dancing? JJ shook his head. Ridiculous. From what he learned, the career of a professional ballerina was short. Just little over a decade at the most.

Verochka was still young, but the clock was ticking.

And what happened when her career was over? The answer was obvious to JJ. She'd be devastated, heartbroken, maybe even traumatized. After so many years dedicated to ballet, her emotional distress will be immeasurable.

He has to save her from that disaster. How? Simple. He must make her pregnant as soon as possible. If it were up to him, she'd be carrying his child as of yesterday.

Patience, buddy, patience.

For now, he must plan his strategy carefully. First thing was to make her fall in love with him. She was halfway there already, so that wasn't a huge problem. Second, to marry her, and get her to his bed. No necessarily in that order.

But he must act soon. Her audition for The Royal Ballet was coming up in the next few weeks. What if she was accepted, and needed to move to London?

A challenge, definitely. Well, then. He was up to it. Long distance relationships never attracted JJ. With *Verochka*? It was unthinkable. Unacceptable. He wanted her by his side. All the time. Damn.

And how to accomplish that? He'd think of something.

Like what? Bribing the international panel of choreographers to reject her?

He shook his head. His consciousness refused to allow him to stoop that low. That was the ultimate betrayal. She'd never forgive him. Okay, what, then?

Hell if I know.

Engrossed in his brooding, JJ didn't notice how they reached their destination. The car was idling near the grey building of *Verochka's* school before he realized it.

Damn. Focus, JJ, focus. You have a precious cargo on board.

He turned to *Verochka*. Slumped in her seat, his precious cargo was down for the count. Her breathing was even, almost soundless, her face relaxed, with a small smile curving her lips. His heart melted.

JJ reached over, tucked a single lock of hair behind her ear. She didn't stir.

My God, she is so young, so utterly defenseless. So alone.

All his protective instincts rushed in a hot flood.

No, not anymore alone. Whether *Verochka* wanted it or not, she had him now.

For better or worse, for richer or poorer, in sickness and in health.

Forever.

Overwhelmed, he couldn't tear his eyes from her. Watching her sleep was a more intimate experience than kissing those luscious lips.

A lump the size of a football lodged in his throat. He wanted to stay like that forever, guarding her sleep, watching over her. But the dark circles under her eyes spoke volumes. She needed rest more than anything. With a silent helpless oath, JJ touched her shoulder.

"Verochka."

CHAPTER TWENTY-SIX

S lowly, her long lashes trembled, then lifted. Heavy with slumber, those enchanting violet eyes gazed at him with confusion.

"Where am I?"

"In the car. You fell asleep."

"Oh." She rubbed her eyes and sat straighter. "I'm sorry."

"There is nothing to be sorry about. You're tired."

"Oui." Her enchanting eyes locked on his face and held. The sensation of being scanned with a laser beam was mildly disconcerting. Chills broke over his skin, but he was unable to look away. Like two magnets, her violet eyes held him immobilized.

After a moment of charged silence, *Verochka* reached over and touched his hand. "And so are you. Tired, I mean. But even more so, you are upset, and disappointed. And...hurt."

To say that he was shocked was an understatement. Tired, he understood. But disappointed and hurt? How did she know that?

A sad smile tugged at her lips. "It is hard, isn't it, to get your trust broken? Especially by someone close to you."

Dear God! Did she see inside his mind?

Finally, he found his voice, "Are you clairvoyant?"

She frowned, mulled it for a moment. "No, I don't think so. Just...intuitive. My father called it Violet Eyes Gift. He was...overly intuitive, too."

"A mere intuition doesn't explain how do you know about broken trust and all."

"I'm not sure. Your emotions...they are too strong. I can almost *see* them. I don't know how to explain it better."

He didn't know what to think, or how to react. She shifted in her seat. "Who upset you so much? Your mother?"

"No. A business associate. Someone I trusted."

"What did he do?"

"He helped himself to the client's funds, and funneled it into his account. It's not even the money. We reimbursed the client immediately, but the damage was done. The reputation of the Morris bank will suffer for it. Dammit." With an oath, JJ pressed both thumbs to his eye sockets. "In banking, trust is everything. The son of a bitch defrauded one of the oldest clients, and God only knows how long it would take to rebuild that relationship."

It took him whole day to clean up the mess. First, he flew to Virginia, to personally inform the client, and bring his apologies. Then, he jumped back on the plane, and returned to New York for an emergency meeting with the board of directors. After such a trying day, he was not in the mood for a trip to SoHo. But fate, or the Universe, guided him through the night streets of Manhattan, until he found himself parked at the Broom Street Bar.

And here he was, hours later, in the car, with a woman who held him captive from the first moment he set eyes on her. He was still upset, but not hurt anymore. Strange, but telling her about his troubling event lifted the weight of grief and guilt from his shoulders. He marveled at this phenomenon.

When was the last time he shared his problems with anyone? Never. Didn't want to. Didn't need to. Until now. Until *Verochka*.

The silence in the car stretched, comfortable and comforting.

He smiled, until *Verochka*'s heavy on a derision reply shattered the atmosphere.

"Stupid."

"I beg your pardon?" Did she just call him stupid? Really? More amused than upset, he squinted at her. "Why am I stupid?"

Impatiently, she shook her head, "Not you, your associate."

"Oh. Well." He assumed the conversation was over, but *Verochka* was on a roll.

"Greedy, but mostly stupid. Did he think you wouldn't notice? *Comme si jamais!*" Her little snort was rude, snooty, and charming at the same time. Like her French. But what grabbed him by the throat, and warmed his heart, was her utter certainty in his acumen. That was worth a helluva lot.

"I must be honest, I almost didn't. Frankly, I'm more disappointed in myself for being so blind."

She twisted in her seat then placed her left hand onto his forearm. "But you trusted him. When we trust people, we become vulnerable. There is nothing more painful in the world than betrayal."

JJ averted his gaze. His thoughts turned back to his earlier decision regarding her ballet career. Will she consider him a traitor? Will she ever forgive him if he went through with his plans? Damn.

Clueless of the turmoil her words created, *Verochka* asked, "What did you do with the traitor?"

"Made sure he will never be able to work in this or any other state."

"Good." Her nod was curt, her eyes gleamed with satisfaction. "He deserves to be miserable for the rest of his life."

He almost laughed. *Fierce little thing.*

"What if I'd tell you I murdered the bastard?"

"I wouldn't believe you. Violence is for weak people. You are strong, and fair, and honorable." A soft sigh later, she finished on a barely audible whisper, "I would never fall in love with you otherwise."

CHAPTER TWENTY-SEVEN

What on earth prompted her to admit that? *Verochka* cringed. She never said those three special words to a man. Then again, she never met anyone like JJ.

Despite all odds, that man managed to get past all her defenses, smashing them in the process, and stealing her heart. And her sanity.

She plopped onto the floor in her tiny attic room, drew her knees up, then hugged them to her chest. There was so much to do before her afternoon rehearsal, but try as she might, she couldn't bring herself to move a single muscle.

So, here she was, sitting in her room that smelled like a rose garden, thanks to another enormous gorgeous bouquet delivered that morning. JJ promised her roses every day for the rest of her life. *Verochka* eyed the pearly white blossoms. Obviously, he took his promises seriously.

Mon Dieu, by now everybody was probably speculating about her and the handsome rich landlord, trying to figure out what was going on.

She fled to the sanctuary of her room to escape the curious glances. But how long was she able to hide?

Hide? Ridiculous! She was not hiding, just...avoiding her teacher. After one glance at her yesterday, Madame Valeska frowned in disapproval, and excused her from training class. Her stern order to take a nap, and pull herself together still rang in *Verochka's* ears.

She winced in recollection. Nothing escaped Madame's laser-like eyes.

Pull herself together, indeed.

Like that might erase the images of JJ. Or delete the memory of last night. Or pacify the confusion churning in her gut.

Merde.

To lose her head along with her heart was one thing. But to willingly confess it?

La folie!

"Violence is for weak people. You are strong, and fair, and honorable. I would never fall in love with you otherwise."

She cursed under her breath. Of course, she might tell herself that at the time she was just tired, and not thinking clearly. But what was the point of lying? Resigned, *Verochka* shook her head, and hugged her knees tighter. The truth was by revealing her feelings to JJ, she reached the point of no return.

Might as well accept it.

Okay. Now what?

And now, you must decide what to do next.

She snorted. Yeah, like he left her any choice.

His reaction after her foolish admission sent a wave of shivers along her whole body.

In a slow motion, the memories unfurled in her mind...

Stunned, JJ turned to her. After a short pause, his apparent shock faded into a helpless disbelief. Holding her eyes, he framed her face with both hands.

"Say it again." A firm order. A desperate plea.

He looked lost, and scared, and insecure. Utterly vulnerable.

The combination tagged at her hear. Verochka *sighed.*

Softly, she repeated, "I'm in love with you." As his chocolate eyes flared with triumph, she hurried to add, "Not that I'm pleased with it, mind you."

"Of course not." His grin was positively wicked, but his eyes stayed serious. "Are you going to marry me?"

She opened her mouth to deliver a resolute 'no', but instead she shocked herself with a reply, "I will think about it."

JJ's laugh tickled her ears. "That's progress. But don't think too long."

"I didn't say yes." So, what if she sounded like a petulant child? She was desperate. Not to mention, terrified.

His brow lifted a fraction and a crooked smile tagged at the corner of his lips.

"You didn't say no."

No, she didn't. Didn't want to. More than anything, she wished to say yes.

Yes. A thousand times yes!

Panic stole her breath. Mon Dieu, was she really contemplating his proposal? She just met him a few weeks ago! What did she know about him? Absolutely nothing. Well, except that his real name was Reginald, and he was rich like Croesus; that he owned a bar, and played sax like a god. And that he was heart-stopping gorgeous. And generous to a fault. And kind, and strong, and fair. Wasn't it enough?

Enough for what? To marry him? You must be mad.

Agitated, alarmed in earnest, Verochka grasped at the thin thread of common sense, "But...but I still don't know you."

It sounded lame, not to mention, totally childish.

JJ seemed to mull that for a second. "I disagree. You know me better than anybody."

His fingertips trailed along her face in a light caress, awakening every nerve ending in her body. Verochka couldn't suppress her shiver if her life depended on it.

"But I'll make sure by Christmas you'll know everything there is about me."

A promise? A thread? Probably both. In self-defense, Verochka *covered his hands with her own. But instead of removing them from her face as she intended, she leaned into his palms. As soon as she inhaled his unique fragrance, she was lost.*

Helpless. Vulnerable. Totally at his mercy.

Say something, you imbecile!

With an effort, she swallowed around the lump in her throat, and opened her mouth for a reply. Soft, almost chaste, his kiss robbed her of the last shreds of her sanity...

The recollection of that last kiss still made her weak, and lightheaded, and confused. And wanting more. Much more. It shamed her that she felt disappointed when instead of kissing her again, JJ walked her to the door, and wished her good night. Shamed her even more, that she watched the lights of his retreating car for a long, long time.

Stupid girl.

Pathetic fool.

A river of heat gushed over her face. Even her ears were aflame. She was burning alive, more frustrated than ever before. She missed JJ.

Darn his chocolate eyes.

And that's why she vowed to stay away from him. For as long as possible. Who was she kidding? She'd be lucky if she managed a few days. Today was day one, and she already had no idea how much longer she'd hold on to her resolve. Stubbornly, she bore down. So, what if she missed him? Big deal. She needed to concentrate on her upcoming audition. Only a few weeks before she performed before the panel of The London Royal Ballet. Her entire future depended on it.

So, shake it off, and think only of that audition.

Madame Valeska counted on her. The school's reputation depended on her. She must do her best in order to be accepted into that famous distinguished troupe. Ballet was her destiny. It was in her blood. It was her one and true love.

Is it?

And what happened if she was accepted, and must relocate to London?

They were forced to live in two different countries, on two different continents.

Will JJ forget about her then? Will he turn his attention to another woman? There were millions of beautiful socialites better suited for the position of a future Mrs. Morris.

And how would you feel then?

She jumped up then kicked her wooden trunk with her right foot. Pain shot up from the sole of her foot to the top of her leg. *Merde!*

Cursing under her breath, *Verochka* grabbed two fistfuls of hair, then gave it a hard tug.

That was all his fault! Everything was JJ's fault. How dare he barrel into her life and disturb everything? How dare he to make her fall in love with him?

Shaky, limping, she flopped onto her bed, then curled into a tight ball of misery. Tears she stubbornly refused to shed misted her eyes. What was she doing?

Moping, that's what. Sniffing, *Verochka* burrowed her face in the pillow as the flow of tears finally broke free. Now her face will be red and blotchy, and her eyes puffy.

Stop it this instant!

Crying was undignified, and pointless. And crying over a man? Demeaning.

Disappointed in herself was a new experience for *Verochka*. Even the fall after a badly executed *jette* that morning was less disgracing. She uncurled her body, then swung her legs off the bed. Her pity party was over. Done with. The end.

She swiped tears from her face. No way she'd allow herself to behave like a pathetic ninny. She was a ballerina, first and foremost. A performer, and a darn good one. So, no more moping, and no more distractions from her main goal.

In thirty minutes, she was expected at the rehearsal. In fourteen days, she must dance the most important audition of her life. And in a month, God willing, she'd be in London, preparing for the most coveted role by every ballerina: Odette in Swan Lake.

All of her life was dedicated to that single goal. It was so close, she almost tasted the victory. She should be ecstatic. Instead, *Verochka* felt forlorn and cheated, like she realized that the Hope Diamond was nothing more than a fake gaudy bauble.

Cheated? What a nonsense!

She shook herself off, then grabbed her pointe shoes, and stomped out.

Verochka came to an abrupt halt on the staircase as an unwelcomed thought popped into her head. *The winter ball.* She forgot all about it! When was it again? November fifteenth. Just five days before her important tryout.

Merde.

She refused to renege on her promise. No matter what. After all, she agreed to accompany JJ as his date, never mind that she did it in anger. Of course, she could easily bail out, but...wasn't that a sign of weakness? *Verochka* Osipoff was made of sterner stuff. And she always kept her word. So, she'd go to the darn ball, and then firmly inform JJ that their relationship—or whatever you might call it—was over.

Ignoring the hollow ache under her left breastbone, *Verochka* resolutely marched forward.

CHAPTER TWENTY-EIGHT

JJ was twitchy and frustrated and distracted. He sat in a meeting held in his Manhattan office and barely managed to hide his growing impatience. The incident with the defrauded client was taken care of, the missing funds found and wired back, and the traitor was fired with the black mark on his record.

He was lucky not to be charged with a criminal offence, the bastard.

Not calling the authorities still didn't sit well with JJ, but involving them meant getting on the FBI radar, and that was the last thing any financial institution whished for. Especially the large investment bank of Morris.

Of course, their internal investigation was no less thorough, and the punishment dealt no less strict, but still. JJ pacified himself with the thought that everybody got what they deserved. The client was not happy, but content, and didn't cancel his accounts. Thank God. The board of directors accepted JJ decision. So, everything was back to normal. He didn't give a damn.

The ring he purchased for *Verochka* burned his pocket. He itched to put it on her finger and make their engagement official. But he was a realist. She wasn't ready for that step yet. She struggled, obviously torn between her feelings for him and her rational mind. Between her ballet and him. And because he wasn't sure of the outcome of her struggles, JJ grew increasingly uneasy.

And jealous, dammit. So, what if it was silly?

No, not silly, pal, but laughable. And irrational. And immature.

And even realizing the sheer stupidity of it, JJ was unable to do a damn thing.

Two days since he last saw *Verochka*. Missing her was akin to pain. Throbbing like an open wound, that sweet ache was unbearable. JJ turned his gaze to the window. But the amazing view of the New York skyline failed to evoke the usual sense of wonder and pride in his accomplishments.

Instead, it filled him with an annoyance, and a terrible need to escape. He wished to be anywhere but here. He wished to be in SoHo right now, and the board meeting be damned.

JJ groaned. Concentrating on business matters was a lost cause. His mind, along with his heart, was far away from the conference room. Wondering if it were appropriate to call the meeting to an end, he scanned the written agenda on the desk in front of him, and winced. Damn. There was another matter that must be addressed. Thankfully, it was a minor issue, and the vice president of the Morris bank was the one to speak on the subject. Oh, well.

As the older man's voice droned on, JJ schooled his features into a calm mask, but there was nothing he could do about his thoughts.

Dammit, how much longer?

Another moment, and he'd bolt from his chair, and run out of the room. And how unprofessional was that?

Patience, buddy. Patience.

But lately, that commodity was in a short supply. Not good.

JJ steepled his fingers, pretending to listen. On the inside, his gut was churning with a barely controlled impulse to dash away.

Two days since that memorable episode in his car. Two impossibly long days as *Verochka* confessed, albeit unwillingly, that she loved him. JJ still couldn't believe his luck. Not grabbing her, then and there, and kissing her until they both forget everything, was the hardest thing he ever did.

Letting her go back to the school instead of driving to his place and making love to her all night was an effort worthy of Hercules. But he managed it. Somehow.

And cursed himself ever since. He tried to play the sax. His trusty old friend never failed to keep him centered and calm. But this time, even music failed.

Yesterday at the bar, he kept his eyes glued to the door in desperate hope to see her. But she never came.

Her absence was akin to betrayal. His mood plummeted as a dull ache spread inside his gut like a cancerous tumor. The familiar weight of sax felt all wrong, almost alien. JJ unclipped it from his neck, and put the instrument into the case. What was the point in playing? His heart wasn't in it.

Gloom settled around his heart like a wet blanket. He went to the bar, then ordered a stiff drink. Winston frowned when JJ upended two fingers of whiskey, then signaled for another. But the burning heat of a prized Dalmore 62 failed to squelch his disappointment, or fill the void inside. *Verochka* was not here. Despite the boisterous crowd, the bar seemed empty and stifling, like all the air was sucked out of it. He wanted to see her. *Needed* to see her. The depth of that need scared him. Never before was JJ so desperate, or so vulnerable.

You never loved anyone before, laddie.

The absolute silence in the room finally caught his attention.

JJ dragged his gaze around the huge office. All eyes were aimed in his direction, curious, questioning. The distinguished members of the board of directors sat around the huge mahogany conference table clearly waiting.

Damn, he totally forgot where he was. JJ cursed silently, then cleared his throat.

"Well, that brings our meeting to an end, gentlemen. Thank you."

The impatience in his voice was unmistakable, but there was nothing to be done about it. Barely containing his restlessness, JJ curtly nodded at the group in general. Chairs scraped across the carpet and the room finally cleared, and he was left blessedly alone.

At last!

JJ gathered his overcoat then punched the intercom button.

"Ms. Black, please cancel all my appointment for the day. I'll be leaving the office shortly."

"When should we expect you back, Mr. Morris?" His admin's voice sounded coolly composed and unflappable, as usual.

"Tomorrow."

"Very well, sir. Should I call your chauffer?"

JJ considered it for a few seconds. "No, thank you. Just ask to bring my car around, please."

He wanted to spend time with *Verochka* without any witnesses. Just the two of them. Away from everything and everybody.

"Certainly, sir."

Once in the car, he gunned the engine, and contemplated his next move. Glancing at the dashboard clock, he noted it was almost 6 PM. Good. Rehearsal was over by now. On the spur of the moment, he decided to take *Verochka* to dinner. A nice dinner at his favorite French restaurant.

She wanted to get to know him better? Well, then, what was the better way than over a meal?

Ridiculously pleased with his decision, energized, he arrived at the grey ballet school building in record time. JJ skipped two steps at a time and ran to the main doors, unmindful of how unprofessional he might look.

The almighty president of the Morris Holding, shaking impatiently like a green youth, grinning like a fool? He chuckled. A sight to behold for sure.

You are practically wearing your heart on the proverbial sleeve, pal.

Madeline would swoon from sheer embarrassment. And the board of directors? Mortified. JJ didn't give a damn.

With barely controlled eagerness, he pulled the heavy door open, then stepped inside.

CHAPTER TWENTY-NINE

Seated at the corner booth in the restaurant, bewildered and uncomfortable, *Verochka* fought to get her bearings. How on earth did JJ manage to talk her into it?

Talk? Are you kidding?

He didn't talk at all—just strode in, propelled her toward the entrance, and pushed her into his car. *Rendre grace a Dieu* she had changed into her regular clothes, or she'd be sitting here practically naked. Well, not exactly *naked*, but her leotard and tights left nothing to the imagination. Totally acceptable for class or stage, it was absolutely improper for a posh French restaurant. She looked around. Everything gleamed and sparkled. Everyone from the uniformed staff to the guests were clad in a formal black, wearing the identical expressions of utter importance. The exhibit of long gowns and dazzling jewelry put a premiere night at the Met to shame.

Verochka was so out of place here, it wasn't even funny. In her threadbare jeans and old sweater, she was ridiculously underdressed. It was a wonder the maitre'd let her in. If his initial startled look was any indication, she must have looked like a pitiful ragamuffin. She'd never be allowed to step a foot inside, if not for JJ. Suave and coolly indifferent, he totally ignored the horrified maitre'd, and steered her toward their table. Thankfully, it was a booth, so she was partially hidden from the view of other patrons. Self-conscious, she slid all the way inside, and pretended to read the menu. It might as well be written in hieroglyphs. Giving up, *Verochka* closed the heavy leather binder. *Mon Dieu*, now what?

JJ looked totally relaxed, and right at home, as he cooly sat across from her. In flawless French, he ordered a bottle of wine, specifying the desired year of production, and then listened to the waiter's spiel of today's special. But even the conversation in her native tongue failed to pacify her nerves, or make her more comfortable. After the waiter ran out of steam, JJ turned to *Verochka*, and asked permission to order for her. Enormously relieved, she nodded.

"*Escargots Bourguignonne, foie gras-de-canard...*"

Sweet Lord, how much food was he ordering? And what was that last thing, *couiless de mouton*? Mutton balls? *Absurde.*

She wasn't hungry to begin with, but now the mere thought of putting some strange *balls* inside of her mouth turned her stomach. *Merde*. She wished to be anywhere but here. Can't he see she didn't belong here?

Miserable, she tugged her sweater sleeve lower, then brushed imaginary lint from her knee. But all her attempts to look more presentable were futile. She cursed under her breath. Vanity was a luxury *Verochka* couldn't afford, but, dammit it, she was a female! No matter what they say, appearances were important. Was it her imagination, or were some patrons casting curious glances in their direction? She looked at JJ. Had he notice it, too?

He sat there totally relaxed, utterly calm, and unperturbed.

Damn, just look at him! Dressed to a T in one of his lord-of-the-manor suits, with a silk Hermes tie that probably cost a small fortune, every gorgeous strand of hair in place. And smelling like a dream. Or sin. Or both.

Her own *o de perfume* of cheap soap and over the counter deodorant made her painfully aware of the chasm between them. She'd give everything at that moment to be dressed in one of the beautiful gowns, a tiny evening bag, and the long heeled expensive shoes. Wistfully, she imagined herself all spiffed up and elegant, and smelling like Chanel No 5.

Dream away, you silly goose.

All her wardrobe, besides her dancing clothes, consisted of two pair of jeans, a couple of sweaters, and a few t-shirts.

And a single gorgeous dress that belonged to her late mother she couldn't bring herself to part with. As to a perfume, the last time she owned one was in France, when her parents gave her a bottle of *Mademoiselle* Chanel for Christmas. *Verochka* was fifteen. Oh, the precious time.

Resolutely, she shook herself and closed the door to the bittersweet memories.

Ragamuffin or not, she was a performer. She chose to play a role, and pretend she belonged in this setting even if just for a single evening. Mentally, *Verochka* stepped on stage, tilted her head in a haughty manner, and straightened her back.

With a panache of a true Parisian, she returned some of the most avid glances.

Let them wonder to their heart contends. See if she cared! She pulled what she hoped was an indolent smile onto her face as she held her hands in a white knuckled grip. After a while, she turned her eyes to the elaborately set table, and a bubble of fresh nerves tickled her throat. *Oh, my!*

Set for two, it was a masterpiece in itself. The delicate china plates, the baccarat crystals, the linen tablecloth. Even though she was far from being clumsy, *Verochka* was afraid to break a dish, or a glass, or, God forbid, to spill something. The array of gleaming silverware on both sides of her plate was most intimidating. How many forks and knifes and spoons did one need? A riot of flapping butterflies seemed to take a permanent residence in her stomach. She failed to remember the last time she ever felt so agonizingly uncomfortable.

But JJ seemed totally oblivious to her uneasiness, or the occasional curious glance. Keeping his eyes on her, he leaned closer. "Do you like it here?"

Like it? Was he kidding?

"Um, it's very... nice."

Unnerving. Daunting. Scary as hell.

"Nice?" JJ's laugh rumbled deep in his chest. Unmistakable humor lit his eyes. "I'll be sure to inform the proprietor of your high opinion."

Verochka snapped her stiff back even straighter. "Laughing at me, are you?"

"Not at all." But his grin said otherwise.

She squinted her eyes. "Fine, laugh all you want. We'll see who's laughing last." Fuming, she grabbed the wineglass, and took a healthy gulp. The exquisite *Bordeaux* tasted like velvet and cherries, and was meant to be savored. She drained it down in three swallows. The Parisian in her squirmed. The performer applauded.

JJ laughed. "You look so adorable."

"I look like Orphan Annie," she grumbled, averting her gaze. Ashamed of her own behavior, she carefully put the now empty glass down. "All these women... spiffed up, polished, sophisticated. Compared to them, I must look like a sparrow."

"You look like a beautiful swan amongst the peacocks."

Shocked, she lifted her eyes, gauging his mood. Was he kidding? Even though smiling, JJ's eyes were direct, shining with palpable intensity. Before her brain registered, she blurted, "You... really think so?"

Merde, now he would think that she was fishing for a compliment.

In response, JJ reached over, and covered her hand with his own. After a heartbeat of silence, his replied, "I really do."

Serious. Calm. Sincere.

Suddenly warm all over, *Verochka* tugged her fingers free.

"Then there is something wrong with your sight. You ought to check it with an oculist."

"There is nothing wrong with my sight. And all these women?" he gestured at the room in general, "I don't see them. I see only you."

Panic sized her by the throat as the dark chocolate eyes held her immobile.

A sensation of being sucked into a whirlpool made her lightheaded.

And scared. And exhilarated. And oh, so tempted!

But the common sense prevailed. "I don't belong here."

"You belong with me. Always. Forever."

His firm tone bore no arguments. If she let herself, she'd believe it, too. And then what? What if she was just a distraction to him? Was he really in love with her, or just seduced by the newness of the experience? Many rich and famous men in history were drawn to ballerinas, blinded and tempted by the image of something ethereal, fragile, unreal. But as soon as the enchantment wore off, the boredom and disillusionment set in. Many a career was destroyed, many a heart shattered. And the rich men always married the women of their own circle. The example of Tsar Nicholas and Matilde Kschessinska jumped to her mind.

No, she was better off on her own. Alone.

"You're being unreasonable." The catch in her voice betrayed her turmoil.

"What I am is man crazily in love. For the first time in my life. And for the last."

And just like that, all her rational thoughts scattered and evaporated.

"*Mon Dieu,* JJ—"

Smoothly, he interrupted whatever she was going to say. "Have you noticed the other gentlemen in this room?"

"W-what gentlemen?"

His lips stretched into a satisfied smile. "Precisely."

Verochka's heart skipped a beat, then thundered painfully in her chest. Even under the threat of guillotine, she was unable to look anywhere but him.

JJ took her hand again, and brought it to his lips. Her knuckles tingled.

"People in love are usually oblivious to anybody else."

"You mean that I...that you...that we—"

"Yes, *mon cherie*. You and I."

CHAPTER THIRTY

Her thoughts swirled, her heart stuttered, her blood churned. The ringing in her ears was almost deafening. Still holding her hand, JJ asked quietly, "Have you decided?"

Helpless, lost, she tried to focus on his last question. What was she supposed to decide? "Decided...what?"

"To marry me."

And just like that, the spell was broken.

With a deep sigh, she claimed her hand back. "*Mon Dieu*, you have a one-track mind."

"I'll take it as a 'not yet.' Oh, well. I'm a patient man. I'll wait."

Resigned or disappointed? Probably, both.

"What if I never say yes?"

"But you will, *ma petite.*" He lifted his glass in a mock salute.

Short of pulling her hair out, *Verochka* was out of options. "How can you be so sure?"

"Because you're as crazy about me as I'm about you. Admit it, *Verochka.*"

"Okay, yes, I'm in love with you, but..."

"But?"

"But being in love and belonging together are two different things."

His brow curved into a dark arch. "How come?"

"We are a polar opposite of each other!"

"True. And?"

"And? Like that is not enough, I might be soon living in another country."

He nodded. "Challenging, but not impossible. We'll manage."

"Please, JJ. Be realistic. My life is on stage, and constant rehearsals, and—"

He rolled over that like a freight train over tracks. "My life is in the office, and constant meetings. So what?"

"So...so..." *Merde*, now what? She was desperately trying to search for a reason, when her mind came up with the most daunting obstacle. "People will think that I'm marrying you for your money."

He shrugged, all negligence. "Probably. What do you care? We both know the truth."

Oh, how she wished to believe it! He almost succeeded in convincing her. What did she really care what the people will say? She had no family, no close friends. She has no one, except her mentor, Madame Valeska, and recently, Winston. And they both seemed to approve of her relationship with JJ.

Verochka was sure they won't doubt her sincerity should she agree to accept his marriage proposal. But JJ's circle...That was another matter altogether.

He held a position in society. He ruled a huge business empire. He was a wealthy man from a prominent family. From everything she learned, the Morrises were considered to be on par with modern royals.

What would his mother say if her only son married a penniless dancer?

And how would the society of mega rich and famous react? *Verochka* didn't have to be clairvoyant to know the answer. Scandalized.

Even in 1962, in the middle of the twentieth century, a *mésalliance* was frowned upon, and highly discouraged. Will they ostracize JJ? Oh, Lord, will they?

Will he still love her, when all his friends and family turn away from him? Or will he regret his rash decision to marry the poor orphan girl from France? What if he learned to despise her with time? Be ashamed of her? She couldn't bear it.

Never. I will never subject him to that humiliation.

The only way to avoid that disaster was a clean break.

Her heart splintered into small sharp fragments.

Already mourning, *Verochka* lowered her eyes. "I wish it could be that easy."

"The truth is always easy. Tell me one thing, do you love me?"

Oh, God, he was tearing her apart. "You know I do."

"Then we'll work through the rest. We have plenty of time until Christmas."

She almost choked on her grief. By Christmas, she'd be a half the world away, in London. But even if not accepted to the troupe of The Royal Ballet, *Verochka* needed to leave New York. Suddenly crystallized, that decision seemed like the best possible solution. For both of them. No matter how it hurt her, or how scary the project of uprooting herself from everything dear and familiar was.

If she did it two years ago, she can do it again. She was no longer a grieving destitute girl of eighteen. *Verochka* was a mature woman, strong and resilient and resourceful. While before she had only herself to think of, now there was JJ.

She vowed to sacrifice everything to insure his happiness and wellbeing.

Even if she must hurt him initially.

Better hurt now than hate me later.

One day in the future he might even thank her. If their paths ever crossed.

As to her career? There were plenty of other companies around the globe, like Australian Ballet, or National Ballet of Canada, or The Paris Opera Ballet.

She'll find an employment, no doubt, even if not as a soloist. She'd dance in the corps de ballet if necessary. But not in the USA.

You can do it.

But Dear Lord, how?

One step at the time, Verochka. *You'll think of something. For now, you must get through this evening.*

Suddenly, the atmosphere of the restaurant seemed gloomy and somber. The lights cast an eerie glow, the conversations muted, the temperature cooled. Shivering, *Verochka* crossed her arms over her chest. Cold waves of goosebumps puckered her skin.

Across from her, JJ narrowed his eyes, cocked his head in a silent question. A suspicious frown formed a deep V between his brows. "*Verochka?* What is it?"

Plastering a fake smile on her face was an effort of major proportions.

"Nothing. Just thinking about...future." At least, that was the truth.

"Why, then, such a forlorn expression? Our future will be spectacular, I promise."

Our future? A bubbling sob threatened to burst free. Ruthlessly, she shoved it back.

"Where do you want to go for the honeymoon? Italy? Greece? Caribbean?"

She masked her whimper with a humorless chuckle. "What if I say North Pole?"

"Then we'll go to the North Pole. Come to think of it, being stranded in a snow storm inside of a small cottage with you sounds definitely appealing."

"I didn't say I'll marry you."

"You didn't say you won't."

"JJ, please—"

"Pleasing you is my utmost wish, *ma petite*. In any way."

"*Mon Dieu*, you are impossible! What am I going to do with you?"

"A few things come to mind, but..." his grin turned positively wicked, "I'll refrain from voicing them out loud."

His chocolate eyes sparkled with mischief and forbidden promises.

Verochka's breath hitched, her heart thudded. Under the thick layer of her sweater, her breasts swelled as her nipples puckered to the tight hard points.

The images that popped into her head were positively embarrassing, and highly inappropriate. Never before had her mind conjured something so blatantly explicit like the picture of JJ and herself, naked in bed. *Mon Dieu!*

She cringed, but the vision refused to fade. A wave of heat flooded her face. For a split moment she wondered what it would be like. Skin to skin, heart to heart, limbs entangled, breaths meshed...

A loud laughter from somewhere behind yanked her back to reality.

Ruthlessly, *Verochka* shoved the images from her head, and shut the imaginary lid.

"A lot of things can happen between now and Christmas."

Did he hear the catch in her voice? The desperation? She held her breath.

But JJ gave her one of his most engaging smiles, and replied, "Well, then, we must spend the remaining time together. As much as possible."

CHAPTER THIRTY-ONE

True to his word, JJ sought her out every day for the next week. They spent all free hours together. After *Verochka's* morning class, he took her to breakfast, then brought her back for her afternoon rehearsals. More often than not, he stayed in the audience with Madame Valeska's permission. How on earth did he manage to do that, was a mystery to *Verochka*. But she found she was glad for his presence, and soon grew accustomed to it. Seated in the corner of the spacious room, with its mirrored walls and barres, amidst the scattered pointe shoes and leg warmers, he should have looked out of place. But instead, he appeared right at home, like he belonged. Like he owned the place. Well, he did. But still.

With quiet intensity, JJ observed every move, never taking his eyes off her.

Never self-conscious about her dancing, *Verochka* became painfully shy under his scrutiny. She wanted—craved—his approval.

Granted, his was not the opinion of a professional, but a smile or a word of praise from him meant more to her than all the accolades from her teacher.

But JJ's deep irritation with her male partner proved to be a constant case of annoyance to *Verochka*. The very first time Madame allowed JJ to watch the rehearsal, he almost exploded afterward.

"He's practically pawing you!"

"He does nothing of the sort!"

"Nothing of the sort? That blonde Adonis had his hands all over you! Hell, he even touched your butt."

"He held my thigh, not my butt. And for your information, it calls support of a partner. For goodness' sake, JJ, it was a *pas de deux!*"

"I don't care what you call it, *pas* or *trois*. I don't like him touching you, like he has a right."

"But he does have a right."

"The hell he does! And if touches you again, I'll break his arms."

Strange, but instead of being angry, *Verochka* found herself secretly pleased.

What do you know, the almighty JJ Morris was jealous.

Thankfully, the last couple of days, Madame insisted on polishing her solo *adagio,* so there were no more complaints from JJ. Call her perverse, but she missed their irrational bickering. She was getting too attached to him. Too dependent. Too vulnerable. What happened later, when she must disappear? How will she bear it? She didn't know if she could. Her body will survive, but her heart...

It begged her to reconsider, but Verochka's resolve held firm.

She'd do whatever she must in order to spare JJ an embarrassment. He didn't deserve to be hurt, or humiliated. One of them must be realistic, and that one was her. After the winter ball, she intended to break off with him. Because she loved him too much. Because she had no choice.

JJ was totally clueless that their time together was limited. But *Verochka's* inner clock was set for the next ten days. The winter ball, then the tryout, and then...

And then, she must leave her school and New York for good. That invisible clock ticked mercilessly in her head, counting every tiny second.

But there were still ten days, and *Verochka* was determined to make the best of the allotted time. Was she being selfish? Probably.

Wouldn't a clean break now be better? Possibly. But God help her, she couldn't bring herself to do it.

And what was the harm in spending the last days with this wonderful man she loved? Or to pretend that they really have a future together?

Just for a little while, she'd grab the happiness with both hands, hug it to her heart, and enjoy every single moment that soon will become distant memories.

Bittersweet memories.

JJ waited for her in the lobby after today's training class. It turned into his usual practice and one she looked forward to.

"What do you say we go for a ride?"

"I say, it sounds like a marvelous idea."

"Well, then." Chivalrously, he offered her his bent elbow. "Let's go, then."

Expecting to see JJ's familiar dark sedan, she was taken aback when he gently propelled her to the small car parked at the curb. Red, polished, and gleaming like a mirror, it stole her breath.

"Oh, my! What a beauty! Is this your new car?"

"No, this is your car."

Shocked, she turned her wide eyes at him. "Are you...kidding?"

"Not in the lest. As soon as I saw it, she reminded me of you. Just look at her, all fluid and sensual and exotic. Just like you, my Beautiful Swan."

"But...but, JJ, it's...a car!" She sputtered, barely able to form a word. "But, *Mon Dieu*...a car?"

"I know. Not just any car, but the Lancia Aurelia B245. The most terrific sports car to date. Do you like it?" JJ's delighted grin split his face, turning it almost boyish. Her heart squeezed.

"What's not to like, but...but I cannot accept it."

"Why?"

"Are you serious? It's too an extravagant present, and awfully expensive."

"I can afford it."

"But I can't! Accept it, that is. And even if I could, where would I keep it?"

"For now, we'll put it in my garage. You need to apply for a driver's license anyway. It'll take time. But later—"

"JJ, please! I value your generosity, and your kindness, but this is...a car."

"Get used to it. As my wife, you are entitled to it."

"But I'm not your wife!"

"Correction: my *future* wife."

Just tell him the truth. It's getting out of hand!

She braced herself. "JJ—"

But in a move as smooth as his cashmere overcoat, he dipped his head, and planted a quick hard kiss against her lips.

"Just a matter of timing, *ma petite*. Just until Christmas."

"Dear Lord, JJ, are you listening to me?"

"Of course I do. But for now, let's take your new car on the road, shall we?"

Without waiting for her reply, he turned her around with both hands, and all but pushed her toward the little red beauty. Too late *Verochka* realized that she was standing at the driver's side. She was about to point that out, when JJ opened the door, and assisted her inside. Quickly going around, he jumped in the passenger seat.

"What are you waiting for? Let's take her for a spin."

"But I...I cannot drive."

"I'll teach you. It's much easier than your *fouette*. Trust me."

Exhilaration warred with the common sense. *Verochka* squirmed, still uneasy. But what the heck? When might she have an opportunity to ride a car again? Probably never. With sudden abandon, she let go of her uncertainty, and turned the key JJ already inserted into ignition. The little beauty came to life with a gentle purr.

"Okay, what's next?"

"Next, you place your hands on the steering wheel, press the clutch pedal with your left food, press the brake pedal with your right, and—"

That was as far as he managed, before *Verochka* floored the gas all the way.

Like a spirited filly who'd been given free rein, the little car surged ahead.

"Woah, easy, easy, *ma petite*. Nice and easy."

Oh, who needs nice and easy when you can fly?

The mighty engine sang, the smooth wheel obeyed her hands, as the car tore through the streets like a compact bullet.

Exhilarated, almost giddy, *Verochka* maneuvered the car at the speed of a wind.

What do you know? She liked it! No, she plain loved it! The sensation of being totally in control of the powerful machine was intoxicating. Liberating. Pure ecstasy. Like *grand jete,* when defying the law of gravity for the precious few seconds, her body soared, weightless, unbounded, untethered.

Now she flew longer, faster and joyous, and totally free.

Her laughter was unrestrained, and a little wild. In her peripheral vision she caught JJ's grin.

"You are a quick study indeed, Little Swan. But for a novice, you must be more cautious."

"Scared?" Recklessly, she pressed the gas pedal, elated to the point of euphoria.

"Concerned. I'd hate for us to end up in an accident."

"Don't worry, there will be no accident." But she released the pressure on the gas.

"How do you know?"

She shrugged. "I just do."

"Your famous intuition?"

"That, and my famous self-control." Slowing down even more, she applied the brakes, then stopped the car completely. She released a soft breath and turned to JJ. "You'd better take over. I'm not familiar with this road."

"It's okay. You have plenty of time to familiarize yourself with it."

And just like that, her joy plummeted. Plenty of time she had not.

Just another ten days.

In a heartbeat, her mood turned to gloom, like a candle extinguished by a windy gust. JJ opened the driver's door, then assisted her to the passenger's side.

He seemed relieved being at the wheel at last. With a warm smile, he patted her hand. "You did great, *Verochka*. You are a natural. Next time, we will take a longer trip, I promise."

She managed to plaster a fake smile to her face and nod.

There will be no next time. There will be no more trips. The day of her disappearance loomed ahead like a dark cloud on the horizon.

Sharp pain knifed through her heart. Sadness enveloped her in a heavy cloud.

Forlorn, she shut her eyes for a brief moment, fighting the unwelcomed tears.

Don't fall apart.

"Where would you like to go?" JJ voice snapped her to the moment.

"Home."

"Are you sure? Maybe we'll stop by the bar first? Winston's getting cross with me for keeping you all to myself."

She was not in a mood for socializing, but *Verochka* realized she missed the older bartender who became so dear to her heart. How long since she saw him? Three, four days ago? No, five. God knows when she'd have a chance to visit again. Maybe never. A short moment later, she nodded her agreement.

"Okay. Let's stop by the bar."

CHAPTER THIRTY-TWO

JJ couldn't wait for the night of the winter ball.

Two more days, laddie.

JJ cursed under his breath as he paced nervously in his Manhattan office. He wished to speed up time. But. He sank down in the leather chair—his father's chair—and contemplated pouring himself a drink. Whiskey or cognac? He shook his head, rejecting both choices. A drink was certain to amplify his restlessness, and add to his agitation. Damn, he was behaving like a green youth. Impatient. Eager. So what? He was a man who was in love for the first time. Madly. Desperately.

He was entitled to behave irrationally, wasn't he?

Two days until he introduced *Verochka* to society as his fiancé. He could hardly wait. Yes, the brows were sure to raise, and yes, his mother displeasure was sure to be enormous. Who cared? He was anxious to declare their engagement, to make it official once and for all.

JJ decided to propose before that night. Call him a selfish bastard, but it was imperative for him that at the ball she wore his ring. Even if he was forced to beg and plead and grovel.

The stubborn little vixen!

She still hadn't formally agreed to marry him, but he wasn't discouraged. Irritated a bit, but not depressed. The main thing was, she loved him. Of that, he was sure.

Dammit, what was stopping her, then? Her ballet? Doubtful. Her upcoming relocation to London? Maybe. But still unlikely.

He much preferred *Verochka* to stay in New York, but her heart was set on The Royal Ballet. So, as much as it pained him, he decided to share his life and time between two countries. Not a big problem when his company owned a fleet of planes. He had easy ability to zip to and fro in a matter of hours.

And with the modern convenience of telephones and telex machines, his business communications were not problematic, even though less convenient.

But, hell, he intended to move heaven and earth in order to spend as much time with *Verochka* as possible. Fortunately, he loved London, dense fog and humid climate notwithstanding. He already put out feelers for a nice property to purchase in Chelsea. *Verochka* should be right at home in that neighborhood with that special touch of artistic side to its overall opulence. And it was just a few short miles from Covent Garden, where The Royal Ballet of London was located. A true win-win. He told her they will find a way, didn't he? Why then, she was still reluctant to marry him? He blew out an exasperated breath. And why for the past few days was *Verochka* behaving kind of... funny? More often than not, he'd catch a look on her face that seemed... sorrowful. Like she was disheartened. Or remorseful. And definitely sad. It bothered him a great deal. When pressed, she laughed it off. But the glimpse of desperation in her violet eyes was unmistakable. She was driving him nuts. But he decided to let it go. For the time being.

She'd confide in him, he intended to make sure of it. As soon as he whisked her away from everybody for their honeymoon. *Verochka* will love Venice, and the private little villa in Laguna Blue he bought recently for her. Delighted, he chuckled, imagining her surprise. She revealed to him once that her biggest dream besides ballet was to travel. Well, it was in his power to turn that dream into reality, starting with their honeymoon in Italy. But one day, they will go to all the beautiful places around the globe. Together.

Enormously pleased, JJ fingered the little maroon box in his pocket. Soon he'd slip the beautiful ring nestled inside on her finger. Damn, he was dying from impatience.

Soon, very soon.

Agitated, he jumped to his feet, and started to pace again.

The wedding was all but planned to the last detail. St. Patrick's cathedral already secured the day after Christmas, December twenty-six, for the Morris wedding. The best restaurant in New York, *La Caravelle*, eagerly agreed to host this special event. The flowers, *Verochka's* favorite roses, were arriving from Spain.

No one was privy to all the plans except Winston and Mrs. Black. Sworn to secrecy, nether his old friend, or his trusted admin who knew JJ since he was in diapers, would ever betray his confidence. And today, the most gorgeous wedding dress the house of Chanel offered, finally arrived. JJ smiled. His Little Swan was in for a big surprise. As he visualized *Verochka* in her wedding gown, he lost his breath.

What will happen on December twenty-six when his vision became a reality?

He'd be lucky to last the ceremony at the church. He grinned, more relaxed than in days. Yes, finally everything was ready for the wedding.

Well, except for the bride, who still hadn't formally agreed to marry him.

JJ shrugged that nagging thought aside. She will. He had no doubts about that. Sooner or later, he'd wear her down. Of course, he'd rather it was as soon as possible, but he was a patient man. Or he used to be, before he met *Verochka*.

His Little Swan, his tiny enchantress with the violet eyes.

Smiling, he remembered their first meeting in his bar, and his firm decision to stay away from her. What an idiot. Absently, he rubbed the left side of his chest. The love for her was like a sweet pain, always there, always throbbing.

Needing her on the most essential level didn't surprise him anymore. Protecting her, shielding her. Worshiping her. He wanted to give her the world, to make sure she had every single thing his fortune has to offer. He wanted her to be his wife, his lover, his partner. He vowed to give her the most luxurious and grandest wedding of the century.

But first, the stubborn Little Swan must accept his proposal.

He swore under his breath. Two days until the winter ball seemed like an eternity.

Now, if I can only survive until then.

He turned around, contemplated his choices. Work? Impossible. His mind was buzzing like a beehive, his concentration shot to hell. In his current state, relaxing was as unattainable as exercising a *fouette*. Maybe, even less so.

What, then? His eyes drifted around the spacious room, until it landed on the black leather case in the corner. Eureka! The sax was just what the doctor ordered. Energized, JJ pick the case up, and grabbed his coat on the way out. He'd swing by the school first, and pick up *Verochka*. She just might enjoy visiting Winston. And he will enjoy performing for her. The first notes of the song unfurling in his head made him smile. *Only You.*

Yes. That's exactly what he'd play for her tonight. She was his dream come true, his one and only. His everything.

Now, if she only said yes.

CHAPTER THIRTY-THREE

F inally, the night of the winter ball arrived.

Dreading it, *Verochka* still prepared for the event with the utmost care and concentration. As she surveyed herself in the bathroom mirror, she critically studied every lock of hair, every detail of her face. Enhanced by cosmetics she wore only on stage, her eyes and lashes looked strange and unfamiliar.

Her sweeping up-do put her features on a stark display, from her forehead to her pointy chin. Eyes too big, nose too small, mouth...She squinted at it. Well, it was the right size, but painted in bright sherbet shade it seemed... puffier. And more prominent. Experimentally, *Verochka* licked her lips. The faint flavor of peaches on her tongue was pleasant, but alien. An eerie sensation of looking at the face of a stranger added to her discomfort.

Who are you? Do I even know you?

The stranger looking back made *Verochka* uneasy. Quickly, she turned away from her reflection, and concentrated on her body clad in a vintage Chanel gown. Her mother's dress. Her most cherished possession. From her neck to her toes, it enveloped *Verochka* in a soft warm hug, comforting, calming. Like her mother's arms. She drew on that warmth and comfort. Feeling steadier, she ran her hands over the dress in a light caress. The long straight column in the palest blue fell past her ankles. Its gossamer silk sleeves covered her arms, from shoulders to wrists. But because of the see-through material, every inch of her skin there was visible. Deceptively demure front with it square cut neck, managed to accent her almost non-existent breasts. The back of the gown dipped low, completely baring her spine. That contrast added the note of sensuality with a typical French flare.

Was it too much? She chewed on her lip, then shrugged it off. The gown was beautiful and charming, even if a bit provocative. But not immodest.

Never before had *Verochka* the nerve to put this gown on. It was hidden in her wooden box, wrapped in a protective case. Feeling like she was conducting a sacrilegious act, she unwrapped it yesterday to let it air. *Mon Dieu*, it still smelled like her mother! Immediately distressed, she almost put it back. But the mere thought of confessing to JJ that she had nothing to wear for the ball was humiliating. It was enough that she borrowed a fur wrap from Madame Valeska. And her pearl neckless. And her earrings. *Merde*.

Verochka pacified herself with the thought that she didn't ask, but was offered the marvelous mantle and priceless jewelry. As soon as Madame found out about the ball, she came up to the attic, and deposited the heavy bundle onto the bed.

"You have to look the part, Miss Osipoff. Wear it."

It was impossible to refuse, especially when she realized that her gown was too light for the weather. Just for one night. Just to look the part, as Madame put it.

She will not embarrass JJ looking like a pitiful street urchin. So, she accepted the loan, grateful, but uneasy. The finishing touch of the pearls and earrings completed the overall picture to perfection. *Verochka* fingered the neckless, touched her earlobes. Delicate, shaped like pears, the gems gleamed mysteriously, adding the note of sophistication. She must admit, she looked elegant, polished, and stylish. She looked the part. Now, if she could only pull her confidence to match the image. Taking a few calming breaths, *Verochka* closed her eyes.

You can do it. For JJ. You'll wear this marvelous gown and pearls like you were born in them.

By God, she will pull it off. She must. She will.

Asking her mother's forgiveness for wearing her dress was silly, but she did anyway. *Maman* would understand. Because tonight was special. In more way than one. Tonight, she was accompanying JJ to the extravagant event as his date.

And after that event was over, she must say good bye to him.

It will break his heart, but that was for the best. He will heal in time, with some other woman, more worldly, and beautiful, and worthy of his name. In the end he'd be grateful to her, and maybe even remember her with fondness.

As to her own heart...It was already shattered beyond repair.

Hot tears of misery pushed against her eyelids, but she stubbornly refused to indulge. Later, when she was alone, she'd let the floodgates open, and hope not to drown in her own grief. But for now, she must stay strong.

Snapping her back straight, she tilted her head and squared her shoulders.

Her teacher's voice drifted through her mind:

You must dance every time like it is your last.

It *was* her last time, even though she won't be dancing tonight. She'd be playing a role, the most daunting role in her life. And then—

The loud knock shattered her thoughts into a million twirling shards.

Cold, *Verochka* stared at the closed door with trepidation. Her composure evaporated like a morning fog, leaving her lost and trembling from head to toe.

She hugged herself. Mon Dieu, *I'm not ready. I can't do it!*

What possessed her to accept his invitation? Did she really think she could go through with this charade? Stupid, so stupid!

"Verochka? It's me."

JJ's deep voice floated into the room. Her gut knotted, her heart squeezed. Lightheaded, miserable, she looked at the door like it was a gate to Hades.

Oh, Lord, please help me.

Through the ringing in her ears, she heard her father's voice:

Pretend that you're backstage, waiting for the last curtain call. Now, inhale, hold it, then exhale. You can do it, ma petite cherie.

She closed her eyes, drew air in her lungs, and with a noisy *whoosh* emptied her mind of everything. Her doubts, her fears, her panic.

As a familiar calm settled over her, she felt blissfully numb and composed.

She was ready.

The curtain was up.

Show time.

I'm sorry, my love. I'm so sorry.

CHAPTER THIRTY-FOUR

Finally!
Sitting across from *Verochka* in a limo, JJ barely kept himself still.

Inside, he was a jumble of nerves and excitement. Finally, the day of the winter ball has arrived. Nothing dampened his mood, not even the miserable weather. Cold and gusty, the wind blew in from Canada that morning, bringing with it a nasty thunderstorm. The lightning put on a real show, forking the black sky with a spectacular explosion of electricity. Booming, grumbling, the thunder accompanied that eerie firework with a furious roar. Outside, the rain fumed, heavy and brutal, and ominous.

But inside the limo, it was blessedly quiet and toasty warm.

As they drove toward the Paradise Hotel in a steady unhurried speed, JJ contemplated his choices. Where and when to propose? Now, or later?

Christ, he wanted his ring on her finger with something close to desperation. Dammit. If he said something now, she might bolt. Refuse? Probably. Despite her composure, he could almost hear her nerves dancing a vigorous jig. If he was not mistaken, *Verochka* was trembling inside that glorious set up of her dazzling gown and excellent fur. As soon as he caught a glimpse of her, all spiffed up and polished, he swallowed his tongue. Literally. That exceptional gown—Chanel, if he wasn't mistaken—did wonders for her complexion, not to mention her body. Slender, fluid, regal, she was a picture from the Renaissance painting. Her elegant beauty, bone deep and quiet, shone mysteriously like a moon through the starless sky.

Mesmerizing.

Tantalizing.

Spellbinding.

And her eyes! Dear God, her magical violet eyes, bewitching, enchanting.

They would have burned her at a stake a couple of centuries ago for her eyes alone.

She was a vision, a dream come true.

She was woman he wanted more and more with every breath he took.

She was his mate, his destiny. His everything.

Blood hummed in his veins in a furious rhythm; his loins tightened painfully.

Wincing, JJ adjusted his pose, crossed his legs, but the pulsing between his thighs refused to abate. Damn, he was sporting a hardon. Embarrassing. Humiliating. Not to mention, highly uncomfortable. And they were just a few minutes away from their destination, for goodness' sake.

You'd better cool off, laddie.

Easier said than done.

With an effort, JJ unglued his eyes from *Verochka's* face, and concentrated on a safer spot, just below her chin. Adorned with an exceptional pearl neckless, her long swan like neck brought a flood of fantasies of a highly erotic nature.

And her breasts? Small, firm, and pointy, they were just the right size for his palms. His hands fisted until his knuckles went white. His dick twitched, straining against his trousers.

Damn. Not safe at all. Think of something cool, something soothing, something inanimate. Like her neckless.

He concentrated on the triple string of pearls like his life depended on it.

Absently, he wondered where it came from. Those pear-shaped baroque earrings alone must have cost a few hundred thousand. Adding the neckless, the set skyrocketed to a cool half mill. Huh.

She caught his gaze, lifted her arm to her throat, then let it drop. "It belongs to Madame Valeska," she answered his silent question. "She insisted I wear them with the dress. And her fur mantel." Nervously, she squirmed. "Do you think it's too much? I feel like it's too much. Should I remove it?"

"No, no. It's just right. This excellent gown goes perfectly with those pearls."

"It's my mother's dress. It might be vintage, but it's..."

"It's classic, and ageless. And it suits you perfectly."

A smile that played on her face was beautiful, and a little wistful. "Thank you."

"That's a simple truth, but you are welcome."

And he was right. She was born to wear pearls. A long string of pearls he glimpsed at Cartier had *Verochka's* name on it. He'd buy it tomorrow. To compliment her wedding dress. And her skin, after he stripped that cloud of silk and lace from her. His imagination went into overdrive, conjuring the image of *Verochka,* nude and glorious, with the pearls shimmering against her breasts, sliding past her navel, and lower still... Oh, yes.

Please, God, yes!

And suddenly, in the midst of his erotic fantasy, JJ had an epiphany. Of course!

He sat straighter, cleared his throat, and, curbing his excitement, plunged ahead.

"But this jewelry set, as gorgeous as it is, is still not complete."

He put his trembling hand into his breast pocket then palmed the ring.

"You must have this to complete the picture." Lifting her left hand, JJ slid it onto her finger.

After one sharp intake of breath, *Verochka* snatched her hand back.

"No, please JJ, I can't!" She tried to remove the ring, but the platinum band sat snuggly, refusing her attempts. He covered her hand with his own.

"Why? Why can you wear Madam's neckless and earrings, but not my ring?"

"Because...because it's too expensive!"

"And those pearls are not?"

"Oh, they are, I know they are, but it's a loan. Just for one night."

"*Verochka*, the set is not complete without the ring. And it will mean a lot to me if you have it on. Please."

Dammit, was he begging? He was. Well, almost. JJ didn't give a damn.

Holding his breath, he watched her struggle with the decision. After what seemed like an eternity to him, she lifted her eyes. They were troubled, but set.

"Okay. I will wear it, but just for tonight. If it means that much to you."

Hallelujah!

"Thank you."

A breath he was holding spilled out in a loud *whoosh*.

"And only as a loan."

Damn, that's not what he was aiming at, but still. A victory of sorts. He'd take it. For now. But he'd be damned if he let her remove the ring later.

Loan, my ass.

"Okay." Did he say it too quickly? Probably. Damn.

Verochka frowned, squinted at him, suspicious and weary. "I mean it, JJ."

"Okay." He repeated, more slowly this time, with an innocent (he hoped) smile.

He failed. Her frown deepened. Just as she opened her mouth, the limo stopped.

Saved by the car.

Relived like a student who was spared a trip to a principal office, JJ grabbed the door handle. "We are here."

His loud announcement plunged *Verochka* into a state of obvious panic.

"On, *Dieu*." She shut her eyes. All the color seemed to leach from her face. JJ's heart turned over in his chest. Poor Little Swan.

Lifting her chin with two fingers, he looked into her wide terrified eyes.

"You have nothing to be nervous about, *ma petite*."

"Easy for you to say. You are used to this scene. But I'm so out of place here. Even dressed up and wearing expensive jewels, I don't belong. Everybody will figure it out in a snap. Oh, Lord, JJ..."

He trailed his fingers along her jaw, tucked one runaway curl behind her ear.

"You will put everybody to shame, darling, I promise you. Every single female in that ball room will be green with envy."

And every single male will be eyeing her with appreciation and awe. And lust.

But JJ kept that little tidbit to himself. No need to make her more nervous. She was already stressed to the breaking point. Besides, he planned to be glued to her side all evening. Stating his claim? Hell, yeah. So what? Let anyone try to cross him.

Or pouch on his territory.

Or embarrass *Verochka* in any way.

At that moment, the chauffeur opened the door, an enormous umbrella in hand, and put a stop to his contemplations. JJ stepped out of the car then took the umbrella, and turned to assist *Verochka*.

Like a general preparing for battle, she squared her shoulders, jutted out her chin, and took his hand. Firmly planting both feet on the ground, she lifted her eyes at the entrance of the hotel. JJ followed her gaze.

Lit from within, it gleamed like a priceless jewel. Or an artificial sun. He was always put off by that glare. Haughty, cold, arrogant. Unapologetically snobby.

A modern playground for the rich and famous, posh, and opulent, it was his mother's domain. Given to her as a gift when JJ was born, his father christened it The Paradise. More than thirty years later, the hotel was still like a Zion in Morris kingdom. JJ despised it with every cell in his body. Madeline loved it as much as she was capable of loving. Definitely more than she loved her only son. Oh, well.

The thought of Madeline brought a rush of disturbing feelings. There was still a shadow of hurt lurking beneath. That little unloved boy still lived inside of him, but hidden well under the veneer of a successful man.

An acceptance of the inevitable didn't mean forgiveness. That weighted on him, but he learned to live with it. One day, he might find the strength to unburden the load from his soul, and forgive his mother. And finally, find peace.

But that day was not today.

Bracing himself, JJ took a fortifying breath. The upcoming confrontation with Madeline was a given. She won't be pleased with his choice of a date, but she'll act accordingly, all cordial and regal. To make a scene in front of the society was out of the question. She'd save that for later, after the ball.

That thought put a great damper on his mood, but for *Verochka's* sake, JJ pulled a smile onto his face. "Ready?"

Without a moment of hesitation, she took his offered hand, gripped it hard.

"As I'll ever be."

"Well, then, my Beautiful Swan, let's go."

And rock the bloody boat.

CHAPTER THIRTY-FIVE

As soon as she stepped through the doors of the hotel, *Verochka* schooled her face into a cool indifferent expression. But, *Dieu* it cost her. Inside, she was quivering with trepidation. She had never seen anything more spectacular in her life. Everything was lush and brilliant, and unapologetically in your face opulent.

A huge Christmas tree sparkled with thousands of shimmering ornaments. Festive green garlands and wreathes with huge red ribbons adorned all the walls of the vast space.

The atmosphere inside the huge ball room buzzed with excitement and merriment. A throng of people strolled about, champagne flutes in hand, laughing and obviously having a jolly good time. The soft murmur of the live string quartet added a shadow of intimacy.

Her stomach knotted. *Mon Dieu*, what a décor! What a luxury! And the women? Dazzling. Gorgeous. Magnificent. The long evening gowns, the gleaming jewelry. Everywhere she looked screamed wealth, and demanded admiration.

No less impressive in formal black tails, the gentlemen presented an image of affluence and prosperity. Even the waiters were clad in tuxedoes, holding the flutes of golden champagne on polished to a mirror silver trays.

Chic fashion and glamour held their high court like a reigning king and queen.

Almost blind from all that brilliance, *Verochka* squinted her eyes in defense, and concentrated on keeping her mask firmly in place. Feeling like a country bumpkin, she gazed at the surroundings in barely contained awe.

What am I doing here?

Hot panic bubbled inside her like a vat of boiling water. The swarm of butterflies in her stomach went ballistic. Her throat, dry as a bone, tight as a fist, refused to allow her a single swallow. She was on the verge of falling apart.

Merde.

Get a grip, you foolish girl.

Bearing down with all her might, she fought her anxiety like a woman possessed.

Do not gawk. Do not embarrass JJ. Think of it as of a performance. You can do it.

Her silent pep talk finally managed to get through the numbing fear. Bolstered by it, *Verochka* snapped her spine straight, tilted her head, as if she were about to step on stage, and arranged her lips into a smile.

And *Verochka* Osipoff turned into the Swan Princess Odette.

Holding onto JJ's bended elbow, she started to stroll, all regal and calm, until a stunning redhead planted herself in their path.

"JJ! My God, it is you! Where have you been hiding, stranger?"

Totally ignoring *Verochka*, the woman hung onto JJ's neck, all the while laughing in her rich throaty voice. Slashed on one side, her blood red gown showcased a long-tanned leg almost to a thigh. Artfully made-up hair looked deliberately windblown and provocative. Red as her dress, her lush mouth was curved into a smile that somehow seemed predatory. *Verochka* almost expected to see sharp little fangs. She despised the woman on sight.

The redhead's elbow jab that struck *Verochka* in a middle was deliberate, as was a sly once over she speared at her before turning her tawny cat eyes back to JJ.

Dismissed me, did you? Well, we'll see about that.

More amused than put off, *Verochka* stepped aside, and prepared to be entertained.

"I'm back in town, my darling." Almost purring, the siren pressed her hourglass body to JJ's, then steepled her fingers on the back of his neck.

A shameless hussy.

In a deliberate move, JJ firmly unwound her arms from around himself, and stepped back. "Not for long, I'm sure."

The flash of anger in woman's eyes was hot, but brief. Quickly camouflaging it under a fake smile, she shrugged her bare shoulders.

"Oh, I don't know. It depends."

Undaunted, she hooked her arm through JJ's unbent elbow, and turned her back on *Verochka*. Again.

Ridiculous.

Did she really think her rude attitude was attractive? Did she really think JJ might fall for it? Idiot.

"Why don't you and I meet later?" Her half whisper was loud enough for *Verochka* to overhear, as it was intended to.

If you're aiming for jealousy here, sister, you have to do better. Much better.

"Whatever for, Celeste?" Polite, but impersonal, JJ question obviously struck a nerve. Frowning, the woman stopped, and faced him directly.

The first notes of irritation crept into her voice. "Oh, I don't know. To reminisce? You and I have so much to talk about, my darling."

"On the contrary. We have absolutely nothing to talk about."

"Oh." Her fake pout was as distasteful as it was coy. "Why do you say that, JJ? You are hurting my feelings. We meant so much to each other!"

JJ's snicker was brittle and humorless. "Don't flatter yourself, Celeste." He removed her hand from his elbow, then stepped away. "As to your feelings, for me to hurt them you must have them in the first place."

"Of course, I have feelings! I had them for you then, as I have them now."

"I highly doubt it, but be that as it may, I simply don't care."

Purposely, JJ reached with his hand for *Verochka,* and drew her closer to his side. "Celeste, let me introduce you to Miss Osipoff. *Verochka,* this is Celeste...what's your last name now? I lost count."

"It's still the same, Coventry." Frigid and mean, Celeste's smile missed her eyes by a mile. Squinting like she just noticed *Verochka,* she ran her insolent glare up and down her body, then up again. "Osipoff? Never heard of it. Is it Czech? Or Serbian?" Disregarding *Verochka,* as if she wasn't there, she placed her question to JJ.

Two can play this game, you audacious floozy.

With a small smile, *Verochka* inclined her head in a regal manner. "It's Russian, as a matter of fact."

Unwillingly, the redhead turned to *Verochka.* "Oh, really?"

"*En realite.* It is my pleasure to meet an old...ah," a deliberate hesitation later, she continued, "acquaintance of JJ."

"I'll have you know, that we are more than mere acquaintances. We lived together for a year, and were lovers!"

Still smiling, Verochka infused as much indolence in her voice as she was capable of. "How wonderful for you."

The sizzle of Celeste's anger was hot enough to scorch skin. With the narrow to slits eyes, she zipped her gaze to *Verochka's* left hand.

"What a marvelous ring! Cartier, isn't it? Well, at least you have a good taste in jewelry."

"And in men, Miss Coventry. But I'm afraid I cannot get credit for this gorgeous ring. JJ gave it to me."

Was it small and petty of her not to acknowledge that it was on loan to her, just for tonight? That it was the mere completion of her pearl set? Possibly. Probably.

So what? *Verochka* shrugged mentally. The ring was on her left hand—not right—so as far as she was concerned, it was not a symbol of engagement.

But obviously, Celeste wasn't aware of the custom. Or steeped in jealousy, she forgot about it. *Verochka* looked briefly at her left hand. The perfectly round large pearl adorned by a circle of sparkling diamonds gleamed mysteriously, like a moon on a star kissed night. It took her breath away. It made her yearn, and wish for the impossible. Oh, well. With an effort, she ripped her gaze away from it, and looked back at Celeste. And barely prevented her facial muscles from twitching.

Fury stared back at her, menacing, chilling.

No doubt the woman would have gone for the jugular, if not surrounded by a crowd. The hatred pulsed in Celeste's overly bright eyes, transforming her stunning face into a vicious, ugly mask.

Checkmate, sister.

Uneasy, but pleased, *Verochka* decided to borrow a page from Celeste's own book. She faked a smile, and turned to JJ, negligently dismissing the fuming redhead.

Brows high, he gazed at her with an open admiration, as his chocolate eyes danced with barely concealed humor. *Verochka* decided to up the ante. Beaming, she addressed JJ in a soft intimate tone of voice, "Darling, as much as Miss Coventry's company is entertaining, we must mingle, and say hello to your mother. Don't you think?"

Bringing her hand to his lips, JJ brushed a gentle kiss over her knuckles.

"Absolutely, my dear. You will excuse us, won't you, Celeste?"
Without waiting for a reply, he turned around and led *Verochka*
away.

CHAPTER THIRTY-SIX

"**B**rava, *ma petite*. You were spectacular."

"Why thank you, *mon ami*. You were not half bad yourself."

"*Darling?*" Wiggling his brows, JJ grinned at her. "I like it."

"Don't get your hopes up. That was just a matter of speech."

Unperturbed, he laughed. "I really liked your matter of speech."

"Of course, you did." She couldn't hide her own grin if her life depended on it.

Strange, but her anxiety seemed to disappear, chased away by that silly encounter with Celeste. Thinking about her, *Verochka* frowned. No, she wasn't jealous. Just curious. Okay, just a little bit jealous. But still.

Before her brain processed her intent, she blurted out, "Whatever did you see in her? She's all show without substance. And mean as a snake on top of it." She winced. Mon Dieu, *did I just ask that?*

Casting a quick glance at JJ, she gauged his reaction. Angry? Annoyed? No, more like pensive, like he was pondering her question.

"Hmm. All show and no substance, and mean as a snake?" Then he grinned. "You know what? You are so right, Little Swan. In a matter of minutes, you figured out what took me several years. How did you manage to become so mature at such a tender age?"

227

"Maturity has nothing to do with age, as intelligence has nothing to do with education," she retorted. "And I am a woman. I can detect fraud in my own gender faster than any male."

He cocked his head and pursed his lips. "Because all men are generally dense?"

"Because all men are generally nearsighted. All you see is the carefully made-up exterior. And what lays beyond that, stays literally invisible."

"Huh. Well, you got me there, my wise beyond years Little Swan. In my defense, I can say that when I first met Celeste, I was young and stupid. And her carefully made-up exterior, as you so aptly put it, was...well, irresistible. But in time, that shiny shell lost its glitter."

"But not soon enough." It was not a question.

He raised his brows and aimed his eyes at her. "Why do you say that?"

"Because you were hurt. I'm not sure what is it she did, but she hurt you."

"You never fail to surprise me." He stopped and peered deeply into her eyes. "Your famous Violet Eyes Gift?"

"No, just common sense. The women such as her, empty and mean, are usually self-serving users." She shrugged, then cocked her head. "Let me guess, Celeste counted on becoming Mrs. Morris, but you didn't oblige?"

"No, I didn't." JJ tucked her hand more securely through his arm, and resumed the unhurried stroll. "To tell you the truth, the thought of marrying Celeste never even crossed my mind. We lived together and enjoyed each other. No strings attached that suited us both. Or so I thought."

"So, what did she do? Break it off?"

"No. Celeste won't do anything so simple or honest. Tired of waiting, or more likely bored, she cheated on me, and then married some rich, hapless fool."

"A betrayal, then."

"A betrayal, yes. Thinking back, I realized that I was more upset than hurt. My pride was bruised, but that was about it. I didn't love her, so I recovered pretty fast. But if it would be you..." JJ stopped then turned to face her. The intensity in his dark eyes sent shivers along *Verochka's* spine. "If it were you, *ma petite,* I wouldn't survive."

The absolute sincerely of his words struck her like a fist in the solar plexus, and plunged her into a deep dark well of despair.

Guilt pressed on her from all sides, stealing her breath.

"JJ, I..." Suddenly cold, she tried to tug her hand free from his grip, "I'll never..."

What? Betray you? Leave you?

But she was going to do just that. When she broke the news to him about ending their relationship, she'd do exactly that.

No, more than that. She'd break his heart, and his trust. She'd hurt him beyond measure.

And how on earth will I survive that?

Torn apart, *Verochka* lowered her eyes, shut them tight. Hot tears gathered behind her closed eyelids.

Mon Dieu, *am I doing the right thing? Maybe there is another way?*

JJ's low voice tugged her back to the moment. "I know, Little Swan. You are honest, and honorable, and loyal. You are incapable of deception. There is not a single selfish bone in your body. And," with two fingers he lifted her chin, "you love me." Tender and earnest, his smile cut her to the quick. All her resolve crumbled like a sand castle, leaving her shaky and unsure and bereft.

"JJ, we must talk."

"Must we?" His fingers grazed her jaw, as he tucked a lock of hair behind her ear.

"Yes." She swallowed around the lump in her throat. "I have to tell you..."

"Okay, but it has to wait." He shifted his eyes from her face, looking above her shoulder. His face lost all the merriment as his body became rigid.

"Don't be alarmed, *ma petite,* but you are about to meet Madeline."

There was no more than a single heartbeat to process that information before the striking older woman glided to stand beside them.

JJ's mother.

"Madeline." He inclined his head in a formal greeting. Impersonal and ruthlessly polite, his voice could cut diamonds.

"Reginald."

Crystal clear and icy cold, Madeline's voice sent a wave of goosebumps along *Verochka's* skin. "I see you deigned to present us with your company after all."

Slowly Madeline switched her gaze from JJ to *Verochka.* Dark as her son's, her eyes sparkled like two black glaciers on the frighteningly beautiful face.

Enormous diamonds dangled from her ears like two icicles. Perched high on her head, a small tiara sent a brilliant shower of light. Draped in a long white gown, dazzling from head to toe, Madeline made an imposing picture. Left bare, her perfectly sculpted arms showcased unblemished skin. It seemed that every digit on her hands was adorned with a gleaming ring. Two bracelets around her elegant wrists completed the overall image. The woman was hands down striking. And formidable. And cold as Arctic winter. The first word that popped into *Verochka's* mind was cruel.

"I see you even brought a date. Why don't you introduce us?"

Even though Madeline addressed JJ, her frozen stare never wavered from *Verochka.* Shrewd, calculating, her eyes seemed to strip her bare, and chilled her blood. A shiver surged through her body in a freezing wave.

Helplessly, she gazed at the cruelly beautiful face, mesmerized, repulsed, but unable to tear her eyes away. Even without her infamous Violet Eyes Gift, *Verochka* knew that this woman was incapable of loving. And she despised *Verochka* on sight. More accurately, she hated her guts. While Celeste's fury was hot and blazing, Madeline's loathing was frigid and passionless. And thousand times more dangerous.

Alarmed in earnest, *Verochka* debated the wisdom of pivoting and running as far away from this woman as possible, when JJ's voice shattered her trance.

"Madeline, let me introduce Miss Osipoff. *Verochka,* my mother, Madeline Morris."

CHAPTER THIRTY-SEVEN

Without tearing her eyes from *Verochka*, the older woman inclined her head. Regally, coolly. Silently, with her chilling stare alone, Madeline managed to make her feel inferior. Lacking. Unsuitable. Less.

Damn the woman. Who the hell did she think she was? The Queen of Sheba?

Grinding her teeth from blurting out something she's definitely regret later, *Verochka* snapped to attention, and returned Madeline's glare.

"I'm pleased to meet you, Mrs. Morris." Keeping her fear firmly under control, she tilted her head in an arrogant manner. She'd be damned to show this woman her real feelings.

"The pleasure is all mine, Miss Osipoff." Madeline's expression said otherwise. How on earth she managed to infuse so much disdain in a single phrase was a mystery. JJ's mother was not pleased. If anything, she was irate, and dissatisfied with her son's choice of a date. But she kept her game face firmly on.

Skewering *Verochka* with her eyes, Madeline asked in a neutral tone of voice, "And where did you meet Reginald, if you don't mind my asking?"

"Why, not at all, Mrs. Morris." *A shock therapy was just what the doctor ordered.* "We met at the bar."

Momentarily taken aback, Madeline blinked in confusion— or shock— before, once again, she schooled her features into a smooth impersonal mask.

"Oh? How...unusual." The deep V of her frown transmitted an apparent distaste. "And do you often patronize that type of... establishments?"

"No, just JJ's bar." *Verochka's* wide smile almost split her face in two. "It's homey, and classy, and simply wonderful. Don't you agree?"

"I can't say, Miss Osipoff, as I've never visited that *place*." She pronounced it like it was a dirty word.

What a snob!

"Oh, you are missing a lot, Mrs. Morris. You absolutely must stop one night. The ambience is terrific, and the music..." *Verochka* purposely sought JJ with her eyes, barely restrained herself from winking at him, "is simply magical. You son has so much talent! The sax in his hands sings like a living breathing person. The first time I heard it, I was lost. It was love from the first sight." She winked at JJ, who was visibly biting the inside of his cheek, as his chocolate eyes danced with laughter.

"Well, I'll take your word for it." Like a surgeon's scalpel, Madeline's voice cut through. "And what do you do? Besides patronizing my son's bar, and listening to his music, that is."

"I dance."

Momentarily thrown off balance, Madeline blinked. "I...I beg your pardon?"

"No need. You see, I am a ballerina."

"Oh, how...marvelous." The disdain paired with a barely visible wrinkling of her patrician nose was hard to misinterpret.

"Thank you." *You despicable snot.* "It is in my blood. I came from a family of ballet dancers. My parents were principals in *Opera Nacional de Paris*."

"I see. And are your parents... still in the profession?"

"No, they are both deceased."

"Oh. Do you have some other family, I hope? Here, or in France?"

What is it? A freaking interrogation? *Verochka* bore down on her annoyance.

Behave. She is JJ's mother. Don't alienate her further.

Further? The woman already hated her guts, for crying out loud. *The hell with it.*

"Alas, I'm all alone. Or I was," deliberately lifting her eyes to JJ, *Verochka* held his gaze, "before I met your son."

What the hell are you doing, you little imbecile? Baiting the Ice Queen? You are leaving after tonight, remember? All your little show is pointless.

And just like that, *Verochka's* bravado evaporated in a flash.

Deflated, she sighed. She must talk to JJ, as soon as possible. She must get him away, where they'd be alone. But Madeline was not finished with her yet.

"What ballet company are you with, Miss Osipoff?"

"Oh, I'm still studying with Madame Valeska. She is—"

"I know very well who that woman is." A heavy layer of disdain coated Madeline's voice like an icy sleet.

Bristling, *Verochka* jumped with both feet onto a defensive line. "Madame Valeska is one of the best dancers in the world! She was a *Prima Ballerina Assoluta!* And now, she is one of the most sought-after teachers—"

Once again, Madeline cut her off. "Don't get so excited, Miss Osipoff." Raising one brow, she watched *Verochka* like she was a distasteful specimen under a microscope. "I merely pointed at the fact that I know of her. That's all."

That was not all, but *Verochka* swallowed her angry retort. Frankly, she didn't care if she antagonized the Icy Snob, but she was JJ's mother.

Merde.

"So, you are still in school."

"Yes, but not for long. In a few days, I'll perform before the panel of The Royal Ballet. If chosen, I'll be hired as a lead dancer in their Swan Lake production."

"And if not?"

Damn the woman. Must she strip me of all hopes?

"Well, then I—"

This time it was JJ who interrupted her. "That's out of the question. *Verochka* is the most talented dancer in her school, and the obvious favorite for that position. Soon, she'll grace the London stage, and bring all other companies competing for the privilege."

"Good for her." Madeline shrugged, and sent her icicles of earrings swinging.

"Good for us both," JJ corrected, "as I will be relocating to England with *Verochka*."

Oh, no. *Mon Dieu*, no! *Verochka* whirled to JJ, but Madeline's sharp rebuke interrupted whatever she was planning to say.

"What?! Are you out of your mind, Reginald?" As the first crack in her composure, her eyes flared with the angry sparkle. Incredulous, she glared at JJ.

"On the contrary, Madeline. My mind was never so clear. Or so set."

"I see." She zipped her molten eyes to *Verochka*. As her gaze traveled to her left hand, all the color drained from her face. "I see," she repeated more slowly. "Reginald, I must talk to you in private. Now. Will you excuse us, Miss Osipoff?"

Without waiting for a reply, Madeline executed a perfect one-eighty, and sailed off. An almost tangible cloak of displeasure trailed after her, sizzling like an electric current. Uh-oh. The Ice Queen was pissed off. Royally.

JJ cursed under his breath. "I'm sorry, *ma petite*. For everything." He shook his head. "Madeline can be... difficult. I apologize for her behavior."

"No apology is necessary. It's not your fault."

"Nevertheless, I'd better see what she wants from me."

I bet I know what she wants from you.

Verochka's shoulders wanted to slump, but she held them straight. She'd be damned if she let JJ see how that horrible woman affected her. She knew his plate was full as it was. She could wager her best pointe shoes that the upcoming conversation will be highly unpleasant. And all because of her.

Merde.

"Why don't you mingle, and enjoy yourself?" JJ voice cut into her turmoil.

"Here, have a little champagne." He pivoted, grabbed a flute from the passing waiter, and thrust it into her hand. "I promise I'll be back in no time."

With that, he went after his mother.

Left alone, *Verochka* panicked. Mingle? Enjoy yourself? Really? She didn't know a blessed soul here, and she didn't want that blasted champagne. What she really wanted, was to get far away from this place, and erase meeting JJ's mother from her memory. Both ambitious wishes.

How long will they have to stay? As soon as JJ is back, she must ask him to take her home. She endured the damned ball as long as she could, but enough was enough.

The task of breaking up with him loomed ahead like an ominous cloud.

After she met Celeste, and especially Madeline, the social chasm between her and JJ became unquestionable. Indisputable. Unchangeable.

They belonged to different worlds. They had nothing in common.

Like two parallel lines that never meet, their lives will never connect.

A pure miracle that they met at all. Fate interfered by placing her before his bar that memorable night in October. Such a cruel joke. But *Verochka* didn't regret it. She wouldn't change a single moment even if she was able to.

How can she curse fate, if it gave her JJ? Just for the short period of a single month, but still. Happiness couldn't be measured by time. The gift of love was priceless and eternal. It changed her. Irrevocably. The girl who stepped into the bar in the middle of that clear and crispy autumn nigh was a pale shadow of the woman she was today. Because of JJ. Loving him was the best thing that ever happened to her. And because she loved him, she must do everything in her power to protect him. Even from herself.

Especially from herself.

CHAPTER THIRTY-EIGHT

As soon as he caught up with Madeline, JJ asked without preamble, "What is it you wanted to talk to me about?" God help him, he already knew.

Madeline speared him a pointed insolent glance. "Isn't it obvious?"

He masked his irritation as best he was capable of. "Not to me it isn't."

"Well, then, let me enlighten you, Reginald. Your behavior is simply outrageous. Bringing your little mistress here, and flaunting her in front of our distinguished friends? Scandalous! What will Celeste think?"

JJ saw red. "She has a name, Madeline. And she is not my *little mistress*. She is my fiancé and my future wife, so you'd better come to the terms with it."

To control himself from snapping and wringing her neck, JJ curled his hands into tight fists. His nails dug into the soft skin of his palms, and he welcomed the pain. If nothing else, it grounded him enough to continue this unpleasant verbal battle. "As to Celeste? I couldn't care less what she thinks."

"What about me, your mother? Do you care at all what *I* think?"

His answering laugh was dry and brittle. It abraded his throat like he swallowed a mouthful of fragmented gravel.

"Madeline, let me *enlighten* you. Pushing me out your womb thirty-two years ago, doesn't automatically make you my mother. So, no, I do not care what you think either."

Two ugly patches of scarlet flared on her cheekbones. "I will never agree to this *mésalliance*! I will never give you my blessing!"

"Let me repeat myself: I do not care. I will marry *Verochka* with or without your blessing."

"You will drag your name and the name of your family through a scandal? And all because of that little ballerina? Are you that selfish? That irresponsible?"

"If I am selfish, you have no one to blame but yourself. I learned from the best teacher. Now, a responsibility? Here is where you're wrong. I am nothing if not responsible. I met a woman, and fell in love, and want to make a future with. As a responsible adult, I plan to marry her. As soon as possible."

"But she's a nobody! Good Lord, Reginald, she's a *ballerina*!" The word came out like it was something dirty and shameful. JJ clamped his jaw so tight it hurt.

"Not just a ballerina, Madeline, but a brilliant one. She is simply incredible."

Just thinking about *Verochka* quieted his anxiety, and drained his anger.

Her face swam in front of his eyes, and unable to help himself, JJ smiled.

Madeline snorted. "You are simply besotted." Her glare was a mix of pity and disdain. "And how long will your silly infatuation last? A month? A year?"

"What about a lifetime? And I'm not infatuated, Madeline, I'm in love."

"Please, spear me. You were never one for dramatics. In love? You? What nonsense." Her laughter was mean and cold and insulting.

JJ gritted his teeth, and reminded himself to stay calm and unaffected. Like any predator, Madeline thrived on weakness of others. He'd rather saw his right arm off with a dull knife than allow her to see his vulnerability.

As abruptly as it started, her merriment died. "Frankly, I don't get the attraction. I suppose, she is cute enough, but, Good Lord, she's just skin and bones!"

"Ah, but such a marvelous skin over the very strong and healthy bones. And that accent?" Picking up the flute of champagne he didn't want, he lifted it in a mocking salute. "A killer."

Madeline shrugged her shoulders in a dismissive manner. As if disturbed by the motion, all her jewelry sent brilliant sparks around her frame.

"You're being ridiculous, Reginald. For goodness' sake, if you want her, accent and all, just sleep with her, and get her out of your system."

JJ gripped the fragile stem of flute hard enough to snap it in two.

"It might surprise you, Madeline, but some women are impossible to get out of the system. *Verochka* is that woman."

He congratulated himself on sounding calm, while inside he was seething.

"Poor misguided boy!" Full of fake sympathy, her drawl set his teeth on edge. "Did it even cross your mind that she's just using you? You are rich and influential. She's penniless, and all alone in the world. Of course, she latched her little claws into you, and holding for dear life. Frankly, I can't really blame her for wanting to better herself, but—"

His temper simply exploded. "*Better herself*? Are you serious?"

"Absolutely. Your status, your wealth, your name—it's a dream come true for the likes of her."

Dear God, was it possible he really came from that despicable snob of a woman?

Spent, JJ drew in a deep breath. It was no use to argue with Madeline, or get upset with her. She was what she was. End of story.

He should be immune by now, but God help him, her barbs were still sharp and merciless, and capable of drawing blood. Dammit all to hell and back.

Stilling himself, he put the full flute of champagne onto the tray of the passing waiter. "I'll have you know that *Verochka* is absolutely immune to my status, my wealth, and my name. As a matter of fact, she still didn't agree to marry me."

"Of course, she didn't. As a smart girl, she's playing you."

"Have you ever thought that a woman might love me—just me—for who I am, and not my money?"

"Get real, Reginald. Your name is a synonym for money."

More weary than upset, JJ looked at Madeline, searching her eyes for any shadow of warmth or compassion. There was none. Never was, never will be.

"This conversation is going nowhere." With every intention to leave, JJ turned, but her words stopped him in midmotion.

"What if I inform the board of directors?"

"You can certainly do that. But what would you tell them? That your adult son decided to get married against your wishes? Now, who's going to look ridiculous?"

Madeline cursed under her breath. "Be that as it may, you are leaving me no choice. We'll see how the distinguished gentlemen of the Morris bank will react."

"Be my guest. Now, if you excuse me, I have to find my fiancé."

"Reginald, please reconsider. If you want her that much, keep her as a lover, but marry someone from our own circle."

"I bet you have a name of that someone." He raised a brow. "Let me guess, Celeste?"

"And so what? She comes from a wealthy and respectable family. She's educated, and beautiful and sophisticated, and—"

"Selfish, conceited, and..." *Verochka's* description jumped to mind, "... mean as a snake."

"Dammit, Reginald. Celeste won't embarrass you before your peers!"

"No, just cheat on me, and betray me like she has done already."

She shrugged it off, like it was nothing more than a small inconvenience. "That was in the past. And if was partly your fault."

Incredible!

Unbelievable!

"Are you serious? How was it my fault?"

"The woman lived with you for almost a year, and for all that time you failed to propose. Of course, she wanted to teach you a lesson!"

"A *lesson*? Is that what you call it?"

Had he really thought she couldn't surprise him anymore? What a damn fool.

"I can't believe it!" JJ's laughter was more of a roaring bark. Hearing it, several heads turned in their direction. Madeline bristled.

"You're creating a scene, Reginald. It's unbecoming for a man of your position. As to relocating to England, of all stupid things? Out of the question."

Squeezing her eyes to a narrow slits, Madeline repeated, "Out of the question!"

After a single calming breath, she waved her hand in a magnanimous gesture.

"You may even leave her that hideously expensive ring. But you must break things off with her immediately."

He didn't know if he was disgusted or disappointed, or both. But one thing was for sure: he was done. Done with Madeline, and everything she represented.

Done with his old life. And his old self. Completely. Indefinitely.

As if the heavy weight was lifted from his shoulders, JJ felt almost lightheaded.

Why did it take me so long?

Calmly, resolutely, he turned to face Madeline for the last time. She met his eyes.

Triumphant. Mean. Chilling.

Did I really think she was beautiful? The woman is plain ugly.

Thank God she was out of his—and *Verochka's*—life. Forever.

He was unable to hide his repulsion any longer, but common curtesy prevailed.

She was his mother, for better or worse.

"Our wedding will take place on December twenty-six at St. Patrick's Cathedral. You are welcome to attend."

"We'll see about that!" Full of venom, her parting response raised all fine hairs on his neck.

Without another word, JJ turned, and walked away.

CHAPTER THIRTY-NINE

JJ politely nodded at acquaintances as he scanned the room for *Verochka*. Where was she? The need to find her, and take her away from this stifling artificial place overwhelmed him. Almost shaking from it, he walked through the crowd. Dammit, where did she go? Did she leave without him? He wouldn't be surprised. First, Celeste, then Madeline. She was probably fed up with everybody—him included—from the tips of her hair to her little toes. After a few minutes of searching, JJ was about to give up and walk toward the entrance, as he focused on the unmistakable slender figure clad in bewitching blue gown. And sensed something was off.

Stiff as a statue, she stood frozen to the spot, facing an unknown woman in front of her. Even from a distance he recognized the shock written all over her face. Her wide-eyed stare was glued to the other woman, like she was seeing a ghost.

What on earth...?

Uneasy, JJ hurried ahead, unceremoniously elbowing aside the partygoers. When he was a couple of feet from her, *Verochka* jolted, then swayed. Jumping forward, he caught her just in time to prevent her fall. Fluid like water, graceful even in her faint. Something cold unfurled inside of him, chilling his bones. Was she hurt? Sick? Dear Lord!

"What the hell happened?" He glared at the other woman. She was older, probably in her early fifties, dressed in a deep purple gown.

A long rope of excellent pearls hung all the way from her throat to her waist. Tall and slender, she was more striking than beautiful. The impossibly curly hair the color of a burnished gold rioted around her narrow face. Motionless, she stood where she was, with her unblinking stare aimed at *Verochka*. Obvious shock claimed her features.

She opened her mouth to reply, but nothing came out, except of a low half moan whimper. Lifting her trembling hand, the older woman pointed at *Verochka*. Damn it, what was it? JJ ripped his gaze from her.

His first concern was the priceless cargo in his arms. Everything else must wait. He knelt carefully, holding *Verochka* in his embrace. Her head lolled like a ragdoll. JJ adjusted his hold, turned her face with one hand, and gently tapped her pale cheek.

"*Verochka.* Come on, sweetheart. Open your eyes. Please."

She didn't stir. Fear raged a war with common sense. Should he call for an ambulance? Should he even move her?

And the million-dollar question remained: what the hell happened to reduce his fearless Little Swan to a listless broken doll? While he debated the wisdom of yelling for a doctor, a rustle of fabric caught his attention. She stepped closer, and knelt. Fueled by a helpless anger, JJ stared at her ready to deliver a blistering reprimand. All the words struck in his throat. Painfully familiar, the pair of unusual violet eyes—*Verochka's* eyes—gazed at him from the face of a stranger.

"My God..." Breathless, he couldn't tear his eyes away.

"I'm sorry. It was such a shock. I don't know what to say."

"Who...who are you?"

"My God, all my manners seem to have evaporated along with my logic. The name is Margaret Coleman Nelson." Her clear and strong soprano sent shivers along his spine. *Verochka's* voice.

My God, was it possible?

Am I hallucinating?

A stirring in his arms drew his attention away from the older woman. JJ shifted his gaze to *Verochka*. Still pale, she blinked in confusion, then focused on him.

"What...what happened?"

"Oh, thank God. I was about to call for a doctor."

"Doctor? But why?"

"You fainted, *ma petite.*"

A sharp intake of breath on his right and he shifted his glance back to the older woman. She seemed whiter than snow, her violet eyes misty.

"*Ma petite...*" she drew a ragged sigh, "That's what my father called my mom."

At the sound of her voice, *Verochka's* whole body jerked sideways. Wide-eyed, she stared at the other woman mesmerized.

Instant alarm sharpened his voice. "*Verochka?*"

That drew another sharp breath from the older woman. "My Lord, *Verochka?* Is that her name? I've heard it so many times!"

Their little group started to draw attention. JJ cursed under his breath. God forbid, Madeline got a whiff of it.

As if coming out of a trance, Margaret blinked, then rose to her feet in a fluid motion. "Why don't we get a breath of a fresh air? We all need it. Especially, *Verochka.*"

That prompted his hazy brain to awaken, and send orders to his limbs.

"Of course." Cradling *Verochka* in his hands, JJ came to his feet, and followed Margaret's suit. After a couple of steps, *Verochka* put both palms on his chest.

"Please, put me down. I can walk on my own."

She was still dazed, but her voice sounded almost normal. Relieved, JJ gently deposited her on her feet, but kept one protective arm around her waist.

The three of them proceeded toward the exit. Without a word, JJ accepted their overcoats from the hotel staff, and assisted both ladies into their furs.

Finally, they left the glaring atmosphere behind.

Crispy clear and fresh, the air held just a hint of turbulence. Like an echo, a distant rumble of a thunder reminded him of the earlier storm. The starry dome of sky hung above, picture perfect, and comforting.

They stopped. A million questions buzzed in JJ's mind, but he restrained himself. Strong undercurrents between *Verochka* and Margaret were almost palpable.

He should probably leave them alone, but God help him, he couldn't.

Something bugged him about the strange woman. Margaret Coleman Nelson.

The name was unfamiliar. She looked like a wealthy socialite, like she belonged to the rich and famous club of his mother's, but at the same time she was ...different. Somehow. He couldn't put his finger on it. JJ was sure he'd never met her before. Had *Verochka*? Highly doubtful. She rarely left SoHo, and as far as he knew, she never attended any social events such as this one. Why then her unusually strong reaction to Margaret? Dammit, she fainted! His strong and stubborn little warrior who faced life head-on, just collapsed like a deflated balloon after one glimpse at the other woman. Did she recognize her from somewhere? Maybe from France?

He switched his gaze from *Verochka* to Margaret. Dear Lord, the similarities between their eyes—the shape of them as well as the color—were eerie. Shocking. And their voices? So much alike, it was astonishing.

Like they were related.

Only they weren't. Or were they?

But no, *Verochka* had no family, no siblings, or other relatives. She had only him. All his protective instincts surged up. No, he refused to abandon her now more than ever. He didn't know what the story was, but if there was any chance that his Little Swan was somehow in danger, he'd be glued to her side, and shield her any way possible.

Finally, Margaret drew a breath, and turned to face *Verochka*.

"I don't know what to say, my dear. I don't even know where or how to begin, but—"

Full of wonder and confusion, *Verochka's* whisper cut through her phrase.

"Daisy?"

CHAPTER FORTY

Where did that name come from?

One moment, she was staring at the older stranger, and the next, the face of a young woman, painfully familiar and dear, swam in front of her eyes. Those sunny ringlets, that perky little nose, and especially those eyes...

She knew and loved that young woman. Like she was her own. Like she was family.

But I have no family!

Daisy.

Her name was Daisy. No, not her name, but a silly nickname, like an endearment. It jumped at *Verochka* from somewhere deeper than her soul.

A jumble of images rose from her memory. A tiny baby with feathery golden curls...a mischievous tooth gaped toddler...a striking young woman in jeans ripped at the knee, and a black t-shirt...

The other woman's voice—so familiar!—broke the silence, and put a stop to the confusing kaleidoscope of pictures in her head.

"No, sweetheart. I'm Margaret. Daisy was my mother. Well, her real name was Nika, or Veronika, but my father christened her Daisy because she reminded him—"

"Of a wild flower. Because of her curls, she really looked like a daisy."

"Yes. We didn't know much about her family, except that her parents were from New York, and her grandmother was from France. Her name was *Verochka*."

"Just like me!"

"And that she passed her unusual eyes to my mother, and her cousin."

"Alex."

"Yes, his name was Alex, Alexander Morris."

"What?" JJ gasped. "Did you say Morris?"

"Yes. My mother's maiden name was Morris."

"But...it's my name."

"And it's a fairly common one. In here, as well as Florida."

Florida...Amelia Island...the ocean, the seagulls, and the peculiar octagonal house by the sea...

She thought it was just her dream, but it wasn't. *Verochka* shivered.

"Florida? Why Florida?" Wide-eyed and confused, JJ stared at Margaret.

"Because that's where I'm from."

"And...and your father?" *Verochka* touched her temple where the pinpricks of memories pulsed, struggling to get free. "Elijah...Eli...Coleman."

Margaret smiled. "Yes. My father, the famous and prominent son of a Fernandina Beach family, preferred to be called Eli. So, you've remembered."

"Remembered...what? I'm confused. I feel like I'm losing my sanity."

"No, my dear, you're just remembering....the other time."

"What other time?"

Instead of giving her a direct answer, Margaret cocked her head. "Have you heard about Violet Eyes Gift?"

"*Mon Dieu!*"

"Of course, you have."

"Yes, but..."

"My mother Daisy had the same violet eyes like me, and you. My father called them amethysts. According to my mother, all people with this color, carried a special gift."

"But...I don't have any...special gifts."

"No?" One of russet-colored brows arched in an achingly familiar manner.

"Just my intuition, but there is nothing special about it."

"I beg to differ. But, in any event, my mother could manipulate time. There was one incident when my father was about to be mauled down by a passing vehicle—"

"And she slowed the time, so he saved the little dog he was chasing, and got back unscathed."

"Yes, exactly." She beamed at *Verochka*.

"And what is your...special gift?"

"Oh, nothing so spectacular, I'm afraid. I can foresee some events, but only related to the family." Margaret's smile was sad, and full of secrets. "I knew the gender of my unborn grandchild from the second my daughter announced her pregnancy, but I cannot see a single thing about myself." She dropped her gaze. "Had I known that I'd meet you tonight, I..." She shrugged, a gesture *Verochka* recognized as her own. "I would have definitely prepared for it. Although, I doubt very much that any preparation would save me from the shock of recognition."

"So, you're saying that you and *Verochka* are related?" JJ's voice took on edge. "Pardon me, Madame, but that's nonsense. *Verochka* has no family. I'm not sure what you are trying to accomplish, but—"

"My dear Mr. Morris, I can assure you that I'm not trying to accomplish anything nefarious. And you are mistaken. Your fiancé has a family. Or she will be. Soon."

"You're speaking in riddles, Mrs. Nelson. I'm sorry, but this conversation is upsetting *Verochka*. I must take her home."

Upsetting? More like poleaxing. Stupefying.

She didn't want to finish the conversation with the strange woman, and at the same time, she was scared and befuddled and shocked, and barely restrained herself from huddling into JJ's protective arms, and beg him to take her away. As far as possible. She was afraid to remember. Afraid to believe.

Afraid that she was losing her mind.

"By all means, Mr. Morris. And I'm very sorry if I upset you, *Verochka*. But I am really happy that I finally found you."

Verochka's attention zeroed in on the long string of pearls around Margaret's neck.

Was it her feverish imagination, or did she really recognize the neckless?

"Your pearls. Your mother's?"

"Yes, and my grandmother's before that. As was this ring." She lifted her right hand. A precious amethyst set in silver. Old ring, circa 1800.

Verochka would have recognized it even with her eyes closed. The engagement ring Eli Coleman put on Daisy's finger once upon a time.

Mon Dieu!

Verochka slammed her eyelids closed against the barrage of memories and slumped against JJ's unyielding frame. "Please take me home. Now! Please, JJ."

Margaret drew a deep breath. "Be well, my dear. And I am sorry again to cause your disturbance."

"What...what is your full name?" For the life of her, *Verochka* didn't know why it was so imperative. She just knew that she must.

"Margaret Vera Coleman Nelson. I was given my middle name in honor of my great-grandmother."

Great-grandmother...Vera...*Verochka*...

"And your unborn grandchild...it's a boy, isn't?"

"Yes."

"And he'll be named after your father. Eli. Elijah Lauder. Senator Lauder."

"Senator? Huh. I didn't see that. Thank you for the insight, *Verochka.*"

Margaret. Daisy. Eli. Senator Lauder.

It was all too much.

Drowning in memories, bombarded with familiar faces and snippets of conversations...

But domineering it all was a clear and loud chiming of the clock.

The Coleman grandfather clock.

And how did she know that?

Torn between those images and reality, *Verochka* felt like she was about to lose all substance, and untethered, weightlessness, soar high above.

Above time...

CHAPTER FORTY-ONE

JJ almost carried *Verochka* down the stairs. She didn't resist, that fact bothered him greatly. Her state of bewilderment might be more severe than he supposed, dammit. As they descended, Margaret Nelson's clear voice floated behind.

"Farewell, my dear. Until we meet again."

"Not if I can help it," JJ muttered under his breath.

He assisted *Verochka* into the waiting limo, slid in next to her, then gathered her into his arms. She trembled as if freezing from the cold and all but burrowed into him. Her splayed hands on his chest were like two blocks of ice. Even through the material of his shirt, he felt the chill seeping through. JJ never saw her like that. Lost. Scared. Despondent.

His silent curse was more of a helpless oath. One thing was clear as a crystal: he cannot—will not—leave her alone tonight. Not in her current condition.

A violent shudder convulsed her body, almost reverberating through his bones.

"Can you stay with me?" Tiny as a child's, muffled against his chest, her voice simply broke his heart. "Just for tonight. Please?"

Halleluiah!

"As long as you want, *ma petite*. As long as you need me."

JJ squelched his excitement and turned to the chauffeur. "Home please."

With a barely perceptive murmur, the limo glided away from the curb.

In fifteen minutes, they stopped before his Midtown high-rise on Park Avenue. Sleek and imposing, the building rose like a spear, reaching the sky. Absently, JJ wondered why he chose it as his residence in the first place. Prestige? Pride? Both? Probably. The penthouse. His home, he smothered a snort, with more space than a single occupant needed. It was a place where he slept, showered, and drunk a single cup of coffee in the morning. His days were spent at the offices of Morris bank, and his evenings, more often than not, at his bar. Sure, the penthouse was a sound investment, but no more than that.

JJ rarely brought anyone there. The place was impeccable, posh and luxurious, and as charming as an ice sculpture. It had no soul. It was not a home.

Come to think of it, *Verochka's* tiny attic room possessed more personality, and was livelier that his extravagant but neutral condo.

Suddenly unsure of the wisdom of bringing her here, JJ briefly contemplated going to the hotel for the night. Waldorf, or maybe Ritz-Carlton. Quickly, he disregarded the thought. Call him a prude, but to take his future wife to a hotel for the night seemed somehow...vulgar.

Let her see the condo. If *Verochka* didn't like it—and he was sure that was a yes—then he'd start looking for another place tomorrow.

Reluctantly, JJ left the cozy ambience of the limo, and beating his chauffer to it, opened the passenger side. "*Verochka?* We're here."

"Here where?" Slowly, she slid from the seat, and blinked owlishly at the looming high rise. "What...what is this place?"

"Here is where I live."

"But, no! I can't! I must be at the school. The class starts at six sharp, and I—"

"Will be in time for it, I promise."

Squirming, she drew her fur mantel tighter around her slender body. "But...but..."

A sinking sensation spread fast through his gut. She was about to refuse. Faking nonchalance, JJ asked, "Don't you want to see where I live?"

"Yes, but..."

"But what?"

"It is inappropriate." She lowered her eyes, bit her lip. He wanted, more than anything, to smooth that little indentation from her teeth with his tongue, and then delve inside that luscious mouth. Deep. Ripping his eyes from her lips cost him greatly.

He cleared his dry throat. "It is very appropriate. You are my fiancée soon to be my wife. And," seeing her mouth open for a retort, JJ plowed ahead, "this place has five bedrooms, in case if you're afraid that I will behave in an ungentlemanly manner."

"I'm not afraid." She blew away the stray curl from her face. "And you are too much of a gentleman to behave any different."

That statement warmed his heart, even though JJ firmly disagreed with it.

Knowing that she slept nearby made it torture to stay put in his own bedroom, and keep his hands off her. But. JJ knew what needed to be done.

She was distraught, and stressed out, and unsettled.

Verochka's request to stay with her tonight had nothing to do with passion, unfortunately. She didn't need a lover. What she needed was a friend. She turned to him for comfort and safety. Because she trusted him. The devil take his soul if he abused that trust. But bastard as he was, JJ couldn't prevent his imagination from conjuring the most erotic pictures of the two of them together.

Naked. On his bed. In the shower. On the floor.

Fueled by those fantasies, his shaft hardened, pushing against his trousers.

JJ winced. Good thing it was dark, and he wore his long overcoat. A cold shower was definitely a must. *Dammit.*

His mood dampened, but his little friend didn't take the hint. If anything, it strained more painfully, pulsing, demanding satisfaction.

No way no how. Not tonight. But soon.

Somehow pacified by that silent promise, JJ tried to shutter his unruly imagination. He lost. Hell, he'd better lock the door to his bedroom tonight. And throw the key out of the window. But JJ was afraid even that drastic measure might fail.

He cursed inwardly then turned to *Verochka*. "So, if you're not afraid of my nefarious advances, what's your objection?"

"I...don't know. But it feels...wrong."

"Come on, Little Swan. Live dangerously. Consider it an unplanned adventure."

"No, thank you. I have as much adventure as I can stand for the night." With a weary sign, she looked at him. "But I would kill for a hot shower, and a cup of tea."

Almost giddy, JJ bore down on the victory shout that tickled his throat.

"I can provide both," he sent her a grin, "and you don't even have to kill anyone."

A shadow of a smile flickered over her lips.

"Alright then. But only if you promise I won't miss the class tomorrow."

"Scouts honor." He lifted three fingers in imitation of a traditional salute.

"Somehow I doubt that you were ever a boy scout, but..."

She shrugged in that typical Gaelic gesture he was crazy about. Chuckling, JJ brought her hand to his lips, and kissed her knuckles. Her hands were no longer cold, her face lost that shattered expression of helpless bewilderment. Even though tentative, her smile was real and warm. And it was aimed at him. Enormously pleased, JJ barely contained his jubilation.

"I promise to drive you to school in the morning myself."

With that, he offered her his bent elbow. After a moment's hesitation, she accepted it. Feeling like he won a major battle, JJ steered her toward the building's entrance.

CHAPTER FORTY-TWO

S he hated the condo on sight. Cool, sleek, and sterile, the penthouse was a place where Madeline undoubtedly felt right at home. Hard to imagine JJ living here. The only bright spot was the library where books and music ruled supreme.

Indisputably masculine, adorably cluttered, it was warm and lived-in and welcoming. The black velvet case of JJ's sax lay open on what looked to be a special podium, allowing *Verochka* a glimpse of the shiny instrument nestled inside. A white baby grand Steinway in the middle of the room added a subtle feminine touch.

Rows of mahogany book cases lined the walls. Everywhere she looked, books met her gaze. The glass cover of the turntable was overflowed with sheets of music. Despite her mood, *Verochka* smiled. She well imagined JJ here, playing his sax, or listening to his vast collection of records. Or just relaxing on the bench before the piano with a tumbler of whiskey.

Slowly, she pivoted, and glanced at him. "I love this room. It's wonderful."

"I'm glad. This is my favorite." He tilted his head and raised his brows. "Why don't we make you more comfortable?"

Only after he removed the mantel from her shoulders, *Verochka* realized she still had it on. A little apprehensive, she murmured her thanks.

She felt ridiculously exposed, like the protective armor was lifted from her body. *Verochka* shivered. Her arms crossed over her chest, hugging herself tight.

She didn't belong here anymore than she belonged in that swanky hotel. She was so out of place. What on earth prompted her agree to come to here? She should've insisted to be taken back to school. But no, her curiosity took the better of her, and now she must suffer the consequences.

Happy now, you silly goose?

Miserable, she scanned the long hallway where JJ disappeared with her mantel.

Correction: Madame Valeska's mantel.

She didn't own a single item that was on her. Everything was on loan. Well, except her dress. But even that gorgeous Chanel belonged to her mother first.

Absently, she fingered the neckless, touched her earlobes adorned with the expensive gems. Her eyes dropped to the ring JJ put on her finger. It simply took her breath away. But it too was just a loan. Just an accessory to the costume she wore for the tonight's performance. Well, the curtains were down. The show ended. It was time to get back to reality. She cast a glance in a big mirror on the opposite wall. Who was that woman staring back at her? Upswept hairdo, long dress, shimmering jewelry. Startled eyes enhanced by cosmetics she barely recognized as her own. A beautiful stranger trapped in her body. A fake façade.

Admit it, Verochka, you are a fraud.

Vehemently, she shook her head. No, her current image was a fraud, the image she couldn't wait to shed. *Verochka* Osipoff might be poor, with just a few things to her name, but she still has her pride, and her self-respect, and a good head on her shoulders. And no matter how it hurt, she was always honest with herself.

She didn't belong. Not here, and not with JJ.

That became brutally and obviously apparent as soon as she stepped her foot into his condo. The difference between their lifestyles was overwhelming. Glaring. They had nothing in common. It was hard for her to even imagine the world and lifestyle he was accustomed to. She didn't fit into that world any more than he fit into hers. End of a story.

Almost bereft, *Verochka* turned from the mirror, and hugged herself tighter.

"You can take your shower now."

Startled, she pivoted. JJ stood nearby, minus his formal jacket and tie, holding something in his hands. Lost in her turmoil, she hadn't noticed his return.

What was he talking about? Did he say shower?

"P-pardon me?"

JJ cocked his brow. "You requested a shower, and a tea, remember?" Coming closer, he tucked a lock of hair behind her ear. "You were even willing to kill for it." A highly contagious mischievous grin lifted the corner of his lips.

Despite everything, *Verochka* laughed. "I think I'll restrain myself."

"I'm sure glad to hear it. You can use any guestroom."

A shower sounded lovely. Hot, and long, and steaming. Pure bliss. She almost shivered in anticipation. Realization that there were no clean clothes to change into burst her bubble.

Merde!

Her smile fell.

JJ grinned.

"Here, you can wear this." He put a bathrobe into her hands. "Granted, it's a man's size, but at least you'll be warm, and covered from head to toe."

Heavenly soft terrycloth was an answer to all her prayers. Immediately, *Verochka's* mood perked up.

"Let me find some socks. I'll be back."

Verochka sniffed the robe as his steps echoed down the long hallway. It smelled like JJ. Her heart swelled. Hot tears pressed heavily against her eyelids.

The love for him, so huge and overwhelming, filled her to the brim.

Helpless. Lost. She was drowning in it.

They have no future together. To pretend otherwise was unwise and cruel. To herself. And especially to JJ. The only answer was to leave him, as soon as possible.

Merde! She still hadn't told him her decision to break off their relationship.

Her mood plummeted, her resolve crumbled. With a tiny *ping*, her heart broke into thousand little pieces.

Mon Dieu, *how can I do it?! How can I not?*

JJ returned with a pair of thick socks.

Now or never.

After a deep fortifying breath, *Verochka* turned to face him. And lost all trail of thought. All the love in the world shone back at her from his chocolate eyes.

Oh, God, please help me.

"JJ, we need to talk." Her vocal cords hurt as if she had swallowed broken glass.

"And we will, after you take your shower, and drink some tea. Come on."

His little push propelled her forward. "The second room on your left. You'll be more comfortable in the small guestroom, I think."

Her resistance was no match for his strength. With a deep sigh, she capitulated. Fifteen minutes. Twenty at the most, and then she'd break her news to him. Feeling lower than dirt, she stumbled to the bathroom. Done in muted colors of mauve and gold, it was several times larger than her whole apartment, and million times more luxurious. *Verochka* couldn't help herself. She gawked, afraid to touch anything.

And how long do you plan to stand here, behaving like an imbecile? Get moving.

Tentatively, she touched the gleaming faucet, then turned the water. She carefully removed her precious gown. Madame Valeska's jewelry came next, but when she attempted to remove JJ's ring from her finger, it refused to slid off.

The hell with it. *Verochka* stepped under the steaming sprays, and moaned from sheer pleasure. Hot and strong, the water pulsed against her back, loosening her knotted muscles. The billowing steam rose, enveloping her body in a warm moist embrace. She closed her eyes, turned her face directly under the shower head, and tried to free her mind. The events of the stressful evening slowly began to fade. The ball, the opulence of the hotel...Celeste... Madeline...

Margaret.

She jolted, opened her eyes, unmindful of the stinging sensation from the hot water pelting over her face. Margaret, the woman with violet eyes, and sunny curls.

Who was she?

And why did meeting her leave *Verochka* disturbed more than Celeste's snide remarks or Madeline's frozen disapproval? Something about that woman...

Something...elusive and confusing, and—

As if on cue, the myriad of images began to unfold in her mind.

Daisy... Alex... Eli...

She knew those people, loved them.

The stately octagonal house by the sea...the cries of seagulls...the ocean...

She never saw the ocean in her life. Or did she?

Amelia Island, a tiny spec of land in Florida.

A sudden shift of images, and the magnificent mansion took up center stage. White, dignified. Majestic. Daisy loved this house. The Coleman house.

And how do I know that?!

Shaken, trembling from the onslaught of strange visions, *Verochka* snapped the water off. Despite her steaming shower, she was chilled to the bone. Her teeth began to chatter. Goosebumps the size of Manhattan covered her skin.

Scared. She was scared like never before. No, not just scared, but petrified.

Mon Dieu, *what's happening to me?!*

The thought that she was going insane grabbed her by the throat. Margaret's voice echoed in her mind, "*So, you've remembered.*"

Remembered, or lost her mind?

The violet eyes, painfully familiar. The name. *Margaret Vera Coleman Nelson.*

She heard that name before. Where? When?

"*I was given my middle name in honor of my great-grandmother.*"

Impossible. Outrageous. Unbelievable!

On rubbery legs, she stumbled from the shower stall, and without toweling, bundled into the plush bathrobe. It swallowed her body from the neck down, dangled over her fingertips. Her hair dripped water onto her face, but she didn't care.

JJ. Must find JJ. Where is he?

CHAPTER FORTY-THREE

By the time she found him in the kitchen, *Verochka* was shaking uncontrollably. Her teeth chattered so loudly, she was sure JJ heard it too. He turned. The smile that started to lift the corners of his lips slipped as if a switch was flipped off.

He dropped the steaming cup he held and hurried toward her.

"*Verochka,* sweetheart, what is it?"

"JJ, oh, JJ, I'm so scared..."

"Hush, little one. You are safe, you are with me." His arms around her felt heavenly. Warmth from his body slowly seeped into her body. When he held her like that, she almost believed that nothing bad might ever happen to her. Safe and secure, she felt incredibly right. Like she belonged. With him. In his embrace. In his life.

"Can you tell me what is it?" Gently, his hand began to rub her back in a slow soothing motion. She shivered from pure pleasure. Her fright melted, then faded like a shadow in daylight, leaving her lightheaded.

I could stay like this for the next several years.

"Why are you scared?" JJ's question brought her back full circle.

"I'm afraid that I'm losing my mind. That woman...Margaret...and those faces, names, places..."

"Just your overactive imagination. That's all."

"That's all? How can you say that? And what about her eyes? Or her name? Or her mother's name? How did I know it?"

"Just a lucky coincidence."

"Do you believe it? Honestly? I met a woman with my eyes and my voice, and recognized her, and remembered strange names and faces, and all that is just a lucky coincidence?"

"What else could it be? So, yes, I admit, her eyes and her voice gave me pause."

JJ drew away, and smoothed the wet strands of hair from her face.

"Believe it or not, there are other people in this world with violet eyes. It's very rare, bit still. Nothing sinister about it."

"But—"

A quick hard kiss interrupted her argument.

"But nothing. You were stressed and uneasy, and meeting that woman just put a cap on your unpleasant evening. That's all."

Oh, God, how she wanted to believe him!

"Are you sure?"

"Positive. Now, why don't you drink that tea, and go to bed. Tomorrow all your fears will seem silly and pointless, I promise."

With a gentle kiss on her forehead, JJ turned to pick up the steaming cup from the counter. An unmistakable aroma of bergamot orange wafted through the kitchen.

She was tired of fighting herself.

She might be distraught and scared, and still in the grips of her confusing memories, but deep inside she knew what she needed. Wanted. Craved. More than her next breath.

JJ.

The man who burst into her life, upended it, and threw it off its axis.

The man who was so far away from her world, they might be two aliens from two different planets.

The man who invaded her dreams and thoughts, who held her heart in the palm of his hand, and owned her soul.

JJ.

They might not have a future, but they had tonight. If that's all Fate allowed her, she'd grab it with both hands. And make it enough.

"I don't want tea."

Turning to her, JJ cocked one brow in question. "No? What, then? Coffee? Wine? Although, I wouldn't recommend any hard alcohol, a sip of brandy might be beneficial."

"No. I don't need any brandy, or coffee."

Something on her face might have alerted him. His smile slowly fell. His chocolate eyes held her gaze as the first sparkles of heat began to gleam in their depth.

After a moment, JJ pulled the shutters over his face, but not soon enough.

The unmistakable burst of desire she glimpsed fortified her resolve.

He cleared his throat. "Okay. No tea or coffee or brandy. What, then?"

Was his voice deeper, raspier, or did she imagine it?

"What do you need, Little Swan? Just name it, and it's yours."

JJ held himself absolutely still, but the slight tremor in his hands revealed another story. Emboldened, *Verochka* recklessly threw away the last shreds of uncertainty.

"Anything?"

"Absolutely."

In three short strides, she closed the distance between them. Now they stood so close, the erratic beating of pulse at the base of his throat, and the molten lava swirling in his eyes were clearly visible. Her skin tingled.

"I need you." Lifting both arms, *Verochka* looped them around his neck, and arched her body into his. Briefly, she wondered where that boldness came from. Or why she wasn't even a little bit apprehensive. She had never been with a man before.

It was her first experience. Why wasn't she afraid? Why was she acting so shamelessly? With an inner shrug, she tossed her caution away.

"I need you," she repeated in a husky voice that barely resembled her own, "only you. Only you."

Breathing hard, JJ made an attempt to step back. But *Verochka* held firm.

"You don't know what you're asking." Another attempt to dislodge her arms went unsuccessful. "You are shaken, and upset, and—"

She raised a brow. "Do I look upset to you? Or shaken?"

He stared into her eyes, long and hard. "No. But—"

"Don't you want me?"

His crude swearing was like a beautiful melody sliding all the way from her ears to her feet. She heard the expression of something curling a person's toes, but it was the first time she actually experienced it. The sensation was decadent. Positively sinful.

Delighted, she smiled. JJ stared at her with a mixture of helplessness and determination. His arms slowly encircled her waist, drawing her even closer. "*Verochka*, you're killing me."

"Well, don't you?"

"I want you more than my next breath." His tortured whisper sounded like it was wrenched from the depth of his soul. "But I'll be damned if I take advantage of you."

If she weren't in love with him before, she'd surely fall right at this minute.

Her heart sighed. Such an honorable man. Honest, decent. Considerate.

And, oh God, so mouthwateringly handsome! *Delicioux!*

And for tonight, he was all hers.

"Okay." She rose on her tiptoes, her lips a breath away from his. "Then I'll take advantage of you."

CHAPTER FORTY-FOUR

As her mouth closed over his, JJ was lost. Defeated. Conquered. Dear Lord, he was just a man. How much temptation can he withstand?

With a deep hungry growl, he crashed his mouth over her lips, and delved.

And devoured.

His tongue dipped inside of the silky cavern, swept over, again and again.

She trembled, violently. Passion or fear?

His consciousness screamed at him to slow down, to take it easy.

But he was beyond reason.

Fisting one hand in her still wet hair, he tilted her head, and deepened the kiss.

Her flavor enchanted him, her little whimpers clouded his mind.

And her smell, something clean and innocent and fragile, simply destroyed him.

Soon kissing ceased to be enough. He needed—craved—to feel skin.

With an effort, he ripped his mouth from hers, and looked at her.

Flushed, disheveled, she met his gaze with eyes that went from violet to deep purple. What he saw in those mesmerizing amethyst pools almost brought him to his knees. Passion, love, need. All the emotions that churned inside of him mirrored in those magical eyes of hers. An instinct to take rampaged like an inferno. JJ fought it like a man possessed, but the battle was already lost.

Unable to wait any longer, he grabbed the belt of her robe, and gave it a tag. His hands shook so badly, he didn't succeed until the third try. With a careless shrug of her shoulders, *Verochka* let the robe slide over her body. Mesmerized, JJ watched as it pooled in a heap by her feet. Brazen, she stood in front of him in all her naked glory. Impossibly slender, fluidly graceful, she was like an exquisite porcelain figurine come to life.

A deep rumble of victory burst from his throat.

He focused his eyes as they traveled from her mussed hair to the elegant shoulders and narrow torso with its tiny waist, down to the long-sculpted legs to the tips of her little toes. Callused and bruised, they were unpainted, and a little reddened from the constant abrasion of her pointe shoes. She was the most beautiful thing he ever saw.

JJ dragged his eyes up, stopping on her exquisite breasts tipped with generous rosy areolas. Puckered to hard points, her little nipples drew his gaze like a magnet. His mouth watered. Shaking from the onslaught of desire, he was afraid to breathe. To blink. To move.

Was it a dream? Just a figment of his imagination? But no. Even in his dreams, he couldn't conjure a vision so perfect, so beautiful. So magnificent.

Alive. She was alive and real. And she was his.

He didn't dare to touch her, afraid of damaging that perfection.

Afraid to lose the last crumbs of his self-control.

Afraid to reach the point of no return.

She didn't have to tell him that she was a virgin. Her innocence was written all over her, more obvious than her distinctive eye color. Despite all *Verochka's* bravado, her kisses were more eager than wanton, albeit passionate enough to boil his blood. And that combination of untainted pureness and shameless lust was simply lethal. And irresistible. And erotic like all the deadly sins combined.

Shaking from the force of it, JJ fisted his hands until the skin over his knuckles almost split over. He was her first. It humbled and terrified him. He wanted to run for cover, and shout on the top of his lungs.

She trusted him. She loved him. She wanted him.

Undone, impossibly moved, JJ swore to make her first experience as pleasant as possible.

You must handle her like a precious thing, carefully, gently. Tenderly.

And how on earth could he do that if his blood churned, and his desire drummed a heavy rhythm in his chest? His shaft strained with a ferocious force against his trousers, pulsing, demanding action. JJ swallowed, and adjusted his stance. He vowed not hurt her.

But you will.

Helpless, his silent oath struck in his throat. "I don't want to hurt you, *ma petite.*"

"You won't." A smile that played over her face was that of a siren. Taking a step closer, *Verochka* splayed both palms over his chest. "You can't, *mon amour.*"

My love. She just called him 'my love.'

His breath hitched. His heart swelled to the size of the Grand Canyon.

But...what was she doing? Was she unbuttoning his shirt?

A cold panic speared his gut, twisting his insides.

Oh, for the love of God!

"Stop." With an effort, JJ covered her hands with his, stilled her busy fingers. "*Verochka*, please. Just... stop."

"Why?" She cocked her head, raised one brow. "Am I doing something wrong?"

A deep V puckered her forehead as she gazed at him with confusion.

He'd laugh if his throat weren't so constricted. "No, no. You're doing everything right. It's just—"

"Just?"

"Just too soon."

"Not soon enough, if you ask me." With a mischievous grin, she returned to her task.

"*Verochka,* please..." Hot against his bare skin, her hands were wreaking havoc with his concentration. "Oh, God. Oh, hell. If you won't stop this, I'm afraid I—"

"Stop what? Touching you? But it's so pleasant. Your skin is like velvet, so smooth and warm. I never knew a man's skin could be so...delicate. And your muscles."

A slow glide of her open palms along his ribcage was the most erotic caress he ever experienced. JJ failed to prevent a helpless shudder.

"*Mon Dieu,* it's like steel! You are so strong. So powerful."

JJ never felt less strong and powerful in his life. Trembling from head to toe, he gritted his teeth until his jaw protested. She was killing him, destroying him.

Too much. Not enough.

More. For goodness' sake, more!

Ready to beg, on the verge of snapping, JJ kept his arms pressed hard to his sides. The temptation of grabbing her was overwhelming. But one little touch, and he could kiss his self-control good-bye.

Finished with the exploration of his chest, *Verochka* murmured something in French, then lifted her sparkling eyes. "You are simply magnificent, JJ." With that she pressed her naked body fully to his. "And you are all mine."

Her small breasts nestled against his chest like two pieces of a puzzles completing the whole picture. Like they were made to fit.

The contrast between their skin—hers milky white, his deep olive—was startling and exciting and somehow just right.

A quick dart of her tongue over her puffy lips was clearly instinctive, and not a deliberate flirting gesture. But that little lick struck JJ as the most provocative act, and sealed his fate. His control snapped like a brittle bone. Reaching for *Verochka*, he crashed his mouth over hers.

The point of no return. Hallelujah!

CHAPTER FORTY-FIVE

His hands roamed over her body, hard, possessive, demanding. He drank from her mouth like a man on the verge of dying from thirst. Bold and hot, his tongue knifed past her lips, sliding, caressing, conquering. Her skin tingled all over, her blood rushed through her veins, her breath turned choppy. Something hot and wet gathered between her thighs. *Verochka's* whole body pulsed like an exposed nerve.

Mon Dieu, *what's happening to me?*

Disoriented, off balance, she clutched at his shoulders with the panic of a drowning person. In the world that unerringly and abruptly fell apart, he was the only solid link to reality. Her anchor. Her lifesaver. Her rock.

Blinded, lightheaded, she strained against his solid frame, instinctively seeking something... Solace? Relief? Fulfillment?

She felt like a vessel without liquid. Desperate to fill that vast empty space inside of her, *Verochka* greedily absorbed every touch, every kiss, every sound. A maelstrom of sensations filled her to the brim, tearing her apart.

She should probably be scared. Terrified. But all she felt was an enormous hunger that only JJ could satisfy. Whimpering, she slanted her mouth, allowing him to deepen the kiss until she didn't know where her lips ended and his began.

Her tongue darted forward, slid past his lips into his mouth. He welcomed the intrusion with a deep rumbling sound of approval.

They were plastered together, skin to skin, both feverish and sweaty.

Their heartbeats thundered in unison. Their breaths mingled.

With a frustrated growl, JJ tore his mouth from hers. Framing her face with both hands, he looked deep into her eyes.

"Last warning." His breathing came in broken heaving, like his lungs were laboring for the next breath. "If you changed your mind, tell me to stop. Now."

Stop? Was he kidding?

"If you stop now, I will never forgive you."

But still, he hesitated. "Are you sure?"

"I've never been so sure in my entire life." Mimicking his gesture, she framed his face with both hands. "I want to be with you."

Just for one night.

Just this one time.

"Please."

Silence stretched. A heartbeat? An eternity?

She wasn't sure how long they stood unmoving, staring at each other.

JJ became a blur of a motion. Bending forward, he scooped her up, lifting her in his arms like she weighted nothing at all.

"As God is my witness, I tried. For as long as I could."

Quickly, he walked down the hall, until they faced the partially closed door to his bedroom. Opening it with his foot, JJ walked inside, and deposited her at the foot of an enormous bed. Momentarily shocked, *Verochka* eyed that behemoth with the first twinges of apprehension. *Mon Dieu*, the bed was larger than two of her apartments put together! The impression of a lake jumped to her mind. The blue color of the silky coverlet reinforced that image. Gasping, she turned to him and all the breath left her body in a *whoosh.* While she gawked at his bed, he shed all his clothes. Totally naked, he stood in front of her, tall, dark, and gorgeous.

Verochka never saw a nude male before. A nude *aroused* male.

The difference between their bodies was staggering. He was hard and huge where she was soft and slender. Wide straight shoulders, roped with muscled arms, washboard flat stomach. Dark ribbon of hair encircled his tiny nipples, that snaked lower over his belly to the thick thatch between his legs.

On my...

A quick glance at his jutting sex stole her breath. Dear Lord, it was enormous.

A wave of hot embarrassment spread over her face and neck.

Without looking in the mirror, *Verochka* knew she was blushing. Furiously. She lowered her eyes.

"Scared?"

Mon Dieu, *make that terrified!*

"Ah, *non.* Just...surprised." With an effort, she lifted her gaze to his face, carefully avoiding looking at *that.* "The sheer size of you is...fascinating."

A strange expression crossed over JJ's face, as a sound close to a moan escaped from his mouth. Immediately contrite, *Verochka* frowned. "Are you in pain?"

"No, not at all." But his face contradicted his statement.

She chewed on her lip. "It must be very uncomfortable. Walking with that... thing."

His booming laugh was followed by another low growl.

"God, Little Swan, if only you knew." JJ winced, and cursed under his breath.

All *Verochka's* protective feelings went on a high alert.

"*Merde,* JJ, you are hurting. I can see that. What can I do to help?" Warily, she cast a glance at his thighs. "Maybe, if I touch it..."

Now he doubled with laughter until his eyes gleamed with moisture.

Verochka bristled. "That's not a laughing matter!"

"Sorry, sorry, *ma petite*." JJ took a deep breath, visibly struggling with his merriment. "You are right, it is not. But if you... touch it, I'm afraid it'll be all over before we even began."

"Began what?"

"Making love."

"Oh."

Now a wave of heat swept over her whole body. She cast a brief glance over her shoulder at the huge bed, and quickly averted her gaze. She knew she was blushing from the roots of her hair to the tips of her toes.

Merde.

Get a grip, silly goose. You are not a schoolgirl. You are a woman.

Yes, she was a woman, and she was about to engage in the act of sex. Willingly.

For the first time in her life. And probably the last. Well, then, she'd make it count.

Squaring her shoulders, *Verochka* reached for her dwindling supply of bravado.

"So, you are not in pain?"

"Not in the way you mean, I'm not."

"Alright." Nodding, she took a deep fortifying breath. "Are you... able to do it just once? Making love, that is."

JJ blinked, blanched, and hooted with laughter. "Lord, I sincerely hope not."

"Well then." She squinted at him, wondering how the simple and obvious solution to this dilemma was lost on JJ. "Let's do it quickly the first time. We can go more slowly the next."

CHAPTER FORTY-SIX

For the first time in his life, JJ didn't know how he was supposed to feel.

Elated? Delighted? Amused?

Dear God, he was so befuddled—more like poleaxed—he didn't know how to behave. Here he was, naked and aroused, in his bedroom, with the woman of his dreams, and he didn't know what to do next.

Really, JJ?

Ridiculously inappropriate under current circumstances, the laughter bubbled in his throat.

"We can go more slowly the next time."

Sweet baby Jesus, it was priceless. Hilarious. JJ bit hard on his tongue to prevent another laugh. But dammit, it cost him. Only *Verochka* was able to make him laugh at a moment like that. Shaking from within, he struggled to keep a straight face. She'd think that he lost his mind. In a matter of speaking, he had.

The very moment he laid eyes on her. But still.

For crying out loud, get a grip, man. And wipe that silly grin off.

He was behaving like a lunatic. At that rate, he'd be lucky to perform at all.

As if on cue, a numbing fear speared his gut. Damn, she was a virgin.

Trembling like a stallion who sensed a filly, JJ silently reminded himself that he was not a green youth at the mercy of his hormones. He was a mature male with a long list of previous amorous encounters, experienced and competent and skilled.

Or so he thought.

Gazing at *Verochka* now, he felt anything but.

Unsure of himself, he was scared and lost.

Like it was *his* first time.

Like *he* was a damned virgin.

Pathetic.

He frowned. How she managed to reduce him to such a pitiful state was beyond his grasp.

He was supposed to be the expert, guiding her through her first sexual experience. Instead, she took the matters into her small elegant hands, and became a master.

Dear God, now what?

As if reading his mind, *Verochka* echoed his silent question, "Now what?"

Thin and quiet, her voice reminded him that of a child. Was she afraid? Had she changed her mind? He looked closer. She stood, pale, and still like a statue, staring at him with wide unblinking eyes. All the confusion and uncertainty he felt at that moment swirled on her face. But her firm determination shone through, like a beacon of light. No, his Little Swan was not afraid. Nor did she change her mind. An enormous and instantaneous relief went through him like a huge warm wave. Yes, she was unsteady, and unsure, and probably weary.

The shock of seeing him completely nude hadn't paralyzed her as he feared.

Nor was she disgusted. If anything, she seemed curious, albeit a bit startled.

She even was more concerned for him, that he was hurting. Sweet innocent girl. Tenderhearted Little Swan, kind and brave and strong.

Was it any wonder he was so in love with her?

His heart melted, his eyes misted. The other, most basic part of him twitched painfully, reminding JJ of its existence. He swore under his breath.

Damn that unruly appendage. He dragged his eyes to *Verochka*. Slowly, she crossed her arms over her chest. "Do you want me to leave?"

"Leave?" Startled, he stared at her. Is that what she thought?

What else could she think, you idiot?

Not only was he confusing her with his silent treatment, but embarrassing her, too.

"No way, Little Swan. No way in hell." He closed the distance in two strides, then gathered her in his arms. "I'm sorry."

"For what?" Her nose, pressing into his pectorals, felt like a tiny icicle. On top of everything, she was cold and shivering. Dammit.

Cursing himself, JJ splayed both hands over her back, rubbing some warmth into it.

"For acting like a moron. My only excuse is, I want you too much, and hate to scare you. Or hurt you."

"I'm not scared." She circled his waist with her arms, pressed closer.

"That makes one of us." That full-body contact was pure torture. JJ's eyes crossed.

"Are you scared?" She peeped at him.

"More like terrified."

Somber, *Verochka* lifted her face from his chest. "Don't be." Her violet eyes shone with compassion and tenderness. "It'll be alright."

She was doing it again, trying to comfort him. Moved, unbelievably touched, JJ kissed her forehead.

"It'll be more than alright, Little Swan. I promise. It'll be earth-shattering, but..." A deep breath later, he added quietly, "after the first time."

She pursed her lips, cocked her head. "What will happen the first time?"

"There will be some pain. Initial. But only for a moment."

And how do you know that, you dolt?

"I wish I could spare you even that, but—"

"That's okay. I'm used to pain. Don't worry, JJ. Just show me what to do."

She never failed to surprise him. He hoped she never would.

Just show me what to do. Right. Okay.

JJ cleared his parched throat. "Ah...for starters, let's lay on the bed."

"Okay." Nimble as a mountain goat, *Verochka* climbed onto the bed, tugged the bedspread out of the way, then lie down in the middle. "Your turn."

Impatient, as graceful as a Mac truck, he plopped beside her. *Verochka* turned on her side, facing him. "And now?"

She gazed at him with the mix of curiosity and shyness. Brave little thing.

JJ smiled, tucked a stray lock of hair behind her ear. All his fears disappeared, like they'd been switched off, and his nerves settled down.

Excitement hummed through his veins in a gentle unhurried rhythm.

"And now, I'll kiss you," he dropped a chaste kisses onto her cheeks, nose, and pointy little chin, "and touch you," his fingers slowly trailed up her torso, from her navel to her breast, "and pleasure you."

When he lightly grazed one puckered nipple, *Verochka* sharply sucked in a breath. JJ stilled. Too soon? Too much?

After a second's hesitation, she arched into his palm in silent demand. He let out the breath stuck in his lungs. His whole body quivered like never before.

He bore down, keeping a firm leash on his inner animal. Its claws were slowly shredding his control to bloody ribbons. JJ gritted his teeth, praying for patience.

"And then, I'll do it all over." To demonstrate, he showered her shoulders, neck, and face with open-mouthed kisses, then gently bit on her delicate earlobe. She shivered. The helpless moan that slipped from her lips was the most powerful aphrodisiac. The unmistakable fragrance of arousal hit his senses and sent him reeling.

Yes. Oh yes. Now.

With every intention of drawing out her very first orgasm, JJ gritted his teeth, braced himself, and slid his palm over her belly.

But when he was about to touch her center, *Verochka* wiggled, dislodging his hand. Puzzled, he squinted at her, and froze. All covered in a glistening sheen of sweat, flushed and panting, she lay amidst the wrinkled silky sheets like a goddess of Eros. Or a courtesan. She took his breath away, and twisted his guts into knots.

Slowly, she lifted her left arm in a wide upward arch. Like a wing.

Mesmerized, JJ followed it with his eyes. A faint glimmer on her hand caught his attention. *The ring.* She removed every stich of clothing, and all the jewelry, but not his ring! Lust, pure and primitive, hit him with the force of a hurricane. His blood swooshed like an overflowed river. Shaken, JJ shut his eyes.

Losing it, laddie. Losing it fast.

"Can I kiss and touch you too?" Like a fist in a solar plexus, her question stole his breath. "I mean, is it allowed?"

Holly mother of God!

JJ swallowed his groan. "Anything is allowed, *ma petite.*"

And when did you become a masochist?

"Anything?" She liked her lips.

This time, his groan ripped free from his throat, loud and tortured.

"Absolutely anything." How did he manage to pass words through his constricted vocal cords was a complete mystery to him.

"Okay, then."

And with enthusiasm, *Verochka* bolted upright, sat on her hunches, and pressing both hands to his chest, kissed him just above his thundering heart.

CHAPTER FORTY-SEVEN

Humming, quivering from excitement, *Verochka* took her lips on a journey from JJ's sternum to his ribcage, then up again. The sight of him simply fascinated her. All those planes and valleys, all those muscles. Unable to resist, she ran her fingers along his torso, touching, marveling. His nipples, dark and tiny, encircled by the ribbon of silky hair; his stomach, flat and firm; his arms, long and strong. Everything was so captivating. Transfixing. So different from her own body.

Speaking of different. She lowered her eyes to his protruding shaft. Thick and huge, it seemed to pulse like a living thing.

Mon Dieu!

She supposed it was too late to wonder if this was going to work. Yes, she was a virgin, but not ignorant. *Verochka* knew the basic mechanics of sex between a male and female body. But the sheer size of that *thing* took her breath away.

Will her body accommodate it? And what if it won't? What then? Will JJ get mad?

Merde.

Deflated, she dragged her eyes from his thighs to his face.

Drawn, dark. Hooded eyes. Unsmiling mouth pressed into a thin line.

The image was that of a person suffering from great pain. Did she cause it? Was her touch unpleasant to him? Momentarily contrite, she snatched her hands from his body, tucked them under her armpits.

"Why did you stop?"

Grave and deep, JJ's voice sounded like he was angry. Or hurting. Or both.

"I'm sorry, I...I didn't want to... hurt you."

"Hurt me? By touching me?"

"Yes." She let out a broken breath. "I don't know what can I do, or what is... allowed."

"I told you, *ma petite*, everything is allowed."

"But your face...you seemed to be... uncomfortable." After a brief hesitation, she confessed, "I've never done that before."

"I know."

"You do? But... how? I never told you that."

"Little Swan, you don't have to tell me. Your innocence is written all over you."

"Oh." Embarrassed, she lowered her gaze. Hot tears pressed against her eyelids like tiny needles. Blinking furiously, *Verochka* shut her stinging eyes. She never regretted her virginity before. The lack of her sexual experience never bothered her, until now. She needed to know. Without opening her eyes, she asked, "Are you upset?"

"Upset? Why would I be?" The bed shifted, as JJ moved to sit beside her. His warm fingers grazed her trembling chin, lifted it. "Look at me, *Verochka*."

Reluctantly, she opened her eyes.

"Do I look upset to you?"

For a long moment she searched his expression. "No. You look rather... pleased."

"And delighted, and happy, and humbled." The corner of his lips curved in a strained little smile. "I am honored and privileged to be your first."

A helpless sob burst from her throat.

You are my one and only.

And my last.

"Make love to me, JJ." A fierce demand. A helpless plea. "Make me yours."

Did he hear the desperation in her voice? Burying all her conflicting emotions under the layer of a reckless bravado, she made the first move.

Looping her hands around his neck, she brought him closer. Then, leaning backward, she tumbled them both onto the bed. His large frame covered her like a heavy blanket. Hot, immediate, scorching.

Weight, unyielding, solid.

Enveloped by his body, steeped in his fever, she absorbed every single sensation, storing it into her memory. For as long as she lived, she'd never forget this moment in time.

This man.

This night.

A single night that fate allowed her. Tomorrow she'd be back to her own world. Tomorrow she must tell JJ that they can never be together. That she was leaving him. Tomorrow. Cringing, already mourning, *Verochka* brought his face closer, and poured all her heart into the kiss.

Don't think about tomorrow. Don't think about anything. Just feel.

For just a heartbeat, JJ hesitated, then opening his mouth, crushed his lips over hers. Searing, that kiss rocked her to her soul. His tongue licked and rubbed and conquered. His hands became busy. Every touch was a sweet agony. Every sound a heavenly melody. Greedy, she soaked everything up like a sponge. Her body became a single bundle of nerves, tingling in places she didn't know she possessed.

The pleasure was almost unbearable. Too much. Not enough.

Mindless, desperate, *Verochka* writhed, trying to reach for something she couldn't name, something wonderful and scary. Something that beaconed ahead.

Weightless and untethered, she hurdled forward, unable to stop. She felt like she was about to burst into a thousand little pieces, and disintegrate into a thin air. What was happening to her?

"JJ. *Mon Dieu,* JJ!"

"I'm here, *ma petite.* I'm right here."

"Please, I can't stand it!"

"Neither can I." Dropping his forehead on hers, breathing hard, he braced his weight onto his elbows. His raspy whisper abraded her ears.

"I'm sorry, Little Swan."

Verochka had a split second to wonder what he was sorry about, when a hot searing pain knifed her body from within. Unprepared, stunned, she cried out. Desperate to find a relief, she tried to shift her legs to no avail. Blinded with pain, *Verochka* pushed at his shoulders, but he didn't bulge.

Mon Dieu, it was unbearable. Horrible. It felt like her middle was split in two. Something heavy and hot pulsed between her open thighs.

"Shh, sweetheart, just lay still. Don't fight it. It'll pass in a moment."

A moment? Was he kidding?

Hiked around JJ's hips, her legs trembled, then slid down, like two overcooked noodles. *Verochka* gritted her teeth. "How... the hell do you... know that?"

"I know, trust me. Just let your body become accustomed."

"Accustomed to what?"

"To the invasion."

"*Merde.*"

Cursing out loud brought some satisfaction, if not relief. But after a few moments, her pain miraculously abated. Instead of a burning agony, it was more of a mild discomfort. Soon even that faded into a mere throb.

Enormously relived, *Verochka* let out a deep sigh. Okay, she wasn't hurting anymore, thank goodness. But was that all? What was the big deal, really?

An acute disappointment settled inside like a cold rainy cloud.

Really? That was all sex was about? Well, she can live without it, thank you very much. Sad now, she bit her lip, heaved a deep sigh.

"I suppose we can get up now." Her nakedness, not to mention her earlier wanton behavior, became humiliating. She was desperate to cover herself, or better yet, get away from here as far and fast as possible.

JJ lifted himself onto his elbows. "What? Get up?" As if confused, he raised both brows. "But why?"

"Well, I figured we're finish making love, so—"

A deep chuckle rumbled in his chest, reverberating through her own. "My darling innocent, we haven't even started yet."

Oh, God. Now she was confused on top of embarrassed. "But...didn't you...didn't we...?"

"No, I didn't. We didn't." He dropped a quick kiss on the tip of her nose, then became all serious. "Are you alright? Has the pain gone?"

Experimentally, she wiggled her butt as much as his pressing weight allowed. "Yes. Completely."

"Good." JJ nodded in obvious satisfaction, and placed a tender kiss onto her lips. "And now, *ma petite,* I'll show you what making love is all about."

He lifted her legs, hooked them around his waist, and pressed his hips forward. *Verochka* gasped. Another thrust made her clutch his shoulders. After a third time, JJ began to move in a fast, hard rhythm.

She had no choice but to catch up. Soon, her hips moved on their own, lifting, meeting each plunge eagerly.

Her body undulated, her legs stretched, her arms arched in a dance older than world.

A *Pa De Deux* of passion.

Slapping sounds of skin against skin, broken breaths, low moans. The air became thick, charged with heartbeats. Soon, the friction between her thighs became unbearable. She was hurdling toward something elusive, something frightening and brilliant and unimaginable. A desperate chant 'more, more, more' pulsed in her ears. His? Hers?

Mindless, lost, guided by pure instinct, *Verochka* grinded her pelvis against JJ's, seeking, straining. She tensed her whole body as if preparing for a leap.

"Let go, Little Swan. Let go and fly."

An anguished whisper. A helpless plea.

And she let go of everything, and flew into the eruption of a brilliant blinding light...

CHAPTER FORTY-EIGHT

Fate was a bitch, headstrong and unpredictable and fickle. JJ raked one hand through his hair, stifled a curse, and turned to the small round window of the plane. White and dense, the clouds behind it looked somehow ominous. Probably, just a reflection of his current mood. Cold foreboding churned inside him, turning his guts to ice. He tore his gaze away from those eerie clouds.

Who could've predicted, that a few hours after he made love to *Verochka*, he'd fly to the other end of the world on such a sad business as death? Dammit.

He should have been in SoHo, with *Verochka*, should have insisted on finishing their last conversation that left him uneasy, and yes, angry. Something was off with her this morning, something he couldn't put his finger on. He never panicked before. JJ prided himself on keeping a cool head at any given circumstances.

Crises were better handled with a firm hand and steely authority. And yes, a cool head. But all his self-control shattered like a broken glass when he faced her this morning. Aloof and detached, *Verochka* suddenly seemed so far away, he was afraid he'd never reach her again. Which was plain silly, since she was standing a couple of feet away. Facing her—so close, but so distant—his fear intensified tenfold. She refused to talk about it, insisted that everything was fine, that she was just worried of being late for her morning class. He was never accused of being a coward, but that morning he surely

acted like one. As much as it galled him, JJ admitted he was afraid.
So, shaky and panicky, he stepped back, and instead of pressing her
further, he drove her to school, and then sped away leaving her alone.

His cowardice left a bad taste in his mouth. Feeling helpless and
unsure was a totally new experience for him. He hated it.

Someone once said that love makes a person vulnerable. Well,
JJ can attest to that. He cursed. Only *Verochka* could evoke such
strong, conflicting emotions from him. Only she could make him
feel mightier than God one moment, and lower than dirt the next.
Maybe it was for the best that he'd be away from her for a while.
Getting to the bottom of their last disagreement could wait.

Tomorrow was her big day, a tryout she had waited a long time
for, and that might well determine her future. The last thing he
wanted was to make her nervous before her important performance.
To spoil the day for her was inexcusable. Unforgivable. He really
hoped she was chosen by the distinguished panel of The Royal Ballet
to be their next Odette. No one deserved it more.

He wished with all his heart for her dream to become a reality.
Verochka worked so hard for it. Her single-minded determination to
reach that goal was admirable. Heck, she even relocated from France
to the States at the tender age of eighteen to be able to reach her
dream.

She was brilliant. She was born to dance. Her place was on stage.

But also with him. They belonged together. There was no doubt
about it.

Until *Verochka*, he had no idea now lonely he was, or how empty.
She filled his life with joy and happiness and purpose. She healed
him.

Completed him.

She made him alive.

She made him whole.

Even before last night, JJ couldn't imagine his life without her. Now, the mere thought of being away from her for even a day was unbearable. He craved her more than his next breath. Like a potent drug, she entered his system, and infected him for good. Yet she was his antidote, his cure, his salvation. The need to be with her, to see her, was overwhelming. JJ planned to see her later, and take her to the bar. He hoped that the friendly atmosphere, and the company of Winston, relaxed her. Maybe then she'd shed the persona of an aloof and reserved stranger she presented him that morning. But fate intervened.

Nothing could make JJ leave in a hurry without seeing *Verochka* except the death of his beloved grandmother.

As soon as he learned about it, he phoned the ballet school, but was forced to leave a message. JJ hoped that whoever took his urgent call forwarded it to *Verochka* soon. Damn, he wished he was able to do it in person instead of relying on a messenger. Or at least speak to the Old Dragon, Madame Valeska. But he was told that Madame was teaching a class. Obviously, no one was brave—or foolish—enough to interrupt it.

JJ heaved a deep sigh, impatiently tugged on the necktie that seemed to cut the flow of air to his lungs. Tired to the marrow, he let his head drop on the headrest, and closed his eyes.

As if on cue, his memory conjured the image of his grandmother.

Fiercely independent, Maureen O'Rourke Morris was tiny, slender, and heartbreakingly fragile. But her unbending will and sheer stubbornness belied her size. In that regard, she reminded him of *Verochka*. Come to think of it, they both was so much alike. Both lived their lives on their own terms; both strong and independent and free-spirited. His admiration and love for them knew no bounds, even though they made his life quite difficult at times.

Maureen wanted to live her last years on the land of her ancestors. So, despite all his protests and concerns, she moved to

Cobh, a small but spectacular seaport town in the heart of County Cork. JJ visited her there, but less often that he liked. He was always busy, always involved in some business dealing that demanded his undivided attention 24/7.

Bastard.

Guilt ate at him like acid. He should've spent more time with his grandmother. She was the second person beside his father who loved him unconditionally.

She was the one who always called him *laddie.*

Sadness crept upward, coating his insides like a heavy fog.

Her death was unexpected, even though Maureen was pushing ninety.

Spry and feisty, with her unruly curls died in unimaginable fiery red, his whirlpool of a grandmother seemed energetic and ageless. But then nature took its toll.

Yesterday, she simply didn't wake up. She slipped from this world to another in her sleep, peaceful, as her long-time housekeeper told JJ.

He should be grateful that Maureen hadn't suffered, that her passing was quiet and painless. But dammit, he was not ready to let her go!

He failed to tell her about *Verochka.* And now it was too late.

A muted conversation somewhere behind him drew JJ out of his reverie. He turned his head. The team of lawyers traveling with him, all dressed in conservative dark suites, were conversing in hushed voices. He supposed he was overreacting, taking five company attorneys with him. But he needed all the help he could get to settle Maureen's estate. As soon as humanly possible.

The local Irish bureaucracy was notorious for its slow, unhurried pace. JJ had no time nor inclination to dance a jig to the government's piper. He needed to return to New York in two or three days. Four at the most. But deep in his gut he knew that he'd be lucky if he was back in a week, if that.

Damnation.

As the Captain announced the delay in arrival due to bad weather, his irritation doubled.

Great. Just my rotten luck.

A distinctive and painfully familiar voice, murmured in his ear.

Don't despair, laddie. A man's mind plans, but the Lord directs.

Startled, JJ jerked his head, looked around, like he was expecting to see his grandmother seated next to him.

Damn, now he was hearing voices. The compliments of his stress? Probably.

And why am I so surprised?

The winter ball last evening, seeing Celeste, confrontation with Madeline.

And don't forget the meeting with that strange woman, Margaret Norris, and Verochka's *fainting.*

Then last night...and this morning. Everything seemed to pile up, one nerve-racking layer over another. The shocking news of his grandmother passing just capped it all.

Face it, man, you are strung out. And exhausted.

He rubbed the back of his neck. His muscles there were hard as pebbles.

Maureen entrusted JJ with her estate by naming him the executor of her will. He could *not* betray her trust. Even if it meant to leave New York in a lurch. Leaving *Verochka.* He was sure she'd understand. When he saw her next, he'd explain everything. Tell her about Maureen, and his most cherished childhood memories of many Christmases he spent with his grandmother, in her house in West Virginia. The small tug at his heart was bittersweet. Despite everything, JJ smiled. Such happy memories. Snowcapped mountains, chilly morning air, hot chocolate by the fireplace...

When they married, *Verochka* and he must travel to West Virginia. She'd love it there.

JJ glanced out the window and blinked in surprise. There, down below the puffy clouds, Ireland slowly unfurled her emerald glory.

Almost there. Thank God.

Pacified by the sight, he closed his eyes. Just for a few moments. The comfortable monotone of the plane's engine lulled his senses. Suspended between the memories and reality, JJ started to drift.

CHAPTER FORTY-NINE

He woke, *half-drunk on bliss, and reached for* Verochka. *But her side of the bed was empty. The sheets smelled of her and of their lovemaking. Intoxicating, potent, that fragrance shot through the fog in his brain, sharpening all his senses. His limbs were loose and languid, but his body was energized, and buzzing. The memories of last night swam in his mind. Delighted, JJ smiled, then winced, as one particular part of his anatomy twitched.*

Damn, insatiable little monster.

He grinned. With his body fully engaged in performance mode, JJ scanned the room, looking for Verochka.

Where was she?

The silence seemed unnatural, almost eerie. Damn, what time was it? He squinted, cast a quick glance at the bedside clock, and yelped in surprise.

My goodness, five-thirty!

Verochka *was due to her class at six. He promised her not to be late, but obviously he overslept. Why didn't she wake him? And where on earth was she?*

He strained his ears for any sound. Nothing. Alarmed, he sat on the side of the bed.

Had she left while he was sleeping? And how would she get to school? She was unfamiliar with this part of town, and dressed to kill in her Chanel dress, furs, and pearls on top of it. A woman walking alone at this hour was asking for trouble. It was dangerous even in this safe and posh neighborhood.

Dammit.

JJ jumped from the bed, unconcerned with his nakedness, then ran out of the bedroom. He checked each room to no avail. Was she in the kitchen? He sprinted forward, and skidded to an abrupt stop.

Dressed into her long evening gown, holding her shoes and mantel in hands, Verochka was trying to open the door.

The breath he was holding left his lungs with a noisy whoosh.

"Where do you think you're going?" JJ didn't mean to sound so harsh, but his confusion amplified by fear left him unsteady. And angry. She was clearly planning to sneak out.

Verochka *yelped, jumped, and turned to face him.*

"Mon Dieu, you startled me." She zoomed her eyes to his body, and quickly averted her gaze. A flush of scarlet colored her cheeks. "And you are nude."

Her sudden bashfulness irritated the hell out of him. "You've seen all of this already."

"Yes, but..." She lifted her eyes. "I suppose it doesn't matter."

Something close to a regret in her hooded violet eyes knotted his gut.

"I repeat, where are you going?"

She quickly regained her composure. Clearing her throat, Verochka *shrugged.*

"To the school, of course."

"Were you planning to walk all the way?"

"And why not? It's not very far."

*"*Verochka, *it's five thirty in the bloody morning, and you're dressed in an evening gown, and wearing close to a million dollars jewelry on you. Not to mention, that sable mantel."*

*With a quick look at herself, she cursed. "*Merde.*"*

"You can say that again." He aimed for patience, but it cost him. "Okay, give me five minutes. I'll drive you."

"Oh, you don't have to."

Something in the tone of her voice, and in her body language made JJ's antennae twitch. Was it his imagination, or Verochka acting strange?

He looked closer at her face. Coolly reserved, totally expressionless, she gazed back at him like he was a complete stranger. Even though a few feet separated them, it seems like that distance became an abyss.

Unmoving, unnaturally still, Verochka seemed to be surrounded by an invisible wall. Almost tangible, it stood between them like an impenetrable barrier.

A sick feeling of dread gathered in the pit of JJ's stomach.

Who was this detached and aloof stranger?

Cool and composed, Verochka held his gaze. JJ almost didn't recognize her.

Where was the woman who burst into flames in his arms? Where was his Little Swan? Shocked, panicking, JJ swallowed around the rock lodged in his throat.

He took a tentative step forward. "Verochka—"

She interrupted him. "We'll be late for my class."

Even her voice was vacant and oddly even. Her empty stare made his skin crawl.

Fueled by fear, JJ's temper erupted. "The hell with your class! Just tell me what's wrong."

"I don't know what you mean."

Her signature Gaelic shrug he adored so much, now irritated him to no end.

"Don't give me that, lady. Last night you shared my bed, and if I'm not mistaken, you enjoyed it. And a few hours later, you're acting like nothing happened, and expect me to believe that everything is fine?"

"Believe what you want." Another little shrug set his teeth on edge. "Last night was a—"

"If you say that it was a mistake, I'll call you a liar."

Verochka *sucked in her breath, bit her lower lip.*

Thank God, the first glimpse of emotion.

But his relief was short lived. Smoothing her features into a neutral impersonal mask, Verochka *recovered her composure.*

"*I was going to say, it was...very intense. For me. I need some time to think about it. I need some space. I hope you understand.*"

JJ couldn't believe what he was hearing. Intense? For her? *What about him?*

"*Think about it! What's there is to think about? We became lovers. Soon we'll be married. Period. The end.*"

A familiar stubborn frown puckered her forehead. "*I didn't agree to marry you.*"

"*You're wearing my ring.*"

"*It was just a loan.*"

"*The hell it was! I bought it for you as an engagement ring!*"

"*I didn't know! You put it on my left hand, not the right, so I thought—*"

"*News flash, Little Swan. In the US of A, we wear engagement rings—and wedding bands—on the left hand, not right.*" *Was it perverse of him to feel such an enormous satisfaction at her discomfort? Probably. He didn't care.* "*You are not in Europe anymore,* ma petite.*"

Her small hands curled into two fists, her slender body quivered like a drawn bow.

Not so aloof, or detached. Or composed. She was all but bursting from within, poised for a fight. Well, then, he'd be more than happy to oblige.

"*You should've told me!*" *Dry-eyed, clearly enraged, she rounded on him.*

"*Probably.*" *JJ crossed his arms over his chest, faking negligence.* "*Here, take it back.*"

She dropped everything she was holding, then attacked her left hand, trying to yank the ring from her finger. As fate would have it, the ring refused to slide off.

"Merde!" A string of cursing that flew out of her mouth would make a seasoned pirate cheer in appreciation. "I will take it off later, and give it back to you."

Unbelievably hurt, JJ took a deliberate step back. A dull ache spread over his sternum with lightning speed. He barely restrained himself from rubbing his chest.

"I won't take it. It's yours, whether you marry me or not."

Another thought that knifed through his anger made him shaky.

"You might be pregnant."

She stared at him, opened her mouth, then shut it into a thin stubborn line.

"I am not."

"How could you know that?"

"I just do! I couldn't...just from one time...Impossibless!"

"Nothing is impossible, Verochka."

Wearily, he raked his right hand through his hair. Dammit, and what if she really was pregnant? How did he feel about it? Happy? Pleased? Scared?

He really didn't know. Later. He'd think about it later. When he was less agitated or hurt. Now, he must decide what to do next. Standing stark naked in the middle of the hallway, and arguing with her accomplished nothing. As much as he wanted to press her further, he knew it was futile. She won't listen to reason, and he was too upset to act or speak rationally.

Step back, reevaluate, and then proceed.

Resigned, JJ drew a deep breath. Maybe she was right. A little space was exactly what they both needed.

"You are going to be late. I'll drive you to school." Turning away, he hotfooted it to his bedroom, then quickly dressed.

They drove in total silence. Ten minutes later, he stopped the car at the grey building. Without waiting for him, she wrenched the passenger's door open, and jumped onto the curb. Hiking her long skirt with both hands, she ran pell-mell toward the doors.

"Verochka?"

She stopped, looked at him over her shoulder. Her drawn face was whiter than snow, colder than ice. His heart gave a tiny ping of regret. He'd give everything at that moment to have the old Verochka back. Stubborn, feisty, fearless.

Was it his fault that she turned into this reserved, frozen stranger?

Did he do something wrong? Did he scare her? He should've been gentler, gone slower. He should have kept a firmer leash on his emotions, his passion.

But dammit, he was just a man.

Yesterday, he lost the grip, and now he must pay a price. But he'd be damned if he lost her. That was unthinkable. Unacceptable.

"This is far from over. I'll be back later, and by God, we will finish our conversation."

The silence hung between them like an impenetrable fog. Dense. Oppressive.

She hesitated, then as if coming to a decision, Verochka nodded.

"Yes. We will finish it."

She sprinted forward, tugged the heavy door handle, and disappeared from view. JJ clutched his cashmere coat closer as he shivered. But not from cold.

Verochka's last words echoed inside of his head with an ominous finality.

CHAPTER FIFTY

The morning of her lifechanging tryout finally arrived. Today was her opportunity for the future she wanted by dancing before the panel of The London Royal Ballet. She should be energized, humming with excitement, and nerves. Instead, *Verochka* felt sick, indifferent, deflated.

And sad. Unbelievably sad. And lost. And tired to the marrow.

The mere thought of putting her costume on, and painting her face with stage make-up was unbearable. The last thing she wanted right now was to dance.

Not today, or tomorrow, or ever.

That realization scared her more than anything.

Absurde!

She was born to dance! Ballet was in her blood. It was her vocation, her dream, her everything.

Cursing, *Verochka* jumped from the narrow cot where she lounged for the past hour. Queasy, she fell back, as her head began to swim in circles.

Merde.

Belatedly, she remembered that she hadn't eaten anything since yesterday. But the mere thought of food made her gag.

And how will you manage to exercise the pirouettes and jete lightheaded?

Okay, maybe, some yogurt? Or an apple? She contemplated on it, but disregarded both choices. No, she couldn't swallow anything right now. Not even yogurt. A shower was sure to make her feel better. Gingerly, she rose from the cot.

Steady, thank God. Her knees were a bit wobbly, but her head stopped swirling. Good. She striped off her clothes then dumped them on the floor.

Naked, she padded to the bathroom. Was it her imagination, or the miniscule space seemed somehow shabbier? Had she ever noticed the rust on the tiny porcelain sink, or the speck of mold in the corner of the wall? Or how shabby her shower curtain was? In contrast to JJ's bathroom, hers was plain, pitiful, and ugly.

Never before was she embarrassed about her modest accommodations. Until today.

No, she will not compare her bathroom—or her lifestyle—with JJ's.

She will not wish for the impossible. She should be grateful to have this cozy room, and this tiny bathroom, and the roof over her head. It was hers, and hers alone. It was enough.

Verochka shivered as she stepped under the thin trickle of lukewarm water, but forced herself to stay still. So, what if it was almost cold? She endured more hardship than that. She was made of sterner stuff. *Verochka* Osipoff was not a sissy.

Why, then did she have to remind herself of that? Or of the wisdom of modesty and humility?

Get real, you silly goose. Stop dreaming, and wishing for the impossible.

She'd never live in JJ's condo, or sleep in his bed, or luxuriating in that mind-boggling bathroom. She will never be with JJ. Period.

Maybe, it was a mistake going to his place yesterday or making love with him, but there were no regrets. Not a single one. Not the initial physical pain, or the heartache that became her constant companion.

But what if JJ was right, and she was pregnant?

She looked down at herself, placed a palm over her flat taught stomach.

Mon Dieu, was a tiny life unfurling inside of her? Was it even possible?

The implication was shocking. What will happen with her career? The London Royal Ballet was out of the question for sure. She supposed, she could dance for a few months, hiding her condition, but after that?

And was it a danger to the baby?

Her daily training classes were vigorous, almost brutal. Endurance was the key. And what if she fell, and hurt the baby? Her hands moved by their own volition, protectively covering her belly.

She can't. She won't. If she was really pregnant, her baby—JJ's baby—must be her main and only concern.

And how will you care for the baby? How will you raise it? Where? In this tiny attic room?

Fear and confusion clouded her mind. After a moment, *Verochka* removed her hands from her middle. It was quite pointless to fret about it now. If her pregnancy became a reality, she'd face it. Alone. She refused to drag JJ into it. She vowed not to disturb his life. If she was pregnant, the baby was hers. Only hers.

To blame JJ was unfair, and dishonest, and simply wrong.

She willingly agreed to go to his penthouse. More, she was the one to initiate the kiss that spiraled out of its trajectory. She deliberately and without an ounce of embarrassment, dropped the robe from her body. Naked, brazen, she practically invited him to make love to her.

Invited? You demanded it, you little slut!

Blushing from recollection, she shut her eyes, calling herself a thousand bad names. What possessed her to act in such a wanton manner?

You must be ashamed of yourself.

But she wasn't. If anything, she wished to do it all over again. Craved it.

Merde.

Forget about it. Forget about everything. It will never happen again.

But how to forget?

You must. If you love him, you will.

Her misery and longing waged a war against her resolve and common sense.

JJ deserved better than her. He deserved a woman who will be his equal. More educated, more sophisticated, more beautiful. And certainly, richer.

He was Reginald Morris, a wealthy man from a prominent family.

She was a poor orphaned girl from Paris, who lived in an attic, and slept on a borrowed cot. Yes, she loved him. More than life itself. But was it enough? Enough to breach that social abyss between them?

Enough for his peers to accept her?

Enough for him to be happy?

She knew the answers to all those questions. She knew what she must do.

So, as soon as she next saw JJ, she'd break up with him. For good. Forever.

Shutting her eyes, *Verochka* concentrated on her breathing. Her heart wept, her emotions churned, but her mind was set. She'd do anything for him, for his happiness and wellbeing. Even lie that she doesn't love him.

A sob burst from her throat.

Mon Dieu, *how will I do that?!*

How could she not?

The water became completely cold, sluicing down her chilled body, meshing with her tears. She shut the faucet off, then stepped onto the tiled floor. Wet, her bare foot slid precariously, and the momentum carried her forward. With a yelp, she clutched the sink with both hands to break her fall. *Merde.* A twisted ankle was all she needed for a full measure of misery. Quickly, she toweled off, and gingerly tiptoed out of the tiny enclosure. As soon as she stepped into her room, her gaze collided with the roses that filled every nook and cranny of her meager space.

They seemed to riot everywhere, saturating her room with potent fragrance. Unable to help herself, *Verochka* inhaled a lungful of sweet aroma. True to his word, JJ continued to send her a fresh bouquet every day, even though he himself failed to make an appearance since yesterday. It bothered her. Was he mad at her? The last time she saw him, he was clearly upset. Was he breaking up with her?

But what if something happened to him? Maybe he was sick, or hurt, or...

One horrible scenario after another bombarded her. She must find out the truth. But how? *Winston!* But of course! He will know. Why didn't she think of that before? She must go see him. Immediately!

What about your tryout? Have you forgotten about that?

Shaking from impatience, *Verochka* cursed under her breath.

No, as much as she wanted, she couldn't go to the bar now. Okay, later.

She'd sneak out after her performance. She looked at the roses, trailed her fingers over the soft pink petals. Soon, the deliveries of flowers will cease, and the enchanting fairy tale she so unwisely believed in will come to an abrupt end. There won't be a happy-ever-after. Unlike Odette, *Verochka* will not turn into a beautiful princess at the end, but remain an ugly duckling for the rest of her days. Lonely. Lost.

Miserable.

And maybe pregnant.

With an effort, she shook off her dread. She made up her mind to deal with whatever happens after tonight. She'd survive. But right now, she must forget everything—her broken heart, her sorrow, her fear—and dance. If not for herself, then for Madame Valeska. *Verochka* owed so much to her. She'd be damned to embarrass her mentor in front of the distinguished panel of judges.

Get a grip, Little Swan. Dress up, make yourself presentable, and go downstairs.

In a couple of hours, the concert hall will be filled with people who flew half way around the world to watch her perform. She needed to pull herself together.

But *Dieu*, how she wished to curl into a ball on her bed, draw the cowers over her head, and just be left alone! Later. She'd grieve later. She'll allow herself the luxury of tears and sorrow. Snapping her spine, and straightening her shoulders, *Verochka* lifted her head high. Now she must go and show everybody what the little orphan girl from Paris was capable of. She must dance her little heart out as if it were the last time. And so she will.

Verochka shimmied into her training tights, pulled the t-shirt over her head, and picked up her pointe shoes. With herculean effort, she pushed all her conflicting emotions to the far corner of her mind, and put an imaginary lid on it.

She drew in a few deep breaths and struggled to bring herself under control.

Her father's comforting voice murmured in her ears.

In, and out. Repeat. You can do it, ma petite princesse. *Again, in and out. Good.*

A familiar before performance anticipation flowed into her veins, as a deep calmness settled over her body. Her breathing slowed, her emotions quieted.

In her mind, she was no longer *Verochka* Osipoff, but the swan princess Odette.

Regal and ethereal and proud.

She was ready.

A sharp knock on the door shattered her concentration. She tensed.

It wasn't JJ. Somehow, she knew that.

Who, then? Did Madame Valeska sent someone to fetch *Verochka*? Probably.

She tried to shake off her uneasiness. That must be it.

Another knock, more insistent this time. She shivered, as a sudden dread crept from her gut to her heart. *Verochka* eyed the closed door with trepidation.

Why was she so scared?

Why was she so reluctant to open the door?

CHAPTER FIFTY-ONE

A s soon as *Verochka* unlocked the latch, the door flew open, banging loudly against the wall. Her dread intensified, as she stared at the last person she expected to see. A cold fear grabbed her by the throat.

"What's wrong? Is it JJ? Something happened to him?"

"Well, hello to you too, Miss Osipoff."

Madeline Morris sauntered inside, her measuring gaze sweeping from *Verochka's* hair to her feet. Her red lips twisted in expression of acute distaste. "Nothing wrong with *Reginald*. Except..."

She scanned the room and narrowed her eyes to slits as she took in every detail. A disapproving frown etched onto her smooth forehead.

"Except?" *Verochka* prompted, clamping down her irritation. Something was wrong. Only one thing could make the Ice Queen Morris deign *Verochka* with her company. Or one person, JJ. Was he sick, or hurt? Is that why she was here? Frightened, she held her breath and watched the older woman.

"Please, Mrs. Morris, just tell me, is JJ well?"

"Physically, he's fine. But..."

An instantaneous relief swept through *Verochka*, leaving her shaky. "Oh, thank God!"

"But I'm afraid, his emotional state is quite... unstable."

Unstable? What is she talking about?

"What do you mean?"

"Let's be frank, Miss Osipoff," Madeline's expressionless voice belied her hard stare, "my son made a terrible mistake."

"And that mistake is...?"

"Why, you, my dear."

Bristling, *Verochka* drew to her full height. "*Moi?* Why is that?"

"Because you are simply wrong for him. You are too young, too immature, and I bet, impulsive. You're a ballerina, for crying out loud!" She pronounced *ballerina* like the word tasted foul on her tongue. "You are not fit to be a Morris. Reginald's infatuation with you is unfortunate and unwise." Madeline slid her gaze at *Verochka's* left hand where the pearl ring still adorned her finger. "It went too far. And it makes me concerned."

"In-infatuation?"

"But of course." Arching two dark brows, Madeline made a mocking *tsk-tsk* sound with her tongue. "You can't seriously think that he's in love with you, can you now?"

With just a few words she managed to taint something beautiful and pure, and turn it into a shameful farce.

Condescending bitch.

Seething, *Verochka* glared at Madeline. "And why can't he be in love with me?"

"Because you're a nobody. A little dancer from France, a penniless orphan trying to crawl up from the pit of poverty. I can understand your intention, Miss Osipoff, even applaud your optimism, but not if it concerns my son." Her voice mirrored the expression of her face: hard, chilling, forbidding. "Let's get it clear, Reginald is off limits to you. He can indulge his baser needs—I can't stop him there—but that's all. Sex is all you're going to get out of him. And a few expensive trinkets." A negligent gesture toward her left hand. "You can keep this ring as a consolation prize, but your unfortunate association with my son must stop. Immediately. Or..."

she let the word hang for a few seconds, "...I will do everything in my power to bury you."

Faking nonchalance, *Verochka* crossed both arms over her chest and cocked her head.

"A threat, Mrs. Morris?"

"A promise, Miss Osipoff."

"Just out of curiosity, what will you do? Hire some unsavory character to kill me?"

"Why, no, my dear. I don't need to hire anyone. If I wanted to get rid of you, I'll do it myself." A curve of her blood red lips was cruel. Evil.

At that moment, *Verochka* had no doubt that Madeline was capable of violence.

It shone through her dark soulless eyes. Under all that sparkling and civilized exterior, Madeline Morris was cold-blooded and vicious. And she hated *Verochka*.

An involuntary shiver slithered through her body. Goose bumps the size of pebbles covered her skin. Try as she might, she couldn't hide her body's response. Madeline noticed, lifted the corners of her lips in a parody of a smile.

"But I trust you are a smart girl, Miss Osipoff, so I'm sure we won't need any drastic measures."

"I might be pregnant."

For the life of her, *Verochka* didn't know what prompted her to blurt it out.

To shock the woman? Impossible. Ice sculptures can't be shocked.

To soften her heart? A futile attempt. The woman was without a heart.

Chilled to the marrow, *Verochka* struggled to keep her gaze straight on the woman face.

So beautiful, and so ugly.

Pursing her lips, Madeline seemed to process the information for a few seconds.

"Oh? How unfortunate for you." Not an ounce of warmth flickered in those bleak dark eyes. She shrugged, dismissing the problem. "Well, I'm prepared to pay you quite handsomely for *any* inconvenience."

With that, she dipped her fingers into her purse, and drew out an envelope.

"You're calling it an...an inconvenience? Your own grandchild?" *Unbelievable!*

"What else? And make no mistake, my dear, if you *are* pregnant, it'll make your baby a bastard—not my grandchild. And definitely, not Reginald's child."

Verochka saw red. "It's not for you to decide!"

"But it is, Miss Osipoff. It surely is. And if you won't accept this money, and get the hell away," her voice became menacing, "then think about this. I can and will make Reginald's life a pure hell. I can and will force the board of directors to fire him from his position of the CEO of Morris Holding. He'll turned into a pariah, an outcast. And all because of you."

"But he is your son!"

"Then he had better remember it, and act accordingly. But," a shrewd glance at *Verochka,* "I hope you and I can spare him from that unfortunate fate and humiliation."

Unable to believe what she was hearing, *Verochka* stared at the envelope in Madeline's outstretched hand like it was a deadly snake posed to bite.

"You... you want me to...accept the payment for leaving JJ?"

"Not only leaving, but staying away from him. Far, far away. Well, what are you waiting for?" The first notes of irritation crept into Madeline's voice. "Take it."

Verochka switched her gaze from the envelope to the woman's face.

Was it some kind of a joke?

"Just out of curiosity, how much are you prepared to pay me for that?"

"Ah, finally a voice of reason." Impatiently, Madeline thrust the envelope into *Verochka's* hands, and waited for her to open it.

The numbers on the check made her eyes pop. Stunned, she let out a low whistle.

"Fifty thousand? Is that what your son's freedom is worth? How generous of you." Sour bile rose to her throat, as sarcasm dripped from every syllable like a poison.

Madeline frowned, then shut her purse with a loud clack that reverberated through *Verochka's* skull.

"Not enough? Fine. I'll pay you more. Say, another fifty thousand. You'll never earn that kind of money, even if you dance every day for the rest of your life." Dropping her voice to a conspiratorial whisper, Madeline skewered *Verochka* with her glinting eyes. "I can even help you to disappear. England? France? Italy? Name any county. With this kind of money, you'll be set for life. And if you're pregnant, I know a doctor who'll be able to help you."

Leaning forward, Madeline clamped her cold fingers around *Verochka's* wrist.

Revolted, she recoiled, and sharply pulled her arm away. Her skin burned as if scorched, her mind reeled.

A doctor?

Nauseated, *Verochka* gazed at the older woman. "What are you talking about?"

"An abortion, of course, you silly girl."

Mon Dieu!

Was there any limit for the woman's cruelty? Disgusted, *Verochka* watched Madeline in mute horror.

"Well?"

"Well... what?"

"Do we understand each other?"

She'd wonder later where the calmness came from. Numb all over, *Verochka* slowly nodded. "I'm not sure about you, but I do understand you just fine."

With steady hands, she ripped the check into tiny pieces, and threw them at Madeline's face like confetti.

"You're a horrible woman, Mrs. Morris, and a poor excuse for a mother. I don't need your money. I wouldn't take a penny from you even if I was destitute and dying from hunger. Even for the sake of JJ's baby I might carry. I hate to put your mind to rest, but the truth is, I was going to break up with your son. Not because of you, or your threads, but because of him."

Tears of sorrow pressed against her eyes, but her indignation kept them from spilling out.

"I love JJ too much to bring even a shadow of misery to his life. I might be nobody to you, but I have more loyalty and pride in my little pinky than all your rich socialites combined. I love your son, Mrs. Morris. Not his money, or his position, but him. A concept, I'm sure, that is totally alien to you."

One of the pointe shoes tucked under her armpit dropped to the floor. On autopilot, *Verochka* bent to pick it up. "And now, I must go downstairs and dance at a tryout. I trust you'll find your way out."

Already at the threshold, she pivoted, and glanced at the older woman. Distorted and ugly, her face was aglow with murderous rage. But instead of fear, all it evoked in *Verochka* was pity, and a deep regret.

"I hope I'm not pregnant, Mrs. Morris. The thought that any child of mine might carry your genes is simply revolting."

A low sound rippled in Madeline's throat. Almost a growl, it burst free, loud and menacing. "Why, you little slut! You'll be sorry!"

Ignoring the insult, *Verochka* clutched her pointe shoes in both hands, and hurried toward the staircase landing. The concrete steps were steep and precipitous. Used to navigating the staircase for the past two years, *Verochka* paid no attention as she put her foot down the first step. Her brain took only a split second to register a rustling of clothes, before a strong shove at her back propelled her forward. Her pointe shoes flew out of her hands, bounced down the steps with a hollow sound. Flailing, her arms fluttered like two wings in a desperate attend to find any purchase.

But there was none.

In a rolling, ungraceful mass, *Verochka* hurtled down the endless stairs, as the sickening *cracks* of breaking bones echoed in her ears.

A metallic taste of blood filled her mouth. An excruciating pain barreled down with the speed of a lightning, as wave after wave of blinding agony assaulted her body. An explosion of light burst behind her closed eyelids like brilliant firework. As her head struck something hard and unyielding, *Verochka's* vision dimmed to a narrow tunnel. And suddenly, all movement stopped.

The following silence hurt her ears more than any blasting noise. A symphony of pain reached its crescendo. Unable to move, half-conscious, *Verochka* lay still, as something dense and pointy prodded her in the ribs. A stick? No, a shoe.

With a herculean effort, she dragged her eyes open. The familiar face hovering above met her gaze.

So beautiful, so ugly...

Madeline sneered at her.

"Neither pregnancy nor my son need ever concern you again."

Then she straightened, and unhurriedly strolled away.

She left me...to die...

Hurting all over, *Verochka* opened her mouth to call for help, but her vocal cords refused to function. She felt like a million glass shards were stuck in her throat and making breathing unbearable.

Pain... so much pain...

Her eyes fluttered closed. She began to float. Barely conscious, *Verochka* held on to the last shreds of her willpower, struggling to stay awake.

I don't want to die...I can't...

The darkness descended, mercifully dragging her under its protective folds.

No! Someone will find me... Someone will help... Please, God...

But deep in her heart, she knew that the battle was lost.

No one will find her in time. She was dying. Alone. Broken. Lost.

Her last thought was about JJ.

I will never see him again...

CHAPTER FIFTY-TWO

JJ woke with a start. He bolted upright, like he was poked in the ribs with a hot rod.

Still in the grips of his nightmare, he quickly switched the nightstand lamp on. What was it that woke him? Something vague, and elusive, and scary as hell.

For the life of him, he couldn't remember. The blurry dark images twirled in his hazy brain, like a macabre kaleidoscope. *Menacing.* He ran both hands through his hair. Cold sweat trickled down his spine. Shivering, he scanned the room.

Where am I?

Disoriented, he gazed at the unfamiliar surroundings. As the realization slowly seeped through, he let out a breath with a loud *whoosh.*

Hotel. Of course.

He totally forgot checking into Crosshaven House. Recently restored to its former glory, the beautiful five-star hotel boasted the luxury worthy of royals. But the spectacular accommodations were lost on JJ. The panoramic view from his window overlooking the harbor, the meticulously renovated antic fourposter, the priceless oriental rugs—nothing seem inviting, or pleasing the eye.

Had he become too jaded? Too accustomed to luxury?

More than likely, the events of the previous couple of days soured his disposition. He was still stressed, and tensed, and worrying about *Verochka*.

Did she receive his message? He hoped she did. How did her tryout go?

Dammit, he wished he was there, with her, celebrating her success.

But fate decided differently.

Cursing under his breath, JJ swung his legs over the side of the huge bed. Cold sticky sweat covered his back like a layer of artificial skin. His heart was about to drum its way out of his sternum. Dammit, what was it? Like a snake, the images from his dream slithered through his foggy brain, malicious, chilling.

He squinted at the wall clock. Four thirty. Oh well. Admitting that sleep was out of the question, he dragged himself to the bathroom. He needed a shower, and coffee.

And maybe an early morning walk to clear my head, and forget all about the crazy woman from yesterday, and her prophesy.

He stared at himself in a bathroom mirror, as the memories of last evening slowly unfolded before his eyes...

After his grandmother's funeral, JJ craved solitude. He couldn't bear to hear another word of condolences. Maureen's service drew a huge crowd. He wasn't surprised to see so many grieving people. Everybody loved his grandmother, and wished to share with him how much she touched their lives.

JJ endured it as long as he was capable of. Overwhelmed, he made his escape before his own grief had a chance to flatten him. He drove away and cruised the city for hours without any destination in mind. Finding himself near the historic center of Cobh, he decided to stroll around the city. Typical for November in Ireland, the weather was clear and cold, with a brisk wind ruffling the waters in the harbor. JJ loved the old part of the downtown, knew his way around it even at night.

Exiting his rental car, he locked it, and slowly walked down the cobblestone street.

In the middle of the short business strip, a small sign above the bar caught his attention. The Swan. Such an unusual name for a traditional Irish pub. Immediately, his thoughts turned to Verochka, his own Little Swan. What was she doing? Was she missing him? Was she okay?

Curiosity prompted him to open the weathered green door, and step inside.

The atmosphere was just what he expected: noisy, busy, and full of typical Irish flair. In the middle of the little dim room, the six wooden tables were crammed close together. Sitting around with the pints of Guinness' in hands, the patrons seemed to have a jolly good time. Their ages varied from near legal to ancient.

All of them were tapping their feet to the accompaniment of the live band tucked in the corner. Instantly swept into the lively music, JJ barely caught himself from tapping his own feet. He grinned. Was it him, or was the Irish jig really so infections? After his eyes adjusted to the dimness, he walked up to the bar. Frankly, he didn't want a drink, but common curtesy prevailed. If he was spending time in a drinking establishment, he better order some adult beverage, whether he planned to consume it or not.

The ruddy-faced bartender of indeterminate age took his order, as his shrewd icy blue eyes scanned JJ. "An American, are ye?"

"Guilty."

"What brought you to our fair town, laddie? A pleasure or a business?"

"I wish I could say pleasure."

The bartender nodded. "A business then. Well, as I see it, you could do both."

"I guess I can. The name is JJ Morris."

"Sean McGregor, the owner of this pub. I am pleased to meet ye."

"*Likewise, Mr. McGregor.*"

"*Sean, please. Everybody calls me Sean. Mr. McGregor was my old man.*"

"*Sean, then.*" *JJ reached out, shook the offered hand.*

"*A sad business, is it?*" *Sean said after another brief glance at him.* "*I can see it in your eyes.*"

JJ arranged his mouth in a little smile. "*As sad as it gets. My grandmother passed away.*"

"*God rest your granny's soul.*" *Real empathy softened his eyes. Then Sean squinted at JJ.* "*So, that makes you part Irish, is it?*"

"*A quarter only, I'm afraid.*"

"*Buh! Who cares about arithmetic, son? An Irish blood is thick and true, even if a dollop.*"

JJ smiled. "*Couldn't agree more. I always felt... right here.*"

"*And no wonder. The land of your ancestors holds a special place in your heart. It's magic, if you ask me. Well, then, laddie, let old Sean build you a pint of the best Guinness you can ever taste.*"

With the flair of a true virtuoso, the bartender got to the task of building the drink only an uninformed—or ignorant— called beer. Thick foam crowned the tall glass of dark liquid as Sean pushed it toward JJ.

"*Thanks. It looks amazing.*"

"*Tastes even better.*" *He winked, and lifted his own glass.* "*Slainte.*"

"*Slainte.*"

The drink was rich and potent, with the distinct aftertaste. Excellent.

JJ lifted his brow. "*I've never tasted a Guinness quite like this.*"

Clearly delighted, the older man nodded. "*Told you. Old Sean knows his business.*"

"*He sure does.*"

"*And what do you do in America, son, if you don't mind me asking?*"

"*Not at all. I own a bar.*" His omission of the other business enterprises was deliberate. For just this evening, JJ wished to be a modest bar owner, and nothing else.

"*You don't say?*"

"*I do.*"

"*Well, then, I'm sure glad you stepped into my pub tonight. Your drink is on the house, son.*" Lifting his glass in a salute, Sean clicked it against JJ's. "*Slainte.*"

"*Thank you. I hope one day I can return the favor.*"

"*Who knows, maybe you will.*"

"*Can I ask you a question, Sean?*"

"*Sure, go right ahead.*"

"*Why* The Swan? *The name seemed unusual for the traditional Irish pub.*"

Before replying, Sean sighed. "*Oh, that's a lovely story, son.*"

A sad little smile ghosted over his lips.

"*You see, my wife, God rest her soul, was an artist. No formal education my Maggie had, but a talent. Raw, and huge, like the cliffs of Mohr. Whenever she could, she'd grab her palette, paints, and pencils then draw for hours. I sometimes joked that she loves her painting more than me.* "

He chuckled, as a faraway expression swam into his face. "*She laughed it off, Maggie did, and tell me that painting was her blood, but I was her heart.*"

Clouded with memories, Sean's eyes became unfocused and misty. Embarrassed, like he witnessed something intimate, JJ averted his gaze. It took Sean a moment to shake off his pensive mood.

With another deep sigh, he focused back on JJ.

"*See here?*" He pointed at something behind JJ.

Turning his head, JJ did a double take, as his eyes found an oil painting of a white swan. Not big in size, maybe eighteen inches by twenty-four, it was spellbinding. Enchanting. Mesmerizing.

"That's my Maggie's work."

Magic shone from every stroke of the brush. The pure talent of the artist took JJ's breath away. But the biggest surprise came next, as he noticed the little golden crown perched atop of the bird's head.

Odette! Dear God, was it possible?

Stunned, he turned to Sean, but the question stuck in his throat. Unaware of his shock, Sean continued with the tale.

"One day, while Maggie was painting by the lake, she found a swan. Hurt it was, with a broken wing, and about half-starved to death. She brought the bird home, nursed it back to life. Claimed that the swan talked to her, Maggie did, and that she understood it. Now, I'm not sure if that was true, but they seemed inseparable. They would sit together for hours, happy and content. My Maggie said that the bird was enchanted, that she was a princess, no less." Sean cackled, rubbed his chin. "Sure, a bit on a fanciful side Maggie was, but I loved her, and pretended to believe it. When it was finally time to set the swan free, it all but broke my Maggie's heart. After that, she moped around the house, teary-eyed and sad. Tore my soul apart, she did. One day, I said to her, "Why don't you paint your swan princess?" And with that she did. Took her two months to finish it." He eyed the oil canvas, drew a broken breath. "Ain't it magnificent?"

"It's magical, and brilliant."

Sean nodded. "It surely is."

He filled another glass with a drink, pushed it toward JJ, even though the first one was still half full. When he spoke again, his voice sounded low and husky.

"After my Maggie passed, I hung the painting here, where I can see it every moment of the day. And I renamed the pub from McGregor's to The Swan."

Touched, moved, JJ simply nodded. "That is a beautiful story indeed."

They both fell into silence.

The commotion near the door cut into the moment, and just like that, the pensive mood was broken.

CHAPTER FIFTY-THREE

As Sean turned toward the direction of the noise, his weathered face illuminated with a dazzling smile. "Well, now, this is a grand surprise. Siobhan, darling! I'm sure please to see you."

The woman that hovered near the door, was tiny with the wisps of snow-white curls sticking out of her knitted hat. She reminded JJ of a leprechaun. Draped in a dark parka two sizes larger than her miniscule frame, the woman could be anywhere from eighteen to eighty.

What a peculiar creature.

She took a couple of steps toward the bar, the corners of her lips lifting in a sunny smile. It lit her face from within, transforming Siobhan's features to almost pretty.

"Siobhan, sweetheart, come and meet JJ Morris. He is visiting from America."

Out of the corner of his mouth, Sean muttered quietly to JJ, "Be kind to her, laddie. Siobhan here is... special."

"How so?"

"She is a seer."

"A what?" JJ took a split moment to digest this information, before the woman's steps faltered, and she gazed at him with something close to a shock on her face.

He was sure his own expression mirrored hers, as he stared into the bright and dazzling violet eyes.

Dear God!

The woman's smile slipped, then her mouth tightened into a thin disapproving line. No longer warm or welcoming, her face turned grim.

"You should not be here." Surprisingly strong and deep, Siobhan voice sent a ripple of goosebumps along his skin.

Not trusting his own voice, JJ just watched her in mute astonishment.

"Now, Siobhan—" A hesitant smile on Sean's face fell as she interrupted him in a grave voice.

"Trouble. Great trouble."

The woman's unblinking stare didn't waver from JJ's face. "Someone close to you. Someone you love. Pain, so much pain!" She shut her eyelids, moaned, as if suffering from agony. "Unbearable..."

Not a superstitious man, JJ admitted that Siobhan's theatrics spooked him. Cold all over, he tried to block his fear, but failed.

Damn the woman.

With an effort, JJ kept his eyes on Siobhan. No way was he getting her crazy mumbling get the better of him. Special, Sean said. "Be kind to her. She is a seer."

Yeah, sure, a seer, my boot.

Just a clever con artist, playing the tourists. Or plain crazy. Probably, both.

Siobhan opened her eyes, met his gaze square on. All the fine hair on JJ's body spiked to painful points. Deep purple, her smoldering gaze held him immobile.

"You should not be here. Go back. Return as fast as you can. There is a little time yet."

JJ failed to suppress a shiver.

More angry at himself than her, he was about to ask more time for what? *when she visibly shuddered, blinked, and once again, became an ageless harmless creature from the Irish folk tales. Totally ignoring him, Siobhan aimed her dazzling smile at the bartender, who stood frozen to the spot.*

"Sean, my dear friend, why don't you pour me your finest whiskey? The nigh is cold for these old bones."

As if coming out of a stupor, Sean jolted, and hurried to pick up a thick crystal glass from the shelve. "I will surely do that, my sweet. And what about a bowl of a hearty stew to go with it?"

"Oh, that'll be delightful!" Clapping her hands like a child who was promised a coveted cookie, Siobhan came closer, and hopped onto a barstool. Turning to JJ, she beamed a serene smile at him. "And who are you, handsome?"

He didn't remember how he left the pub, or when he got back to his hotel room.

He supposed, it was ridiculous to get so disturbed by the encounter with the strange woman, but here was nothing to be done about it.

Damn her.

Sure that sleep was out of the question in his current state, JJ remembered plopping onto the bed fully dressed, minus the loafers. Brooding, he tried to convince himself that Siobhan was just plain nuts, and her declaration about *trouble* and *pain* was nothing more than a cheap spectacle, or a fiction of her hazy mind.

No way was she anything but what she seemed on a surface: an odd little creature, half-pitiful, half-fanciful. A whack job if he'd ever seen one. But still.

JJ didn't remember falling asleep until a strange and terrifying dream he still struggled to recall, jerked him wide awake in the middle of the night.

He knew—felt—that something really bad happened back home.

JJ turned from the mirror, and hurried out of the bathroom. Shower can wait.

He must phone Winston immediately. Hell, everything can wait until he found out what was going on in New York. Cursing, JJ stuck his bare feet into the loafers. Why didn't he call yesterday? Dammit. Impatient to get downstairs to the lobby, he quickly calculated the time difference. Was it too late in New York? Too early?

The hell with it.

A muffled knock on the door stopped him dead. JJ slowly turned, and eyed the door with trepidation. Nothing good prompted a wake-up call at four in the bloody morning. Another knock, louder this time, knotted his gut in a tight fist. Something was definitely wrong. JJ walked to the door dreading the news he was about to receive. When he unlocked it, his heart stopped, then lurched upward.

The uniformed hotel employee met his gaze. "I apologize for disturbing your sleep, sir, but there was an urgent telex for you, with the instructions to deliver it immediately."

In his hand the porter held a folded piece of paper. With a slight nod, the older man offered it to him.

JJ eyed the outstretched hand like it was a live grenade about to detonate. His own hand shook badly as he finally forced himself to accept the telex.

Slowly, reluctantly, he unfolded the note, skimmed the printed words.

Verochka is injured. She is in ICU.
Malgorzata Valeska

His brain froze, unable to comprehend the message. Injured? ICU?

As if in stupor, JJ squinted at the signature line. He read it twice.

Malgorzata Valeska.

Had he known Madame's first name before? He didn't remember. Such an exotic name...Polish? Czech?

And what does it matter, you idiot?

Trembling, JJ read the message again. And again.

No. God, no! Please! Not Verochka*!*

A discreet coughing ripped him out of his shock. Lifting his head, JJ blinked at the uniformed man standing by the threshold. With an expression of polite attentiveness on his face, he watched JJ, obviously waiting for his instruction.

What are you waiting for? Do something!

Prompted by his screaming mind, JJ shook himself off. No time for panic. No time for second-guessing. No time.

Pain, so much pain…Someone you love…You must return…

In the distance, he heard the voice he barely recognized it as his own. "I must phone the States. Right now."

"Certainly, sir. Please follow me."

CHAPTER FIFTY-FOUR

JJ didn't remember how they reached the lobby. A strange feeling of being detached from his own body, and watching himself from afar, was probably a defense mechanism. Blessed numbness spread all over him, from head to limbs.

Once, he read that the human brain shielded itself from the trauma by shutting down. Now he was able to attest to that. He waited until the night manager talked to the operator over the phone; waited until the call was connected.

"Mr. Morris? You can talk now, sir."

He watched as his right hand took the phone from the older man. As if wondering of its origins, he stared at the receiver, then slowly brought it to his ear.

"Hello." Reserved and cold, his voice belonged to a stranger that took place inside his body.

"Boss? I guess you've heard already." Despite the less than stellar connection, Winston's grief came through the line, loud and clear.

"I have." JJ swallowed around the lump in his throat. "What happened?"

"Nobody knows. That ballet teacher, Madame something, called me earlier looking for you. From what I learned, *Verochka* didn't show up for her tryout. So, the Madame went to look for her, and found her sprawled on the staircase landing, unconscious."

"Is she...?" The spasm of JJ's vocal cords cut off his question. But Winston understood.

"She's alive, but broken all over. She's in a hospital, in NYC Health. The doctors are afraid to operate until they stabilize her."

Alive. Verochka was alive.

That was all that mattered.

To fight off the dizzy spell, he gripped the desk corner to stay upright. "How bad?"

"Bad enough." Winston fell silent.

"Is she awake?"

"No, and thank the merciful Lord for that. With her injuries, the pain would be horrible. They placed her into a medical coma."

In a flash, his mind conjured the image of *Verochka,* laying in a heap at the staircase landing, broken, bloody, lifeless.

Pain, so much pain...

Just for a brief moment, JJ shut his eyes against the horrific visions swimming before him. Like bullets, Siobhan's words pinged inside of his skull.

You shouldn't be here...You must return...

At the time he disregarded that crazy muttering, chalking it up to the woman's obviously unstable condition. More fool was he. Those unique violet eyes should have been his clue. Siobhan was really special.

A seer.

He should have been paying attention, instead of shrugging it off.

And what was the point of berating himself now? Self-flagellation was futile and absurd, an indulgence he couldn't afford.

Get a grip. Get moving. Verochka *needs help.*

Bearing down, he blocked out all emotions, and deliberately erased the image of *Verochka* from his mind. He wouldn't be able to function if he concentrated on it. She was alive. That was the most important thing. She needed help.

There is little time yet...

He jolted as his heart kicked into a thundering beat. "I'm coming home."

Without waiting for Winston's reply, JJ disconnected the call. The night manager was still hovering nearby. Good. He addressed the older man, "I must return to the States right now."

"Very well, sir. Anything I can do to assist you?"

"Yes. Please notify my team of attorneys that I had an urgent situation back home. They will have to finish our business here on their own."

Sorry, Grandmother.

"Certainly, Mr. Morris."

"And please phone my pilot. I need the plane ready as soon as possible."

"Absolutely, sir."

He sent an urgent telex to Mayo clinic in Minnesota before he left the hotel.

He'd rather transport *Verochka* there, to the best orthopedic hospital in the country, but wasn't sure if her injuries allowed her to be moved to another location. So, he arranged for the best surgeons to be flown to the NYC immediately.

Already sitting in the plane, JJ connected via the onboard communication center with the New York hospital. The doctor who took the call sounded grim. There were no changes in *Verochka's* condition. She was still in a coma. Before hanging up, JJ notified the doctor of the arrival of the Mayo clinic's team. The other man was not thrilled, but JJ didn't give a damn. *Verochka* will be tended by the best medical personnel in the States. He will not accept anything less. And if he must ruffle some feathers in a process, so be it. His main concern was *Verochka*. Everything else was irrelevant.

Like a general preparing for battle, he planned his next actions, calculating every tiny detail with deadly precision and a cool head. For the next several days, he'd spend all his time at the hospital. The business must function without him. Not a problem. The Morris Holding was well established and solid; it will survive without him. And even if it won't, who cares? He'd gladly sacrifice anything, himself included, in order to bring *Verochka* back to health.

He'd happily exchange places with her in a heartbeat. But that were his emotions talking, not his rational mind. So, he shut down his feelings, and concentrated on reality. An eerie calmness settled over him. It plunged him into a state where every thought was honed to brutal clarity, and every problem held a transparent solution. JJ embraced this abnormal phenomenon.

For as long as it lasted, he was able to hold his fears and emotions at bay, and function. Only after *Verochka* was out of danger, then he might allow himself the luxury of falling apart.

The flight seemed endless. Eight hours turned into an eternity. Unable to close his eyes, JJ stared into a round window, seeing nothing.

How could *Verochka* fall? Had she slipped on the steps? Was she late for the performance, and ran? Somehow that scenario didn't ring true.

She was always so disciplined, so careful. Hard to imagine her rushing down four flights of stairs, especially before her big event.

What then?

He wracked his brain, but came up blank. A thought that she might have been pushed crossed his mind, but was quickly rejected. Who could do such an atrocious thing?

Another dancer consumed by jealousy? Possible, but highly unlikely. The school that Madame Valeska ran as Commander in Chief was a temple for all her pupils.

And everybody loved *Verochka,* starting with her formidable mentor to the last novice student. Or did they?

Bombarded with those troubling questions, he contemplated the wisdom of notifying the police. Or maybe, hiring a private investigator to look into the matter. Disregarding both, he decided to wait until *Verochka* woke.

Only she knew the truth. Only she knew if it was a simple unfortunate accident, or something more sinister. Until then, he needed to concentrate only on her, on her health and recovery. He'd do anything and everything to get her back on her feet. To walk again.

But will she be able to dance?

Cold dread settled in his gut like a heavy boulder. For *Verochka,* ballet was as essential as air. Maybe, even more so. How did she phrase it?

Ballet sets my soul on fire.

What if that fire was extinguished? The thought was chilling.

Physically, she will survive, he'd make sure of that. But emotionally?

The million-dollar question.

Don't borrow any trouble. You don't know her predicament yet. Think positive.

But deep down, JJ knew—felt—that *Verochka's* ballet career was over.

Poor Little Swan.

CHAPTER FIFTY-FIVE

*V*erochka didn't know where she was. Everything around her seemed eerie and quiet and grey. Such a dreary place, but surprisingly peaceful.

Where am I?

Was it a dream? Or maybe a stage? The decorations seemed too bland, and there were no wings, no curtain. No, not a theater. But what, then?

And how did she get here? The last thing she remembered was dressing for the tryout. Did she dance? She didn't remember. Surely, she would recall her most important performance. And why was she suddenly so scared?

I don't want to think about it. Don't want to remember.

Whatever happened, had brought her to this place. Grey, tranquil, quiet.

The stillness around her was absolute and impenetrable. She strained her ears.

Nothing. Not a single sound.

How odd.

But she was not frightened—just a bit uncomfortable. And hazy.

Don't want to be here. Must move. But where should I go?

Surrounded by the thick silvery fog, she was unable to see anything. It was like she was swallowed by the dense mist, cocooned in its embrace. Was she alone in this place? Felt like it. Confusion made her restless. It became imperative for her to leave this unnaturally tranquil place. A shadow of a flickering light ahead drew her attention.

No, I'm not alone!

There was someone out there, down the path. She squinted at the barely visible gleam. For a second, it disappeared, then twinkled again, like a tiny star through the cloudy sky. A candle?

Must go there.

She kept her gaze on the weak light, and started to walk. Every step she took was like swimming though a jelly, clingy and resistant.

An invisible weight dragged at her feet, slowing her progress. Something was pulling at her to turn around, and go back, but *Verochka* stubbornly plowed forward. Cold seeped through her paper-thin nightgown, but she ignored it.

With a single-minded determination, she navigated toward that mesmerizing flicker of light. It seemed to take forever to reach it.

Finally, she emerged from the fog, and gasped. Blinding, the rays of brilliant golden blaze seemed to shoot upward. Illuminated by that radiance, the long tunnel lay ahead, beaconing, promising, encouraging. She gazed at it in wonder. What an enchanting place! *Verochka* smiled. She must go there. She must leave that grey, miserable place, and go down that tunnel. The pull was irresistible. Tempting, alluring, enticing. Mesmerized, she couldn't tear her eyes off of it. But still, she hesitated. What awaited at the end of that tunnel? Freedom? Peace? Or great sorrow? Surely the place that was awash with dazzling golden light couldn't be scary, or sinister. Or could it?

Only one way to find out.

Unable to wait a second longer, *Verochka* took a step forward.

Seemingly out of nowhere, a sudden pain knifed her from the inside. Sharp and brutal, it stole her breath, halted her steps. *Verochka* screamed from the agony, but failed to hear her own voice. The silence was absolute. Unnatural. Deafening.

From the great distance, she heard an urgent cry:

"No! Please, God, no! Do something!"

What can *I do?*

Cringing from the unbearable pain, unable to move a single muscle, she froze.

She recognized that voice. Male. Deep. Familiar. She heard that voice before.

But where?

"Verochka! *Come back!"*

The pain intensified, burning, scorching. Her chest was on fire. It felt like a lightning bolt shot all the way through, repeatedly. Again and again and again...

Suddenly, she was yanked backward, away from the light and that tunnel.

No!

She wanted to fight, but her body betrayed her.

An excruciating pain tore her apart. Unbearable. Unimaginable. Please, God, let the suffering end!

"Verochka! Don't give up. Fight, dammit!"

That voice again. Scared.

Insistent.

Desperate.

She wanted to ask what was the point of fighting, but couldn't open her mouth to form the words. Tired. She was so tired, so empty. So lost.

Just let go. Close your eyes, and let go...

Resigned, *Verochka* shut her eyes, and succumbed to the inevitable. She was never meant to go through that tunnel. She never saw what was at the end of it. She was destined to exist in that eerie, grey place forever.

As if by miracle, her pain disappeared. Relieved and exhausted, she started to drift. The sensation of weightlessness...floating...like a slow dance...

Pleasant. Peaceful.

"That's right, Little Swan. Slow and easy. Just breathe."

Little Swan...only one person called her that. But who? Why can't she remember?

But she wasn't alone anymore. That familiar baritone...Murmuring, encouraging. Pacified, she turned her face toward the sound of that voice.

Something warm and soft brushed against her cheek. She smiled, as she finally remembered. JJ. His name was JJ. And he was right here, with her, wherever it was.

Now everything will be fine...

CHAPTER FIFTY-SIX

"Oh, thank God you're awake!"

A female voice. Clear, high-pitched, familiar.

Verochka squinted at the woman nearby. For a second, she failed to place the name with that face. Strong cheekbones, high forehead, hazel eyes.

I know her.

"You gave all of us such a scare, Miss Osipoff." The older woman sniffed, but quickly recovered her composure. "Don't you ever do such a thing again!"

"I...I am... sorry..." Was it her voice? Scratchy, husky. Unused.

Confused, *Verochka* concentrated on the face of the woman she loved.

What was her name? Why can't I remember?

"Madame...?"

"Yes, it's me, my dear. Madame Valeska."

Of course. Her teacher. How could she forget?

"And don't worry if you are foggy on the names or details. Doctor Schwarz warned us of a possible memory loss. But don't fret, it's just a temporary thing, and not such a big deal, considering your injuries."

"My...injuries?" Her hazy brain struggled to connect the dots. What was Madame Valeska talking about?

And where am I?

She remembered the previous place, all grey, and quiet. This was different. *Verochka* looked around. White walls, pale yellow curtains, and a lot of beeping.

Noise, rendre grace a Dieu.

"You don't remember?" Madame Valeska gazed at *Verochka* with sad sunken eyes.

"What am I... supposed to...remember?"

"Your accident."

Accident? Mon Dieu, *no!*

"What accident? What happened?" Agitated, *Verochka* scanned her surroundings. "Where am I?"

The beeping sounds intensified, gaining in speed and volume. It was coming from somewhere on her left. With a brief glance in that direction, Madame turned back to *Verochka.*

"Shh-shh, don't get excited. Everything is fine now." The hand she placed on *Verochka's* forearm felt warm and comforting. "You are in the hospital, my dear. But you are okay. As to your accident..." with a sigh, Madame Valeska averted her eyes. "You fell."

"F-fell? After a... *fouette?*"

"No. You fell down the staircase and landed hard on the concrete floor and probably bounced your head."

"*Non! Impossible!*"

"I'm afraid so. I'm sorry, *Verochka.*"

Madame never called her by her given name, only Miss Osipoff. An alarm went off in her brain. Something was very wrong. Cold fear climbed all the way from her gut to her throat. With an effort, she swallowed around the icy lump.

"When... did it happened?"

A deep sigh later, her teacher answered, "The day of your tryout." After a long pause, Madame Valeska added in a rough voice, "Two weeks ago."

"Two...weeks?!" Unbelievable. Impossible. Incomprehensible!
"What day is it?"

"December first."

"Mon Dieu!" Her tryout was in November. "Did I... perform?"

"No. You were late, and I went to fetch you. But found you
unconscious at the bottom of the staircase."

"Oh, Lord! I... am s-so sorry, Madame!"

"For what?"

"For f-failing you. You... did so m-much for...m- me, counted on
m-me, and I—"

"What a nonsense! You didn't fail anybody. You just had an
accident."

Verochka shut her eyes, as a sudden kaleidoscope of images
bombarded her brain.

...A woman's face, beautiful and ugly at the same time...

A harsh voice...*You little slut! You'll be sorry* ...

A sensation of flying...

Mon Dieu, *was it an accident?*

Restless, she tried to sit up, but her body refused her brain's
command. A shadow of pain, just a faint throbbing followed her
failed attempt. A pillow under her head, a blanket over her body...
She dragged her eyes lower.

She was lying flat on her back, on a strange hard bed with two
side rails.

A hospital bed.

She *was* in a hospital. Two weeks, Madame Valeska said.

Okay, alright. Calm down.

She tried to lift her arm with no avail. Why can't she move?

Oh God!

"Why can't I move? What's wrong with me? Am I paralyzed?"

"No, my dear. Thankfully, your spine is intact. You had a broken nose, and a shattered cheekbone, but the plastic surgeon took care of that. You face will be as good as new in no time."

Verochka's gaze traveled downward, stopping on the gleaming metal contraption. She gasped. Both of her legs were encased in a hard cast, and held by a scary-looking mechanism in an elevated position. "My legs!"

"Are totally okay now. The best orthopedic surgeons in the country made sure of that. You have a long road of recovery ahead, I'm sorry to say, but you will walk. That's the most important thing."

"Walk? What about dance?"

Madame averted her gaze. The charged silence was her answer.

A broken sob escaped. "I will never dance again, will I?"

Forlorn, Madame Valeska shook her head. The regret on her face was palpable.

"No, not professionally, I'm afraid. But you will live a full and productive life."

A low wail burst from *Verochka's* lips. "What life? Without ballet, my life is not worth anything!" She wanted to rage and rave, to break something.

Hard as a slap in a face, her teacher's voice lashed out, "Stop it! Stop this instant! Feeling sorry for yourself is totally useless, Miss Osipoff. And quite selfish. Your life is not worth it? What rubbish! Ballet is not everything."

"How can you say that, you who dedicated your whole life to it?"

"Yes, I did, and that's why I am in a better position to know." Her voice became softer. "Trust me, my dear. Ballet is—was—my life. Only ballet, and nothing else. And I will regret it to my last day. I cheated myself out of love, and family, and children. At the end, I was left with an empty house, bittersweet memories, and deep regrets. If not for the school..." She drew a broken breath. Misty, her hazel eyes seemed bottomless as she glanced at *Verochka*. "Loneliness is the worst thing in the world, my dear. Remember it. I wouldn't wish it on my worst enemy. It is my penance, my life sentence. Don't let it be yours."

Her teacher's stare became vacant and unfocused, as her voice trailed into silence. Full of sorrow, her expression was unbearable to watch. Then, as if shaking her mood off, she squared her shoulders, and looked back at *Verochka.*

"You are so lucky, Miss Osipoff."

"Lucky? Me? Are you kidding?"

"Not at all. Ballet was your vocation, your passion. But your true treasure lays somewhere else. In your heart. You have found love. Unconditional. Pure. Unselfish. You have found your soulmate, and your destiny."

A warm smile lifted Madame Valeska's lips, transforming her face. "You are incredibly lucky, my dear. To love someone is a great joy, but to have your love returned is a greatest blessing." She sighed, patted *Verochka's* hand.

"Mr. Morris quite literally moved heaven and earth to save your life. All the surgeons that operated on you? He flew them here from all over the country, making sure you have the best medical team available. And he never left your side during all this time, day or night. He will hate to miss your awakening."

A wave of tenderness covered *Verochka's* battered body. Her heart trembled, then sighed. She was never alone. JJ was always with her. She heard his voice, when she was in that strange dreary place. It was he who urged her to fight. He who brought her back from the entrance of that eerie tunnel. She was sure now that if she stepped inside, this world was lost to her. Forever. He was her link, her lifesaver, her fate.

He is my everything.

Hot tears of joy and happiness pressed against her eyelids. "Where is JJ?"

Madam grinned. "I bodily threw him out of your room to take a shower, and get a couple of hours of rest. That man was wasting before my eyes, looking like a shadow of his former self. Quite pitiful, if you ask me. And God only knows how much weight he lost. But still such a handsome devil he is."

She leaned over the bed railing, and tucked the lock of hair behind *Verochka's* ear. The gesture was as unexpected as it was rare. Madame Valeska was not a toucher.

In a gentle voice, she said, "You found a true treasure, my dear. Don't let your sorrow overwhelm you. Don't close your heart. You love him, don't you?"

"Yes, I do, but—"

"No buts, Miss Osipoff. Love is the most important thing, the only thing worthy of any, and all, sacrifices. The only thing that keeps this world moving. Love is so much more than ambition, so much stronger than any suffering. It's a heavenly gift, my dear, but only if you're brave enough to accept it. You, Miss Osipoff, are the bravest soul I have the privilege to know." Her wink was so out of character, it was almost shocking. "My money is on you, Little Swan."

CHAPTER FIFTY-SEVEN

Verochka learned of the true extent of her injuries later from her surgeon Dr. Schwartz. In his professional no-nonsense manner, the old doctor recited all the damage her body sustained, and the procedures that were done to repair that damage. A pure miracle that the doctors managed to put her back together, because it was easier to state what was *not* broken in her body.

Her face was healing nicely, and much faster than her legs and hips that were now implanted with tons of titanium. The doctor's joke that *Verochka* may now consider herself a bionic woman was amusing, if it weren't so unnerving. But still, she was grateful. It could have been much worse. She could have hurt her spine, and left paralyzed for life. She could be imprisoned in an invalid chair for the rest of her days. Would she be able to find the courage to move forward?

Or just give up?

Verochka honestly didn't know the answer, didn't even want to consider that possibility. What was the point? She was alive, and well, with all the limbs attached to her. That was more than enough.

She knew there was a long and tough road of rehabilitation ahead, but she will walk. For JJ, for herself. And for her beloved mentor, who proved to be her staunch supporter and a mix of cheerleader and mother figure.

From Doctor Schwarz she also learned about her sudden cardiac arrest the day after the surgery. In medical jargon, she flatlined for three minutes. Translated to a layman's terms, she died. A defibrillator applied to her chest brought her back. That accounted for a burning sensation of lightning strikes she experienced while trapped in that eerie grey place. Now she knew it was not a dream, but a medically induced coma.

The paddles that sent electrical impulses through her heart left two angry burns.

Verochka considered them her most valuable accessories.

If her days in the hospital taught her anything, it was to never take life for granted. It was precious and fleetingly short. How stupid was it to spend it on regrets and doubts and misery? How silly to dwell on what ifs? Especially, when you have the gift of love. She turned and look at JJ sleeping in the nearby chair.

Her heart trembled in her chest. He was her gift, her love, her destiny.

He saved her life by gathering the team of best doctors in the country, and bringing them to New York. He stayed by her side while she was in a coma. He never left the hospital, even when she woke. *Verochka* couldn't imagine her life without JJ in it. So what if the society of rich and famous frown upon their union? How downright foolish it was to pay attention to other people's beliefs and opinions. Who cares? Obviously, not JJ. Then, why should she? Why should they sacrifice their happiness? No way! She was done with questioning herself.

She loved the best man in the whole wide world, and was loved back.

Madame Valeska's words often played in *Verochka's* mind.

Love is so much more than ambitions, so much stronger than any sufferings. It's a heavenly gift, my dear, but only if you're brave enough to accept it.

Was she brave enough? *Verochka* grinned. You bet. She will accept, and hold, and treasure it for the rest of her life.

With the days that followed her awakening from coma, her memory slowly retuned. And she remembered everything.

Madeline pushed her down the steps. Deliberately, maliciously. When *Verochka* refused to accept her money in order to leave JJ, she quickly unraveled. Madeline's ugly sneer was burned into her brain forever. Had she been trying to save her son from a possible embarrassment, or was she more concerned about her own status? The answer was obvious.

Women like Madeline didn't care about anyone but themselves.

How this truly evil woman was related to JJ was incomprehensible.

Verochka firmly decided not to reveal the truth to JJ.

When he asked her, she answered that it was an unfortunate accident, that she just slipped and fell. Lying went against her nature, but was there anything to gain by telling JJ about his mother's treachery? He'd be devastated. Maybe even blame himself. No doubt, he'd confront Madeline, she'd deny everything, and accuse *Verochka* of deceit.

She couldn't care less about that despicable woman, but JJ was another matter.

To shatter his last illusion about his mother was sure to hurt him deeply, and leave invisible scars on his heart and soul. She'd rather die, than subject JJ to that pain.

As to justice? *Verochka* shrugged. As far as she was concerned, it was already served. Maybe, not in the traditional way, but still. Against all odds, she survived, and will spend the rest of her life with JJ. So, all Madeline's efforts turned out to be futile. Instead, she accomplished the very thing she tried to prevent. She brought *Verochka* and JJ together, and made them even closer.

Has she realized that? Undoubtedly. It must be maddening to Madeline to see all her careful planning backfire in her face. For women like her, the defeat was simply unacceptable. Unbearable. Humiliating. She'd rage and rave, but to no avail. Madeline lost, spectacularly, and will live the rest of her life agonizing about the little French orphan who bested her.

And that, as *Verochka* was concerned, was true justice.

CHAPTER FIFTY-EIGHT

On Christmas morning, JJ seemed preoccupied. Unnaturally quiet, his expression pensive, he sat by *Verochka*, holding her hand, and gazing at the Christmas tree. Delivered by Winston a few days ago, that tree stood eight feet high, and smelled like childhood and magic.

The medical personnel tried to stop Winston, claiming it was against the hospital policy to have a live spruce in a patient's room, especially of that enormous size. But at the end, they capitulated. Whether it was due to Winston's formidable features or JJ's charm, was anybody's guess.

Madame Valeska soon made an appearance, hefting a huge box of decorations, and all of them spent a delightful several hours dressing the tree.

All except *Verochka*, who supervised the whole process from her bed.

Like a child, she was elated to see that dazzling symbol of Christmas decorating her hospital room. She wanted to gaze at it for hours, and never get tired.

But JJ's unusual behavior bothered her. Closed off, he was brooding in solitary silence. Her intuition screamed at her that something was off. But what?

What was he hiding from her? Frowning, *Verochka* watched him with growing concern. The smart thing to do was wait until he decided to share whatever was bothering him, but she was growing impatient. As far as she was concerned, the best approach was addressing any problem straight on.

Finally, that charged silence became unbearable.

"JJ? What's wrong?"

"Huh? Nothing." A fake smile on his face only confirmed her suspicion.

"You don't fool me. Something is on your mind, I can see it. So, I repeat, what's wrong?"

"Really, *Verochka,* nothing is wrong." He raked one hand through his hair.

"Why then are you so quiet? You didn't utter a word for almost an hour."

"I'm sorry. I didn't mean to ignore you, *ma petite.* It just..." He shrugged, as his voice trailed into silence.

When the pause became too long, *Verochka* prompted, "Just...?"

JJ let go a deep breath. "I just realized that tomorrow was supposed to be our wedding day."

"And that's why you're acting so peculiarly?"

"I guess. It's silly, but," he shrugged again, avoiding her eyes, "I wanted to give you the best wedding of the century, a fairytale affair with lots of guests, live music, a huge reception, and—"

"*Mon Dieu,* JJ, I was going out of my mind with worry!" *Verochka* let go the breath she was holding, and grinned at him. "Who needs a grandiose wedding, anyway? I will be more than happy with a simple intimate ceremony. We can ask Madame Valeska to stand for me, and Winston for you, and the hospital chaplain can marry us right here."

For a long moment, JJ simply goggled. His mouth opened, then closed, then opened again. As if he had trouble hearing her, he leaned closer.

"What...what did you say?"

"I said, we can be married right here. If you didn't change your mind, of course."

"I..." he swallowed audibly, "I didn't. Of course, I didn't! How can you even think that! " He shook his head, grabbed both of her hands. "I will be more than happy..." All elation drained from his face. "But what about your wedding dress?"

"My only choice of dress for the foreseeable future will be this indecent hospital gown, I'm afraid." *Verochka* winced, as she glanced at herself. As bridal attire went, hers was unique, alright. She gave a mental shrug. Who cares? "But at least, it's white."

"I bought a spectacular Chanel wedding dress for you."

"You did? Really? Aww, JJ." She squeezed his hands. Turning his palms up, JJ entwined their fingers. Her engagement ring that stubbornly refused to be removed since the day JJ put it on, gleamed through their joined grip. "If I promise to wear that spectacular Chanel dress on our first anniversary, will you marry me?"

His response was short and immediate. "When?"

"Well, you planned our wedding to take place on December twenty-six, right?"

"Yes."

"Then, tomorrow it is." A bevy of butterflies fluttered in the pit of her stomach. "If the chaplain is available, that is."

"He will be," leaning forward, he lightly touched his lips to hers, "even if I have to promise him a pint of my blood."

Then, he frowned. "I forgot to tell you something important." His dark chocolate eyes became troubled. Immediately alert, *Verochka* searched his expression. If she wasn't mistaken, JJ looked almost...embarrassed. A worrying line puckered his brows. His lips pressed together formed a tight line. Then he cursed under his breath. Puzzled, she frowned. JJ rarely swore.

"What? What is it?"

In a deep low voice, he finally answered, "I resigned."

"*Excuzes-moi?*" Whatever she expected to hear, was not that. Wide-eyed, she watched him in a stupor. "You...you did what?"

"I resigned from my position as the CEO of Morris Holding."

"But...but why? Did they force you to leave? Is that because of me? Did Madeline have anything to do with it?" Agitated, she made an attempt to sit up, but failed. The metal contraption attached to her legs, prevented any movement.

As a testament to her bewilderment, *Verochka* didn't blurt a single curse. All the words stuck in her throat as she gazed at JJ's face, waiting for his reply.

"No to your last three questions. As to why," he looked at their joined hands, then glanced up at her. A self-conscious smile curved his lips. "Because I became tired, and a little bored. Truthfully, I stepped into my father's shoes only because Madeline almost botched the business during her initial two-months tenure.

"I had to do it to save the enterprise my grandfather built from the ground up, and my father made a success of. At the time, there was no one who could do it. But now, after more than three years, the business can practically run itself. And I have a very strong person to take my place. He's brilliant, loyal, and determined. I trust him. I still will be holding the position on the board of directors, but not involved in a day-to-day operation. Thankfully, I don't need to work in order to survive. I have enough money to lasts several lifetimes."

"Are you sure?"

"Quite." He grinned, kissed her knuckles. "We won't starve, I promise you."

"That's not what I meant. Are you sure you *want* to quit?"

"I've never been more sure of anything in my life. Well, except when I met you, and knew that you are the one and only for me."

"But what will you do?"

"Travel all over the world with you. Build a family, and raise the children we will have one of these days. Spoil and pamper you. Play music, run the bar with Winston. Just enjoy life in general."

"That sounds terrific, but won't you get bored?"

"Not really. But if, and that's a huge if, I'll think of something." He shrugged, clearly unconcerned. "For now, I will be a modest bar owner, playing my saxophone to the patrons." He raised a brow. "Are you okay with marrying a musician instead of a business mogul, *ma petite*?"

The laughter that bubbled inside of her finally burst free. "Are you kidding me?" Delighter, *Verochka* wiggled her shoulders. "If I could, I would be dancing a happy jig right now!"

Sitting beside her on the bed, JJ carefully drew her closer, dropped his forehead against the crown of her head. "You will, my Little Swan. On the day of our first anniversary, you and I will waltz in Vienna, to Strauss' The Blue Danube. I swear to you."

"I'll hold you to that."

JJ smiled. "And I'll hold you to wearing that Chanel wedding dress on our first night as a husband and wife." His voice took on a husky undertone, as he gave *Verochka* a positively wicked wink. "Removing it from you became my most cherished fantasy."

She knew she was blushing. Even the tips of her ears became hot and tingly.

Secretly thrilled with the prospect, *Verochka* schooled her face into a serious mask. "Far be it for me to deny you your fantasy, *mon amour*."

"Deal?"

"Deal."

Both solemn, they shook their hands, then exploded into a boisterous, carefree laughter.

CHAPTER FIFTY-NINE

"So, did you wear your wedding dress on your first anniversary?" Abby gently prompted after a long moment of silence. *Verochka* turned from the bay window where she stood, gazing at the dramatic view of the ocean. With an effort, she brought herself back to the present. The journey down memory lane brought a flood of conflicting emotions. Happiness, joy, sadness.

Composing herself, *Verochka* took a couple of deep breaths.

"I sure did, and on all following as well. For the next fifty years."

She smiled through the mist of tears at the memories. They were mostly sweet, with just a dollop of a bitter aftertaste, like her favorite dark Belgian chocolate.

Like JJ's eyes.

True to his word, on December twenty-six 1964, he flew *Verochka* to Vienna, where they stayed at the famous Sacher Hotel, and danced to the music of the Waltz King Johann Straus. During the next fifty years, that became their special tradition. After JJ passed away ten years ago, *Verochka* traveled all over the world, but never went to Austria again. To this day, the sounds of the Blue Danube made her unbearably miserable and depressed.

Abby's next question pulled *Verochka* out of her reverie.

"And did JJ fulfill his most cherished fantasy?" The expression of wicked curiosity danced in Abby's eyes.

Verochka chuckled. "For a pregnant woman, my dear, you're asking the most inappropriate questions."

Abby shrugged. "My pregnancy did not happen due to the immaculate conception, you know."

"I should hope not." Shaking from laughter, *Verochka* gazed at the girl who became her granddaughter. From the moment Abby popped up in the twenty-first century, the love for her was immediate and overwhelming. They simply clicked, and shared a special relationship that only reinforced with time.

Two years ago, after Abby married her grandson Alex, she became family.

Their first child was due any day now, and *Verochka* could hardly wait to hold that precious baby in her arms. Her first great-grandchild.

Well, actually her second, as Nika's daughter born in 1911, was her *first*.

Margaret Vera Coleman Nelson.

When fate brought them together, on the day of that infamous winter ball in 1962, Margaret was older than *Verochka*, her own great-grandmother, by three decades.

Talk about timeless miracles.

Unlike *Verochka*, Margaret recognized her immediately.

That special violet eyes gift? Or the family memories passed down through her parents? Who knew?

While *Verochka* fumbled through the fog of bewilderment, bombarded with the images she was afraid to acknowledge, Margaret quietly disappeared from her life. Only once she reached out, sending *Verochka* her wedding gift: the priceless heirloom Coleman pearls. A small note tucked inside the antic jewelry box simply stated:

To my dear Verochka with all my love and best wishes. Those pearls rightfully belong to you. I'm sure my mother and father would approve.

Always yours,

Margaret Nelson

Abby's voice brought *Verochka* back to the present.

"I never knew how badly you were hurt. I thought you had an unfortunate accident, and broke your legs, but I had no idea of the true story."

"No one has, Sweetie. I never told anyone before now."

"Wow," Abby shook her head, frowning. "So, you didn't say anything to JJ?"

"No. What was the point?" *Verochka* shrugged. "He was hurt enough."

Clearly incensed, Abby clenched her hands, glaring. "Damn that horrible woman! She had no right to treat you that way! Or her own son."

"Water under the bridge, my darling. I can never forget nor forgive, but I don't dwell on it. I led a very happy life with the man I loved to distraction. I've been truly blessed."

"What about ballet?"

Verochka sighed. "I won't lie and say that I didn't regret losing my career. Ballet was my passion for as long as I remembered. I loved dancing, but as my beloved teacher, Madame Valeska, once told me, ballet is not everything.

"And when she retired, she entrusted her school to me. Surprisingly, I found that teaching is no less rewarding than performing. I'm very proud of the school."

"You did a great job, *Verochka*. How many pupils would still be dreaming of ballet if not for your foundation for the talented children?"

"Well, the foundation was established by JJ, not me, as a present for the fifth anniversary of my surgery." She smiled, remembering that day. "The best gift ever."

"He knew you well."

"Oh, he knew me, alright. That man was incredible. I wish you could have met him."

"I wish so too." They both fell into silence.

"Ouch!" Abby's sudden intake of breath interrupted *Verochka's* musings.

"What? What is it?"

"I'm not a hundred present sure, but I think the baby..." Abby swallowed, and looked at *Verochka* with huge terrified eyes. "He or she is quite determined to be born."

"Like... now?!"

"Like right now, I'm afraid."

"Okay, alright, Sweetie. Stay calm and breathe." Her own panic bubbled close to the surface. With every ounce of her willpower, *Verochka* forced herself to calm down. "When did you feel the first contraction?"

"I don't remember exactly, but I think...earlier this morning."

"You think!" Fear like she never experienced before threatening to plunge *Verochka* into a blind terror.

Merde! The girl was in labor for several hours!

"Doesn't matter what I think, Grandmother, because my water just broke."

Stupefied, *Verochka* dragged her eyes to Abby's legs. Something wet and dark was rapidly increasing in size between her pajama clad thighs.

Oh, God! Now what?

What did she know about child birthing? Only that it hurt like hell, and went forever, like her own horrendous labor. But she had twins. Thank goodness, there was only one baby inside Abby. A huge baby, but just one. Okay, alright. That was a plus. Wasn't it? Shaking, *Verochka* swallowed through the enormous fist in her throat.

Get a grip, silly goose. Act like you know what you're doing.

Cursing like a seasoned sailor in her mind, she plastered a big fake smile on her face. "Okay, Sweetie. Don't panic. We can do it. Piece of cake. Let me call the ambulance, and —"

"But what about Alex?"

Murphy's law proved true. Alex was in Jacksonville.

Even if he jumped in a car and broke the speed of light, he still won't be able to reach Fernandina Beach in time.

Merde. Well, then.

Squaring her shoulders, *Verochka* jutted her chin forward. "We'll manage without him. And anyway, who needs men at the time of a crisis?"

The ride to the hospital passed in a blur. By the time they arrived, Abby was in full blown labor. *Verochka* donned the surgical scrubs hurriedly thrusted at her by the nurse, and went to perform the scariest role of her life: a breathing couch. She'd rather twirl in an endless *fouette* on her titanium infused legs.

Verochka cracked silly jokes between contractions, and breathed with Abby until her own lungs screamed in protest, and cheered everybody on, while her granddaughter labored to bring a child into this world.

Her left hand gripped in Abby's desperate clutch became numb from the lack of blood circulation. *Verochka* didn't make a peep of protest. For the ten longest hours of her life, she held on, stubbornly refusing to bend under pressure.

Only when the tiny wail announced the arrival of the baby, *Verochka* finally broke down. She hated crying in general, but this was such a happy occasion, she let her tears flow freely down her face. A squirming nine-and-a-half- pound giant of a boy, red-faced and seemingly angry at the world, was quickly checked out, and pronounced healthy. When the doctor offered her to cut the baby's cord, *Verochka* shuddered, but bravely accepted the umbilical scissors. Agonizing, trembling inside, she prayed not to embarrassed herself by fainting. Only after she did the honors, *Verochka* allowed herself a first breath.

Laughing and crying, Abby accepted the baby, then cradled him in her arms.

"Isn't he the most beautiful thing you've ever seen? Look at him, Grandmother!" She gently ran a finger along the baby's fuzzy head. "Look! He even has hair! Oh, you are so precious, my darling. So gorgeous!"

Verochka almost snorted, but caught herself in time. Gorgeous was not even cutting it close, but who was she to offer her opinion? The beauty was in the eye of a beholder, they say. Especially if that eye was a mother's.

Much later, when Alex finally burst into Abby's room, *Verochka* left them alone, allowing the new parents some privacy. Grateful for a few moments to herself, she tiredly plopped into the waiting chair. Her legs were killing her, not to mention her abused left hand. She could swear she still felt the grip of Abby's fingers.

But it was so worth it. *Verochka* smiled, closed her eyes.

As if on cue, JJ's beloved face swam in front of her eyelids.

So, my darling, we are great-grandparents. You did good, my Little Swan.

I was terrified out of my mind.

I know. And still, you carried yourself like a brave little solder. I'm proud of you.

Oh, JJ. I wish you could be here. I miss you so much!

I miss you too, ma petite. *I love you.*

She must have drifted off. Someone called her name, and shook her by the shoulder. Bewildered, *Verochka* jerked awake, and looked at the familiar violet eyes she passed onto her two grandchildren. Grinning, Alex stared at her from above.

"I am a daddy!" He rubbed his bald head with both hands, then hooted with laughter. "I am a daddy, *Verochka!*"

His dazzling smile was so contagious, she couldn't hold back her own grin. "Sure you are, darling. Congratulations."

"But let me tell you, Gorgeous, I couldn't in a million years cut that umbilical cord with your panache."

Startled, *Verochka* blinked at him. "How...how do you know?"

Alex sat in a nearby chair, as his face grew serious. "I saw. Everything."

Of course, he did. Why was she surprised? Alex's Violet Eyes gift that manifested itself two years ago, was his ability to travel the great distances in his mind when the people he loved were in danger.

Feeling for him, *Verochka* patted his hand. "Poor baby. It must have been terrifying for you."

Alex's head bobbed in a jerky nod. "The scariest thing that I've ever lived through." After a deep breath, he turned his laughing eyes to her. "But that's all in the past. Now, I want you to come with me, and meet my son."

"Huh. I'll let you know, my adorable baldy, that I met him already. Way before you did, Daddy."

"True. But do you know his name?"

"So, you're finally agreed on a name? Fantastic!"

The baby name battle was the constant subject of *Verochka's* amused annoyance for the past nine months.

"We have. Come with me, Gorgeous." Tugging *Verochka* by the hand, Alex propelled her toward Abby's room.

The picture that greeted her there brought a fresh flood of tears to her eyes.

Abby, tired but radiant, cradled her sleeping newborn now swaddled in a hospital blanket. A knitted blue hat perched atop his head was so funny, *Verochka* chuckled.

Taking the baby from Abby's hands, Alex angled his son's tiny face toward her.

"*Verochka*, let me introduce you to the newest addition to our family. Meet Jacob Joseph Morris. We'll call him JJ."

For the second time that day, *Verochka* broke down.

"Thank you, my darlings. Oh, thank you so much!"

Gazing down at the baby through the sheen of happy tears, her only regret was that JJ wasn't here to see that miracle.

A sudden shimmering sensation along her spine was akin to a caress.

Smiling, *Verochka* brought her hands to her shoulders, placed them atop. And when her fingers were intertwined, she knew without a doubt that JJ was here, watching down at his namesake.

Deep and familiar, his beloved voice whispered in her ears.

You did good, Little Swan. You did darn good.

Silently, she replied, "We did good, *mon amour,* you and I. Together."

The baby stirred in his father's arms, then issued a high-pitched wail of protest. Laughing, *Verochka* wiped her tears. To her, it was the best music she ever heard.

A music of a new life, new beginnings. New love.

ACKNOWLEDGEMENTS

To come up with a story and write it down is easy. To make it into a book—now that's entirely different story.

The creative process is a lonely road, sometimes straight and smooth, often like a hike in the hills, but always solitary. And that's how it should be. But every road, no matter how long or hilly, comes to an end, and then...

...you realize that it's not the end— far from it! — but a crossroads, and you need to choose carefully where to turn, or how to proceed and not to get completely disoriented. You need help to choose the right path, a map to orient yourself, a guidance and a gentle nudge (or a mighty push) to start moving again. In short, you need other people. Then, the real adventure begins.

I've been truly blessed. By the time I came to my crossroads, I was so lost, I was about to turn back. But fate decided differently: she sent me Sloane Taylor, my editor, who very soon became my mentor and my guardian angel. She took me by my hand and dragged me to the right path, showing me the way. And all the time while I stumbled along the thorny path, she was walking behind me, cheering me on, whipping my tears, or kicking my behind. I've never had so much fun, or been so frustrated, in my life, but every second of it was worth it.

Thank you, Sloane Taylor, for sticking up and not giving up on me. Thank you for everything. This book is as much yours as it is mine. Without you it wouldn't see the light of a day.

My heartfelt thanks to Justine Alley Dawsett, who created such a beautiful cover.

And as always, my sincere gratitude to the men in my life, my husband Leo and my son George. Thank you for believing in me, guys.

ABOUT THE
AUTHOR

S tella May is the penname for talented author **Marina Sardarova** who has a fascinating history you should read on her website[1] STELLA MAY Author[2]. Click onto About Stella in the header for the details.

Stella writes fantasy romance as well as time travel romance. Love and family are the two cornerstones of her stories and life. Stella's books are available in e-book and paperback through all major vendors.

When not writing, Stella enjoys classical music, reading, and long walks along the ocean. She lives in Jacksonville, Florida with her husband Leo and their son George. They are her two best friends and are all partners in their family business.

Learn more about Stella on her website[3] STELLA MAY Author[4] Follow her blog[5] SEEK MAGIC EVERYDAY – Seek Magic Everyday (home.blog)[6] Stay connected on Facebook (20+) Stella May Author | Jacksonville FL | Facebook[7] Twitter[8] (20)

1. https://www.blogger.com/blog/post/edit/19076326/1152448649577793874

2. https://www.stellamayauthor.com/

3.   https://www.blogger.com/blog/post/edit/19076326/1152448649577793874

4.   https://www.stellamayauthor.com/

5.   https://www.blogger.com/blog/post/edit/19076326/1152448649577793874

6.   https://stellamayauthor.home.blog/

7.   https://www.blogger.com/blog/post/edit/19076326/1152448649577793874

Marina Sardarova (@MarinaSardarova) / Twitter[9], and Pinterest (952) Pinterest[10].

Also by Stella May

UPON A TIME SERIES
'Til time Do Us Part
Time & Again
No Other time

STAND ALONE NOVEL
Rhapsody in Dreams

COMING SOON
THE ROSTOFF SERIES
New Dawn
New Hope
New Life

8. https://www.blogger.com/blog/post/edit/19076326/1152448649577793874

9. https://twitter.com/MarinaSardarova

10. https://www.blogger.com/blog/post/edit/19076326/1152448649577793874

Don't miss out!

Visit the website below and you can sign up to receive emails whenever Stella May publishes a new book. There's no charge and no obligation.

https://books2read.com/r/B-A-COXF-GPTHC

BOOKS 2 READ

Connecting independent readers to independent writers.

www.ingramcontent.com/pod-product-compliance
Lightning Source LLC
Chambersburg PA
CBHW051522250626
47156CB00001B/189